THE BUGBEAR HUNTER

or

THE SEDUCTION AND REDEMPTION OF CONGRESSMAN DAVID CROCKETT

DAVID BARNETT GOLDMAN

Published by Hill Country Press, an imprint of StoneyCreekPublishing.com

ISBN: 978-1-965766-17-0
ISBN (ebook): 978-1-965766-18-7
Library of Congress Control Number: 2025910075

Cover design by Ken Ellis. Author photo by Steve Barrett.

Printed in USA

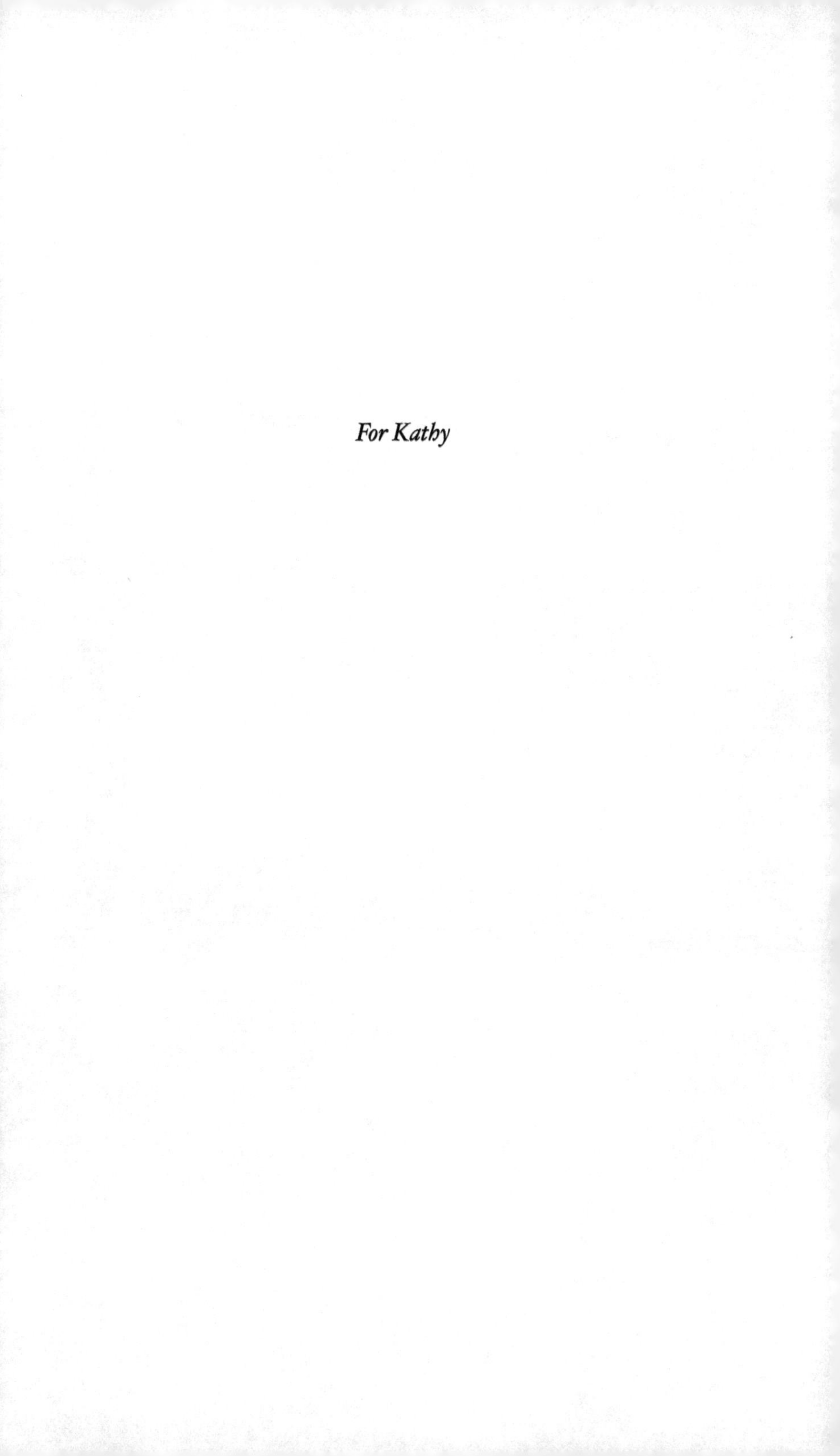

For Kathy

I was appointed by the president to stand on the Allegheny Mountains and wring the Comet's tail off. I did so, but got my hands most shockingly burnt and the hair singed off my head so that I was as bald as a trencher. I div right into the Waybosh river and thus saved my best stone blue coat and grass green small clothes. With the help of bear's grease I have brought out a new crop, but the hair grows in bights and tufts like hussuck grass in a meadow, and it keeps in such a snarl that all the teeth will instantly snap out of an ivory comb when brought within ten feet of it.

—Davy Crockett's Almanack of Wild Sports of the West, Life in the Backwoods & Sketches of Texas, 1837

1833

Chapter One

The frontier fellow tossed the tail of his fur hat over his shoulder and brought two chairs forward to the center of the stage. He sat on one, and then as the lady was about to sit on the other chair, he threw his legs on it.

"Ah, the soldier tired," sighed the lady. "Perhaps, sir, you would prefer an armchair?"

"No, madam. If it was just after dinner, I should like to put my legs out the winder." He crossed his outstretched legs. He wore deerskin leggings and a fringed hunting shirt.

"His legs out the window," she said to the audience. "A very cool proceeding, certainly. May I offer you a cup of tea?"

"Much obliged to you, Mrs. Wollope. However, I never raise the steam with hot water. I always go on the high-pressure principle—all whiskey."

"Ah, a man of SPIRIT. Are you stationed here in Washington City, sir?"

"Stationed? Yes, but I don't mean to stop long. Old Kaintuck's the spot." He raised his hand and swung it around vigorously. "West Tennessee's another spot, too, by the Eternal. There the world's made upon a large scale."

"A region of superior cultivation," she said after the applause had died down. "In what branch of science do its gentlemen excel?"

He stood up and gave her a deadly serious frontier look. "Why madam, of all the fellers either side of the Allegheny hills I myself can jump higher, squat lower, dive deeper, stay longer under and come out drier."

"Why you, sir, are a—"

"I'm a horse. Fact is, I'm half horse, half alligator, a touch of the earthquake with a sprinkling of the steamboat. And if I ain't, I wish I may be shot."

"And your ladies, sir?"

"The gals? Oh, they go it on the big figure too—no mistake on them. There's my late sweetheart, Patty Snaggs. At nine-year-old she shot her a bear, and now she can whip her weight in wildcats." He took off his hat. "There's the skin of one of them," he said and waved the hat high above his head.

Upstairs in the gallery, Dr. William A. Caruthers loosened his cravat with one hand and wiped his brow with the other. The theater was stifling tonight, the fires roaring, the air thick with segar smoke despite the signs prohibiting it. This was Will's second night in Washington. He was on his way home. Or rather, on his way to his lodgings *du jour*, the Corporation of New-York being little more than a procession of temporary addresses to him. And as much as he missed his family, he wasn't chafing at the bit to get back. At least not until he saw the woman he had tried to forget for the last ten months and fourteen days.

"Doubtless your soil and people correspond, Colonel Wildfire," Mrs. Wollope said to the frontier man.

"The soil?" Colonel Wildfire said. "Oh, the soil's so rich you may travel underneath it."

"Travel underground, sir? I must put this down."

"Yes, madam, particularly after the spring rains. Look you here now, t'other day I was a-horseback and paddling away pretty comfortably through Nobottom Swamp when suddenly— I wish I may be curry-combed to death by 50,000 tom cats if I didn't see a white hat getting along in mighty considerable style all alone by itself on the top of the mud. So up I rid, and being a bit jubas, I lifted it with the butt end of my whip when a feller sung out from under it, `Hallo, stranger, who told you to knock my hat off?' `Why,' says I, 'What's come of the rest of you?' `Oh,' says, he, `I'm not far off—only in the next county. I'm doing beautifully—got one of the best horses under me that ever burrowed—claws like a mole—no stop in him—but here's a wagon and horses right under me in a mighty bad fix, I reckon, for I heard the driver say a spell ago one of the team was getting a leetle tired.'

"So says he, `you must be a pretty considerable feller on your own, but you had better keep your mouth shut or you'll get your teeth sunburnt.' So, says I, `Goodbye, stranger. I wish you a pleasant ride, but I prognosticate afore you get through the next sandbank you'll burst your biler.'"

"What a geological novelty," Mrs. Wollope replied.

Novelty? said Will Caruthers to himself up in the gallery. Such aptitude would be a *godsend!*

Aye, if horses could burrow and pigs could fly and other such fanciful things were of common occurrence, Will would leap at the chance to burrow his way back home, too, someday—anything but risk encountering his creditors in broad daylight. Last month that had nearly happened. His stage driver had driven him home to Virginia as if he'd been out to break some speed record, so they reached Lexington well before dark. They arrived there just as old Mr. Barclay was entering his store. Will still owed him over two hundred dollars, and had they arrived a quarter minute earlier, there might have been an incident.

Well, in all likelihood there wouldn't have been, Will thought. Last month had been his first journey back to Rockbridge County since he removed to New-York—hardly the triumphant return he had planned—and he had nearly forgotten how tolerant Virginians could be with their prodigal sons. It was four years ago that he took the insolvency oath, packed what few belongings that had escaped the auctioneer's hammer and carried his wife and children north to re-make his fortune. They had been a family of four then. Today they were six. How in God's name he was ever going to keep so many bodies and souls together on his own, he hadn't an inkling.

Which was why he had decided to venture home last month to talk to his brother. He had hoped that John might take pity if not on him then on his young family. Just how much help they needed, Will had thought it ungentlemanly to spell out in his letter, and so a figure had not been agreed upon until the day before he left Lexington. The figure turned out to be insufficient—cheeseparings and candle ends, Will thought. It was not enough to cover much more than his traveling expenses and next month's rent. Most of John's money was tied up in his latest business venture— or so he said it was—a gold mine somewhere in North Carolina.

A gold mine, Will thought. Will's meager income was tied up in household expenses.

Still, it had been a tonic to be back home in Rockbridge again, if only for a week, to watch the sun rise over the Blue Ridge and set over the Alleghenies. And in Lexington you could still cross the street without having to worry about being run down by some ill-tempered meat monger's horse-and-dray or a speeding omnibus, for there were times even in the middle of the workday that you could look up and down the length of Main Street and not see a single moving thing. *"Kaintuck may indeed be the spot,"* Will thought, but Virginia was another.

"A waltz?" said Colonel Wildfire. "What sort of varmint's that —a jig or a war dance? Come, madam. I know you're a screamer."

"Thank you just the same, sir," said Mrs. Wollope, "but I never dance."

"Hullo, stop your steam," Colonel Wildfire shouted down to the musicians in the pit, who had just begun their waltz. "That's no dance at all. I want something strong. Here, stranger, I'll trouble you to play *When Wild War's Deadly Blast Was Blown* and bear pretty considerable hard upon the treble."

One of the musicians told him they didn't know it.

"Then play what you like, only let it go quick on the thunder and lightning principle."

Will smiled, but not at Mr. Hackett's bogus frontier dialect. For Will was paying scant attention to anything that was happening on stage. Rather, he was thinking about something he had done in Rockbridge County last week. And for the first time in fifteen years, yet—aye, half his lifetime ago! Last week Will climbed the first ten or twelve feet of the Natural Bridge as if he were a schoolboy again and carved his name upon it. Then he rode into the deep woods, built a fire, wrapped himself in two blankets, his greatcoat and an oilcloth, and revised in his mind the eighth chapter of his second novel: a historical romance set in seventeenth century Virginia with the working title *The Recluse of Jamestown.*

When the sun came up, Will had a breakfast of cold turkey and light bread. Riding back to Lexington later that day, he remarked to himself that he hadn't felt so youthful since the first year of his marriage. By the time he reached town, however, he was his old gloomy self again. Guilt had settled into him like dyspepsia, guilt because he was feeling so blissful while his wife and children were languishing in a cold dirty city where they couldn't intrude upon his solitude and remind him of what a sorry provider he had come to be.

Enough! Will said to himself. What was so reprehensible about taking a well-earned leave of one's responsibilities for a few weeks? Even the beast in the field has to occasionally get out from under its yoke.

Well, a sorry provider might indeed be a suitable object of scorn, he thought, but there are worse things, things that should be kept far in the back of a married man's mind. But how does one keep such a devil's little red-haired green-eyed angel from one's consciousness when she is so close and the yoke and harness so far?

Her name was Ivy. She was fresh out of finishing-school and ten years younger than Will. Will hadn't looked into those green eyes of hers or run his fingers through her red hair in almost a year, not since she set up housekeeping with her mother in Alexandria, Virginia. When she removed from New-York, he had assumed that he would never see her again, but it was inevitable he would see her tonight, if only from a distance; she was backstage at this very moment, no doubt, awaiting her turn in the final skit. Not that he had come to the theater expressly to see her. Not that she even knew he was here in Washington City. Which he supposed was for the best. After all, he had sworn her off almost a year ago.

"If you ask me," Colonel Wildfire said, "I think you had all better pack up your plunder and tote off to West Tennessee. I'll divide all my land among you on the Big Muddy and the Little Muddy free gratis for nothing. And look here. The ground's so rich there that if you but plant a crowbar overnight perhaps it will sprout three-penny nails a-fore morning."

He stepped forward to the edge of the stage.

"Look here, ladies and gentlemen, strangers," he went on to the audience now, "I know I'm a pretty hard sample of a far-Western fellow, but I didn't want to scare nobody. And as you see, I'm in want of a leetle more genteel education. I hope I may be indulged occasionally in a trip to Washington City."

Mr. Hackett removed his fur hat and bowed. The audience rose and thundered out an ovation. After they had settled down, he turned to his left, fixed his eyes upon the stage box and bowed once more. The long-haired, middle-aged guest of honor slowly rose and returned the bow. Which set off the audience again.

"I wish I may be shot!" somebody shouted from the pit.

Will gazed down at Mr. Hackett with his outlandish long-tailed hat and fringe and then back up at Colonel Crockett in his stylish tailcoat. He had to admit it gave him gooseflesh to watch the two of them pay homage to each other. It was almost as if Colonel Crockett were bowing to himself. And in a sense, he was, thought Will. Art had imitated life—stretching the truth a considerable distance, to be sure—and life was now returning the compliment.

Will got out his opera glass and took a better look at the real colonel. Crockett looked as if he had gained twenty pounds since Will last saw him, the only time, in fact, that he had ever made the colonel's acquaintance. That was six or seven years ago at Will's uncle's house in Staunton, Virginia. His uncle had met Crockett through Mr. Houston, a prominent former neighbor who had just then been elected Governor of Tennessee; ever since the election it had been fashionable around Staunton to claim to have known the governor since he was in swaddling clothes, but many of Will's people truthfully did. As for Colonel Crockett, few beyond the confines of his congressional district had ever even heard of him then—Will certainly hadn't—for that was three years before Mr. Paulding wrote the play. The colonel had only recently been elected to his first term in Congress and had been on his way to Washington City to take his seat.

If there had been anything remarkable enough about Colonel Crockett back then to warrant his current widespread popularity, Will had not taken notice of it. As for his appearance, the colonel had been dressed as fashionably as any of Will's wealthier patients, looking considerably more like a courthouse lawyer than the Indian-fighting bear hunter he was purported to be. As for the now-famous Crockett sense of humor, Will had heard precious little of it, for the colonel had been grievously ill that evening. He had been suffering from intermittent fever, the same ailment that, according to rumor, had nearly kept him from attending the play tonight; and had he not been suffering from it, Will, in all likelihood, never would have met him. Will's uncle had told the colonel's traveling companion that he had a young kinsman who was a physician, and the man had him sent for at once. When at length Will arrived at Staunton, there wasn't much he could do for Crockett except to provide him with quinine and laudanum to help him sleep. Fortunately, his fever finally abated late the next day, and he was able to continue his journey the following morning.

"Move your legs, old son. I don't want to break any bones."

Will's friend James French had returned to his seat precisely as Ivy was taking her place upon the stage for the last feature—a musical farce—which was just getting under way. Jamey had been in the lobby cajoling a connection of Mr. Hackett's into allowing him to arrange a European tour for their theatrical company. So much drivel, thought Will. He had known Jamey French for nearly ten years—since Jamey was in his teens—and his big, clumsy friend was still as full of himself as he was on the day they first met, backstage at Papa French's theater in Petersburg, Virginia.

"Oh dear, I seem to have forgot something," said Ivy—center stage now—her first line of the skit. She tapped her forehead. "Now wherever did I put that silly thing?"

Will melted. So much for my solemn oath, he thought.

"William. Pssst, William." Jamey slapped him on the shoulder with the back of his big hand. "Get an eyeful of that one." He reached for Will's opera glass and peered through it, then offered it back.

Will frowned and waved it away. "I can see fine without it," he said.

"She's going to the reception with me," Jamey said. "Be a good fellow and take a better look. I want your honest opinion."

Will gulped and took a glimpse. He handed the opera glass back. "A little wholesome for you, isn't she?"

"Appearances can be deceiving, old son." Jamey put the glass to his eye. "Her name is Ivy Green. Can you imagine? Ivy *Green*!"

"That's just her ... that's probably just what she calls—"

"Ten minutes, William. Ten minutes was all it took. The stage manager introduced us and all it took me was *ten minutes*!"

"I wish I had your initiative." Will said. He was only five years Jamey's senior—barely into his thirties—but at the moment, he felt like an old man in a cocked hat. He already had a hint of a second chin although he hadn't gained more than a pound or two since medical school, and lately his wife had been telling him to pick up his feet when he walked. He wasn't so sure he had the stamina to compete with a six-foot two-inch Greek god.

"You're coming along too, Will, aren't you? Perhaps she has a friend."

"I've a splitting headache. I think I'll turn in early."

"You'll be missing the event of the season."

"I hardly think—"

"You will, by Jove, so if I were you, sir, I would reconsider. And if it's your immortal soul you're fretting about, Saint Peter was once flesh and blood, too, so he'll understand. And if it's your wife you're fretting about, you shall be just as happily married when you walk through your front gate next week as you were when you walked out it. Depend upon it."

Will shook his head and wondered where he might find a good book to keep him company tonight.

So much for the "Rake of Rockbridge County," he thought.

Colonel Crockett's reception was held at Gadsby's Hotel, in one of the public rooms. The room was dimly lit, as if old Mr. Gadsby were hoarding his lamp oil, and it was full of segar smoke as thick as in the theater. Will didn't recognize a soul. He waited a half-hour for Jamey to turn up or for Ivy to turn up, and when neither did, he decided to call it a night. As he rose to go to his room, an ancient humpbacked little man in an ill-fitting black frock coat, the skirts of which reached the floor, approached him. He held a candle in each hand. He smiled and a diamond chip sparkled from one of his front teeth.

"My dear sir," he said. "I apprehend your friend has got himself into some mischief." He handed one of the candles to Will. "Come along. I shall take you to him."

"What on earth has happened to him?" Will said. The old man didn't answer. He walked out of the room into the dark hallway, stopping once to turn to see if Will was coming.

Something wasn't right; nevertheless, Will followed him down the hallway, which was so convoluted that he soon lost his bearings, so much so that when they emerged from a short cut through another public room, he gave up on logging his steps. At the end of the hallway was a carpeted staircase. They descended it until they were three flights below the street. They walked through a tunnel and up some more stairs, which led them into the hotel's interior courtyard. The courtyard was well lit by a dozen torches. Two men in high-crowned beaver hats were sitting cross-legged on the ground, a bushel of apples between them. They stood up when they saw Will and the old man approach. They were both exceptionally tall. Will asked the old man where Jamey was.

"I was not referring to that particular friend of yours," the old man said.

"Oh my God, Damen," Will said when one of the men in the hats turned around. "What are *you* doing here?"

Damen responded with a dark snaggle-tooth grin. By now Will had surmised that he was having another one of his nightmares.

"Gentlemen, please continue," the old man said.

The two took positions on opposite sides of the courtyard, about forty yards apart. They were both armed now with long flintlock rifles. The old man stood between them. At his signal each placed an apple on top of his hat.

The old man got out of the way. "Whoever shall miss," he said, "must place the apple upon his bare head for the other to take aim at."

They both missed, high. Impossible, Will thought—at least

for Damen; Damen was a crack shot at forty yards. If anyone knew that, Will did. Will, after all, had invented him, Damen being nothing more than a character in his first and as yet unpublished novel, *The Kentuckian in New-York*. Will looked up at the windows that faced the courtyard. None of the guests were stirring despite the thunder of the firearms.

They placed apples on their bare heads this time and took aim once more. Again they missed.

"So it's a stalemate," Will said. "And now I shall go back to my room."

"Patience," the old man said holding up his hand. "There is one last round." He explained that for the final round an apple must be placed upon a third party's head as a target for both marksmen. "It will take but a minute of your time."

"I think this has gone far enough," Will said.

"My dear sir, the rules," the old man said.

"What rules?"

The old man merely smiled, his diamond tooth scintillating in the torchlight. Will couldn't take his eyes off it. He found he couldn't move. He was mesmerized, something he did not even believe in. Somehow, he managed to close his eyes, but when he opened them, he found he had not woken up; rather, he was sitting on a cider barrel with an apple on his head. Damen and his rival had meanwhile gotten into a fistfight over who would shoot first. The next sound was neither the crack of a rifle or of Will's skull splitting but a knock on his door. He sat up straight and tried to catch his breath. Another knock, louder this time. Will rubbed his eyes and got up to see who it was.

"Rise and shine and fill up your chamber pot," said Jamey French at the door. From the slur of his speech and the stench of his breath he was profoundly deep into his cups. Will asked him what ungodly hour it was.

"Half past the bewitching hour," Jamey said, "and time to get back into your clothes."

"Go away," Will said.

"I fully intend to. And you, sir, are coming with me. The frolic has moved across the street to Crockett's lodgings, and now so shall we." He threw himself down on the bed.

"I thought you had other plans."

"Plans? What plans? 'Tis a pity to have to inform you of this, but that's the trouble with you, Caruthers. You plan every last minute of your dreadfully dull little life. Well, let me tell you something, my friend. If I feel like caruth ... like carousing when the rest of the world is sleeping, sir, then I damn well will, sir."

"I was under the impression you were going to be entertaining a certain young lady."

"taining a certain young lady."

Jamey belched. "She had a headache. Typical female ploy if you ask me." He laughed. "I should have called you, shouldn't I've? I should have sent for the doctor."

"Perhaps you should have," Will said.

And perhaps the doctor should pay her a visit tomorrow morning, he thought. She shouldn't be difficult to find. She most likely had a room at Gadsby's with Mr. Hackett's entourage or perhaps with some other local players who, like she, lived outside of the city. And with any luck, she missed him as much as he missed her.

"Let's not just stand there," Jamey said. "Get a move on it, old son, before I lose my patience with you."

"Then lose it. It's too confounded late for me, so if it's just the same with—"

"Stuff and nonsense. It's never too late for a business proposition."

"A business proposition? At half past midnight?"

"The man wants to meet you. I told him about you, and he wants to see you directly."

"He can wait till tomorrow."

"He wants to see you *now*. He may change his mind by tomorrow."

"Then let him change his mind. No one is stopping him."

Jamey yawned and covered his face with both of his hands.

"Don't be a damned fool, William," he said into his palms. "This is a monstrous opportunity for you. He's out with his family all day tomorrow, and then he's leaving the city. You'll be gone by the time he returns. So on with your clothes. Up and on with them."

Will walked across the room to the stove. The fire had gone out; no wonder he was so cold. He wasn't so very lucid either, for he had taken some laudanum; clearly, he wasn't in any condition to go out. And yet how could he squander such an opportunity? Lord knows he needed the money. A friend of Jamey's was looking for someone to do a bit of writing for him. Jamey had pointed him out at the theater. He had been one of Colonel Crockett's companions in the stage-box and, according to Jamey, was the colonel's adviser as well as the author of his recent biography. Apparently, he wished to publish a sequel. He had originally planned to retain Jamey, but as Jamey would be leaving for London in a few weeks, that was impossible. That was all Will knew about the matter, and he preferred to wait until his head cleared before hearing more.

"Well, I still think it can wait till tomorrow," he said as he looked around for his shirt.

"Here, take some medicine," Jamey said holding up a gaudily engraved silver flask. "Physician, heal thyself."

"I believe I'll rely upon my own prescription, thank you. It's easier on my disposition." Will rubbed his eyes. "It does have one drawback, though. It gives me the most God-awful night-mares. I had one a minute ago. As a matter of fact, you were in it."

"Then it must have been God-awful indeed."

Just then Will remembered that it wasn't Jamey who had been about to shoot him in the face. Rather, it was Earthquake, the principal *buffo* in the novel on which Jamey was laboring. Will had read four chapters and a synopsis of a few others in his hotel room earlier in the day and had found it difficult to keep a straight face sitting there in his friend's presence as he read. And not because it was so witty, but because it was so bad. Overly florid and embarrassingly imitative of Fenimore Cooper, it was one more dying Indian story to have to suffer through. And even if you could get past the style, the characters were lifeless and unconvincing. If Jamey expected his readers to believe that his hero, a handsome young attorney from Petersburg, Virginia (like the author, of course) could just so happen to run across his true love from back east some six hundred miles away on the Ohio River so he could rescue her from the Indians (as ordained by Providence, no doubt), then he had better wake up. And as for Earthquake, he was nothing more than a second-rate Crockett analogue.

Will straightened his suspenders and looked down at his friend sprawled out on the bed; Jamey made the four-poster look as if it had been built for a child. He decided that if Jamey fell asleep by the time he had finished dressing, he would not rouse him. Rather, he would camp out on the floor and return to his nightmares—only this time perhaps Damen would knock Earthquake's block off. Which would only be fitting, he thought. What could be more appropriate than to see his protagonist soundly thrash Jamey's as their two creators raced each other to get them into print? And it *was* a horse race, for although Will had already finished his manuscript, it would be just like Jamey, with his obscene assuredness, to conclude a deal on the strength of but a handful of chapters.

Well, if he *does* beat me to the punch, thought Will, I've no one to blame but myself. Will, after all, had made the mistake of showing Jamey his manuscript in New-York last January. Not that Damen was the only ringtail roarer that Jamey had at his disposal to copy—Jamey claimed to know Colonel Crockett personally, and tonight was hardly the first time he had seen Mr. Hackett in the *Lion of the West*—but who was to say he wouldn't have chosen the prophet Daniel as his protagonist if he had not perused Will's manuscript?

Will put on his tailcoat and his greatcoat and regarded his

gargantuan snoring friend. He shuddered at the thought of hopping into bed with him. The floor looked even less inviting. He reached for his hat and gloves. Who could say, he might even *enjoy* himself tonight at Crockett's lodgings. And besides, where else this trip could he scare up some rent money?

He shook Jamey awake.

"I am more an antique Roman than a Dane," Jamey mumbled.

"Come along, old son," Will said. "I've an appointment to keep."

Chapter Two

Colonel Crockett's rooms were in a long, narrow red brick building nearly identical to the other congressional boarding houses along Pennsylvania Avenue. Will and Jamey peered down the hallway into the parlor where upwards of a dozen men were discoursing, some loudly and profanely. The colonel was ensconced in a gilded red armchair. A wine glass in one hand, the other stroking his chin, he for all intent and purposes seemed to be soaking up wisdom from another well-dressed gentleman his same age, about forty-five or fifty.

"Is that him?" Will asked, pointing to the colonel's friend.

Jamey shook his head and straightened a gaudily framed likeness of Justice Marshall. "He must still be upstairs. Relax. Go fix yourself a drink."

Will was reluctant to medicate himself any further—at least not prior to talking business with Jamey's friend. Still, he consented to a small one.

"That's the old spirit," Jamey said. He led Will down the hallway to the dining room.

"Name your creature," said the rail-thin fellow at the sideboard. He seemed about Will's age and had a Mexican mustachio. He spoke with a Tennessee twang, and his coal black hair was greased down in the Western fashion.

"Just a small glass of port," Will said.

"One glass of port coming up." The Westerner picked up an abandoned teacup, sniffed it and then filled it to the brim.

"Crabtree," he said. "R.C. Crabtree. Used to do this for a living. Can't seem to break the habit." He shook hands first with Will, then with Jamey.

"Big hands," he said to Jamey. "I like a man with big hands. Me, I've got small hands. You fellows congressmen?"

Will shook his head. "I was about to ask you the same question."

"Me? No sir, I work for a living. More members here tonight than you can shake a serpent-stick at, though—and nary a one of them of the right persuasion."

He indeed did turn out to be from Tennessee. Moreover, he was an old friend of Colonel Crockett's, though easily twenty years his junior.

"We go way back," he said. "Back to Murfreesboro days. He was in the state legislature back then. I did most of the dispensing, and he did most of the imbibing."

"You certainly have come a long way," Will said.

"I'm still dispensing."

"I meant you have come a great distance."

Crabtree laughed. "Shoot, I've only come down from Baltimore—but by God if I don't clear out soon enough to keep *next* Christmas in Tennessee."

"Murfreesboro is an agreeable little town," Jamey said. "I passed through last year on my way to Nashville."

"I don't live in Murfreesboro no more," Crabtree said. "Didn't see much future there after the government cut out for Nashville. So I cut out, too. Westward. After the sun."

Will asked him if he and Colonel Crockett were neighbors. Crabtree shook his head.

"I do live in his district," he said, "but that don't tell you much considering the fact he represents seventeen or eighteen counties. No, he's up in Weakley and I'm down in Shelby. I've got me a little hostelry business there. Just outside of Memphis —if it's still there, I do. I've been gone thirteen months already, so there's no telling. Not from Baltimore there ain't."

"Baltimore seems quite habitable," Will said, "but I suppose `if 'tis not home, then 'tis not home.'"

"Baltimore would be fine if times was better. I've got me a cotton mill up there, but it don't amount to a belch in a gale of wind. I'll tell you what. It's eating my head off."

"I'm sorry to hear that."

"If you gentlemen will excuse me," Jamey said, "I have to see a man about a horse. *Your* horse," he whispered to Will and walked out of the room toward the stairs.

Crabtree refilled another guest's glass, then he and Will took their own glasses back to the parlor. He pointed out the half-dozen gentlemen with whom he was acquainted—Southerners and Westerners by and large, and most of them members of Congress. Will hadn't heard of any of them. One, however, soon made himself known to him; he sat down next to Will on the horsehair sofa and gave him a fifteen-minute harangue on the virtues of the canvass-backed duck. Then another congressman —a patently inebriated one—rose from his seat at the piano-forte and called for silence.

"Gentlemen, please," he slurred, one arm above his head and the other around the young Englishman whom Will had over-heard him introduce to his colleagues as the newest member of the British legation. "Gentlemen, we shall now witness a demon-stration the likes of which I for one have never beheld."

"It's nothing," the Englishman said. "Any parrot can do it."

"He can mock dead people."

"So can I," said someone from the back of the room. "Mr. Randolph of Roanoke." He slumped in his chair, closed his eyes, folded his hands on his chest.

"Upon my word," the Englishman said, "it may not be within

my power to equal that. Rest assured, however, for I shall not permit *that* to stop me." He cleared his throat.

"Villain be sure," he intoned in a deep coarse voice. *"O God, I am dying. Speak to them, Charles."*

Nobody seemed to know.

"Othello," he told them. "Edmund Kean's final words upon the stage at Covent Garden before collapsing in his son's arms."

"Can you give us a king?" somebody asked.

"I can do George the Third." The Englishman hung his head, opened his mouth, rolled his eyes.

"I can give you Charles the First," said a stout man standing by the fireplace. He pulled his coat over his head.

"No more monarchs," said the Englishman, "but I'll give you a few prime ministers." He did Lord North and William Pitt the Younger. He was about to do the Earl of Liverpool when somebody shouted:

"They're all bloody Britishers. Give us someone we can distinguish."

"Distinguish, sir? I should like to, but unfortunately, I haven't had the opportunity to study any of your famous personages yet. Would anyone care to introduce me to your president?"

Everyone laughed.

"I'm afraid you're on the wrong side of the fence," Colonel Crockett said. "Which I'm proud to say is your good fortune, son. He ain't too partial to you Johnny Bulls. He'll butcher you and feed your entrails to his hounds."

"Yes, sir, so I have heard."

"Well, before he gets a chance, let's have us a tune," said the inebriated congressman. He sat back down at the piano-forte and struck a loud sloppy chord with his fat fingers. Will noticed that his shirt tail was tucked into his red flannel drawers.

"I'll need some help, of course. Those of you who've heard me croak before sure as hellfire will understand that." He hit another chord and then in a broken baritone he cut loose:

> "With a cherry-cheek'd maid I've an eye on,
> I do many things they cry FIE on.
> EGOD! I'm as bold as a li-on.
> A blessing on brandy and beer."

That was the only verse he knew, so after the chorus he sang it again. Half-way through, there came a loud thump from the ceiling.

"I think your landlady is trying to tell us something," the Englishman said to Colonel Crockett.

"No, that's just old Clayborne," the colonel replied. Then he whispered something into his friend's ear. His friend whispered something back and handed him his brass-handled cane. The colonel took the cane into the center of the room and rapped the ceiling three times with it, then looked around for approval, a tobacco-stained grin on his face. A moment ago he had looked like a polished gentleman, but now Will thought he looked more like a mischievous middle-aged schoolboy.

The colonel returned the cane to his friend, appropriated a chair and stood on it. "When I'm president," he shouted at the ceiling, "the very first thing I'm a-gonna do is name you minister to the North Pole. You hear me up there, Shit-borne, you pap sucking old *pole* cat?" He cocked his ear to the ceiling, winced and waited for a response. None came. He turned around and looked down at his audience.

"As for the rest of you gentlemen," he said, "if this nation is ever foolish enough to elect me president, by God, I can guarantee you two or three things at least. First off, my house shall be your house. You're all welcome there any time of day or night. Second, there'll be bear steaks on the menu three times a day. And as for that white haired old bugbear that currently resides there, gentlemen, by the Eternal if I don't run his sorry arse back to the rock he done crawled out from under. And if I don't ..." He cocked his ears down to his guests.

"I wish I may be shot," several said at once.

The colonel straightened himself up, then reeled back; he had to reach for the ceiling to steady himself.

"All seriousness aside," he went on, "I may be an ignorant old brush hick straight out of the woods, but I ain't too ignorant to know my friends when I'm a-looking down at them. And you really and truly are my friends. That's on account of you know me inside out and *still* you put up with me. Gentlemen, I love the whole lot of you. And thanks for staying up with me tonight. Light me a segar, Tree," he said to Crabtree. Then he dismounted the chair and almost fell down.

Will shook his head and smiled; until then he hadn't apprehended how intoxicated the colonel was. *President Jackson* had taken some getting used to, but *President Crockett,* he thought— *God save us!*

∾

"Dr. Caruthers of New-York," R.C. Crabtree said to Colonel Crockett a few minutes later.

The colonel stood up to shake Will's hand. Will was surprised to find the celebrated bear hunter to be no taller than he, which made him about five-ten or eleven—funny, but he had remembered Crockett as standing well over six feet. And his dark hair was longer than Will had recalled and was parted down the middle now like a back country preacher's.

"That's not truly where I'm from, New York," Will said, startled at how embarrassed he felt. "I am a native Virginian, sir. You probably don't recollect, but we met once in Staunton about six years ago."

"Why sure I recollect," the colonel said. "I'm not so good with names, but I never dis-remember a face. I reckon we had us a few horns that day."

"Begging your pardon, sir, but you didn't feel much like drinking that day. Or eating, for that matter. In fact, that was why they sent for—"

"You ever been to Abingdon, Virginia, son?"

"Yes sir, I have. Many times."

"They give me a testimonial dinner a few weeks ago on my way up to Washington. They really like me in that part of the country. Where did you say you was from, Mr. ..."

"Caruthers. I'm from Rockbridge County."

"Rockbridge County," the colonel said. "Now don't that bring back a recollection or two. I drove a herd of cattle to that country when I was not yet twelve-year-old."

"By yourself?"

"I come back by myself. My father hired me out to this old Dutchman, and the scoundrel tried to keep me beyond my term of service, but I got away from him, by God. I had to walk seven, eight mile through deep snow to accomplish that. Fact is, the snow was so deep that the seat of my britches wiped out my footprints. Now that's been thirty-five years, son, and my *toes* ain't been properly *heeled* ever since."

The colonel waited a moment for Will to either laugh or groan at his pun—or so Will surmised—and when Will did neither, he shrugged.

"Mighty pretty country, though, Rockbridge County," he continued. "I was there four or five weeks if I'm not mistaken. You still live there?"

"No, sir, I don't. As a matter of fact I—"

"You a drinking man, Caruthers?"

"Oh ... occasionally," Will said completely losing his train of thought.

"Glad to hear it, son, and I'll tell you what. This is as good an occasion as any seeing as my glass is nearabout as empty as your'n. Come along Tree, let's have us a horn. You'll excuse us, gentlemen."

He hardly needs another one, Will thought as he followed Crabtree and the staggering colonel down the hallway to the dining room. At the sideboard they came upon a tall blond-haired fellow with a bulbous nose and dark bushy eyebrows. He was easily as tall as Jamey, though not as broadly built. He wore a rumpled shirt without a collar.

"Chilton," the tall man said and offered Will his hand. "Thomas Chilton."

"Hoppit," said the colonel, "Shirley Hoppit. Now *thar's* a name that suits him a far sight better, by God. Did you ever see a Baptist preacher of his dimensions that you could keep out of a corn field, son? Well, I for one haven't. I'll tell you what. You may build you a fence high as you please, but this man right here will surely hop it."

Will introduced himself to Mr. Chilton, who turned out to be a member of Congress from Kentucky. Congenial enough, Will thought, but when he spoke, he looked you more in the forehead than in the eye.

"Can I assume, sir," Mr. Chilton said, "that you haven't been around my friend David here long enough to acquire a sobriquet?"

"Yes sir, you can," said Will.

"Then count yourself among the fortunate. Like as not, you'll have one before sunup, though." Mr. Chilton took a sip of his drink. "Well, I do believe you're the man I've been looking for, Caruthers. A colleague of mine and a friend of yours are upstairs in my room. I promised I'd go down and discover you for them."

"Appears to me you done got waylaid." Colonel Crockett tapped Mr. Chilton's dram glass with a fingernail.

"Just a little something to help me sleep."

"That figures," the colonel said to Will. "That's about all the man ever does when he ain't a-working himself half to death. Sleep, work, sleep, work, sleep, work." He nodded his head from side to side as he spoke.

"You know, if common sense was lard," he went on, "Chilton here would be hard pressed to grease up a pan. Even my dogs know they've got to stop and smell the roses, but this man don't."

"My zeal hath consumed me because mine enemies have forgotten thy words," Mr. Chilton said.

"Hook it, son!" cried the colonel. "Spoke like a true soldier of the cross. Or like a six-foot mule. I'll tell you what. White mules don't ever die, they become Baptist preachers. Matter of fact, Reverend Chilton here—"

The colonel grimaced and clutched his abdomen.

"Good God almighty," he said just above a whisper.

Finally he let out his breath. Will asked him if he was indisposed.

"I'm fine, just a little crimped-up is all. Too much oyster sauce, I reckon."

Too much whiskey, Will thought.

"Gentlemen," Mr. Chilton said, "I believe it's getting—"

"You missed a mighty impressive performance," the colonel said and reached for a bottle of something dark and murky. "That young Johnny Bull had us a-roaring on the floor."

"I didn't miss a thing. I could hear you three flights up."

"Well, the boy was good—and I know good when I hear it. I go to the theater every chance I get. You should too, Chilton. Life ought to be more than one monstrous piece of legislation for you to have to slave yourself over."

Mr. Chilton smirked. "I don't have the time. Besides, if the elders of my church knew that—"

"Then make you some time. That's what I do."

"You don't compose your own speeches and amendments."

The colonel finished pouring his drink and smiled. "I don't need to. Not with you and your ink-pen down the hall I don't. And if I've never before properly thanked you, sir, I wish to do so right now, old friend, for carrying me longer than my own dear mother done till she dropped me into this wicked world. But I really do love good play acting, I swear I do. Old Verplanck used to drag me along with him like I was his pet monkey or some such thing, hell bent on turning human. Listen here:

"What light through yonder window breaks? It is the East, and Juliet—I mean, Chilton here is the moon-dog. WAH-OOOOH!"

He clutched his abdomen again. "You know, when you get to be my age," he said, "one monstrous fart is all it takes to throw your back out."

He put his drink down on the sideboard. "If you gentlemen will excuse me, I reckon I'd better go out back. I'd surely hate to have to transact my business too close to the house. Customarily I would go ahead and fault it on the chickens, but seeing as there ain't none available, I had best get these tired old limbs of mine a-moving. So I'll be seeing you gentlemen later."

Will walked him to the door. Then he took leave of Mr. Chilton and regarded the stairway; he had met the ringtail roarer again, now it was time to meet his keeper.

~

"Matthew St. Clair Clarke," the little man said. He had thinning red hair, except at the temples where it was much thicker and nearly white, and he squinted when he spoke. For a second or two, Will thought he was Vice-President Van Buren.

Clarke put his segar in the corner of his mouth and shook Will's hand with both of his.

"Young French here speaks highly of you," he said as he worked the segar with his teeth. "I understand you are a writer."

"An unpublished one," Will said.

"So, too, Shakespeare once was. Any bites?"

"It's gathering dust, sir. At the Harpers. I haven't heard from them in two months."

Clarke pulled a chair out from Mr. Chilton's writing desk, turned it around and sat down on it. His feet barely touched the floor. "Keep your spirits up," he said blowing smoke. "And I wish you two would sit down. I may be a trifle past my youth, but I am not old enough to be your father."

Will and Jamey sat down on Mr. Chilton's bed.

"James here tells me that you and he attended the play," Clarke went on.

"Mr. Hackett was in rare form," Will said.

"Then you've seen it before."

Will nodded; he had attended the opening night performances of the last two revisions. As for Kirke Paulding's original manuscript, he had read it over coffee one morning three weeks before it was first produced.

"I've done some occasional work for Mr. Paulding," he said. "Including spying on the theater goers when he was unable to attend."

"Still trying to keep up with Mr. Irving, is he?"

"Since their youth, sir. Then you and Kirke are acquainted?"

"I know him only through his work. I did correspond with him once, though, but I am quite certain he doesn't remember me." Clarke pulled one of his feet up to the seat of his chair and slipped it behind his other knee. He closed his eyes and chuckled to himself.

"I was just reflecting upon the irony of it all, Caruthers," he said. "Your Mr. Paulding, the consummate Jackson man, makes a national celebrity of my friend Crockett, completely unaware that my friend has already written King Andrew off as a bad investment and gone over to the good-fellows' side—viz: ours."

"He knows it now, sir," Will said.

"And that thought, I calculate, must keep him up nights."

Will nodded. "Once, I overheard a political crony of his ask him how he had felt when he learned that Crockett had jumped ship and was championing the United States Bank. 'Like Mrs. Shelley's Frankenstein,' Kirke replied. 'I have created a monster.'"

"Indeed he did. *Our* monster, thank Providence!"

"Have you seen the latest *Knickerbocker*?" Jamey asked Will.

"Not yet—should I have?"

Clarke picked up the journal from Mr. Chilton's writing desk and handed it to Will. "Our efforts were reviewed quite favorably," he said. "Go ahead and read it."

Will glanced over the review of Clarke's book, the anonymous Crockett biography that had just been re-printed. It was so fulsome it was practically falling all over itself. And it paraphrased Kirke Paulding to a fault, implicitly attributing Colonel Wildfire's comical lines from the play to Colonel Crockett rather than to the quiet emasculated New-Yorker who had actually penned them.

"I couldn't have done it without you, James," Clarke said.

Jamey looked down at his huge hands and smiled. "'Twas but a trifle, Will," he said. "Just an interview or two."

"Mr. French is too modest," Clarke said. "And now he's to peddle them abroad for me, aren't you lad?"

"Matt here has been kind enough to put in a word for me at Harpers. I—"

"And I do need the income now that I am off the government pay roll. James must promote the rest of their list too, of course. After all, I am not the only unoccupied writer in this nation with a family to feed"

Will smiled to himself. According to Jamey, Matthew Clarke could afford to remain comfortably unoccupied for the rest of his life. He regarded Jamey over the top of his magazine. Jamey had told him he was going to England in an editorial capacity— something about a joint publishing venture with some British firm. In truth, however, he was but another lowly foreign agent on a mission to knock upon doors.

"Which brings me to why I asked you here, Caruthers. Mr. French here is going to be leaving us after the first of the year and we don't expect him back until, when James?"

"Next fall."

"Yes, and next fall will be entirely too late for our purposes. I had intended to engage him for a particular project of mine, you see. Now that I must look elsewhere, he thought perhaps it might be of some interest to you. Has he broached the subject yet?"

Will and Jamey looked at each other. "Not in any great detail," said Will.

Clarke pointed to the door with his segar; Jamey got up to close it.

"I wish it to be ... how shall I say? A political tract in sheep's clothing." Clarke leaned forward and lowered his voice. "In all candor, Caruthers, I am somewhat uncomfortable speaking to you about this. I have nothing of your political background, sir, than Mr. French's rather vague assurances. Quite frankly, I find your close association with such a rabid Jackson partisan as Mr. Paulding to be a trifle disturbing."

Will raised his right hand. "Rest assured, sir, I am no Jackson man," he said. "I have rejected him on all three occasions for the same reasons that you have, I gather. Because he is the most ignorant man ever to stand for the presidency, let alone to have gotten himself elected."

Clarke nodded. "If my feeble-minded Uncle Petrus had killed two thousand lobsterbacks at New Orleans and sent their commanding general home in a casket of rum, he might have gotten himself elected president too. So you are one of us, Caruthers."

Will tightened his lips into a semblance of a smile and raised his eyebrows. "I am not a politician, sir," he said. "I am a physician."

"And a good one, no doubt. But I suspect your pen is as mighty as your scalpel. And you are in all likelihood as capable of expressing another man's thoughts as you are your own—that is, sir, if the gulf between them is not so terribly great."

Clarke squinted and drew on his segar. "Well, in any event you seem to be a level-headed young man. We intend to send Colonel Crockett on a tour of the Northern states to plead our case among the workmen and are in need of someone like you to chronicle it. I wish I had the time to do it myself, but I am afraid I've too many irons in the fire."

He brushed some ashes off his trousers.

"I'm going to tell you something," he went on. "What I am asking you to do is of the utmost importance to the very survival of the National Republican Party. Because if we don't make any inroads among the lower classes, we are finished: pure and simple. Suffice it to say, the time has long since passed since the days when we could afford to choose our political associates by the contents of their pocketbooks. Rich or poor, these days a vote is but a vote."

"If Mr. Clay had only had you for an adviser, sir, he'd be president today," Jamey said and sat down on the bed.

Clarke coughed and shifted in his seat. "Mr. Clay had far better things to do than to listen to the humble Clerk of the Lower House. And I am quite certain he has seen the same handwriting on the wall."

"I do hope he has. And he had best move swiftly, sir, before the opportunity passes us by."

"I wouldn't worry about it passing us by, Mr. French. Believe me, we haven't seen anything yet." Clarke made a motion with his closed right hand as if he were turning a screw.

You haven't seen anything yet, thought Will. Will, however, had seen plenty. He had seen five of his patients lose their livelihoods and his next-door neighbor lose his home of fifteen years. Mr. Clarke was right, though. It was going to get worse before it got better. A prodigious number of businesses had already gone under, and many more were in immediate jeopardy. As for the government, no one was doing a blessed thing to alleviate the situation. Quite the opposite, in fact. Each party—President Jackson's and the opposition coalition's—seemed more disposed to feed the panic, to place the blame on the other party and bring it to its knees.

"Gentlemen," Clarke said, "I submit that the workmen of this country are disposed to listen to the truth for a change."

"Aye, the truth," said Jamey.

"Particularly if they hear it from one of their own. To wit, if a man as popular as our Davy Crockett assures them it was the president of the United States and not Mr. Biddle's bank who deprived them of their jobs and pilfered their life savings, they will believe him. To paraphrase the Bard: politics makes strange bedfellows. And I cannot imagine two stranger ones than Crockett and Nick Biddle, can you?"

"Not for the life of me," Jamey said.

Will turned his head and covered his yawn. "So you want me, sir, to write this political tract," he said hoping to get the business at hand over with so he could go back to sleep.

"Well, not exactly. You can leave the political content to us. What we expect from you is nothing more and nothing less than a spellbinding well-written story—with plenty of humor, of course."

"Then William is your man," Jamey said.

If William chooses to be your man, Will thought. He rubbed his eyes and wondered how many gold eagles his scruples were worth and how much time he was going to have to spend with the hard-drinking colonel.

"I suppose I must accompany him on the tour."

"If you so wish," Clarke said. "It should be well reported by the newspapers, though, so there is no need to inconvenience yourself. But understand, I am not looking for a verbatim journal. If you don't use your imagination, sir, I calculate your book will be one long yawn."

He smiled at Will and then studied the lit end of his segar. "Contrive him into an extraordinary situation or two, Caruthers —solely on paper, of course. Have him ... uncover another administration plot to debase the currency. Or have him risk his life rescuing somebody's grandmother from a pack of Irish ruffians—anything to dramatize the nobility of his character."

The nobility of his character, Will thought.

"And when precisely does this tour commence?"

"I shall write to you as soon as I find out myself. The sooner the better as far as I am concerned."

"And I'll second that motion," Jamey said. "The administration isn't holding back its big guns and neither should we."

"How much time will I have?"

"Plenty," Clarke said. "Several months at the very least. You may begin tomorrow if you wish."

"No thank you, sir. I shall likely sleep through tomorrow."

"And so too shall I." Clarke opened his watch and raised an eyebrow. "Great Scott, would you look at the time! Annie must be wondering what's become of me." He gathered his paperwork from the desk.

Will stood up. "One last question, sir, if you don't mind."

"Mind? Heavens no—but do keep it brief."

"I heard Colonel Crockett say something preposterous downstairs."

"So what else is new under the sun?"

"Does he really intend to stand for the presidency?"

Clarke put out his segar in an empty dram glass and smiled. "Our friend thinks quite a lot of himself these days."

"I've noticed that, sir, but the *presidency?*"

"Boggles the mind, doesn't it? Apparently, a friend of his in the Mississippi state legislature has convinced him that a motion to place his name in nomination would carry."

"And would it?"

"What do *you* think?"

"Well, maybe in Mississippi."

Clarke shook his head. "Not even in Mississippi, but I calculate it's best to humor him. I cannot begin to tell you what a time I am having trying to get his consent for the tour."

"You mean he hasn't given it yet?"

"Well ... *implicitly,* more or less—but not in so many words. I do have all the confidence in the world that he will, though. I've never known him to turn down a public dinner, have you French?"

"I don't believe it's within his power."

"Nor do I. Believe me, the prospect of two or three weeks of free liquor and food should prove to be irresistible to a man such as he. And being fawned over as if he were the baby Jesus."

Will asked about his compensation; Clarke told him it would be generous. He would brief him about the particulars once the itinerary and the budget for the project were set.

"And if the publisher doesn't come through," he said, "I shall pay you, sir, out of my own pocket."

They exchanged calling cards and bade each other a good night.

"MAY I BE OF ANY ASSISTANCE, SIR?" SAID WILL TO COLONEL Crockett. He had been on his way to the front door when he saw the colonel alone at the dining room table, his head thrown back, a wet towel over his face down to the tip of his nose.

"Not lessen you've got you a rifle-gun and you're a-willing to use it." The colonel removed the towel; the color was completely gone from his cheeks, and he was shivering. "I'll be all right after a while. Just a little touch of the ague. I've been a-wrassling with it all week. I reckon the worst of it is over."

"You belong in bed, sir."

"Aye, and that's just where I'm a-going. As soon as I can get myself to confront those stairs."

"May I give you a hand, sir?"

The colonel waved Will away. "I'm fine," he said. "Really and truly I am. I mean, it's not about to kill me. Least-ways, that's what I told Mother Ball. She was relieved since she's never had a boarder die in this house yet. I reassured her that if I took a turn for the worse, she could always have me carried out to die in the gutter."

Will smiled. "I can give you something to make you feel better. It's just across the street in my hotel room. I won't be but a minute."

"You say you're a doctor?"

"I treated you for a similar affliction five or six years ago on your way up here. I believe it was your first term."

"That was you?" The colonel straightened himself up. "You like to killed me, son."

"I hardly think so, sir."

"You damn near bled me to death. If you got leeches on your mind, don't you come near me. I'm a-warning you, son. I been down that road before."

"You must be confusing me with someone else. I don't use leeches. When I saw you, another physician had already—"

"I'm not confusing you with nobody. I took ill like you say on my way up here, and you drained what little life I had left in me. How do you expect me to be mistaken about a thing like that? All you leeches is the same. I believe it tickles the devil out of you to watch a man bleed to death, I swear it does. Only difference between a doctor and the angel of death is a doctor makes you pay for it."

Will was tempted to let the colonel sit there and suffer. At length, however, he put on his greatcoat and promised to return shortly with something to help him sleep and a month's supply of anti-fever pills.

What a sorry excuse for a human being, he thought as he walked down Pennsylvania Avenue toward his hotel. And the rest of them weren't much better—there probably hadn't been a sober congressman in the house tonight. Curiously enough, Will had once wanted to be one himself, a member of Congress. He had been fifteen then. His father had brought him here in March of 1817 to witness the inauguration of the president. Will had hoped to shake hands with Mr. Monroe but never got close enough to so much as get a good look at him. Breakfast with the representative from their district was the best that could be arranged for them. Unfortunately, the man didn't have much to say to Will, who just sat there in silence, longing to be old enough and wise enough to discuss something of more significance with a congressman than how well he was doing in school.

Will had thought he would be a congressman, too, by now. He had understood that his chances of carving a niche in history for himself were slim, but he would at least have the satisfaction of knowing that he was doing the same thing with his life that Patrick Henry and Thomas Jefferson once did with theirs. The naivete of youth, perhaps, but those were idealistic times. As opposed to *these* times, Will thought; pick up most any newspaper today and you will find less real news and more self-serving partisan diatribe than an honest man can stomach at a sitting.

Will paused in the middle of the avenue and looked up at the dark silhouette of the Capitol Dome. Some of the elegant rows of poplars that Mr. Jefferson had planted were gone, cut down for firewood a few years after Will's visit, but otherwise it still could have been 1817. Except for a few lamps at the hotels, the avenue was still pitch dark; and although the center part had been macadamized, it was still as thick with dust—hardly the "Paris of the West," he thought. What Washington more closely resembled was Rome during the Decline.

Hail Caesar, O just and gracious Lord. A postmaster-ship wouldn't be asking too much, would it?

Or some rent money, Will thought, for trying to convince thousands of honest workmen that the bogus hero poised to stab them in the back was their friend. He laughed so sharply that he startled himself. Is that what he had come to, he who had dreamed of walking in the footsteps of Patrick Henry and Thomas Jefferson? His father had known Mr. Jefferson briefly during the latter's declining years. Will himself had once written to the great man for a character reference.

But what would Mr. Jefferson think of him now, he who was about to grind out lies for the poor to suck up like so much sausage? And what would Will's father think of him, he who was about to hire himself out to the Bank Party? Will shook his head and stepped onto the sidewalk in front of Gadsby's Hotel.

Politics may make strange bedfellows, he thought, *but bankruptcy makes even stranger ones.*

Chapter Three

He has a Mexican mustachio and speaks with a Tennessee twang, and his coal black hair is greased down in the Western fashion.

R.C. Crabtree

Rogers Clark is what the letters stand for. George Rogers Clark Crabtree, after the famous general. My mother's father served as an officer under him during the Revolution, and it was on account of my being born on his birthday that I ended up with his name, although I dropped the George before I reached my majority. I wonder what the odds are against such a thing occurring, me being born on that same day. Three hundred sixty-four to one, I suppose—unless the folks did some mathematical ciphering and waited till nine months previous to my arrival to commence their relations.

I mention odds. I wonder what the odds are you wish to hear more about *me* than about my friend Crockett. Not much, I suspect. Fact is, a considerable number of you no doubt fancies the thought of trading places with him. To this I must say: perish such thoughts, for they will not serve you well.

If I was to ask you how well you thought my famous acquaintance was doing these days, you would likely say he was cutting himself a wide swath. You would be right, of course, if you was talking about gaining fame. But if it was fortune you was talking about, then you would be dead wrong because the man is up to his ears in debt. Part of that's of his own doing. Friends tell me he drinks and gambles a good portion of his income away, but that's not the whole story. The rest has more to do with forces he has no more control over than the weather. Believe me, I know what he is going through. I'm going through the selfsame thing myself. I should like to think I'm handling it a little better, though.

IF YOU WILL INDULGE ME FOR A MINUTE OR TWO, I WISH TO tell you a few things about myself before I get back to my famous friend and stay there. To begin at the beginning, the year I was born was also the first year of this present century, and this, combined with what day it was has always led me to believe that I was destined for something out of the ordinary. So far that has not proved to be the case. Today I am still nothing more than a poor-to-middling coarsely dressed tavern keeper. The tavern is but a little old rum shanty with a few extra rooms added on for sleeping just outside of Memphis, Tennessee. I will say this about it, though: it does have an impressive view of the mighty river.

I call my establishment the Sign of the Crabtree, and it bears but scant resemblance to the likes of Gadsby's Hotel and Brown's Indian Queen here in Washington City, although it's an improvement from what it used to be. Years ago, it was a regular cut-you-and-hurt-you sort of place where they would check you for weapons at the door, and if you didn't have one, then they would *give* you one.

I should tell you that it's my sister Kate that runs the place these days. This is because for the past thirteen months I have been in Baltimore, Maryland. If you're wondering how I ended up so far away from my home, it was on account of my other sister Sarah who resides in that city. A year ago last fall I received word that her husband had just given up the ghost from the cholera. He left her with a failing business that she could not manage on her own, so I had to set out and go manage it for her. It's a cotton mill and it has seen better days. I'll tell you what. If things don't turn around by summer, I'm going to liquidate what's left of her assets and carry Sarah back to Memphis with me. Out west a good woman is a mighty scarce commodity, and I would bet my last bit of bullion that the boys will come from miles around to have a look at her.

You would think that I'd be itching to get back home to Tennessee, wouldn't you? Well I am, but it irks me to have to cut and run like that. I've been counting on turning that mill around —and I reckon as how I could have done so by now if only it hadn't been for Nicholas Biddle and the Bank of the United States. Thanks to that man, money is tight as a tick and getting scarcer every day. The Bank newspapers are trying to frighten the people into hoarding what little there is that's left so as to feed the panic and blame it on President Jackson. As much as it pains me to admit it, I fear they are succeeding. I hope the people wake up before they vote the Bank Party into power.

You know what I would do if I was the president? I would haul Nicholas Biddle into court before a jury of unemployed mechanics that lost their jobs on account of him. Then I would have the judge order him hanged, drawn and quartered. And don't think for a minute I would lose a single night's sleep over it.

I'll tell you one thing that I *have* lost some sleep thinking about, and that's what has become of my friend Crockett. This is his third go-round in the U.S. Congress, and each term he has slid a little farther down that slippery slope which the preachers tell us about. The Bank Party has got him under their thumbs now, and if I hadn't seen it with my own two eyes, I would never have believed it. Just last night I met the man that has hoodwinked him the most. They call the vice-president a magician, but he ain't one-up on that little snake-in-the-grass Clarke—who, by the way, is no kin to my namesake, praise the Lord. One minute he's telling a windy about some Dutchman neighbor of his like he's nothing but a simple farmer himself, and the next minute he's twisting your arm to vote for some pet measure of his and quoting from the U.S. Constitution like he wrote it.

I wish you could have seen that slippery Mr. Clarke at the reception they had for Crockett last night. That little man must know every politician in town. From what I understand he keeps a book on them. He knows their every weakness—and what's more, he knows how to use them to his advantage. I could plainly see that he knows Crockett's weaknesses. He never let my friend's glass get below half-full all night. From what I've been able to piece together, he has been working on him for years. At first, I thought it was merely a case of him making Crockett out to be a greater man than he truly is in order to turn his head and get him to compromise his principles away, but now I suspect it was something even more underhanded than that.

It was my old friend Ned Keeble who told me the thing that caused me to question what respect I yet had for Crockett. Ned and I have been staying at our friend Dave Dickinson's lodgings here in Washington City for the past several nights. Dickinson is just now commencing his first term in Congress and Ned, who is now editor of his own newspaper, came up with him from Tennessee to see him installed. When I knew the two of them back in Murfreesboro, they were both mere schoolboys trying to arm-twist me into giving them a taste of the spirits I was then dispensing at the Elk's Horn Tavern.

Dickinson's brother-in-law you may have heard of. His name is John Bell, and I should tell you that he's as ambitious a man in politics as he is in fortune seeking. He and Colonel Polk both want the Speakership of the House so badly they are apt to break out in hives just thinking about it. By the way, Polk is also the name of Dickinson and Bell's landlady—no relation I am told—and I have seen them make great sport of this by lowering their voices and placing their forefingers to their pursed lips when she entered the room!

It was John Bell we was talking about when my friend Ned told me the shameful thing that Crockett had done. We were off in the parlor with our brandy and segars, just the two of us. After suffering through a whole supper-full of Dickinson and Bell's money-making schemes, I confessed to Ned that all that money-talk was making me feel a mite envious of them. He says I should stop talking nonsense.

"They're both strapped for cash," says he, lowering his voice. "I don't want this to leave this room, but between you and me, John Bell is into the Bank of the U.S. for over twenty thousand dollars."

I wasn't surprised. I knew that Bell's brother was on the board of the Bank's Nashville branch, and that they did a raft of land speculating together.

"I'd likely be into the Bank five figures deep myself," says I, "if I had blood kin with a key to the vault."

"Or if you had a fighting chance to become the next Speaker of the House."

I agreed; blood may be thicker than water but the glue that holds a political faction together is often thicker yet. I am speaking of the coalition of Nationals and Nullifiers (the money men, that is, and the secessionist traitors) who have aligned themselves against the president. Bell has been busy lining up votes among them of late despite the fact that he still claims to be a Jackson man.

"You reckon John's done signed his immortal soul over to the coalition yet?" I asked Ned.

"Just his heart so far," Ned answered me. "I don't expect you'll hear a peep out of him on the Bank question this session."

"No telling what might turn up once the books are thrown open."

"No telling."

I told Ned how surprised I was to hear that Crockett was standing up for the National Bank this session, and he with but little more than his famous name to show for himself in this world. While it may be common knowledge that he tends to vote with the coalition, still I've never known him to defend *any* bank before in his life, let alone the monster one. In my mind's eye I can clearly hear him say:

"I keep all skunks and bankers at a distance."

"He probably never got an interest-free loan before."

I thought I hadn't heard Ned right. I made him repeat what he had said.

"I'm telling you he walked right into the Washington branch, and they gave it to him no questions asked, no fixed terms. I guess you'd have to say he's all bought and paid for now."

"You mean to tell me they flat out made him a *present* of it?" says I.

"That's as apt a word as any."

I then come to find out that Crockett's first week back in Washington—by this I mean but a few weeks ago—they forgave him the entire transaction, principal and interest both. Aye, the whole confounded thing was struck from the books—and by personal order of none other than Nicholas Biddle himself. I asked Ned if he was quite certain of this. Ned said he was.

"Dickinson told you that?"

"Crockett told me himself. He seems to be proud of it."

Then Ned pointed out that right about the time that Crockett got the loan was when the Bank started trying to buy up other candidates for election and re-election from Maine to Georgia so as to seize control of the Congress and vote itself a new charter. That was nearly three years ago, not more than a month or two before Crockett publicly deserted President Jackson and his party.

I tried to convince myself that there was no connection, but the more I thought about it, the more I feared there really was. I asked myself if this could possibly be the same man I had known for so long. When I knew Crockett in Murfreesboro, he would no more have sold his vote to the money men than he would have sold his old mother down the river. Once he was as good a friend as our poor backwoods farmers ever had in the state legislature. If somebody had told me ten-twelve years ago that one day he'd be voting with the Bank men in the United States Congress, I would have laughed in that man's face. Hell, I might even would have knocked him down. Crockett stood by his principles back then even when it was bad politics to do so. He didn't have a compromising bone in his body. I know this for a fact. I know this because I have been privileged to call him my friend ever since he first came to Murfreesboro as a newly elected legislator.

Well, I reckon a man in need will sometimes soften up and put the good of his family and himself before the good of his country, and Crockett has been in need as long as I have known him. The last time I saw him previous to this week, it struck me how pitiful poor he still was, particularly for a man who had come up so far in the world. That was in the summer of 1831 when he was canvassing for re-election. Well, not only did he lose his seat in the U.S. Congress that summer, but he was so deep in debt he lost his home as well. The best he could do after that was to go lease some overgrown patch of thick woods belonging to a neighbor and start all over there from aught. When I went to visit him, he was just about ready to go pitch his tent there and start clearing off the land. That was when he and his wife broke up housekeeping. She moved in with some kinfolk —and if you ask me, that's half the problem right there. Crockett's wife is a good Christian woman, and when he let her get away from him, I believe that was when his serious backsliding commenced.

As I said, I have known the man a long time: ever since 1821 to be exact. I am certain of the year because I had just turned twenty-one along with the century. That was soon after I first arrived in Murfreesboro. I come up from Ducktown, which is in the Cherokee nation down near the Carolina and Georgia borders. (I don't have a drop, but my step-mama is a full-blooded Cherokee) I come up because I had taken a notion that I might involve myself in politics, and seeing as Murfreesboro was at that time the capital of the state, I figured it would be as good a place as any to make a start. I took a job at the Sign of the Elk's Horn to make ends meet. The proprietor there was a friend of my father's. They had fought together at New Orleans under Billy Carroll, and before that he spent a year or two working in my father's tavern back when I was a mere child.

In the fall of 1823 I started reading the law in the office of Mr. William Childress, but after a few months I came to comprehend that I don't have it in me for such things. Fact is, there's far too many gaps in my education as I have never set foot inside a true and proper school before. So I concluded that I was best off doing what I done best, namely keeping a tavern; however, it was three years and two hundred miles before I was able to get out from under the yoke of another man's employ.

My first year in Murfreesboro was an exciting one, for that was when the legislature elected Billy Carroll to his first term as Governor of Tennessee. People forget, but what they are calling Jacksonism these days had more to do with Governor Carroll back then than with the old general himself. General Jackson, in fact, was on the other side of the fence at the time. Those who know him solely as the president and the "Hero of New Orleans" may find this hard to believe, but it is an undisputed fact. He was —or so we all apprehended—nothing more than a tight-fisted land-grabbing aristocrat and a tool of the Overton Party. Judge Overton was the richest man in the state, and we all thought Jackson was under his thumb. The whole lot of them had more allegiance to their plundering pack of land speculators than they did to the welfare of their fellow Tennesseans.

As for the Carroll Party, it was a mighty strange mix, from true friends of the people like Crockett to money men like John Bell. They all claimed to believe in the governor's forward-thinking policies, but most of them paid him little more than lip service. What they believed in most was getting elected and staying elected, which isn't much different from how things stand nowadays if you stop and think about it. The only difference is today they all claim to be Jackson men—except Crockett, of course—and at election time they claim it the loudest. Let me tell you something. The Jackson party of today, or the Democrat-Republicans—or whatever you wish to call them—is every inch as motley a crew as the Carroll Party used to be—at least in the state of Tennessee it is—and Dickinson, Bell and company are no more Jackson men than I am a college professor.

I was a Carroll man in those days, of course, and so was my friend Crockett. The taproom where I worked, I must tell you, was strictly a Carroll room. Stands to reason, for with one of his old lieutenants operating the tavern how could it be any other's? That was where I first met Crockett, right there in the taproom of the old Elk's Horn. He used to spend a measure of time there. He used to drink a fair amount even then, but rarely before the sun went down. Except for one day not long after I first met him, which was, I'd say, a dozen or so days after the legislature convened. He was the first one in the room that evening and the last one to leave. He had been in a frolicsome enough mood at first, entertaining his colleagues with his laughable stories, but at the end of the night his good humor took leave of him.

"Three thousand dollars," Crockett moaned over and over again. "More than I'm worth in the whole world."

He had recently built a grist mill and a powder mill, too, said he, of considerable size and he had borrowed heavily to finance them only to have to learn that they both had been destroyed by a terrible flood. He had, in fact, just received the bad news that very day.

"Swept away to all smash," said he. "I feel like something the cat drug in and the dog wouldn't eat."

He must have kept me there two hours that night pouring out his troubles to a boy he hardly knew from Adam. I'll tell you one thing, though. He may have lost everything he had, but he didn't stoop to finagle a corrupt loan from the Bank of the U.S. to cover his debts. Not then he didn't. He worked them out honestly and then packed up his family and moved to the Western District to make a fresh start on some refuse land even he could afford.

Well, I suppose he has finally had enough of being poor as his backwoods neighbors. Either that or he has run out of refuse land to escape to.

He made his move to the Western District at the end of the last session of his first term. I figured I would never see him again; which would be a shame, as we had come to be good friends. Well, I was wrong about that being the last of him, for one day the following September as I was opening up my taproom, in he steps—and as none other than the newly elected legislator of a district one hundred and fifty miles away from his previous one! None of us had ever heard of such a thing occur-ring before; here you must remember he was not a well-known personage yet, not even in his own state. We asked him to explain how he done it, and if you have ever before met the man, you know he hardly needed to be asked.

"It all started out as a joke," he began.

The way he told it, it was February of that same year, 1823, and he was sitting in a tavern in Jackson, Tennessee when in walks three candidates for the state legislature. They get to talk-ing, and then somebody suggests that he offer for the legislature as well. Crockett declines; says he don't live close enough to any settlement "to represent nothing but critters." Then he gathers up whatever provisions he traded his animal skins for and rides home.

"It was about a week or two after this," Crockett went on to us (we numbered about a dozen now and we was gathered around him like he was the King of Egypt), "when this stranger comes by my house and informs me I'm a candidate. I figured he had a little too much of the creature in him, but he swore he was sober as a judge. Then he takes out a newspaper from his pocket and shows me where I was announced. There it was in black and white, gentlemen, so I figured it had to be true. But the more I thought about it, the more I become convinced that someone was out to have himself some considerable fun at my expense. It kept me up all night, but by morning I decided I would go ahead and do it. The way I figured, I'd make it cost that man at least the value of the printing. Not long after that, I hired out a young boy to take my place on my farm and set out to electioneering.

"So off I went down every little holler in the country, and it wasn't long before the people there was a-talking much more about the bear hunter and much less about them other politicians. Next thing I know, the three of them went and caucused up together to choose the strongest candidate so the anti-Bear Hunter vote wouldn't be split. Dr. Butler was the one they chose and the other two backed out. Which was good for them, I reckon, because they was both so dead between the ears they could throw themselves upon the ground and miss."

"Doc Butler's money didn't do a thing for him, did it?" somebody standing next to me said.

"I reckon not," says Crockett, "but let me tell you something about that man. He just happens to be the most masterful fellow I know of ever to stand for office in that country—and being kin to Andy Jackson don't hurt him none."

Right about then, Crockett asked me to go fetch a bottle of whiskey and enough glasses for all present, myself included. When I got back, he had already started explaining about how he out-electioneered his opponent.

"If you can make them laugh, you can get 'em to vote for you," said he.

It turned out he could even make that man Butler laugh. Out west where I come from, office-seekers spend a considerable amount of time together; they generally deliver their speeches one after the other off the same platform. Well, after a number of such public meetings, Crockett had committed his opponent's entire speech to memory word for word—or plum nearly—and delivered it ahead of him on this one occasion leaving the doctor so be-spited and tickled, both, he could barely pull himself together to deliver a substitute speech.

As for old Crockett's speech, if you are expecting me to repeat it word for word you have another thing coming, because he just summed it up for us. Here is one thing I do remember, though:

General Butler (I say "General" because some folks called him that, for he was once a military man too, another stumbling block for Private Crockett to have to surmount), he liked to recall how as a young doctor, he once stayed up all night trying to cure a dying child and not only saved her, but also changed his whole life to boot, this by teaching him to never again give up on nothing. Well, when Crockett got to this story in his speech, he changed things a little by turning the child into a rooster.

"So I stayed up all night with my feathered friend," said he, "a-doctoring him back to health. I done this with such remedies as blowing my own breath into his beak and spooning my special whiskey potion down his throat and reciting a chant I done made up to break the devilish spell that had come over him. Then, by the Eternal if on the next morning at daybreak that rooster didn't commence to crowing again as usual. Which meant that I no longer had to worry about sleeping through entire days no more. No sirs, I now had plenty of time to make up enough jokes to get me elected to the legislature!"

"But that kind of foolishness ain't the half of how I done the man in," Crockett went on to us there at the tavern. "The sawbones' problem was he would run his mouth too long on subjects far over the heads of the simple folks that come out to hear him so that pretty soon their good humor had done took off and left them sour as two-week old clabber-milk on the Fourth of July.

"Well, like I said, I delivered that speech of his myself once, and after I seen the deadening effect it had on the people, I knew it would never do for me as a regular bill of fare. So after that, here's what I done:

"I would go prepared to leave every man on as good a footing as when I found him. I had me a large buckskin hunting-shirt with a couple of pockets holding about a peck each, one of them with a big twist of tobacco in it, and the other one with my bottle of red liquor. What I knew was, if I met a man and offered him a dram, he would have to throw out his quid of tobacco to take one. So I made sure that after he had took his horn of liquor, why, I would out with my twist and give him another chaw. That way he wouldn't be worse off than when I found him. And I would be sure to leave him in a first-rate good humor."

Crockett won that election by a majority of something like two hundred and fifty votes, and it had as much to do with his new neighbors recognizing a kindred spirit as it did with their taste for whiskey, tobacco and a good joke. Aye, for they all knew he had stood up for their rights in the legislature long before he moved to their district.

Right about then was when the politicians around Murfrees-boro started taking serious notice of him. He may not have been the best legislator in the state, but as a vote-getter he had no equal. That was also about the time the Overton boys started snickering at him, which was as sure a sign as any that they feared his growing reputation. They called him the "Gentleman from the Cane," the cane being the West Tennessee thickets they wished he'd crawl back into and stay there; and they called him "Ring-tailed Davy, the Wild Man of the River Country." Try saying that after four or five cock-tails!

All that floutery troubled him at first, but after a while he came to see the value of outplaying his enemies at their own game.

"Reckon old Davy'll ever learn to eat with a knife and fork?" I heard him ask Judge Mitchell in the presence of three news-paper writers. One of the papers printed it a few days later and, believe it or not, it made him even more well-favored. I reckon even then the man knew how to use the press to his own advantage.

I used to see a lot of him in Mr. Childress's office that session, which was just before I gave up reading the law. He and Colonel Polk, who, by the way, is married to Childress's sister, used to come in together. This was Polk's first session in the Tennessee state legislature. When I first met him he was already a power there despite his youth and inexperience as he was one of the few college men in the Lower House. One thing that didn't hurt him, he was just about the first Carroll man to declare for Jackson—and don't think the old general didn't take notice of that. We all thought Polk had sold out to the money men, but it wasn't long before the rest of us lined up behind him, too—even Crockett; I reckon Colonel Polk had a better conception of Old Hickory's character at the time than any other forward-thinking politician in the whole state.

There is one thing I should like to tell you about Polk and Crockett. I know you are going to find this hard to believe considering how much they hate each other these days, but they was close friends back then. Polk would help Crockett with the legislation they was working on, which was mostly to stop the land speculators from depriving poor honest settlers of their homes, and Crockett stood in awe of him even though Polk was two years his junior in the legislature and a good ten years his junior on this earth.

"Now, I ain't lying when I say I'm as strong as an ox and almost as smart as one," Crockett once said to me, "but I'll be shot if Jim Polk ain't the best damn limb of the law in the whole state. Every morning when I rise, I thank my lucky stars we're not a-fighting under different colors, for if we was, the man would cut me to ribbons."

Well, they're sure not fighting under the same colors today (Polk still stands by his principles) and those words sound mighty strange to me now, seeing as the two of them don't hardly speak to each other anymore. Polk is President Jackson's wheel-horse in the U.S. House of Representatives, and ever since Crockett went over to the opposition, he has been a fly on the wheel-horse's tail.

Anyway, there old Crockett was, back in Murfreesboro without missing a session. All through the fall of 1823 and into the winter he was the talk of the town on account of his remarkable re-election from a strange new district. It wasn't long till some of the Party men came around to the opinion that he would make a first-rate candidate for the U.S. Congress. He resisted for a while saying it was a step above his knowledge, but his ambition finally got the best of him, and he gave them his consent. From what I understand, he lost his first election for that position by only *two votes*.

Two votes, thought I. I could have kicked myself. I had blood kin in Madison County, right slap in the middle of his district, and it was just too much trouble for me to go pick up my ink pen and ask them to support my friend at the polls. To this day I can't help but feel it was my fault as much as any man's for him going down in defeat.

That particular election took place in the summer of 1825. Two years later he ran again and won, and I helped him with the electioneering. I was already living in Memphis by then. I hadn't seen him but one time in the years in between, as he had given up his seat in the legislature to run for Congress—and that one time like to killed me. I had wrote to him in the spring of '25 just before he started canvassing for that first election he lost. I told him about my intention of moving west and asked him what he knew of Memphis. I received his reply in September, not long after his defeat. He invited me to his home and promised to take me to Memphis himself to show me first-hand what he knew of the place.

I didn't make it out to the Western District until after the first of the year. When I reached Crockett's home, I was informed that he was off somewhere bear hunting. It was nearly a week before he got back, and when he did, he looked every inch the wild man that the Overton boys characterized him as: he had a full beard, and his hair looked like it had neither been cut nor combed in six or seven months. Wore out as he was, he somehow found enough strength to arm-twist me into lending him a hand with one of his schemes. I don't know how I let him do it, but he talked me into helping him transport a whopping load of barrel staves down the Mississippi to New Orleans.

"We'll spend a whole week in Memphis on the return trip," said he, "and that's a promise, son."

We set out in mid-February, me and him and a half-dozen hired hands that we picked up at Obion Lake where they had built the two boats which we used for the journey. When we got to the lake, they was still in the midst of loading the staves on board, so we felt obliged to roll up our sleeves and help them out. Crockett said there was over thirty thousand of those staves all told, and at the end of a day's work my poor aching back but little doubted him.

So off we went down the Obion. Everything was fine till we got into the Mississippi. None of us had ever been down that mighty river before, and to make matters worse, our pilot proved to be just as ignorant of the business as the rest of us. He had us lash the two boats together, but that made them so heavy it was impossible to do anything at all with them.

That night, Crockett and myself were down in the cabin of one of the boats talking about what a fix we had got ourselves into when the hatchway came slap-down through the top of the boat—and it was our only way out except for a small hole in the side that we would stick our arms through to dip up water.

Before I knew it, we was floating sideways, and we could hear the hired hands running over the top of the boat in great confusion. The next thing I knew, we went broadside at full tilt against the head of an island where a large raft of drift timber had lodged. Water started pouring through what was left of the hatchway, so we made for the hole in the side. Crockett had me make the first go for it, but I could barely get more than my arms through it, so I cried out for some help; by that time the water was almost up to my neck. With a mighty heave-ho, two of the hired hands jerked me through, and then they went back after Crockett. They had an even harder time with him, for he is much broader at the shoulders than I am, but they got him out, too—and in just the nick of time, for before we had a chance to so much as straighten ourselves up on the other boat, the one we was in went entirely under.

We escaped to the pile of timber, and there we sat all night, a mile from land on either side. You should have seen us sitting there naked as jaybirds—and in the middle of February, yet—for our clothes had been torn off getting out of the cabin. As Crockett later said, we was *"froze right smart and starved half-stupid."*

The first good thing that came out of that misadventure of ours—there were other good things to come, which I shall presently relate—was I got to see the town that has become my new home a far sight sooner than I had expected, for we was at that very moment at the head of the Old Hen, or "Paddy's Hens and Chickens" as they call those little islands just outside of Memphis. The next morning a boat came by and carried us to town where I soon met a gentleman who has since become a close personal friend of mine. That gentleman was none other than Major Marcus B. Winchester, our former mayor (although he hadn't at the time been elected yet) and current postmaster. The first thing he did was feed us and give us some clothes and some money to help us get ourselves back to where we started from. The next thing he did was give us a horn or two of his own private stock to help restore our spirits.

I wish now to tell you what else Mark Winchester soon came to give me. By this I mean nothing less than my present livelihood. When I finally settled into Memphis at the end of the summer of that same year, 1826, he showed me around a piece of property of his on the outskirts of town. On that property stood a boarded-up building he was then using as a storehouse for his mercantile business. It had once been a rough-as-they-come rum house. That building today is now the Sign of the Crabtree. It was to be Mark's concern at first with me solely as its operator, but thanks to his generosity the establishment now belongs entirely to myself and my sister Kate. I pay Mark a dollar a year as rent for the property, and you can safely wager that no friend of his from either near nor far has ever had to pay the first farthing for bed and breakfast or perhaps a little something to take the chill away on a cold winter's night.

But that was nothing compared to what he did for my friend Crockett. Aye, for Marcus B. Winchester is as responsible as any man in Tennessee for getting him elected to the U.S. Congress. It all started when Mark invited us to his home on the evening subsequent to our rescue. What happened was, Crockett had him in stitches at the supper table with the laughable stories only he can tell so well; and after the laughing was finished, he touched the man's heart strings with his great compassion for the downtrodden pioneer settlers of the deep woods. At the end of the evening Mark was a true convert—and him a loyal Overton man!

Next morning he made Crockett promise to consider making another go for a seat in the Congress. Not that Crockett needed much arm-twisting, but as his finances had just taken a plummet into the mighty Mississippi, it was unlikely that he'd have the wherewithal to go out canvassing again without the funds that Mark soon promised to provide him with.

Well, provide those funds he did, a considerable amount of them going towards the purchase of liquid refreshment for the voters. And it was my honor and pleasure to help dispense those spirits to the citizens that came from miles around to hear my friend Crockett speak.

"Now this here's not a thing to do with getting them to vote for me," Old Davy—that's what he always calls himself when he's out electioneering—insisted with a wink while holding up one of my jugs of clear white farm liquor. "That would be against the law. I just figure I owe it to them for making them sit there so long a-listening to me run my mouth."

Well, he ran his mouth a-plenty during that summer's canvass, and while the liquor may have helped his cause some, I hardly think his speeches wearied even the few tea sippers that showed up, for he is without an equal when it comes to treating a crowd. I'll tell you one thing. He was surely head and shoulders above his two opponents—although they didn't know that at the time. They took precious little notice of him at first. Fact is, they rarely so much as mentioned his name in their speeches.

One of Crockett's opponents was a major general in the militia as well as an attorney general at the law, and as much as Crockett complained about having to deal with "war work and law trick all at once," the man was no match for him. I saw this myself, heard it with my own two ears. One day early in the campaign, they was up on the same platform together, the three candidates was, in one of the eastern counties of the district. I believe it was General Arnold's turn at the podium when a large flock of guinea fowls came very near to where he was speaking and set up the most God-awful squawking I ever did hear. They so confounded the general that he made a stop and requested that they might be driven away, which they then was.

When General Arnold was finished, Crockett walked right up to him there on the platform and said in a voice loud enough for all the folks to hear:

"Well, General, you are the first man I ever saw that comprehends the language of fowls. Therefore, I feel compelled to apologize for my little friends. Understand, sir, that when you didn't have the politeness to so much as name me in your speech, they felt it was their duty to persuade you to. Only, I wish't you hadn't gone and drove them off like you done when they hollered, 'CROCKETT, CROCKETT, CROCKETT.' I'm sure they was just as primed as me to hear the rest of your interesting remarks."

This raised an ear-deafening shout among the people for my

friend which caused the general to seem mighty discomfited. Right after that, Crockett pulled me aside and said:

"Just look at him, Tree. He don't know whether to check his arse or scratch his watch."

But the general got even more discomfited at the polls that August, and so did their opponent, the incumbent. When the ballots were counted, Crockett won by a substantial margin—some three thousand votes, I believe.

As for the money Mark Winchester loaned him, Crockett paid it all back within a year of his election. This I have heard not only from him, but also from Mark himself. And it hardly surprised me back then because I had always known David Crockett to be a man of his word, a man unwilling to remain beholden to another for long. This is why I find it so hard to swallow the fact that he ever accepted a corrupt loan from the Bank of the United States.

All I can say is that I hope with all my might that Ned Keeble was wrong in what he told me—I don't know, maybe he misunderstood what Crockett told *him*. I suppose I shall have to find out for myself. The next time I see Crockett I'm going to arm-twist him into providing me with an honest answer—and I'm not going to turn him loose until he does exactly that. I can only hope that it doesn't lead to our friendship going the way that his and Colonel Polk's went. I have known him far too long to see things come to that.

The more I think about it, though, the more I wonder if maybe I'm just covetous. There are times when I likely could be persuaded to trade everything I own for so much as half the public attention that my famous friend is enjoying these days. The only difference is I would never abuse my reputation; I would use whatever influence I had to try to improve the lot of my neighbors rather than the lot of myself. Who knows, if I stopped thinking about yours truly for a change, I might even wake up one morning and find myself in better shape than when I first started out, like one of old Crockett's tobacco chewers.

Not that I would set out to turn a profit on my name like Crockett seems to be doing these days on his. I believe that charity does *not*, as the old saw goes, begin at home. It is elsewhere that charity must begin. The way I figure, maybe—just maybe—it will at length wind its way back to my old front door. Not by any of my direct doing, of course. Call it superstition, but it is my firm belief that charity will never come to the man that pursues it.

I'll tell you what, though. From now on, that front door of mine is going to remain open all day long, come hell or high water. Aye, for as much as I like to consider myself an unselfish man, I am also nobody's fool!

Chapter Four

Dr. William A. Caruthers put down his newspaper and flipped open his watch. It was nearly ten a.m. He was slouching on a settee in the reading room of Gadsby's Hotel waiting for Miss Ivy Green, late of the Park Theater Company, currently of the Washington Theater Company, to join him for a stroll on the Capitol grounds. She had said she would be down in a few minutes, but that was almost three quarters of an hour ago. Last night Will had all but dismissed the possibility of ever knowing her again the way he once had, but what a difference a few short hours can make, he thought. He could wait another if he had to.

Will would have spent last night alone if his friend James French hadn't asked him to stop by his room for his notebook and to bring it with him to Colonel Crockett's lodgings when he returned with the colonel's badly needed quinine and anti-fever pills. Will had found the notebook next to Jamey's bedstead in a portmanteau. When he put down his candle, something on the floor caught his eye. It was a white cambric chemise. He picked it up and examined it; it smelled of bergamot oil, a scent with which he was well acquainted. He looked under the bed, then laughed at himself for having entertained the possibility that a certain somebody might be hiding there watching him sniff her undergarment.

He picked up the candle and looked for more evidence of the elusive Miss Ivy's recent presence. Sure enough, there by the door to an adjoining room was a be-ribboned pair of plum satin slippers that he was certain he had seen before, in another hotel room in another city. He stooped and put his eye to the keyhole but could see nothing but pitch black. He tried the door. It was neither locked nor latched, and its hinges creaked so loudly that he backed away as if it were alive and about to strike him.

He sat down on the bed. A quarter-hour he sat there until he remembered that he had come back to the hotel not for some foolish tryst, but to find some medicine for Colonel Crockett. So he got up and let himself out, locking the door behind him. Half-way down the hall, however, he turned around and went back to unlock it. And that was how he left it. Just in case he could summon up enough courage to return.

WHEN WILL GOT BACK TO COLONEL CROCKETT'S LODGINGS with the medicine, the colonel had already gone up to his rooms. Will found him under the covers, a malodorous slut lamp on his bedside table still lit. He decided against waking him; the colonel would probably cane him if Will roused him for no better reason than to give him something to help him sleep. He glanced around the narrow little bed chamber. It was much tidier than he had expected. Except for the piles of newspapers and the scattered note-covered sheets of writing paper on Crockett's desk, it was virtually devoid of clutter—even the clothes the colonel had just shed had been neatly folded and placed on the trunk at the foot of the bed. On the wall opposite the door were two small paintings, one a crudely rendered fall landscape and the other a portrait-sketch of Colonel Crockett himself.

"Mighty good likeness, ain't it?" said the colonel.

Will caught his breath. "Yes, sir," he wheezed out.

"Ain't nothing to do with vainfulness. I keep it there merely to speak to. You know, whenever I get the notion I need a good dressing down. I thought about using a looking glass, but then I figured folks might would think I was a little touched in the head if they caught me speaking to myself like that. Tell me something, leech. Just how old are you, anyways?"

Will told him his age and wondered what that had to do with Crockett's portrait.

The colonel swept back his long greasy hair "Thirty-one," he said. "I'll be shot if that ain't the same exact age I first come down with my ague."

He stopped to do some figuring.

"No. It was 1816, so I must've just turned thirty. My first wife done passed the previous summer, and I had just then got me another."

He had been traveling through northern Alabama, he said, in search of new lands on which to settle when his horse got away from him. Right about then he contracted the fever. If a party of friendly Indians hadn't discovered him, he might have died. They carried him to a nearby house where he remained in a feverish state for the better part of two weeks.

"Then the woman there, she give me a whole bottle of Bateman's Drops about the time I was at my worst, and that seemed to do the trick."

"A whole bottle?" Will said. "I'm surprised that didn't kill you."

"She thought it might too, but either way she figured I would only die anyhow. They throwed me into a considerable sweat, but I felt none the worse in the morning. And from that time on I begun to mend. I wish I could remember that woman's name. I don't reckon you know this, leech, (the colonel lowered his voice) but some folks down south is trying to convince me to make a go for the Presidency of these United States. Now, I don't know if such a thing will ever come to pass, but I'll tell you what. If I am ever forced to take the White House, I should like to find out that woman's name so that the nation might know just who it was that saved the future president's life."

There he goes again, thought Will.

"When I got home," the colonel went on. "my wife hardly know'd me, for I'd lost so much flesh that I had to drink a jug of muddy water to so much as cast a shadow. And another thing: I soon learned that she'd supposed I was dead. My neighbors had returned and had my horse with them, which they finally found, and they reported that they had seen a man who'd helped to bury me. Well sir, they might could've mis-fooled my wife, but I knew it was a whopper of a lie as soon as *I* heard it."

Will examined the colonel and gave him his medicine.

"And do take this laudanum right now to help you get back to sleep."

"Much obliged," said the colonel. "From now on I'll take this here at night and save the corn liquor for snakebite. That may compel me to carry around a little snake, though."

"Pleasant dreams," Will said. "You'll probably have one or two."

Then he went downstairs for a stiff drink. To brace himself—snake or no snake.

WILL SHOOK HIS HEAD AS HE POURED HIMSELF A GLASS OF brandy. There was a time when a sip of water would have been sufficient. Aye, when dropping in on Ivy would have been the easiest thing imaginable—even at three o'clock in the morning—but now he had no idea what to expect from her.

Or from himself. The last time he saw her, he all but threw himself at her feet pleading with her not to leave New-York. And then, as if he were upon the stage in some theatrical production and at the same time hovering high above it, he heard himself voice the possibility that he might abandon his wife and children for her.

Dear God! he thought then as he thought again now. *What demons we harbor within.*

By the time he got back to Jamey's room, most of the courage that he'd suckled from the brandy had evaporated. Nevertheless, he put down his leather satchel, drew a deep breath and took a few meek steps in the general direction of the adjoining room.

He retreated to the window. He muttered an obscenity to himself and mused that his mind was now about as functional as a bowl of porridge. He looked down at the avenue, but it was too dark to make anything out. Except for a little shepherd dog tied to the hitching post. He wondered what business had brought its master here at three in the morning. He smiled at this.

Kindred spirit, he thought.

Then he caught his reflection in one of the windowpanes.

"White-livered little puppy," he whispered—and he didn't mean the shepherd dog.

WILL PICKED UP ONE OF HIS BLACK BEAVER GLOVES FROM THE floor and stuffed it back in his coat pocket. Funny, but he didn't remember tying its fingers into knots. He tugged at his shirt-cuffs and then maneuvered an unruly curl to the center of his forehead. He removed his boots and tip-toed to the door, opening it swiftly so the hinges wouldn't creak too long. He held up his candle and peered inside the other bed chamber, and there she was: sound asleep, her red hair splayed out on a plump pillow.

He tip-toed to the bed. He stopped cold when he saw she wasn't alone. Mr. Hackett, he figured. And that would be just like her, sleeping her way to a leading role in one of his popular comedies.

One more glass of brandy, he thought. Aye, just one more and he'd have shaken them awake and given them the tongue lashing of their lives.

He took a closer look.

Why, of all people! It wasn't Mr. Hackett at all, but that effeminate little tyro who had played Percival seven or eight hours earlier; who would probably be more comfortable, Will thought, sleeping with Mr. Hackett than with Ivy.

Ivy opened her eyes as if on cue. She must have mistaken Will for Jamey, for she mumbled some unintelligible excuse.

"Shh," Will said. He placed his hand gently over her mouth almost dropping his candle on her covers. "It's me. It's William." He removed it when he felt the tautness of her smile.

"William! I know that name," she whispered playfully. "What are you doing here, William?"

Percival moaned and turned over in his sleep.

Will motioned to the door. Ivy shrugged, then threw on her coat and followed him into Jamey's room.

"What am I doing here?" Will said. "It's nice to see you, too, sweet little Miss Green Eyes."

"I didn't mean it that way. *Sweet William come from another land*," she sang softly, "*to court Evita Malaxechevarria.*"

"Ivy sweetheart, I think we should discuss this."

"There is nothing to discuss. I simply felt sorry for him. And nothing happened." She kissed Will's lips. "Don't let's talk about him. Let sleeping little whiffets lie." She kissed him again. "Let's talk about us. Have you journeyed this far hither just to see little old me? Tell me, did you?"

He placed his hands on the small of her back. She stepped away.

"Not here," she said.

Five minutes later she was in his bed chamber and under his covers. All at once she was a different person.

"Come Will, and dock," she said sounding like some Liverpool fish monger. "Dock with your little game-pullet."

"Stop it," he said.

"Stop what, silly Willie?"

"You sound like you're play-acting upon the stage. In a play.... you know, *acting*."

She shook her head and quietly—almost thoughtfully— laughed. "I'm sorry," she said, "but it has been so *long!* I guess I have to get used to you all over again."

Will shrugged and kissed her on her chin. He had known her nearly eighteen months but hadn't seen her in over ten. They had met in New-York, backstage at the Park Theater. She later admitted that she had assumed a role for him back then, too, when they first met. It was quite the opposite, though: more like *Little Goody Two-Shoes*.

"Come visit my apple dumpling shop, won't you William," she said to him now in her fish monger's voice. "It's just up the hill from Cock Lane. You might want to spend some time down there as well."

"And what exactly shall we do there?"

"Well, we could play a little `Up-tails All,' if you'd like. Or perhaps you would prefer a game of `Pickle-me-Tickle-me.'"

Will waited until all such games were finished before asking her about Jamey.

"Upon my word!" she said. "You two actually *know* each other?"

"Since he was fourteen years old. And you, you've only known him for but an hour or two and here you are, all moved in with him. I don't understand how you could do such a thing."

"I cannot believe it," she said. "I cannot believe he actually told you."

"Of course he told me. He has never been one to keep his conquests under his hat."

She pulled the covers up to her chin. "Is that what you think of me?" she said. "As somebody's conquest? Well, let me tell you something, William Caruthers. First of all, I did *not* move in with him. I moved next door. And second of all, you don't have to act so scandalized. I have known him for almost a year already."

"A year? It was my understanding that he first met you tonight. Backstage at the theater."

"Who told you that?"

"Who do you think?"

Ivy closed her eyes and set her jaw like some child's indomitable old governess. "So you have been discussing me, have you? And to think that *I* went and gave myself to *you* after *he* dispatched you here. And that's what he did, didn't he? He dispatched you."

"Now, that makes a bundle of sense," Will said. "He sent me here to carry you away from him. I have never heard anything more ridiculous in my life."

"I am not being ridiculous. And I cannot believe he didn't have the decency to inform you we were already acquainted. I cannot believe he didn't care what kind of woman you would think I had become."

"Ivy, he doesn't even know that we are ... as you said, 'acquainted.' Anyway, what did you expect I would think? And I'll tell you what I can't believe. I can't believe you have involved yourself with someone like him."

"I've done nothing of the sort," Ivy said, sitting up straight. "And even if we ever *had* been truly connected, we wouldn't be any longer, not after tonight. He embarrassed me half to death tonight. He pawed at me like an animal, right in front of every-one. I had to feign a headache to rid myself of him. And by the time I retired, I found I truly had one."

Will turned over on his stomach and stared at the floor. One of his boots caught his eye. It was lying on its side, the heel worn down well past the limits of respectability. Still staring at it, he asked Ivy how long it had been since Jamey had first spent the night with her.

"None of your business," she said. "Not after walking out of my life, 'tisn't."

"Out of *your* life?" he said and straightened himself up. "I never walked anywhere. I'm not the one who moved three hundred miles away."

"You didn't try very hard to stop me."

"You made me promise not to."

"Oh I did, did I?"

"In no uncertain terms."

"And you believed me?"

He suppressed a smile. "I suppose I forgot what a convincing young actress you were."

"And still am." She scooted back down and kissed him on his lower lip. "Now close those angry gray eyes of yours, Sour William," she said. "Perhaps by morning you will be your old sweet self again."

Well, THAT was a mis-prognosis, thought Will now as he gazed out the window of the hotel's reading room.

As for the cure, Ivy would simply have to return to New-York with him. He still needed her; he was certain of that now. His wife was showing him precious little interest these days, let alone passion. Sometimes he hardly blamed her; they didn't have much in common now except for the children and the unpaid bills. The bills she blamed on him. As for the children—God knows they meant as much to him as they did to her—she seemed to have forgotten that he had had a little something to do with their arrival on this planet, too. To Louisa they were Gibsons in all but name. Except perhaps when nine-year-old Horace would try to coax his infant brother to swallow some concoction he and a friend had cooked up, or when little Emma would get into Louisa's box of correspondence with her colored chalk. Then it was Will's fault. Then it was their tainted Caruthers blood getting the best of them.

Well, perhaps she's right, he thought. And he could hardly blame anyone else's blood for getting the best of *him*, too, as he found himself spending more time each day with his manuscript than with his patients. And each time Louisa had to dip into her savings to keep the landlord at bay, he lost that much more self-respect. Lately he felt more like a bumbling dependent son than a husband and father, so much so that he rarely picked up a pen at home anymore. And Louisa ridiculed him about his writing, made him question his talent. Catching him at his desk going over his manuscript instead of their finances, she would give him a look that made him feel as if he were perusing the diary of some Anthony Street harlot.

"Your mind should be on where your next dollar is best expected to come from," she would say, "instead of on that wretched hobby horse of yours;" and it would be all he could do to restrain himself from striking her. So he would put on his coat and hat and walk as many blocks as it would take to calm down, often as far as to the Battery and back.

Keep his mind on his finances? What did she suppose was on it during most of his waking hours? And if his "wretched hobby" had any chance at all of being his salvation—and according to one of New-York's most respected literary lights it very well might—he owed it to himself not to neglect it. He may not have been the most dedicated physician in New-York, but if his practice was suffering, it was his wife's fault as much as it was his. He wouldn't have to devote so much time to his writing during the day if she allowed him to write at home at night. And at home he would find peace of mind instead of having to look for it elsewhere.

Sometimes Will wondered how far his infatuation with Ivy would have taken him had she not removed to Alexandria. He hadn't felt truly at peace with himself since those late afternoon trysts at her lodgings. Sometimes they were more innocent than his wife could have imagined, if she indeed had ever suspected anything. Often, he did little more there than write. But oh, did he write! There Ivy would be, sitting on a rickety old, salvaged chair no more than a few feet away going over her lines from some play, perhaps; and there he would be, stretched out by the fireplace on the faded rag carpet that her mother had made when she was Ivy's age, unleashing entire chapters.

And then he would go home to his wife. Just before supper he might tear off a scrap of the *Evening Post* and scribble down an idea that had come to him on his way home. If Louisa happened to catch him in the act, she might not speak to him for the rest of the evening; or perhaps she would slam his supper down on the table with almost enough force to break the plate in two and say something like:

"Every time you pick up that precious pen of yours, sir (she always called him *sir* when she was angry with him), you are driving another nail into your own children's coffins."

And this she might say loudly enough for those very children to hear her in the next room. Never mind that James Kirke Paulding had once compared him favorably with none other than the immortal Sir Walter Scott. There was a time when Will would have reminded her of that, when he would have pulled from his pocketbook a fistful of bank notes that Kirke had given him for helping him revise one of his manuscripts and waved them high over his head like Mr. Hackett's long-tailed hat and made her take back everything she had said about his paucity of talent. Now he held his tongue. Now he allowed her to believe that every last dollar he brought home had been derived from his medical practice, for in her eyes, a dollar derived from his writing couldn't be more tainted if it had been won at a cock fight.

Well, at least he had his children to comfort him. For the time being, anyway. He supposed it was only a matter of time until she turned them against him, too. And it wouldn't take much. The last several months he had been coming home so late they had little more than a quarter hour to spend together. He would crawl into bed with them and tell them stories he had made up on his way home from work. Then he would go back to the sitting room and hide behind his newspaper and rework them in his mind—as if he were in the Bastille or some such place where the use of pen and paper was forbidden. His wife would be sitting across from him with her *Clarissa Harlowe*, perhaps. There would be a contented half-smile on her lips as she read, and he would wonder if that novel would ever have gotten written had Mr. Richardson's wife not permitted her husband to write at home either.

THE CAPITOL GROUNDS WERE QUIET THIS MORNING, IT BEING Sunday. For the moment, Will and Ivy had them all to themselves. Will looked up at the elegant white marble-and-stone building with its classical Greek columns and its copper dome gleaming in the morning sun. What a contrast, he thought, to the common, red-bricked boarding houses with their sooty black roofs that blighted the east side of the hill. The Capitol looked like an exquisite piece of ivory that had been dumped on top of a rubbish heap.

"You looked so ridiculous lying there with him," he said to Ivy as they stopped at the foot of the Capitol steps. "How did he ever get up the courage to approach you?"

"I thought we kissed and made up."

"I'm just curious, nothing more. Here, allow me." He removed his greatcoat and offered it to her. She waved it away and sat down on a bare stone step without bothering to first brush it off with her gloved hand.

"The little whiffet was in the other room," she said and folded her hands in her lap.

"In Jamey's room? What on earth was he doing there?"

"Getting ... *corned* on your friend's jug of corn liquor."

"But what was he *doing* there?"

"I didn't calculate he would truly do anything," she said rubbing her thumbs together. "I had always considered him perfectly harmless."

"You mean *you* let him in?"

"I felt sorry for him. I went downstairs to get someone to fire up my wood-stove and there he was, sitting by himself outside the front door. He told me he had lost the key to his room."

Will looked down at his scuffed-up boots. Someone had scratched a pair of initials and a heart on the lowermost step where Will's right heel rested. He smiled at this and decided not to press her any further.

"You and your big heart," he said and stood up. "Here, give me your hand."

She gave it and brushed off her coat with the other as she rose. "You're a good man, William Caruthers," she said. "You're a much better person than I shall ever be."

A good man, Will thought. A husband, a father four times over and here he was, strolling arm-in-arm with a barely grown-up girl together with whom he had just crawled out of an adulterous bed.

Aye, but a girl who still delighted in his touch. And a girl who understood the artist in him as only another artist could.

"Tell me something," he said.

"How handsome you are?"

He shook his head.

"How clumsy you are in bed?"

He stopped abruptly "Goodness no, don't tell me that," he said with a short laugh. "I'm not, am I?"

"Not since your opening night."

"I dare say that's a relief." He wiped his brow for effect. "But what I want to know is, well, in your ... well-considered opinion is there room for one more physician in this town?"

She gave him a curious look.

"I'm serious. Permitting you to re-settle so far away was the biggest mistake I have ever made."

She raised her penciled eyebrows and smiled faintly.

"Cross my heart," he said.

"Your wife and children," she said, "are you going to leave them in New-York to fend for themselves?"

"I apprehend you know me better than that. Besides, Louisa would pack tomorrow if I asked her to. Quite frankly, she has had her fill of New-York City."

Ivy let go of his arm. She stooped and picked up a small stone and held it out for a squirrel; it studied her for a moment, then scurried off to a nearby fruit tree.

"You cannot have us both, William," she said, still stooping and hugging herself as if it were not so unseasonably warm.

"I am not asking for that," Will said. "I merely wish for things to be as they were before."

She stood up straight. "And you call that 'not having us both?'"

Will removed his hat and scratched his head through his matted hair. "When have I ever interfered with your life?" he asked her. "You said you were happy. Many times you said that."

"I was."

"And you are not now?"

"People change. People truly do. Now I think it's about time for me to be a wife and a mother."

Will put his hat back on and closed his eyes. And he kept them closed for a few moments as they walked along the crest of the hill, Ivy's arm resting on his arm as if she were leading her poor blind husband somewhere he had never been in all his sighted days.

"And have you ... someone particular in mind?" he asked.

"Perhaps," she said. "That all depends."

He opened his eyes and gazed down at Pennsylvania Avenue. To his right, not more than a half mile away, a milk cow was grazing in somebody's front yard. To his left, beyond the botanical gardens and the canal, goats, pigs and geese wandered freely upon the mall. Every which way you looked, houses were scattered about like so many marbles tossed by a child. If Will indeed removed here, he would have to purchase a pair of high-topped Wellington boots, for the only route to some of those houses was across muddy garbage-strewn fields. He stared at the

Tiber Creek bridge and wondered what course he would have committed himself to by the time he crossed it. Then he remembered it was the Rubicon that Caesar had crossed, not the Tiber.

Well, he must have crossed the Tiber, too, he thought.

"I think perhaps you should give it a little more thought," he said.

"I've a better idea," said Ivy. "Why don't you do the thinking for both of us."

"Would that I could. But do understand there are certain things I am not prepared to do as of yet."

"So you have said, but are you truly serious about what else you said? About settling here in Washington?"

"Upon my word, Ivy. But whether doing such thing alone is within my power I cannot yet say. I suppose time will tell. Perhaps sooner than you may think."

They walked in silence down the flagstone walkway toward the Capitol gate. They walked through a grove of shade trees, the wind blowing briskly through their bare branches. There was a curious scent in the air. It was sweet, sickly-sweet like fruit just beginning to rot.

"How do you know you can depend upon me?" Ivy finally said. "How do you know I won't return to New-York once you've removed here?"

"I guess I don't."

"And how do I know *you* won't return to New-York? It was my impression that you wished to spend the rest of your life there."

He stopped walking. "I said that?"

"You indeed did."

"Well, then perhaps I truly did wish such a thing." He touched her cheek. "But that was when I had a good reason to remain."

"Seriously, William," she said and let go of his arm. "You wouldn't much like it here. It is so provincial."

"You're forgetting I come from a sleepy little village in the mountains."

"Ah, but there's a difference. In your little village I am quite certain that the people there don't fancy themselves as living at court with the king."

She curtsied.

"No, not like too many of them *here* do," Will replied. "After all, there is only one Washington City—and only one King Andrew the First."

He returned a full deep bow.

"Say, I have an idea," he went on. "Let's take a drive out to Alexandria. You can show me the secret little places of your childhood. You can introduce me to your mother."

"I should like to, William, but the truth is I've not the time. Not today, anyway. And now I simply must return to my room to catch a few more hours of sleep. I have a rehearsal at three."

"I thought you weren't performing tonight."

"It's for next week. I'm only an understudy, but it's for an important part. Anyway, I've an even better idea. Why don't you stay over another few days and keep Christmas with Mother and me? You'll never make it back to New-York in time, even if you leave tomorrow."

That stung. And yet he replied:

"There is nothing I should like to do better than to keep Christmas with you."

"Then it's settled."

"Settled," Will said, offering Ivy his arm again. And wondering which way the wind would blow him next.

Chapter Five
THE UNDERSTANDING

Matthew St. Clair Clarke

R eader, have you ever boated up a western waterway on a steamboat? If you haven't, then you should do so at least once in your lifetime, for when you find yourself in the insufferable company of the foul-mouthed foul-smelling hoosiers[1], pukes[2] and suckers[3] whom you are likely to encounter there, you will come to better appreciate your own neighbors. And you will come to agree with Mr. Payne that there indeed is no place like your own home.

I would not be surprised if Mr. Payne had happened to write that particular lyric on board a rat trap similar to the one on which I found myself five years ago this past September. It was typical of the sort you will still encounter plying many of the western rivers today being a small, converted freight carrier. As it had only one deck, I was obliged to share the same cabin with the lowliest of scoundrels as well as with the engine (which I was

---

1. Someone from Indiana
2. Someone from Missouri
3. Someone from Illinois

certain was going to blow us all to smithereens), and as it rained continually, I had to spend most of my waking *and* sleeping hours in that common cabin. Not that I got much sleep, for we were obliged to take our rest (such as it was) upon narrow wooden shelves like so much cargo.

Make no mistake about it, I have no regrets about having taken that excursion. I can say such a thing because confined in that squalid cabin where I had to marshal the full power of my concentration to obduce the din of so many concurrent conversations, I accomplished far more in one day than I might have in ten sitting alone in my garden. Understand, the Muse has no tolerance for Elysian Fields. At least mine doesn't.

I chose to preface my remarks about Colonel Crockett—which follow immediately—as I did because if it hadn't been for that particular excursion of mine, it is quite conceivable that few of you would today know one truthful thing about the man other than, perhaps, his name. For somewhere along the Tennessee River in a stuffy smoke-filled cabin, it came to me that I should introduce my colorful friend to the rest of the world. And that was three years before Mr. Hackett first stepped upon the stage in his buckskins and that remarkable long-tailed hat.

It was early in Colonel Crockett's first term as a representative from the state of Tennessee that I made his acquaintance. That was in late January or early February of 1828, the year of my western excursion. I had never heard of him; to me he was just another name on the congressional payroll. (I was Clerk of the House of Representatives at the time.) He was downstairs in the Capitol when first I met him, having some oyster stew and a pint of ale with his friend Mr. Chilton of Kentucky, another first term member. They were both still Jackson men at the time and consequently moved in different circles than did I, but on this occasion, I was anxious to have a word with them.

Actually, it was Chilton with whom I had wished to speak. He had just finished delivering his maiden speech from the floor of the House and appeared to be quite pleased with himself. I, however, was not at all pleased, for he had accused President Adams's party of squandering our national wealth on, of all things, quills and ink for the members, and as Clerk of the House I took that accusation personally. I had intended to give him a piece of my mind, but he and his friend disarmed me with their geniality and humor to such an extent that I had to put off venting my spleen till another day.

I was particularly struck by Colonel Crockett's sense of humor. He spoke of his rooster, which was so indolent it wouldn't crow at daybreak; rather, it would wait for his neighbor's to crow and then simply nod its head in agreement. And he spoke of his indolent mule, the one he had to hitch backwards to his plow so it could see the sign posted on that implement which said, *WORK*. Once hitched, the mule would try to back away from the sign—and so quickly would it do so that it would plow a hundred acres in a half-hour despite itself. And Crockett did an unflattering yet nonetheless amusing impression of President Adams—he even made himself look like him!

Over the next several months I got to know Crockett well enough to consider him a close personal friend. I was surprised at the depth of his intelligence. He really is quite quick despite the fact that he's always confessing how ignorant he is and that he can barely write his own name. That, I suppose, is part of his charm, but anyone who has spent much time around him knows that he is fully capable of expressing himself clearly enough (albeit within the confines of his limited vocabulary and imperfect syntax), and his penmanship is no worse than mine. We rarely discussed politics in those days, however. He voted up and down with his delegation (solid Jackson, of course) during his first session, and I am certain he saw me as the embodiment of all the selfishness and hypocrisy that poor yeomen such as he tend to associate with my class. Nevertheless, we enjoyed each other's company and were able to set our politics aside long enough to swap lies over an occasional bowl of oyster stew.

It wasn't until late in the session that Crockett and I first spoke deliberately and frankly about his political concerns. If my memory serves me right, it was the last of April, shortly after we had finished with the tariff business. I was sitting at my desk in the Capitol when in he steps without so much as a knock, sits himself down across from me and offers me a segar. I declined and asked him to excuse me for a few minutes while I finished whatever it was that I was doing. But glancing over my papers I could see him out of the corner of my eye. He was sitting there, his legs crossed at the ankle and his booted foot jiggling as if he had to visit the privy.

He said he wanted my sage advice. He said he wanted to discuss his delegation's land bill with me. Well, I dare say you will appreciate my complete surprise, reader, when I tell you that but one day after he had defended that very land bill from the floor of the House—defended it against the cynical barbs of 'those heartless Easterners,'—he was now seeking advice in the enemy camp!

"It don't look like it's going to pass, does it Saint Clarke?" said he, the unaccountable twinkle still in his eye.

I still thought him to be a rabid Jackson man on all points, and such ebullience at the floundering of his delegation's beloved land bill was hardly what I would have expected from him. I asked him if his colleagues were taking the matter so lightly.

"I don't give a hoot in hell about any one of them," said he. "They ain't nothing but a pack of thieving blackleg lawyers."

I reminded him that I, too, was a lawyer.

"Maybe so, but least-ways you don't have a notion to steal your neighbors' land out from under their feet so far as I can reckon. I just figured—"

"That it takes one to know one."

"I wouldn't exactly put it that way," said he without acknowledging my self-deprecating smile. "I just figured you might could comprehend the deviousness of their ways a sight better than I do. I may have read the law some, but that hardly makes me a lawyer."

It was then that he opened up his heart to me as if we had known each other for years. He had come to Washington City for one purpose, said he, and that was to somehow secure for his less fortunate constituents clear title to the refuse land on which they had settled. Many of those constituents were squatters (although he never uses that word), and he was convinced that they had no one in either party to protect their interests but him.

At first, he thought that his associates in the Tennessee delegation were his friends and we *'Federalists,'* as he anachronistically called the Adams Party (or the *National Republicans* as we would soon be known), his chief adversaries. But now he saw those associates of his as the true blackguards and the rest of the Jackson Party as their boot-licking confederates. He had come to believe that should the land bill pass as they had written it (that is, should the public land in Tennessee be relinquished by the general government directly to the state to dispose of as she saw fit), then her legislature would allow speculators to bid the price of the land up to levels that Crockett's constituents could never afford to pay, and they would lose their homes.

This, you must understand, is the predominant reason he eventually turned against his own party. I can assure you with honor bright that we have never had a secret fund to entice him into league with us. He came willingly, reader, and all because of that land bill and the poor West Tennessee settlers he wished to help. But I am getting ahead of my story.

So there I was, sitting at my desk and Crockett on his feet now, leaning toward me, one end of his segar in the corner of his mouth, the lit end practically in my face, and both of his hands flat against the desk as if he were about to heave it.

"It's a bad bill," said he. "It don't deserve to pass."

"Then why in God's name did you defend it?" asked I.

"Because I know'd it wouldn't pass."

I told him he was not making any sense.

"I thought I was the one supposed to be sap-green around

here," said he. "How the devil do you expect my delegation to ever support a measure of mine if I won't support theirs?"

I asked him if he had an amendment. He told me he didn't.

"Well, least-ways not yet." He stroked his chin and drew on his segar; his breath reeked not only of tobacco, but also of onions and some kind of strong drink, as I recall.

"Go on," said I, for 'twas obvious that he intended to do precisely that.

"Go *ahead* is what I shall do," he corrected me, as that is his motto. "Back home they say that when the only tool you've got is a hammer, every problem looks like a nail. I'll tell you what, though. This here problem is much too tricky for any hammer to hit. It's more like having a pair of new boots that you can't get your feet into till first you've worn them a day or two to stretch them. Only thing, how the devil do you get them on to stretch them if your feet won't yet fit? The answer is you track down a cobbler. And that's why I stand before you now, Saint Clarke. Because I believe you're a first-rate cobbler."

"And I am to cobble some clauses together for you?" said I.

"Well, sir, in a manner of speaking, I reckon," said he.

Then he said he would forever be in my debt and that his mother would bless me if only I would draft a substitute bill for him, one that would provide his constituents with a direct dona-tion of the land on which they had settled '*free gratis for nothing*' as Colonel Wildfire would say, thus bypassing the self-serving state legislature.

I asked him what made him feel that such a bill would have any better chance of passing than the original one.

"They'll listen to me," said he.

I tried not to smile. "Who?" asked I. "Who will listen to you?"

"The whole plague-gone House is who. I do believe I made a favorable impression yesterday."

"I am quite certain you did," said I; but then I cautioned him that such an impression would in all probability not be enough.

It is one thing to evoke sympathy for poor settlers, but it is another to charm delegations of penny-wise New Englanders and aristocratic Southern planters into giving away our national treasure. Three or four million acres can give one pause for thought, I told him.

He said he couldn't agree more. "And that's exactly why that confounded bill of theirs won't pass. But mine's a horse of a different color. It won't concern itself with nowhere near that much acreage, just the rough odds and ends my poor constituents have settled upon. Answer me this, Saint Clarke. What harm is there to provide those God-fearing hard-working neighbors of mine with clear title to their land, sir, the land they done improved by the sweat of their brow?"

Before I could give him an answer, he grinned and poked me in the arm.

"You should have heard that pap sucking puppy Davis of Massachusetts," said he. "He got up on his hind legs and praised me—can you believe that, Clarke? He praised me for my *wisdom* of all things—and him a stiff-necked chowder-head Yankee, yet! That's how I come to run here in such a hurry."

"Then perhaps Mr. Davis is the one who should help you draft your amendment," said I. "Have you spoken to him?"

He shook his head. "You're the only Adams man I know I can trust a foot or two farther than I can throw."

"You flatter me, sir," said I, "but you mistake me. I present myself in this House neither as an Adams man *nor* as a Jackson man. 'Tis the secret to my unanimous re-election as Clerk—twice so far, thank Providence."

I asked him if he were willing to risk alienating his entire delegation. He nodded. I urged him to sleep on it for a day, for upon my word, reader, I had already grown too fond of him to allow him to jeopardize his political career without seriously considering the consequences.

He drew viciously on his segar. "They can all go to hell," said he.

I told him not to expect much support from President Adams and his party, but as a personal favor I would help him draft his amendment. I insisted, however, that my contribution to it remain confidential, for though my tolerance of the Nationals was well-known, my lopsided allegiance to them was yet a secret.

"From your heart to my ear," said he, "and there it shall remain."

Then he pulled me out of my chair and hugged me like a bear in one of his stories. Said he:

"If anyone can do the job, you can. I swear, if you can't pack a sawlog to hell and back before breakfast, then I wish I may be shot. When do we start?"

We started that very evening, time being of the essence as the session was nearing its close. I invited him over for supper after which I helped him put his ideas into proper English. Unfortunately, it was all for naught; the following day, the House grew tired of the question and tabled the Tennessee delegation's bill, thus obviating any consideration of Crockett's amendment to it. The deciding votes, I should tell you, were cast by Adams men, so you can easily imagine Crockett's reaction; he was now as furious at our party as he was at his own. Somehow, I managed to calm him down before he alienated the entire House.

"These things take time," I told him; and I promised to work closely with him during the next session.

"And I'm a-holding you to it," said he. "I must admit, though, there's one thing I done learned from all this business, Saint Clarke. "I've learned the true meaning of pros and cons."

"The concept of weighing arguments for and against something?" asked I.

"Not exactly. What's the opposite of pro—it's con, right?"

I nodded.

"Well, if pro is the opposite of con, then the opposite of progress is Congress."

One other thing I should tell you is that the presidential

election was only six months away at that time, and it was already apparent that nothing short of Divine intervention would stand between General Jackson and the Executive Mansion. While there was virtually nothing that I or any other member of my party could do to prevent this, I nevertheless felt confident that we might be able to weaken his hand in the Congress. It seemed plausible that if we could stir up a little dissension in the Tennessee congressional delegation, not only would that serve to embarrass Jackson in his own state, it might also serve to loosen his hold on some of his less committed partisans in other states; the "Old Hero," after all, could hardly be expected to keep the bulk of his army under his boot-heel if he couldn't control his own 'local regiment,' so to speak.

But if Colonel Crockett was going to be our Brutus, then we had a few serious problems. First of all, he was just another nameless, faceless, first-termer to whom no one was going to pay the slightest bit of attention. Secondly, I wasn't so certain he could be depended upon to travel any farther from the Jackson fold than as far as his land bill would carry him (he certainly didn't during his first session), and I was convinced that until he made an unequivocal and open repudiation of General Jackson, he would be of little use to us. Finally, I quite frankly despaired of mustering up more than a half-dozen Anti-Jackson votes for his amendment. Our party, after all, does not have a reputation for charity.

I didn't meet with Crockett again until the fall of that same year, 1828, when I visited him in his backwoods home. He had extended to me his invitation on the last day of the session; poor people, as you know, have little more than their hospitality to offer as an expression of their gratitude. And the man fell all over himself that day thanking me for drafting his amendment and advising him on parliamentary strategy despite the fact that it had not yet yielded him any dividends. I told him I was deeply moved, but my next few months had already been spoken for: my friend Peter Force and I were hard at work on our history of the Revolution, and my summer home in Greencastle, Pennsylvania was much in need of repair.

"I hate to see a man shoot up his summer so quick," said he, "but I'll tell you what let's do, old hook. Let's go shoot up the fall. You ever skulk after a bear, Clarke?"

"I have never skulked after much of anything," replied I. "I prefer to encounter it fully cooked and on a plate."

Said he: "Back home we have a saying. *'Give a man a hunk of meat and he'll eat for a day. Teach a man to hunt and he'll eat all year.'*"

"I've heard that," said I, "but where I come from, it's said about fishing."

"It ain't true about fishing," replied he. "Because with fishing it's: *'Teach a man to fish and he'll spend all day in a boat drinking hard cider.'*"

I told him I would write to him if I found the time to get away. I must confess, however, that I hadn't the slightest intention of traveling over six hundred miles for no other purpose than to shoot myself in the foot and to ingratiate myself with a man who lived only a few blocks from me during the session.

It was Peter Force who talked me into making the journey. Crockett, he said, might be in a more receptive state of mind in his natural habitat. And as long as I was going to be out west *anyway* (this alone, I believe, explains Peter's enthusiasm for my journey) I might as well do a little research for our literary endeavor.

I consented after a few days. In all honesty, I had ulterior reasons of my own. For one, my wife Anna and I had for several months been rather at odds and, quite frankly, needed a rest from each other's company. For two, such a trip would afford me an opportunity to visit my old friend and mentor of sorts Richard Buckner at his home in Kentucky. Dick had been a member of Congress from that state at the time of which I write. He had been my house guest at Greencastle at the close of the previous session and had insisted that I permit him to return the hospitality. Come along with me, reader, and I shall take you to the wilds of West Tennessee.

I LEFT GREENCASTLE IN MID-AUGUST TRAVELING BY PRIVATE coach. It was a pleasant enough week's journey, my only complaint being that our glorious National Road was—and I am afraid still is—much in need of repair. And the Maysville Road was even worse; we were tossed about in that coach like pebbles in a child's rattle. At Lexington, Kentucky I lodged at the house of one of Buckner's old chums, an amateur historian and distant relation of Colonel Boone's colorful friend Simon Kenton. Buckner's friend lived within walking distance of the courthouse, which was where I had planned to spend a full day researching the Revolutionary War in the West. Unfortunately, I didn't find more than an hour's worth of interest there—nothing more than some old muster rolls, really. I had better luck in my host's personal library from which I borrowed a book, a very special book, a book that in a roundabout way would later help to change my friend Crockett's life. I shall tell you about that book in a moment, for I think you will find it of some interest.

After spending over a week at my friend Buckner's estate arguing with him well into the night about everything from Henry Clay's political future to the best way to roast a leg of mutton and getting far too accustomed for my own good to that decadent practice so prevalent in his society of having a julep or two before breakfast, I set out for Colonel Crockett's. Leaving my coach and coachman at the Buckners' (Crockett had advised me that his part of the country was best traversed on horse-back), I caught the mail stage to Louisville. At Louisville I boarded a safety barge for my trip up the Ohio River. It was four decks high, immaculate and free of anything which might be inclined to blow itself up, and it was towed by a steamer peopled by souls far less timid than I. Unfortunately, it was bound for the

Mississippi, and so I was obliged to disembark at Paducah to board that filthy little rattrap which I have already described herein for my trip up the Tennessee.

It was a miserable journey of four and twenty hours. Not that a trip of that distance should have taken so much time in this day and age (it really shouldn't have taken more than half that time), but the boilers became clogged with sediment, and twice we had to stop so they could be cooled down and cleaned. My time would have been less miserably spent had I not been forced by the inclement weather to remain in the cabin. There I occupied myself reading by what little daylight the tiny portholes permitted in. I read Filson's *History of Kentucky* from cover to cover. That was the book I had borrowed from Dick Buckner's friend in Lexington.

You may not be aware of this, but 'twas Filson's *History* that was responsible for the establishment of Colonel Boone's reputation some fifty years ago. It contains the so-called *"Autobiography,"* a document of dubious authenticity that somewhat exaggerates the colonel's prowess as a hunter and explorer in language much too stilted than a backwoodsman such as he would ever have used.

As I read about Colonel Boone's exploits in the wilderness, I found myself picturing not the young man which he had been at the time, but the white-haired octogenarian whose likeness I had seen on the wall of my Lexington host's library. Once aware of this temporal displacement, I darkened his hair in my mind (although I suppose I could just as credibly have colored it blond) and went on with my reading. By the time I had finished escaping from the Indians with him, I had what an old politician such as I can only call a religious experience.

What, I asked myself, if the man who had opened up the West (the hero, mind you, of young boys from Massachusetts to Missouri and former young boys well into their voting age) were still living, and I were on my way to visit him? And what if the man who was now itching for a scrap with General Jackson's henchmen were the legendary Daniel Boone instead of a first-term congressman of whom few people outside his home state had ever heard? Then it hit me like Paul on the road to Damascus:

When I had darkened Colonel Boone's hair in my mind, I had turned him into Colonel Crockett. What I needed now was to turn Colonel Crockett into Colonel Boone.

By the time I disembarked from the steamer, I had resolved to indeed do unto Crockett as Mr. Filson had done unto Boone. I had resolved to compose a biography so compelling that it would transform my new friend into the most famous personage in the state of Tennessee, bar none but Andrew Jackson himself; and in the process, hopefully, it would serve as an anvil upon which the Jackson Party might be broken.

I eventually did write that book, although I am ashamed to admit that it took me four years to complete it. And it will probably take me that long to finish this tale, reader, if I don't stay on course. So back to my story.

I left the steamer near Paris, Tennessee where I sought out John Wesley Crockett, David's eldest son, who was then reading the law with a prominent judge. He had, as a matter of fact, married the judge's daughter but several weeks previous. Aye, he married *up*, just as I myself did.

I found John to be a slightly shorter and considerably slimmer version of his father. His sense of humor is not nearly as well-developed, but he is extremely good-natured, much more so than David. David is funny only when he chooses to be, especially as of late. When he chooses not to be funny, he can be as sour as my Dunker neighbor's crab apple sauce.

From Paris I had fully intended to take the mail stage to Dresden (it must sound to you, reader, as if I were traveling in Europe) where I would procure a horse, but John insisted that I borrow one of his. The road to Dresden was not as bad as I had expected, but the road from Dresden to Trenton (the nearest settlement to Crockett's homestead) was in some stretches little more than a pig path. And there were several un-bridged creeks to ford where my coach, as I had been forewarned, would certainly have been a hindrance.

I reached Trenton after a full day's ride and found the town to be no more than a small cluster of primitive log buildings situated around a public square. I lodged at a filthy little tavern belonging to an equally filthy little man whom Crockett had said would direct me to his backwoods home. This the tavern keeper did the following morning. He had his servant set me out in the proper direction, leading me three or four miles down the road towards Troy and then sending me in a northeasterly direction on what proved to be nothing more than a blazed trail overgrown with pea vines. Pursuant to his directions, I traveled five or six miles until I reached a small creek, which I followed to a place where it drained into a larger one. There I forded the larger creek and within less than a mile found myself at the gate of what appeared to be my friend's log cabin. In the front yard of the cabin a young woman was hanging some washed garments on a clothesline to dry, some of them belonging to an infant. She couldn't have been more than thirteen or fourteen years old, and it struck me how prematurely motherhood comes to a backwoods girl. She turned out to be David's eldest daughter. When I asked her about the whereabouts of her father, she explained to me that he no longer lived there.

"Oh, you will have to travel clear to the next county to visit him," said she.

Well, reader, you can easily imagine how I felt upon hearing that piece of news after I had made such an arduous journey through the dense jungle. And it must have showed on my face, for she burst into a fit of laughter.

"The next county is less than a mile and a half yonder," said she, and she pointed east to where the sun was rising over the timber line. "Light, sir, and have you a cup of cool water."

I complimented her on her sense of humor.

"You can thank my father for that," said she.

After I was sufficiently refreshed, she gave me directions to her parents' homestead sending me down a recently cleared trail into the deep woods. Just as I was about to succumb to the temptation of turning around and beating a hasty retreat lest some Indians or bushwhackers set upon me, I came upon a clearing near a little stream. When I got closer, I could make out a small cabin of un-hewn logs situated on a rise perhaps fifty yards from the stream. Ten minutes later I was having a cup of coffee on the porch with Mrs. Crockett; David was off at a neighbor's house several miles away digging post holes.

Mrs. Crockett, I should tell you, is tall and, like her husband, quite solidly built. While I certainly found her pleasant enough to look at, she is, according to David, "not half as easy on the eyes" as was his first wife, whom he lost to a devastating fever about fifteen years previous. I must say, however, that Elizabeth Crockett (or "Betsy" as he calls her) is possessed of more sensitivity and natural intellect than I would have expected of a backwoods woman. David later showed me some verses she had composed, some of which put my wife's efforts to shame despite the nearly illegible scrawl and atrocious misspellings.

We finished our coffee; then I brought my saddle bags inside, and she showed me my accommodations: her young son's bed in the loft. I had to climb my way up on crude wooden pegs which had been stuck in the wall, a rather daunting proposition at first, but one to which I nonetheless got accustomed after a few tries. Crockett and his wife slept on the main floor of the cabin in the far corner of the single room, their three young daughters across from them in a homemade one-poster he had built out from the wall. On the near side of the room was a pedestal table of satinwood, beautiful and out of place in such a primitive cabin, and in the center of the room was a large bearskin rug.

Crockett arrived several hours later; the chatter of his little daughters, whom he had retrieved from their schooling, woke me from my afternoon nap. As I have said, there were three of them, and they were all under the age of ten. The youngest was named Matilda, and they called her Mattie for short. After I told her that *my* parents had called *me* by that very name when I was her age, she took to me like a duck to water. She reminded me of my own little daughter Ellie (who is not so very little anymore), and she cried when I bade her adieu.

As for David, his appearance quite shocked me. His shoulder-length hair was tied back in a que, in the manner of our fathers; and the stubble on his chin was almost as thick as his long side whiskers. I asked him if he normally sported a beard when public service was not occupying his time. He said not usually; he just hadn't been able to find his razor for a few days.

"It'll turn up if I wait long enough," said he. "All things come to them that waits—including a beard." Then he apologized for the primitiveness of his accommodations explaining that he had started out poor and had been rooting along ever since.

"But damn apologies," said he, "I hate 'em. What I live upon always I reckon a friend can for a week or two. You think you can stomach a bowl of rat-tail soup, Saint Clarke?"

I told him I would certainly try. Fortunately, however, I didn't have to, for we dined on the most delicious roast pork I had ever tasted in my life that night. And I most assuredly did not keep my sentiments to myself.

"Obliged for the compliment," said he. "And if it's a-coming from your stomach, it must be so. Least-ways, there's no use in attempting to debate it since no stomach I ever heard of has ears. Anyways, here's the secret. You must kill the whole hog all at once to get meat of this quality."

"Ha!" said I. "And it's easier on the animal, too."

"Show me a man who mistreats an animal—even one he's fixing to eat," said he, removing the joke from the matter, "and I'll show you a man who mistreats his friends. My way of thinking, you ought to treat your friends like family, which I always strive to do. And for family I always go the whole hog."

After supper, he showed me around his property. He took me over to his little field of corn which he himself had cleared and grubbed, and as we walked, he talked of the quantity he should make and of his peas and pumpkins with the same pleasures that a James River Virginia planter would exhibit showing me around his wide inheritance. He asked me what I thought of his cabin.

My sentiments were that if you had seen one, you had seen them all; but I chose not to tell him that.

"Excellent workmanship," said I instead. And I suppose that despite its primitive nature, it truly was.

"We did the best we could with what we had," replied he. He and his neighbors had built it over the summer. His original home, the cabin at which I had first alighted, he had given to his second son William. William had a young wife and an infant child to whom the swaddling clothes on the line had belonged. His sister Polly, David's eldest daughter from his first marriage, thus was not a child bride after all .

"Make no mistake: having a grandchild is the beatenest of pleasures," he confided to me, "but I'm not so sure how I feel about being married to a grandma."

Later on that evening, Crockett and I sat on his front porch steps sipping some homemade hard cider (Said he: *"The old woman won't permit me to touch nothing stronger."*) and watching the sun go down behind the tree line. I had hoped to gather up enough courage to do what I had come there to do, to wit: to broach the delicate subject of a political compact, but that courage was slow in coming.

We discussed his dogs instead, several of them having seen fit to join us there on the porch. He had seven or eight at the time, most of them enormous since he used them for bear hunting. The largest one was the size and color of a panther. He was called Old Tiger, and he would growl at me whenever I stopped stroking him.

"He likes you," said Crockett. "You know, they think more highly of us than we do of ourselves, dogs do. So I always try to be the person my dogs think I am. Which reminds me of a riddle: how can you tell who likes you more, your dog or your wife?"

I shook my head.

"It's easy. Tie them both up for an hour, then come back and see which one is overmastered by joy to see you. You like dogs, Clarke?"

"That I do, sir. But I haven't been around them nearly as much as you have."

"Astonishing as this may sound, some folks don't like dogs at all. Or people that keeps dogs. They say we don't have the grit to bite unwelcome strangers ourselves."

I looked at Old Tiger. Slowly and deliberately did I remove my hand from his head. He showed me his teeth again.

"Right there's the best dog I ever had," Crockett said shooing him away from me, "except for Old Carlow. Now, Old Carlow I lost five year ago."

He went on to tell me a touching story about the last moments of that poor creature's life. His dogs had just brought down a large bear when Crockett stepped into a sink hole of water up to his chest. "I was so infernal mad," said he, "I had a notion not to get out."

When he did get out, he found that the only dry powder he had left was the load in his rifle. Nevertheless, he was able to bring down the bear with that single shot. He was feeling quite pleased with himself until he encountered his four-footed companion lying on the ground in a large puddle of blood.

"He was cut into the hollow, Clarke. Nothing could save him. I knew what I had to do, but it was the hardest thing I ever done in my life."

He stopped to clear his throat; it was not an easy tale for him to tell.

"So there I was," he continued, "a-feeling about him when what does he do, he starts licking my hand. Then my eyes filled with tears. I couldn't bear to look upon him, so I turned my head away when I done it. He yelled his death note, and no sooner had I pulled my knife out of him when the other dogs jumped upon him, such is the nature of a dog."

"I suppose that's the way God fashioned them," said I.

"Which is why I can't fault them. Fact is, they're living proof that heaven must go by favor. Because if heaven went by merit, folks like me would stay out and our dogs would all go in."

Crockett then offered to take me out on a hunt so that I might get my own bear. I had already suspected that his prowess as a bear hunter might be just the vehicle I was looking for to propel him to national celebrity, but I was not so very eager to observe that prowess at close range. I told him I didn't fancy stepping in a sink hole or ending up like his dog.

"You won't," said he. "I had a case of bear-buck ague too my first time out, but I got over it—and so too shall you."

"Aye, but you, sir, are not five foot-one."

"Size ain't everything, Saint Clarke. My milk cow is big enough to catch a mouse, but I don't believe she's done caught one yet."

I asked him if he didn't think it was a trifle early to set out on a hunt, hoping he might reconsider.

"Well, maybe a mite," answered he, "but by the time the bears are as fat as I should like them, I'll be over yonder in the Congress wondering what in God's purpose ever put me there."

"Or me," said I.

"And it's all their fault," continued he, "the damn coons and bears. I come to find out they done got together and election-eered for me all the previous summer to remove me from the woods so's they might have a reprieve for the next two years."

That night, the one we spent sitting on his porch in the middle of the woods, was one of only two occasions during my entire stay with him that I saw Crockett truly inebriated. I dare say Crockett saw me inebriated, too, at least on that one partic-ular night. In any event, his cider soon gave me enough Dutch courage to turn the conversation around to politics.

"I wish I could bring some of my Eastern colleagues here," I began. "If they could only see what determination and courage it takes for a poor honest man such as yourself to eke a living out of the wilderness, I cannot imagine they would deny you their votes on your amendment."

"Bring 'em out next year at harvest time," says Crockett. "I'll put the rascals to work."

"I just may do that," says I, "but I expect your land bill will come up well before harvest time."

"Aye, my land bill will be *enacted* before then."

"God willing, maybe so. But in my opinion 'tis an unlikelihood."

"That's just your opinion," says he. "I'll have you know I made a canvass on the last day of the session, and the consensus was they favored my measure over the delegation's by a far sight. I've got Jim Polk by the short hairs, by God."

I told him I had made a canvass of my own, and that the consensus I had found was for keeping the measure on the table.

"Well, then you ain't talked to the same members that I done."

"I've spoken to enough of them. Don't you suppose there is the slightest possibility that they were not being completely candid with you?"

He gave me a murderous look. "Confound it, Clarke," said he. "You reckon I was born yesterday—or am I a be-addled old fool?" He took a long swig from his jug and set it down on his other side where I couldn't reach it.

I told him that I most definitely did not take him for either a dupe or a dotard. I merely had meant to warn him that the requisite votes were not going to fall into his lap like so many peaches.

"And you just might have to traverse the political fence to get some of them," said I.

"In a pig's eye!" says he. "My vote, sir, is not for sale."

"I suppose you think they are going to come to you as if you were the Pied Piper of Hamelin."

"The Pied Piper," says he. "They's rats, not peaches."

I laughed. "Pardon my mixed metaphor."

"Your what?"

"Mistaking my peaches for rats."

He slapped the step on which we were sitting with an open hand. "They'll come, all right—the rats and the votes," said he as he rubbed the smooth new wood with his thumb. "A vote for me is a vote against Jackson."

"And a vote, sir, to table the measure is a vote against both of you."

He answered that by upending the jug again; I remember wondering if he had a callous on the bridge of his nose.

"It's not as if we are the devil's emissaries," said I.

"You could mis-fool me," said he. "What are you then, guardian angels?"

I smiled. "Well, I wouldn't go that far. But I will say this: by and large, sir, we are all respectable gentleman—to various degrees, of course."

"Now don't *that* put my mind at ease, Saint Clarke! Trouble is, I know what a so-called respectable gentleman is like, and it's enough to make my flesh creep. No, I ain't a-gonna change my stripes for you or no other man—and that goes on earth, heaven and elsewhere."

I told him I wasn't asking him to change his stripes, that no one expected him to vote with us on Party questions; but as far as less pivotal legislation was concerned, what harm would there be in a little horse trading? That would hardly jeopardize his Jacksonian credentials.

"My Jackson credentials?" said he. "I don't care any more for that snake-bit old man than I do for old Daddy Adams. If he didn't have the plain folks of my state so hornswoggled, I wouldn't give him the time of day."

"Then perhaps you shouldn't."

"What, and end up setting right here on my own porch all next term?"

I told him I understood his feelings precisely. I told him that if I were a Tennessee politician, I would be just as loath as he to confront her favorite son.

"I ain't afraid of no man, sir," said he. He gave me another intimidating glare.

I apologized, but 'twas to no avail. It took him quite a few more swallows to get into a better frame of mind, by which time I had resolved to remain mum about all things political for the remainder of the evening.

We did not again discuss politics until the following week. In fact, it was the day we bade each other adieu—and it was he who broached the subject, not I. We had been on a hunting excursion in the "Shakes," which is what Crockett and his people call the Mississippi River country of West Tennessee where the great earthquake of 1812 took place. He considers that country to be the most bountiful hunting ground in all of the West. Put another log on the fire, reader, and I shall take you there. Let us have ourselves a look at the bear-hunter congressman in his natural habitat.

COLONEL CROCKETT AND I ARRIVED IN THE SHAKES EARLY IN the morning of our second day's journey having traveled about thirty miles. Not counting the dogs (who took turns riding horseback with us) we were a party of five: Crockett, his grown stepson, his brother-in-law, a neighbor boy, and myself. We pitched our tents within sight of Reelfoot Lake. Reelfoot Lake is one of the wonders of the Western District, for it is nearly twenty miles in length and wasn't even a twinkle in Mother Nature's eye until that earthquake of twenty-one years ago.

Before we commenced our first day's hunt, Crockett took me on a tour of the immediate vicinity. As he pointed out the flora and fauna, I could see the same pride in his face that I had observed when he showed me around his humble homestead.

There were canebrakes nearly everywhere we turned. The worst of them he called "harricanes." These are places where severe storms had blown down many good-sized trees leaving an almost impenetrable (at least by the hunter) undergrowth, which provides an ideal shelter for the bears, wolves, panthers, deer and elk that inhabit the region. But the most salient features of the land are the multitudinous fissures and openings in the ground that had been fashioned by the great earthquake. I have seen one such opening thirty feet wide and thirty feet deep. And I have seen a large forest tree split from its roots to its top, half on each side of a fissure.

Crockett told me that he had once killed a large bear in a fissure similar to the one near our campsite, which was at least four feet deep. That was two years prior to the time of which I write, and it was the dead of winter. I told him I wouldn't for all the money in the world jump into that crack with a bear. He said it hadn't been his intention to do that either, but since he had misplaced his rifle in the dark, he no longer could deal with the beast from a comfortable distance.

"Losing my weapon would be all the more reason for me *not* to jump in there," said I.

"I didn't exactly jump in it," said he. "I sort of eased myself into it like it was an ice-cold water hole. And I had my dogs with me to keep him busy, so that his head might could face some other head than mine. Well, I eased on up to him and placed my hand on his rump and felt around for his shoulder—this is all in the pitch dark, mind you—and made my lunge right behind his shoulder and into his heart. Right after that I crawled out of there in a hurry."

But the most torturous part of his ordeal (if you can imagine anything more torturous than wrestling with a bear) was having to cope with the weather, it having been the coldest night of the year. Crockett had tried to go to sleep, but his fire went out and he couldn't kindle another. He had thought he literally was going to freeze to death.

"So I jumped up and hollered a while," said he, "and threw myself into all sorts of motions, but that didn't do a thing but give me a sore throat. So I went up to a tree about a half yard or better straight-through and nary a limb on it for thirty foot, climbed up to where the limbs begun, locked my arms around the trunk and slid all the way down. All night long I did that. When I had me a look at that tree in the morning, do you know what it looked like, Saint Clarke? It looked like every varmint in the woods had been sliding down it for a month, the trunk was so slick."

Just before we set out on our hunt, Crockett permitted me to fire his rifle; `Betsy,' he calls it after his wife. It is a large coarse common one with a flint lock and from its appearance has been much used. In its breech there are two or three wire holes with feathers in them, and several parts of it are wrapped with wax thread for the purpose of healing up wounds it has received in its passage through life.

"But this right here is the tool I set my store on," said he as he grasped the handle of his monstrous hunting knife. He wore it on his belt near his right hand. On the other side was a hatchet which he said was more for balance than anything else, and from his shoulder hung a powder horn and a bullet pouch. He wore a plain heavy homespun linsey-woolsey hunting shirt, a wide-brimmed hat, deerskin leggings and moccasins. I had a pair of deerskin leggings on, too, but everything else I was wearing was store-bought and more fit for the business world. The leggings belonged to one of David's grown sons, and Mrs Crockett had shortened them for me. I must confess I have neglected to return them. They remain in my closet, and every time I look at them, I have fond memories of my journey west.

"Go ahead," Crockett said and handed me his knife. "See how it feels in your hand."

I told him it had good balance, although I had no idea what I was talking about.

"A single bullet may settle up a buck or bear into a right sort of fix," said he, "but I always finish him off with my butcher. It won't give out a sign like a rifle-gun with a crack and smoke when some skulking redskin or vagabond is upon my tracks for mischief—and besides, it's a mighty saver of lead and powder."

After I had finished admiring his deadly weapons, we divided into two parties: Crockett's stepson Little George and the young man's uncle proceeding first while Crockett briefed the neighbor boy (a fellow novice) and me on the rules of the hunt.

"First off, never go on a hunt with someone that's called *'Drunken Billy Goat.'* Especially if he's after deer and you're a-wearing deerskins. And if you're after bear, never look one in the eye, not unless you're meaner than he is—and that ain't you, Saint Clarke, lessen there's a side of you I ain't yet seen."

I assured David there was not.

"Well, maybe by the time we're finished, there will be," he replied.

Then, in a more serious vein, he admonished us not to cry out at the dogs once a "start" was made. The hasty hunter, said he, is more likely to frighten a bear than to kill it. The dogs would stay with him until he gave the word to go, and they would never "give mouth" on a run.

"You won't have to concern yourself about me giving mouth either," said I. "I shall be scared speechless."

"Perhaps," said he, "but I'll learn you as we go along, and you'll be first-rate prime before you know it. Take note I said *learn* you and not *teach* you. There's a powerful difference. When I'm a-learning you, first you watch me do it right, and then I watch you do it wrong—and tell you so. Then you make a note to yourself what each blunder feels like—and I guarantee you'll commit a number of 'em—so that when you stumble into actually doing it right, by God, you'll readily feel the difference—*feel* it, I say."

That afternoon, Little George and his uncle killed an eight-point buck. As for the rest of us, we pursued a "he-bear" of considerable size all day but did not vanquish it. We contented ourselves with thinning out a flock of wild turkeys, one of which we had for supper. The next day we were more fortunate. About an hour past dawn we saw a yearling bear come tearing out of a canebrake and into the far end of the glade in which we were walking. The neighbor boy raised his rifle and took aim, but Crockett restrained him. The dogs, said he, must have first crack at him.

Well, the dogs overtook it before it could go more than a hundred yards taking it by the elbow of its forearm and bringing it to a stop. Crockett then slew it with his knife without having to fire a single shot. Suffice it to say that I was somewhat taken aback by the whole proceeding; I have never in my life been a hunter and prefer to purchase my meat at market. And you would too, reader, if you had seen that poor beast of the forest succumb to its sad fate and then had to help skin it, fleece the fat off it, salt it and scaffold it.

As distasteful as such tasks proved to be, I am nevertheless grateful for having had the opportunity to accompany Crockett on that hunt. Understand, the experience has enabled me to write about bear slaying with considerable authority. Not that Crockett yet knew I was planning to write a book about him. No, I chose to withhold such plan from him until he was foursquare in my party's camp.

The next day Crockett and I left the others by the lake and set out for New Madrid. New Madrid is a Mississippi River town from which we were then about twenty miles. It was at such place that I would board a steamboat bound for Kentucky to retrieve my coach and coachman. 'Twas my originally intention to take the overland route by way of Nashville where I might squeeze in a few more days' of delving through journals and military documents, but I was too exhausted and couldn't for the life of me contend with the long ride back. I asked Crockett to pack what few possessions I had left at his home and to transport them to Washington with him the subsequent month.

As I earlier mentioned, only twice during my western excursion did I see Crockett profoundly inebriated. The first occasion I have already described; the second, I shall do so now. 'Twas on our last full day together, in a tavern in New Madrid. I must admit that I encouraged him in such indulgences, for I had hoped the libations would assist me in my last attempt to fashion a political compact with him. So I bought us a quart of rye whiskey and followed him over to the long table with it.

"Go ahead and taste it," said he as I sat down across from him.

I took a small sip and nodded my approval. He nodded back and signaled that I should have some more. So I took one more little sip.

"That's no way to do it," said he, grimacing. "Give it here and I'll show you how it's done." He freshened my glass with four or five times as much liquor as I had poured myself and downed it all at once. "Don't play with it all day," said he, handing me back the glass.

It was not very long until my friend, as I had hoped, was in a cheerful talkative mood spinning yarn after yarn, or *tall stories* as they call them out west. The ones I remember best were about his electioneering.

"It was three year ago and I was canvassing for Congress the first time," he began. "We was treating the voters and on our first outing I couldn't help but notice that my opponent the incumbent had a powerful grin. Now, I'll tell you what: that there grin seemed to be winning the voters over—which I guess is why some folks calls it a *winning smile*. Now, I knew it was nothing but mere trickery, and as much as I had no wish to mis-fool the voters like he done, I had a bigger wish to stop him from getting himself re-elected to Congress at my expense.

"So what do I do, I practice my own grin into a looking glass. All day long I do this till I apprehend I've done grinned myself into a sore face. But I also apprehend that I've done fashioned a mighty powerful persuasive grin of my own.

"So the next time out, after my speech I greet the folks one by one and try out my new grin on them. Some of them averted their eyes, and when they looked back it was more down at their feet than at me. Those of them that locked eyes with mine for a considerable moment, they're the ones that all got sick, some of them heaving their barbecue all over themselves. It didn't take me long to apprehend that I done grinned them all bilious, so for the rest of that canvass I kept my face perfectly straight. Folks after that figured I had an ornery stand-offish disposition despite all the jokes I still told, so they elected the *Honorable* Adam Alexander to another term instead of the *Questionable* Davy Crockett to his first.

"Well sir, all that grinning sure didn't help me win over any voters, but I soon found it to be a mighty useful weapon against critters—at least smaller ones like raccoons. It got to be that whenever I was after coon, I'd like as not leave my rifle gun at home. I didn't need it. It got to where all I had to do was grin up at a coon, and if it didn't in fifteen seconds time tumble down from the tree dead, then I wish I may be shot."

Colonel Crockett then spun for me another yarn about raccoons—or, rather, about one particular coon. Two years had passed since he lost that congressional election, and he was determined to deprive Colonel Alexander of his seat. It was the summer of 1827, a little over a year previous to the time of which I write. He was sure he could win this time, partly because it was a three-way race. And just as important, he had regained the ability to smile at people without making them sick, reserving the full grin for the purpose of un-treeing coons.

I shall now turn the spinning back over to David:

"Well, there we was, the Honorable Adam and me, positioned at each other's throats again," he began. "This time we was set up in front of a large grog shantee owned and operated by a mean-spirited crafty transplanted Yankee named Job Snelling. Now, Job Snelling had himself a sign chalked-up in large letters: *Pay to-day and trust to-morrow.* This, and his habit of sneaking his hand on his scale when he's a-weighing your purchase, made him ill-respected. But as his shantee is the only grocery for miles around, folks are obliged to trade with him.

"Anyways, when it was my turn to speak, I was not on the stump but a minute or two when there came such an uproar from the crowd that I could not hear my own voice. Those standing nearest to me made it plain that the folks was not prepared to sit and listen to me blabber and jabber about such a dry subject as the welfare of the nation without me a-treating them with something to wet their whistles. So I jumped down from the stump and led the way to the shantee, the folks following me now shouting, *'Huzza for Crockett'* and *'Crockett forever.'*

"So I call out for a quart of Job's best New England rum, and he just stands there like a smoke-shop wooden Indian and points up at the *Pay Now* sign over the bar. Now, ready money in these parts is the shyest thing in all nature, and it was most particularly shy with me on that occasion. Well sir, when the voters saw my predicament, they started drifting away to my opponent. Right then and there I knew that unless I got me some rum in a hurry, I should lose my election. That goes to show you that popularity can sometimes depend on a trifling matter indeed.

"So what did I do? I struck into the nearby woods with my rifle-gun on my shoulder a-looking for coon and, sure enough, within a quarter hour I treed a nice fat one. So I raise Old Betsy and take aim when it occurs to me that there's no need to waste powder and lead—and besides which, the voters weren't so very far off and might be frightened by the blast. So I put Old Betsy down and commence to grin that coon to death faster than you can say, *'Crockett for Congress.'* Then I picked it up from the root of the tree where it fell, skinned it and marched it back to Job Snelling's shantee.

"Then I threw down the coonskin upon the counter and called out for my quart of rum again. This time I got it, for Job well-knew that a coon was as good a legal tender in the West as a New-York shilling any day of the year.

"Well, as bad luck would have it, that quart only lasted nigh on to a quarter of the way through my speech, so I was obliged to go grin down another coon. So off to the woods I again slogged. This time, twice the amount of time lapsed as previous and still no sign of coon.

'Now don't that beat all," thought I. *"The word must be out among the critters: Davy Crockett is in the neighborhood—flee for your lives!'*

"I was perhaps a minute or two away from high-tailing back to finish my speech—rum or no rum—when I chanced to look upwards and spied a coon on the highest limb of a good size tree. So I grinned at it so long that my face begun to ache. Then I come up with a five-foot length of a broke-off limb, stuck one end in the ground and used the other end to steady my chin, and grinned another five minutes or so, but to no avail. I would have then put Old Betsy to the task, but thinking I wouldn't need her, I had left her back at the shantee.

"Curiosity now got the best of me, so I climbed halfway up the tree for a better look, and lo and behold I got the surprise of my life, for I could now see plain as day that it was a consider-able size knot way up on that limb that I had tried to grin down, not a coon. But here's the curious-est part: I could now also see that I had grinned all the bark off that limb and left the knot perfectly smooth!

"Anyways, I went back to the shantee for Old Betsy figuring I would be skunked worse in this contest than last time when I chanced to look downwards and spied one end of my coonskin sticking between the logs that supported the bar. Job had slung it there in the hurry of business. So I gave it a sort of quick jerk, and it followed my hand as natural as if I had been the rightful owner. Then I slapped the skin on the counter and called for another quart of New England rum, which Job straightaway gives me figuring he now has two skins, never suspecting it's but the one, and that he's done swapped for it *twice!*

"So I soon had the crowd huzza-ing for Crockett again and made sure to keep the rum a-flowing. I accomplished this by jerking that coonskin away from that ornery old Job Snelling from the same place he kept a-slinging it. And I'll be shot if I didn't before the day was over get ten quarts for the same identical skin—and from a fellow who in those parts was considered sharp as a steel trap!

"Well sir, that joke straight-out secured me the election, for it soon circulated like smoke among my constituents, and they all agreed that the man who could get the whip hand of Job Snelling could surely outwit the Devil himself and was the real grit for them in the U.S. Congress. So that's where they done sent me."

"Bravo, Davy!" said I, the first (and I believe only) time I ever addressed him as such.

"I wish you wouldn't call me that," said he. "Only I myself can call me 'Old Davy,' though I do make an exception for the critters. And sometimes for the voters, too, that only knows me from my stump-talk. But not for my friends. Not for them that takes me serious."

We traded some more laughable tales there in the New Madrid tavern. (Mine were about my Pennsylvania Dutch neighbors; I shan't inflict them upon you.) But soon the same whiskey that had fired my friend up was sedating him. He sat there in silence occasionally shutting his eyes, drifting in and out of sleep, or so it seemed. Meanwhile, I rehearsed in my mind how I might again broach the subject of our political compact. As it happened, though, he broached it himself. When I caught him with his eyes open, I remarked how beautiful I thought the wilds of the Western District to be. Said I:

"How can one even put a price on such beauty?"

He laughed at this. "You've got the right church but the wrong pew," says he. "The land is so poor it won't even bear the expense of surveying it."

"That is not what I meant," says I.

"I know it ain't," says he, "but it's what I done meant. I'll tell you what. The high grounds is rough and rocky, and the low grounds flood like Noah's fresh. I'll be shot if it's worth more than a penny an acre."

"Well, certainly there is some value in the timber," I offered.

"Value?" said he incredulously. "You folks back east may wish yourselves more timber, but if you lived out west you most surely wouldn't. Like as not, you would wish for some invention to remove a considerable quantity of it off with less labor."

Then he waxed sentimental about his constituents. The poor people of his district loved their land whatever its value, he insisted, because it was all they had, and because their children had been born there.

"Take a good look around you, Clarke," said he. "Ten-fifteen year ago my entire district looked like this. And it would *yet* look so if it wasn't for those poor settlers. They broke up the cane so that 'better' folks might could give them the privilege of watching them drive by in their six-horse coaches."

Most of those settlers, according to Crockett, had once possessed better homes and more fertile fields farther east under titles they had thought to be good.

"But then they got drove off their lands by the appearance of a stranger," said he, "strangers with rock hearts and warrants in their hands of an earlier date than theirs."

This reputedly happened more than once to some.

"They got drove from one home to the next," continued he, "till they was obliged to settle on lands nobody else would claim. That's all we're asking the Congress for, Saint Clarke. The odds and ends between the boundary lines of the better tracts. Is that too much for a man to have to ask for?"

"Not according to my book," said I.

I waited for him to ask me what book I was referring to. When he didn't, I told him it was the one about a certain young man who had also worked with his hands, a certain young carpenter from Nazareth.

He smiled at me and his eyes got misty. Then he finished off our first bottle of rye whiskey.

"I'll tell you what," he then said with a belch. "They's folks around here that would give their eye teeth to learn to read the Scriptures."

He looked down at the tavern floor and spit between his feet. "Still, not ary a one of them's a-willing to give up the roof over their family's heads to accomplish that, though. And if those thieving rascals down in Nashville think I'm likely to sit back and watch them rob Peter to pay Paul, they have another thing coming."

The thieving rascals to whom Crockett was referring were the members of his state's legislature who wanted Congress to cede to Tennessee all the federal land within her boundaries— including the land on which Crockett's constituents had squatted—so that they might auction it off and use the funds as an endowment for education.

I decided to play the Devil's advocate.

"Let's say the land is turned over to the legislature," I supposed. "Why can't your neighbors purchase it from the state? You just said it wasn't worth very much. Surely they would be given fair terms."

"Fair terms?" said he. "Not much they won't! The damn speculators run the government, and they aim to bid the price clear up through the roof. And don't think they can't do it. They's a well-oiled swindling machine is what they are. I'll tell you what, they would purloin pennies off a dead man's eyes."

"That's quite some accusation."

"It's common knowledge. They have all the qualities of a dog except loyalty. And about those terms, I've seen it all before and have but little doubt that I shall see it again. What those rascals done, they went up one side of the creek and down another just like a coon. They gave my poor constituents credit of a year to secure their claims, and they promised to take cows and horses as payment. But when the year come around, those notes was in the hands of others. And those others sued them for cold hard cash, cows and horses not being enough.

"It's a vigorous, hateful measure," he continued, referring to his delegation's land bill. "I ask you, sir, is it fair for the general government to take away their homes? Is it fair to make a donation to the state out of them so they can raise up schools for the children of the rich? I ask you, Saint Clarke, is that fair? Is that an act of charity to the poor?"

I said of course it wasn't fair.

"Now, don't get me wrong, old hook. I'm no enemy of education. I had no more than six months of it myself—which is something I ain't proud of—and I do wish I could have availed myself of more. But beyond that, well, the children of my people never saw the insides of a college, and like as not they never will. And that's where the funds is going, not to the little country schoolhouses like what my little girls attend. I'll tell you what, Clarke. If ever I sit by in silence and watch that measure pass into law, you have my permission to shoot me. No sir, the deeds must go straight into the hands of the true and actual occupants of that selfsame land. Aye, the ones that done improved it and made it a fit place to live on."

The barkeeper brought our second bottle, and Crockett took a long swig from it. Then he shook his head vigorously like a soaking wet dog trying to dry itself.

"I'll tell you what," said he. "When I lay myself down tonight, I do believe I'll have to hang on for dear life."

He wiped his mouth on his sleeve and sat there without speaking another word for quite some time. Then he pointed out the tavern window at one of his dogs; it was sitting in the shade, under a large evergreen tree and cleaning itself.

"Don't you wish you could do that?" said he with a faint smile.

"I've never given it much thought, said I. "Quite frankly, I prefer a long hot bath."

"You know when a dog licks its arse, Saint Clarke?"

"I won't even hazard a guess."

"After he's ate a bad piece of meat, that's when. To get the bad taste out of his mouth."

Then David stood up and staggered over to my side of the long table.

"And that's exactly what I feel like doing myself right now," said he, leaning down on it with both hands, his head cocked toward me, his eyes meeting mine. "You want me to swap votes with your people, Saint Clarke? Fine, I reckon I'll take any dog that'll hunt with me. But I wish there was some other way. I have a mighty bad taste in my mouth already, and I ain't so much as swapped my first vote yet."

A bad taste indeed, thought I, for his was to be a singular act of courageousness. Understand, reader: Andrew Jackson was the most admired man in his state—nay, in the entire nation—and a personal break with him might prove fatal to my new friend's political career.

Then thought I more pragmatically:

Aye, but perhaps such break shall help bring that irascible Old Roman down with him.

I held my tongue.

"I'll tell you what," he finally said after a few more agonizing (for me) moments of silence. "I'm beginning to feel like a cat in hell with no claws."

Then he pointed a forefinger at me and shook it. "Now, don't you go and expect me to vote with you on the tariff. I don't berry in such a patch as that."

"No tariff," said I.

"And I won't support your damn Yankee harbor bills. Road bills neither—not lessen they go through my district," he insisted. Then he sat down again, this time next to me, and took another long drink from the bottle.

"I'm a-gonna tell you something," he continued, "and you had better listen close. I had me a neighbor once, back when I was living in Lawrence County. Now this here neighbor, he had him several large dogs, and all of them had collars with his name engraved upon them. As I've already done told my delegation—every last one of them I told them this—I ain't never had a collar 'round my neck marked 'My Dog' with the name Andrew Jackson—and it don't say John Quincy Adams on it neither, is what I'm a-telling you."

I told him I didn't expect him to wear any man's collar.

"You done got *that* right," replied he. "And so long as you people keep that in mind, I don't reckon there's any harm in us a-coming to some sort of an understanding. I only hope my constituents understand, too."

"They will, sir, when your land bill is enacted."

He laughed. "Aye, sir, I'll be a fancy-pants congressman for life."

"And the bears around here will be able to breathe more easily."

"Aye, the bears," he said wistfully as he looked out the tavern window at the woods.

He continued to gaze out that window for quite some time while I drifted off into a doze. Then he startled me by grabbing my shoulder and shaking my hand.

"That wasn't so hard, was it Saint Clarke?" said he. "I always know'd you would come around to my way of thinking."

I wondered if he was being ironical.

Yes, of course he was, I finally concluded.

Simultaneously drunk and ironical. But was such a thing possible?

Until I bade him farewell the following morning, my mind remained open. My mouth on that particular subject, however, remained shut.

Chapter Six

THE FASHIONING OF A FRONTIER HERO

Matthew St. Clair Clarke

When last I wrote, I related how Colonel Crockett and I became close personal friends, and I chronicled the forging of our political understanding. Now I shall briefly recount how by both happenstance and design the Hon. David Crockett, Member of Congress from Tennessee, in no more time than it takes a babe to learn to walk and say a few broken sentences, became virtually a household word in these United States.

During the second congressional session of my friend's first term, David and I did some horse-trading. Upon my word, reader, I never pressed him to vote for any measure he thought might jeopardize his political standing back home—not initially, anyway. His amendment to the Tennessee delegation's land bill came up for consideration in early January of 1829, several months after my return from the western frontier. By then, I had called in some old debts and accrued some new ones, lining up what few votes I could deliver to him in those early weeks of the session. As it happened, that handful of votes proved sufficient to do the trick. Not to carry his amendment, mind you (although for a while I thought it possible), but to create a fissure in the heretofore rock-solid Tennessee delegation big enough for a bear to hide in—or a bear hunter.

You should have seen Mr. Polk sitting on his hands, trying to hold his temper as he watched my affluent Northeastern colleagues rise in defense of the champion of the poor Western farmers; he was too timid to publicly express his true feelings lest such an outburst evoke sympathy for his new adversary. Unfortunately for my friend Crockett, we were unable to drum up enough sympathy to prevent his measure from being tabled again. That was as far as we got. As for me, well, I didn't mind so terribly much, for I have always preferred a hungry client to a satiated one.

And a celebrated one to an obscure one, thought I as I wondered when I would find the time to get started on his biography.

The following year, however, I nearly gave up on him altogether. He had made peace with his Jacksonian delegation and agreed to support their land bill virtually as written, this after negotiating but a few minor changes. I couldn't believe it. Here, after all, was the very measure he had insisted would drive his constituents into the poorhouse!

"I've got me an election coming up next year," said he, "and if I can't get something passed this session—anything—I'll be assigned to a committee-of-one on my own front porch. Then what use to my people will I be? I'll tell you what, Saint Clarke. Sometimes you have to suck the hind tit."

Thought I: *'Tis time I cease sucking yours, you ungrateful so and so! I shall have to find some other disgruntled Tennessean to convert to our cause.*

Aye reader, I was not about to waste any more time singing the praises of a reborn Jacksonian Democrat. So I laid on the shelf what few chapters of his biography I had completed over the summer and washed my hands of him forever—or so I thought.

We avoided each other for the greater part of that session.

We spoke occasionally but no longer had the same rapport which we had developed over the previous two years. Then something interesting happened. It was the last of April or the first of May 1830 (Crockett was re-elected the previous summer) and his delegation's compromise land bill—the one that he, at best, had been *temporarily* supporting—had come up for consideration. It failed by twenty votes.

"I can't dance and it's too wet to plow, so what's to be done now, Saint Clarke?" boomed out a familiar twangy-toned voice the next morning, breaking my concentration as once it did two years previous—quite conceivably to the day.

I looked up from my desk and there stood Crockett looking down at me. And once again there was whiskey on his breath. This surprised me (a little) because one year previous, shortly after my return to Washington from my western excursion, he swore on my family Bible that he had given up ardent spirits for good.

"I thought you were still shunning me," said I.

"I ain't never shunned you," replied he. "You're the one that's done shunned me."

I told him I wasn't going to argue with him over who had cast the first stone.

He said he wasn't either. Then:

"I'll tell you what you can do for me, though, if you would, old hook. I'm ready to jump ship again, so if you'll be so kind as to fashion me a substitute measure—my *own* land bill, not just another amendment to that sorry piece of privy work I've been pretending to support—I shall be forever in your debt."

He held up a forefinger. "Correction," he said. "Forever *once more*, is what I shall then be."

"For a bill that is more favorable to your constituents?" asked I more or less rhetorically.

He nodded.

"And that has a better chance of carrying than your opponent's bill does?"

"If it won't carry, it ain't worth no part of nothing," he declared.

I told him I would indeed consider fashioning such a measure for him—but it would cost him. In the following session he would have to vote with us on important Party questions, viz: the tariff, internal improvements, the Bank, etc. And those votes, I reminded him, would become a matter of public record for his adversaries to use against him. Come election time, he would no longer be able to masquerade as a Jackson man.

"I shall never need to masquerade as nobody but myself," said he. "Not with the margin of votes I accumulated this time around. And that's after the collar boys slung the same old mud at me—you know, that I'm a no-account drunkard and such. But the voters weren't buying it. Nay, not after I convinced them that no amount of spirits can make me drunk."

The next day, my friend Sam Vinton of Ohio rose and introduced my substitute measure. It was similar to Crockett's original amendment in that it was concerned exclusively with the land on which his constituents had already settled; however, it stipulated that those squatters must purchase the land from the federal government instead of receiving it as a grant. Crockett was satisfied because the price was fair and locked in by law. As for the rest of the House, no one could claim we were giving away our national treasure. We were merely converting it into another medium: cold hard cash.

When the yeas and nays were tallied, our measure failed by only three votes—and in a Democratic-controlled House, yet. After that, however, Polk "collared his dogs" and made certain that the Tennessee delegation's land bill would never again reach the floor for consideration lest we vote it down once more and introduce our own—who knows, perhaps we would *win* by three votes next time!

Crockett was livid. Said he: "I shall never so much as walk on the same side of the street as that lick-spittle chore boy Jim Polk."

As for Mr. Polk, he considered Colonel Crockett a political Judas. Understand, if our measure had passed, it would have provided not one penny to his state's coffers. To make matters worse for Jackson's right-hand man, within a fortnight David delivered a passionate speech against passage of the president's *Indian Removal Bill*, which once again antagonized his entire delegation.

By way of an explanation, the Tennessee delegation had pledged their allegiance to speculators who had coveted the Indian lands for decades. Jackson insisted he was acting in the Indians' best interests as well when he signed the bill that supposedly would ensure their safety from encroaching whites by requiring them to be "shepherded" to the far side of the Mississippi. Crockett vigorously disputed this.

"How long you reckon it's a-gonna be till we white folks crowd them out of their *new* land?" asked he of me. "Less than a generation, I'll lay. And then what? I'll *tell* you what, Saint Clarke. Since all the sufferings of a hungering people excites no pity in our president, all the miseries of famine brought on by his own acts are bound to be the instruments of their extermination."

I complimented him for his compassion but was somewhat puzzled by it.

"Considering the fate of your late grandparents," said I, "I am surprised—though pleasantly—that you chose to come out so vociferously against him on this particular question." Understand, reader: David's forebears were massacred a half-century ago by a band of Cherokees.

"And I would've dispatched those savages to Hell with my own two hands," said he, "if only I had yet been born. But another band of that same tribe once saved my life when I was stricken in the woods by the ague, so I reckon we're . . . well, not exactly even. But plum nearly."

Here I must mention my concern that his open break with

his delegation over Jackson's Indian policy might threaten his political career.

"I suspect your constituents's views coincide more closely with the president's views on this issue than with yours," said I.

"Like as not they do," admitted he, "but when they re-elected me last year—and they done that by near a two-to-one margin— they chose me to vote my conscience. And that's exactly what I done in this case and all others. Mark you my words: they'll soon come to see that if Old Hickory-face can deprive the red men of their land so summarily—they're next!"

I wasn't so sure. Which is why I convinced my good friend Mr. Gales, publisher of the *Register of Debates in Congress*, to omit David's remarks from the printed record. Regardless, I am happy to report that the chances for another rapprochement between Crockett and Polk since then have diminished to next to nil. Rather, Representative Crockett is foursquare in our camp.

Which meant it was high time for me to put my nose to the grindstone. I calculated that with the next presidential election just two years away, I had better start singing his praises on paper again. And did I this time? Well, sometimes the best of plans never make it from head to hand, and such again was the case with my Crockett book that year. To my great surprise, however, this proved to be of no consequence whatsoever, thanks to Mr. Paulding's play,

The following, if you will, is a true account of the genesis of the *Lion of the West* (which has since been re-titled *The Kentuckian*), the play that first brought national celebrity to my friend "Davy" Crockett. It is by no means my intention here to boast, but I happened to have had a hand in it myself. 'Twas a sleight of hand, though, for should my contribution ever be revealed, I'd have for an enemy not only the play's author but my dear friend the play's protagonist as well. So mum's the word, gentle reader!

'Twas the spring of that year, 1830. Near the end of the session, I was approached by the poet Richard Henry Wilde,

Member of Congress from Georgia, who told me that he had just then received a letter from his friend in New-York, the writer James Kirke Paulding, asking him if he knew any colorful stories concerning the Southern under classes.

Said Mr. Wilde to me:

"You, sir, know more regional anecdotes than anyone else in this city. And if none come to mind, feel free to make some up."

"For what mephistophelian purpose?" I asked him with a wink.

'Twas then he told me that Mr. James Hackett, the actor, was sponsoring a contest to determine who could introduce the most truly American character to the New-York stage. And since the judges were all his friends, Mr. Paulding was expected to walk away with the prize hands down.

I agreed to do this and wrote to Mr. Paulding personally a few days later. I suggested he write a comedy about a backwoods congressman—a true people's man—who had arrived in Washington City on the crest of the great Jackson wave. I mentioned my friend Crockett by name and included some examples of his colorful speech such as *"I wish I may be shot,"* &tc. And I included a clipping of a farcical piece from one of the newspapers which poked good-natured fun at "Old Davy" as a country boy in the city.

After signing my letter *"A Friend of Old Hickory,"* I added a postscript in which I assured Mr. Paulding—a consummate Jackson man—that Colonel Crockett was as staunch a supporter of the president as ever there was. This, of course, was by the time of my writing pure hogwash, but I lost no sleep over it. And you wouldn't have either, reader, if when you masqueraded the truth, you did so, as I did, for such a noble purpose: to imbue Colonel Crockett with such widespread renown that from it he might develop the requisite political strength to help prevent our current chief executive from putting an end to our Republic as we know it.

Exitus acta probat.[1]

Well, Mr. Paulding followed my advice and, as predicted, won the contest. After that, it didn't take long for Colonel Wildfire and Colonel Crockett to be linked together in the public eye. The judges' decision was announced near the end of the year, and the newspaper writers (with a little help from your obedient servant) immediately made the connection. This was four or five months before the play was first produced, so by the spring of 1831, when it opened at the Park Theater in New-York, my friend Crockett was well on his way to *bona fide* national celebrity.

'Twas not the kind of celebrity he desired, though. For while he was perfectly enthusiastic about playing the simple rough-hewn, yarn-spinning bear hunter for his constituents back home at election time, once elected, he preferred that his congressional colleagues saw him as a gentleman. Or as he himself would say:

"Like as close an approximation of one as I can pull off."

Which hasn't been easy, says he now. And he hasn't ceased blaming Mr. Paulding's play for making him an object of ridicule; I cannot begin to tell you what an effort it was to convince him to attend last week's performance. And as for Mr. Paulding himself, when a few months after its opening at the Park Theater he discovered that he had "lionized" a vociferous member of the anti-Jackson coalition, he was livid. It is my understanding that to this very day, he refuses to admit that he'd had my friend Crockett in mind when he penned the *Lion of the West.*

As for me, I was by the summer of 1831 in full anticipation of witnessing Representative Crockett taking this nation by storm —and in plenty of time to help us deny President Jackson the electoral votes of his own state the following year when he was up for re-election. Or at least to embarrass him with a close count.

---

1. The end justifies the means.

Reader, you can well imagine my complete and utter surprise when at the close of that same summer I learned that our Lion had not been able to so much as take his own *congressional district* by storm.'Twas true: Crockett's constituents had denied him his bid for a third consecutive term.

I suppose I should not have been so surprised. After all, that had been the first electoral contest in which he ran openly against the "Old Hero"—an unpardonable sin in the eyes of the Jackson press, which lit into him with a vengeance.

And it was not just the newspapers, for he was (in David's own vernacular) *"hunted down like a wild varmint by every little pin-hook lawyer in the state."* They spread out over his district, those Jackson henchmen did. They made appointments on his behalf for speaking engagements alongside his opponents, this without his knowledge. They met the crowds at the appointed times and places with saddlebags stuffed with handbills and read their trumped-up accusations.

But Crockett couldn't defend himself—because he wasn't there.

Crockett's enemies were indeed there, though. They told the people that he had been afraid to attend. And unfortunately too many believed them. Nevertheless, here is what I wholeheartedly believe:

Had my friend already achieved the stature which he enjoys today, those tactics would not have been sufficient to defeat him. If only the play had been written a year or two earlier, reader!

Or if only I had finished my book in time.

That election, as I have said, took place in mid-1831. Shortly after the first of 1832, I received word from David that he intended to stand for office again a year and a half later. Time being of the essence, I once again resolved to expeditiously finish his biography. Thought I, if it were published and on booksellers' tables well in advance of the election, it just might be a deciding factor in his getting his seat back, this by dispelling some noxious and erroneous notions about him.

Here I must tell you that by then I had come to agree with David that Mr. Paulding had indeed fashioned him into quite the buffoon. And while some of his constituents may have known better, others clearly had been deceived. As for the rest of the country, his newfound admirers certainly had not yet had an opportunity to take his true measure. In fact, I don't think I would to any degree be exaggerating if I told you that as recently as one year ago, David Crockett was the most little-known well-known personage in the United States of America.

I decided to do something about that. Understand, if Crockett were going to be an effective spokesman for our cause, it was imperative that the people discover he was much more than an eccentric character in a popular play. Moreover (as I have already noted), he first had to get elected again, which meant I had to get my book into voters' hands well in advance of the Tennessee congressional elections to be held in August of 1833. This I at length accomplished. Not without a modicum of anguish, though, for I had forgotten many of the details of his early life and had misplaced my notes from our interviews.

I completed the better part of the book in two weeks. Initially, I had planned to dance my way around the gaps in the narrative, but in the end, the punctilious clerk in me would not permit it. Therefore, I had the manuscript copied and, in the spring of 1832, I sent it to a young colleague of mine, viz: Mr. James Strange French, who was then residing in Nashville, Tennessee. It was young French who promptly conducted the final interviews (Crockett was now most cooperative, for his political career was at stake) and filled in those inexcusable gaps. And it was Mr. French who with a light hand revised it and hand-carried the finished manuscript to Cincinnati, delivering it personally to my editor who published it in January of this year, seven months ahead of the election.

You may find it to be of some interest, reader, to learn how my friend Crockett received our tome, and so I shall tell you. He arrived at my door the day after his triumphant return to Washington the first week of December having been re-elected this past August. As I write, that was but three weeks ago, it now being the day after Christmas, 1833.

As they say in the book trade, he gave our efforts (mine and Mr. French's) mixed reviews. He was pleased, of course, that we had helped him win his seat back. And he was pleased that we hadn't mangled too many of the particulars of his life as he had related them to us. But here is what *dis*-pleased him immensely:

"I thought we agreed the book was to correct the damage the play done me," says he, sitting down and making himself uncomfortable in my parlor

"We did," says I, "and I believe we did so with flying colors."

"In a pig's eye you did!" says he, jiggling his foot nervously. "Look at what speech you put in my mouth. You made like I don't even know how words is put together proper. I may not have learned my letters till I was fifteen-year-old, but I've read a heap since. I'll have you know, sir, that I of late have thumbed my way through Ovid's *Metamorphoses*."

"And in the original Latin, I suppose you are about to attest."

He laughed. "If so, I should be advising *you* from now on!" says he. "But still I'm a heap less of a blockhead than I was ten-fifteen year ago."

"I never implied that you were a stranger to literature," says I, "but my impression was that your plain unvarnished use of the English language was not what you objected to. What you objected specifically to in Mr. Paulding's play—or so I thought— were such attempts at high-sounding speech as: *bodyaciously, tetotaciously, obflisticated, exflunctified,* and the like. Understand, not only did I refrain from putting such language in your mouth, sir, but as you may recall from my introduction, I affirmed that I'd never heard anything of the like in my travels west or anywhere else; and that I lamented, sir, that these terms have been made to enter, as a component part, into the character of every backwoodsman."

"Well, huzza for you, Clarke," says he. "But still you persisted in making plum-near every word that sung out of my mouth either mis-used, mis-spelled, or both. And that's just as hurtful."

"My understanding again, sir," says I, "was that when you came here to Washington, you were disinclined to speak just like everyone else. In fact, if my memory serves me right, you said—and I quote you here, sir: '*I aim to get them to talk more like me.*'"

"Talking is one thing," says he, "but putting it into print is another."

He stood up.

"And one more thing, any of this sound familiar to you, Saint Clarke?":

"*I am that same David Crockett,*" he began in a caricature of his frontier accent, "*fresh from the backwoods, half-horse, half-alligator, a leetle touched with the snapping turtle; can wade the Mississippi, jump the Ohio, ride upon a streak of lightning and slip without a scratch down a honey locust; can whip my weight in wild cats, hug a bear too close for comfort and eat any man opposed to Jackson.*"

"That's from the play, of course," says I, "except for any references to either you or the president—whom, as I by no means should need to remind you, you once upon a time actually did support."

"Guilty as charged!" says he. "But that blabber, sir, comes not only from the play. You know full well that you hauled off and stuck it in your blasted book, too. No sir, you really hadn't ought to a-done that. I can't comprehend why you would do such a thing to me, Clarke."

"Because those lines helped make you famous. Why should Mr. Paulding get the credit?"

"Because he's the one that's wrote them."

"I beg your pardon," says I, "but I've seen clippings from the *Nashville Republican,* sir, two-three years before Mr. Paulding wrote the play that attributed nearly identical language directly to you."

He smiled sheepishly. "I must admit I've used them from time to time on the stump—but look here, that's not the same as putting them in a book. Because on the stump I would always follow up with something like:

"*'All seriousness aside, friends and neighbors, I can't do any of them things—just the thought of them plum tuckers me out. But I got your attention, didn't I? And now that I've got it, here's something I don't want you to ever forget. Doggone it, it's done slipped my mind. Wait a minute, it's a-coming back. It's something to do with why you should vote for me.'*

"See, that's my kind of humor-izing, Clarke. Poking fun at myself. Ain't nothing laughable when it's on display all by itself in a book. All it does is makes folks that don't yet know me think I'm stuck on myself."

"Well—" I started to defend myself.

"And another thing." He was pacing now. "That newspaper piece about me at the White House. That was six year ago. I had hoped folks had forgot about it by now but no, you had to raise its ugly head again in that catch-all trap of yours."

That anecdote was from very early in his first term and 'twas what I had clipped from one of the papers and *confidentially* sent to Mr. Paulding a few years later. It related some fanciful boorish behavior on the part of Colonel Crockett at President Adams' dinner table including his eating soap from a finger bowl. I still think it humorous and harmless. Had I thought otherwise, I never would have reprinted it.

"Like I done told you time after time, Saint Clarke," he continued, "only Old Davy himself gets to make fun of Old Davy. Otherwise, it ain't funny—it's a cruel mockery. I'm morti-fied, sir, *mortified* you done put that in the book. I'll tell you what, if it's ever uncovered who exactly wrote that libelous piece, I'm a-gonna wring his neck."

I forced a half smile and hoped I wasn't crimsoning. Yes, reader, 'tis true: I wrote that newspaper piece myself.

"I included it to illustrate how unjustly cruel your enemies can be," said I. "And to justify my inclusion of those wonderful defenses of your character by Mr. Clarke of Kentucky and Mr. Verplanck."

"Wonderful they may be," said he, "but it would be far, far better if such defenses weren't needed. You know, it ain't necessary to repeat a lie over and over again to damage someone's reputation. Denying it will do the same trick, if you keep on repeating it. I guarantee that if you keep denying something—even if you ain't never so much as once been accused of it—folks will soon get the notion that where there's smoke there's fire."

I offered him a glass of Kentucky bourbon, which he accepted gratefully, downing it in two or three swallows. I poured him another; he sat down with it on one of my ladder-back Shaker rockers.

"Now don't get me wrong," said he. "There's parts of your book that actually ain't half-bad—I'll grant you that—but really and truly, I could have wrote it a far sight better myself."

"Well then, why *don't* you write such a book?" replied I, surprised at my own enthusiasm. "In my opinion, the citizens of this country would come to treasure your memoirs. And as for me, nothing would please me more than to assist you in the composing of them."

And I sincerely meant that, reader. True, those memoirs would compete with our own book, Mr. French's and mine; but as it instantly came to me, an autobiography of an already celebrated personage (thanks in part to the two of us) should render him an even more effective spokesman for the *Whigs*, as we opponents of King Andrew's *Tories* now proudly call ourselves.

Crockett raised his right hand. "Obliged for the offer," said he, "but Chilton's already a-working with me on it."

"You mean you've already commenced your autobiography?"

"That's what I just said. You gathering wool, Saint Clarke?"

"And he's planning to promote it for you, Mr. Chilton is?" asked I.

"We ain't got that far down the road with it yet. Speaking of which, though, we aim to carry it 'round the country and peddle it during the next recess, provided it's all printed up by then."

Bells and whistles went off in my head—*train* whistles heralding a grand tour! I shall explain:

Crockett may not have known it yet, but if I have my way, he shall be selling a lot more than books when he heads up north and down east. He shall be selling our party, too. Aye, to the hard-working Yankee workmen. He shall woo them away from Jackson and Van Buren. Perhaps he shall woo away enough of them to enable us to take over the lower house of Congress!

"And you have fixed this tour on your calendar for what month did you say?"

"I didn't," replied he, "but I figure September or October."

I wished him luck but held my tongue about the timing.

Hours later, however, I in bed found myself tossing and turning about that aforementioned timing. Thought I, postponing the tour until the recess would ensure that 'twould be of no influence whatsoever on the congressional elections of 1834. But if, on the other hand, the tour were pushed ahead to this coming spring, it could be a significant component part of our efforts to wrest control of the House of Representatives away from the Jacksonians.

Here I must tell you that winning the House would have implications far beyond the fate of our legislative agenda, crucial as that in itself stands to be. By this, I mean that it just might determine the election of our next president. Again I shall explain:

Mr. Clay, by his own admission, cannot be depended upon to, in 1836, once more serve our party as its standard bearer. Therefore, we may be obliged to field several sectional candidates— favorite sons, if you will—to oppose Mr. Van Buren in the presidential election. If no candidate wins a majority of the electoral votes, the contest will by Constitutional necessity be thrown into the House—aye, just as it was ten years ago.[2] Mind you, the

---

2. In 1824, the House of Representatives elected John Quincy Adams president

stronger our numbers are in that chamber, the better chance that whatever Whig candidate we unite behind shall be elected president there.

Of course, if Mr. Clay does indeed choose to again run for president, such a favorite son strategy will be scrapped. Which would be a shame. Understand, many of us apprehend that the name Henry Clay too much smacks of Kentucky aristocracy in this age of Old Hickory's rustic *hunters* of Kentucky.

O, if only we had a candidate as popular with the yeoman farmers and mechanics as is Andrew Jackson—aye, but a true man of the people this time instead of a populist impostor like the current president—he could demolish Van Buren *one-on-one*. And there would be no need whatsoever to throw the contest into the House.

I ask you, reader, does that not sound like someone you may already know?

To wit:

The Bible tells us to know thyself, and my friend Representative Crockett has recently intimated that he sees himself as the embodiment of such an ideal presidential candidate—'tis true, he has contracted the White House fever! Says he, a friend of his in the Mississippi state legislature intends to place his name in nomination. Moreover, the Mississippian friend of David's believes the motion will carry. David plays this down; nevertheless, he raises the question so often that I apprehend, to paraphrase the Bard, that he *"doth protest too much."*

As for me, I have discounted his musings to all I have told. Still, I fear I am coming down with a touch of the selfsame fever myself. Imagine, if you will, a five-foot one-inch power behind the—

---

over Andrew Jackson after the third-place candidate, Henry Clay, threw his support to Adams. President Adams then made Clay Secretary of State and "heir apparent" to the White House, which generated charges of "bargain and corruption" from the Jacksonians.

Well, not the *throne*, of course, reader. Shall we instead say, *"The Power propelling the Ship of State?"*

Pooh! Enough of such fanciful thinking! The closest Crockett could ever come to the presidency would be as a favorite son candidate of the Western states in our prospective plan to, as I have said, throw the election into the House. And the possibility of our party uniting behind him there? Well, my White House fever is not yet severe enough to permit me to swallow such a whopper hook, line, and sinker!

As for the aforementioned tour, I attempted to bring it up with David this past Saturday night at the theater; we were sitting together in the stage box waiting for Mr. Hackett to come on. I couldn't get his attention, though. He was too distracted by members of the audience who had spied him there and were loudly greeting him from a distance.

I had better luck at Gadsby's Hotel, at the reception following the performance. After Mr. Hackett made his brief appearance, David, who was suffering from an intermittent fever, grew weary of the guests. So we escaped to a private room to wait them out.

"What's on your mind?" said he once he had settled into the quiet. "How you people can put me to good use, I reckon."

I told him he could be of good use to himself *and* to us because his political agendas and ours were becoming more and more intertwined. We both saw President Jackson as a danger to the survival of the Republic. And we both knew there was no time to waste to prevent Jacksonism from surviving its namesake and flourishing under a future President Van Buren.

"Which calls for a spring tour, not an autumn one," said I. "How ever else can we stop the Magician in his tracks?"

"Now, hold your horses, old hook," said he. "How in blazes do you expect me to rise as a viable candidate for the presidency if I can't hold onto my seat in Congress—which is nigh near impossible if I go on a tour during the session. That's one of the ways they beat me in '31. I mean, making so much of the days I chose to take off for well-considered self-important reasons."

"Well, it won't necessarily happen that way this time," I answered. "By election time, you shall be ever so much more celebrated than you are even today, which should more than make up the difference."

At length, he promised to make every effort to complete his book by the end of January, although he didn't commit to a specific date to commence the tour. Thought I:

First things first. Blind ambition will take care of the rest.

So there it is in a nutshell, reader, if fifteen or twenty thousand words can properly be considered a nutshell. Am I responsible for the current wave of enthusiasm for my backwoods friend? Not exclusively, of course; nevertheless, I cannot help but take immense pride in having played Filson to his Boone.

As for Colonel Crockett himself, he should take pride in having stood up for his pioneer constituents throughout his rise to renown. Furthermore, whatever road may lead him to even greater renown (I suspect it will be a northerly one), he will undoubtedly be of considerable service to his country along it— particularly when he spearheads our crusade against the tyranny of the current chief executive.

In closing, please excuse him should you come upon him daydreaming aloud about his presidential prospects, for he is but a simple man with a vivid imagination. To borrow from Mr. Paulding's eulogistic remarks about his fictional Colonel Wildfire:

> *All his whimsical extravagance of speech results from mere exuberance of spirits, and his total ignorance of conventional restraint he overbalances by a heart which would scorn to do a mean or a dishonest action.*

Upon my word, reader, I could not have said it better myself.

Colonel Crockett arrived at Washington and had been there but a short time when he received a note inviting him to dine with President Adams.

"I was wild from the backwoods," said the colonel, "and I didn't know nothing about eating dinner with the big folks of our country. And how should I, having been a hunter all my life? I had eat most of my dinners upon a log in the woods and sometimes no dinner at all. I was afraid that at the president's house I should be awkward as I was entirely a stranger to fashion. So in going alone, I resolved to observe the conduct of my friend Mr. Verplanck and to do as he did. This I indeed did do, and I know I done behaved myself right well."

The colonel's originality of character induced someone to write a humorous but false account of this dinner scene, which could never have been believed by any person who knew him, but which the colonel thought proper to deny as it was used to his prejudice by his enemies. This story, as printed in the newspapers, went as follows:

The first thing I did (said Davy) after I got to Washington was to go to the president's. I stepped into the president's house—thinks I, who's a-feared? If I didn't, I wish I may be shot.

Says I: 'Mr. Adams, I'm Mr. Crockett from Tennessee.'

'So,' says he, 'how d'ye do, Mr. Crockett?' and he shook me by the hand although he know'd I went the whole hog for Jackson. If he didn't, I wish I may be shot.

So I went to dinner there and walked all round the long table looking for something that I liked. At last I took my seat just beside a fat goose and I helped myself to as much as I wanted. But I hadn't took three bites when I looked away up the table at a man they called *Tash* (attaché). who was talking to a woman there in French. He dodged his head, and she dodged hers and they got to drinking wine across the table. But when I looked back again, my plate was gone, goose and all. So I just cast my eyes to t'other end of the table and I see a man walking off with my plate. I says:

'Hello mister, bring back my plate.' Which he did, and how do you think it was? Licked as clean as my hand. If it wasn't, I wish I may be shot. Says he:

'What will you have, sir?' And says I, 'You may well say that after stealing my goose.' And he began to laugh. Then says I, 'Mister, laugh if you please, but I don't half-like sich tricks upon travelers.'

I then filled my plate with bacon and greens, and whenever I looked up or down the table, I held on to my plate with my left hand. When we were all done eating, they cleared everything off the table and took away the tablecloth. And what do you think? There was another cloth under it. If there wasn't, I wish I may be shot.

Then I saw a man coming with a great glass thing with a glass handle below, something like a candlestick. It was stuck full of little glass cups with something in them that looked good to eat (soap). Says I:

'Mister, bring that thing here.' Thinks I, let's taste them first. They were mighty sweet and good—so I took six of 'em. If I didn't, I wish I may be shot.

1834

Excerpt from the Preface to:
NARRATIVE
OF THE
LIFE OF DAVID CROCKETT
OF THE STATE OF TENNESSEE
Written by Himself
1834

Fashion is a thing I care mighty little about, except when it happens to run just exactly according to my own notion; and I was mighty nigh sending out my book without any preface at all until a notion struck me that perhaps it was necessary to explain a little the why and wherefore I had written it.

Most authors seek fame, but I seek for justice—a holier impulse than ever entered into the ambitious struggles of the votaries of that *fickle, flirting* goddess.

A publication has been made to the world which has caused me much injustice; and the catchpenny errors it contains have been already too long sanctioned by my silence. I don't know the author of the book—and indeed I don't want to know him—for after he has taken such a liberty with my name and made such an effort to hold me up to public ridicule, he cannot calculate on anything but my displeasure. If he had been content to have written his opinions about me, however contemptuous they might have been, I should have had less reason to complain. But when he professes to give my narrative (as he often does) in my own language and then puts into my mouth such language as would disgrace even an outlandish savage, he must himself be sensitive to the injustice he has done me and trick he has played off on the public.

I have met with hundreds, if not thousands, of people who have formed their opinions of my appearance, habits, language, and everything else from that deceptive work. They have almost in every instance expressed the most profound astonishment at finding me in human shape and with the *countenance, appearance,* and *common feelings* of a human being. It is to correct all these false notions, and to do justice to myself, that I have written.

Chapter Seven

NARRATIVE OF THE LIFE OF DAVID CROCKETT
(The Work Progresses)
Washington City January 1834

"*I was living ten mile below Winchester, Tennessee when the Creek War commenced. As military men is making so ... AS military men ARE making so much fuss in the world at this time, I give a ... I MUST give an account of*—bear with me, Chilton. I can't hardly make out my own scrawl.

"*I must give an account of the part I took in the defense of the country. If it should make me president, why I can't help that. Such things will sometimes happen, and my pluck is never to seek nor decline office.*"

"I think your pluck should be to delete all mention of that notion, David," said Thomas Chilton sitting there at the foot of his own bed.

Crockett, sprawled out on the rest of the bed, put his manuscript on Chilton's bedside table and then, with both hands, picked up the pillow he'd been using on his stomach as a podium. "Trouble with you, Tommy Chitlins," he said placing the pillow behind his shoulders, "you ain't got much of an imagination."

"The *Lord* blesses us each in *myriad* and *com-pli-mentary* fashions," Chilton replied in ecclesiastical tones, "Now if you'd be so kind as to read me the rest and be done with it. I need my sleep. Apparently more so than do you."

"Ain't no more to recite. That there's as far as I done got."

"Then if you'll excuse me." Chilton stood up and started for the door motioning with a stiff right arm for Crockett to follow suit.

"Wait a minute, I got more. It's all up here." Crockett tapped his forehead. "Go ahead and set yourself back down. You'll find I make a far better dictator than a scribe."

Chilton raised his ample eyebrows but otherwise attempted to remain expressionless. Then he held up a forefinger and shook it at his friend. "One hour," he said. "One hour, sir, and you are *out* of here!"

And that would not be a minute too soon, Chilton thought, because for over a month his Tennessee messmate had been spending two or three hours a night here in Chilton's room struggling with his memoirs and Chilton was growing increasingly annoyed by the distraction.

"Fair enough," Crockett said. "One hour it is. Go pick up your ink pen. I'm as ready as I expect I shall ever be."

Chilton left his pen where it was. "From your head to mine," he said and sat back down on the foot end of his bed.

"I already done give you the facts pertaining to my enlistment in the mounted volunteers, didn't I?"

Chilton closed his eyes and nodded.

"I thought so. Well, anyways this here segment takes place in 1813 or thereabouts—you sleeping, Shirley Hoppit?"

Chilton opened his eyes. "I'm all ears," he said.

Crockett tugged at his borrowed quilt. Chilton then eased off it until it nearly reached his friend's chin exposing both his bare feet at the other end.

"All right, then," David began, clearing his throat. "The way it was, Major Gibson, he come up and wanted some volunteers to go with him across the Tennessee River and into the Creek Nation. To find out the movements of the Indians. So he asks my captain for two of his best woodsmen and for one of them the captain volunteers me. So that's how I come to volunteer for this here adventure."

"And how did that strike you?"

"I agreed with him. I was a right good woodsman even then."

"No, I meant were you afraid? You must have been at least a trifle apprehensive, twenty years old and never been shot at before."

"Not really—and I suspicion that's exactly why I wasn't, because just like you say that first shot hadn't been fired yet. And I wasn't twenty. I was twenty-seven-year-old almost to the day."

"So you went off searching for Indians."

"Aye, for the war party—the Red-Sticks they was then called. The second day out we split up, me taking about half the men— they was about a dozen all told—and Major Russell taking the rest. We was to meet up where these two roads come together some fifteen-twenty mile distant. We got there and waited for the major till dark, but he never showed up, so we struck up camp for the night at the head of a hollow. And let me tell you, they was so many chiggers there that a tick bite was a kind of enjoyment.

"Anyways, we waited there past breakfast next morning but still no sign of the major, so we chose to strike out on our own. We pressed on another twenty mile or so past a Cherokee town to the house of a man called Radcliffe. I can still recall that man's name as if I first heard it only last week instead of twenty years ago. Radcliffe. He was a white man, but he had done married a Creek woman and they lived just at the edge of the Creek nation."

"And where exactly was the Creek Nation?" Chilton asked.

"Like I said, on the other side of the Tennessee River from

where the army was camped. You got to pay attention, old hook. Now get up off of this bed and start writing these things down."

Chilton shrugged, rose and sat down at his writing table.

"That's better. Anyways, this Radcliffe had two grown sons, and one of them had him a pretty young daughter no more than seven-year-old or thereabouts. Now, the sons, they was off somewheres else, so it was just him, his wife and the little girl when we got there, and they was bad scared. They had been ten painted warriors at his house not one hour previous and if they should discover us, not only would they kill us, they would kill him and his family, too, for harboring us. We weren't about to permit that to happen, so we took leave of them and pushed on through the night by the light of the full moon till we reached a camp of some friendly Creeks eight or ten mile distant.

"They was forty-some-odd men, women, and children at that camp and—oh, I forgot to mention this, Chilton. On our way there, we run into these two black-skin fellows a-mounted on Indian ponies, and each one had him a good rifle-gun. They told us that the redskins had taken them from their owners quite a spell ago and now they was making their escape. Now, whether that escape might take them back to their owner or not I chose not to ask, but one of them agreed to go back to the landing where the main army was camped. The other one stayed with me. He was called Reuben, and he could talk Indian as well as English. So I had him talk to some of those friendly Creeks who told him they was very much alarmed that the Red-Sticks would come and all would be killed.

"So we lay down with our guns in our arms. I had just got into a doze of sleep when I heard a scream and I'll tell you what, it was the sharpest scream that ever escaped from the throat of a human creature. Then that big buck Reuben come up and told me that the Red-Sticks was approaching—this is all true so far, Chilton, so help me God.

"Now, the Indian that had fetched the scream was a runner for the friendly Creeks and he told Reuben that a war party had been crossing the Coosa River all day at the Ten Islands and was on their way to confront Jackson and his men. Of course if I knew then what I know now about Old Hickory-face, I might would've let them confront him. Because then this nation wouldn't today be going through such hard times as it is. But I didn't know the man yet, so I was not about to let that happen."

Old Hickory-face, Chilton thought. He wrote it down and underlined it twice.

"So we mounted up and cut out with the Indian runner to report to the army back at the landing, which was, I'd say, some sixty mile distant. When we got back to the Radcliffe place, we come to find out they was all killed and—

"No, they wasn't. The Red-Sticks come, and they done taken their little girl is what happened. That pretty little blond-headed girl."

"I thought you said her mother was a Creek Indian," said Chilton

"She was. So make her a pretty little black-headed girl, suits me. Anyways, they took her with them, the savages did. And old man Radcliffe, he begged me to try and save her, but I told him I had to report back to Colonel Coffee. Well, he kept on a-begging and a-pleading till it like to broke my poor heart, so I sent my men on ahead and took Reuben and the Creek runner with me and doubled back after the war party that done abducted the little girl.

"We never did catch up with them, though, but we finally spied a small group of painted warriors from a bluff directly across the stream that we was a-following. They was only four of them so we figured we stood a fair chance. So we doubled-back again, crossed the stream, moved up to the high ground and come up on them from behind. Old Reuben got the first with a tomahawk from about fifteen paces, which now made it three against three. I aimed to take mine alive, and I was mighty glad I was able to do exactly that because the Creek runner says it's none other than the chief's son!

"So we painted up the Creek runner like a red devil and sent him off with the chief's son's rifle-gun to find the chief, who he soon enough finds, and he tells the chief that although he was able to retrieve the weapon he was mighty sorry he wasn't able to retrieve his son, who was now in the clutches of the white men —but they'll swap him for the little girl. But the chief says no. I reckon he figured that no harm would come to his son so long as the little girl remained alive.

"So I said to myself: *I come here to retrieve that little girl.* Then I said to the Creek runner that he should go back and tell the chief that if they let the little girl go, they can have Davy Crockett. Well, I hadn't been to the Congress yet, of course, and no books was yet wrote about me neither—which ain't too germane a point seeing as none of them could read nohow—so they didn't know what they was a-getting themselves into. Anyways, they consented to make the exchange. Old Reuben and the Indian then took the little girl back to her folks and the war party took me. As for how Old Davy made his escape, I shall have to defer that till later. It ain't come to me just as of yet."

Chilton covered his eyes with one hand, turned in his seat to face his friend, then peaked out from under the hand.

Crockett jerked his head back in mock indignation. "What, can't you distinguish the back-staffed truth when you hear it, Reverend?"

"The scriptures tell us it's not good to eat much honey," Chilton said and reached over to shake one of David's bare feet. "And so for men to search their own glory is not glory."

"The Scriptures tells us lots of things," David replied, "and a measure of them's a sight harder to swallow than what I just been a-telling you."

Chilton shook his head. "There's a world of difference. We swallow them, as you say, because we have faith in God. But why should anyone have faith in *you* once they have come to doubt your truthfulness?"

"What then, you reckon it's better to weary the people to death?"

"Better that than make a fool of yourself. Nobody is going to believe that you voluntarily turned yourself over to a band of hostiles."

Crockett mimicked the cadence of his friend's reply with little popping sounds from his smacking lips.

"Oh, what the devil," he finally said. "I reckon you can leave out the part about the little girl if you so wish, I don't give a continental. I only wish I hadn't made such a burdensome effort calculating it."

"And did you make up the rest, too?"

"The rest is true as preaching, only it really ain't that noteworthy. Do you want to know what really transpired—I'll tell you. Absolutely nothing."

"At all?"

"Not really. After we got the news about the war party, we pressed on all night back the way we come till we got to the main army round about ten o'clock the next morning. And that was all there was to it. The only thing, Chilton ..."

He stopped to clear his throat.

"The only thing, when I reported to Colonel Coffee the news about the Red-Sticks a-coming, he regarded it like it was no part of nothing—and that raised my dander higher than ever. I didn't do a thing about it, though, so really and truly there ain't more to tell."

"He questioned the accuracy of your report?"

"Aye, from top to bottom he did. And I was so mad I was burning inside like a tar-kiln, and I wonder that the smoke hadn't been pouring out of me at all points. But the next day, Major Gibson returned and brought in a worse tale than I did, and it put the colonel into a fidget. And I'll tell you what, Chilton. That opened my eyes and convinced me clearly of one of the hateful ways of the world. When I made my report, it wasn't believed because I was no officer. But when an officer reported the very same thing, why then it was all true as preaching and the colonel believed it every word."

"And you made this same report to General Jackson?"

"I didn't have the honor and privilege. He was still off at Fayetteville. Colonel Coffee sent an express."

"What a pity. Wouldn't it be convenient if the two of you had had a confrontation so many years ago—and he not believing you any more back then than he does now!"

Crockett spat at a brass cuspidor at the side of the bed but instead hit the top of one of his boots. "Well, it's something I'm mighty thankful never happened."

"Do my ears deceive me?" Chilton said. "From the way you've been spouting off lately, I never imagined that you would ever admit to having avoided a confrontation with the old man."

"I didn't avoid it. I just wasn't sent. And my mind is to let the matter rest the way it really and truly happened."

Chilton shook his head. "Well, my mind is that it's best you deliver that report to General Jackson personally. Your readers will appreciate the symbolism."

"I hardly reckon," Crockett shot back. "If they believe it, they'll think it mighty small of me to turn on Old Hickory-face today for no better reason than because he insulted me once in my youth. I'll tell you what, though. I believe they'll know it's a lie-tale soon as they read it."

"David, no one is going to contest your story. It's not as if the army has records of such minutia."

Crockett burst out laughing. "A minute ago you all but told me I could go to hell as quick for lying as I could for stealing," he said. "What is it, son, you fixing to join me there?"

"There's a world of difference."

"The only differ is you done thought it up."

"The difference, David, as that as a minister of the Gospel, I have learned to place words and ideas in the service of Scripture."

"I nearabout forgot. You're one of those fellows that turns lead into gold."

Chilton smiled and wiggled his fingers.

"Let's say I stood up before a congregation and told them of a neighbor I once had," he finally said. "A farmer who lost all his corn. And let's say he lost it because it came from a field he'd plowed with the aid of a mule he stole from a God-fearing Christian. Of what significance and consequence would it be if I never truly ever had such a neighbor? What matters is the moral."

"I fashion my share of morals too—you know that," Crockett said. "You don't have to take up the cloth to practice chin music."

"That's not what I meant."

"I don't give a tinker's damn what you meant. I just wish you'd keep your big mouth shut long enough to hear the rest of my story. Then you'll know how come my mind is such that we ought to dispense with the entire incident."

My big mouth? thought Chilton .

"What happened," Crockett began, "was that after Old Hickory-face made a forced march with his troops to come to our support, and after—mind you, Chilton—*after* he dispatched upwards of a thousand troops to follow the same varmint path through the woods that I took on past Radcliffe's in search of them Red-Sticks did he come to find out that my report was based entirely on false information."

"You mean you made the whole thing up?"

"Me? You know me better than that, old hook. No, It was that damn Radcliffe. Turns out he was the very rascal that sent the runner to the Indian camp with the news that the Red-Sticks was a-crossing the river at the Ten Islands. His object was to scare me and my men away and send us back with a false alarm. If you'll recollect, I done told you the man had him a Creek wife."

Chilton stood up. "Perfect," he said folding his arms.

"Not hardly. I ain't the least bit proud of the part I played in that affair."

"There's not a thing for you to be ashamed of, David. It could have happened to anyone. That it happened to you, however, is *providential*! You were a thorn in the old man's side even then, so why not make *him* look small for carrying a grudge from way back them until now! And if he *does* pick a fight with you, you'll send him on another wild goose chase!"

"Like as not he'll make *me* look like the goose—and wring my neck while he's at it."

"I think your public will be more amused at his expense than at yours."

Crockett scratched one of his long side whiskers with his thumb. "Maybe so," he said, "but I'd still rather you leave it out."

"Stew on it for a while," Chilton replied. He sat back down at his writing table and jotted down a few notes including a reminder to look into Jackson's military record previous to New Orleans.

"So what else did you do in the Creek War—nothing?" he finally asked.

"Not much," Crockett said. "Nothing much different than the next man."

"Good, I'm too pressed for time to listen to much more just now. And tired, so if you will excuse me, I should like to appropriate my bed back."

"Wait a minute, there *is* something I wish you might put down. You familiar with the mutiny at Fort Struther?"

Chilton nodded. He indeed was well-acquainted with the incident, one of his wife's people having witnessed it. A considerable number of Tennessee volunteers had refused to continue their service after their sixty-day terms had expired, but General Jackson wouldn't permit them to go home. He faced them down personally, a pistol in one hand, his injured other hand in a sling. He threatened to shoot the first man to make a move to leave, but nobody was brave enough or foolish enough to call his bluff. Every last volunteer turned around and marched back to camp.

"You know, it don't necessarily need to have happened the way you heard," Crockett said. "Not if it's to have, like you say, a true and proper moral."

Chilton smiled; he knew what was coming next. "So the general was quaking with terror in his tent," he said, "while you faced down the mutineers."

"Don't you be a-placing me on the wrong side of that question, old hook. Anyways, I wasn't even there. I was off at Huntsville with the cavalry. But if I *was* there, by the Eternal if I wouldn't a-been up on my hind legs with the rest of the boys— and while you're at it, go ahead and make the old man back down and eat his words."

"What about the witnesses?"

"What witnesses?"

"The troops. There must have been hundreds there who saw it."

"They won't say nothing. Whose side you think they was on —his'n or mine?"

"I'm more concerned about whose side they are on now," Chilton said. "Besides which, there are such things as military records."

"I know there is, but like you just said before, they're not so considerable as I once thought."

"They are considerable enough to include an attempted *mutiny*."

"Maybe so, but who's to say the so-called president didn't doctor them up to make himself shine? You want symbols, Chilton? Try this one on for size: Old Davy standing up to King Andrew's dictatorly pretensions back then just like he's a-doing right now today. And we walk over that bridge without the first shot being fired."

"How heroic of you, sir," Chilton said. "Deserting the army in the middle of a campaign."

"It wasn't deserting—not by a long shot. All they was fixing to do was getting on home for provisions so they might be better prepared for the next campaign."

Chilton closed his eyes. Sometimes he wondered how much of the Bible had been written in this fashion.

"I'm beginning to think we should perhaps dispense with your military experiences entirely," he said. "I like you better as a man of peace."

"You're a preacher, that's why. But if the preacher vote could so much as get me elected chief privy cleaner of Congress, then I wish I may be shot."

Chilton pursed his lips and nodded slightly; Crockett was convinced that a glorious military career was the only ticket to a glorious political one.

"David, the people elected Jackson because they believed he was one of them. And that is exactly why your constituents elected you."

"The people elected Jackson because of his soldiering."

"That too, but at least he didn't stoop to making up stories about himself."

"He didn't need to."

"And neither do you, my friend."

"I need to tell them *something* worthwhile, don't I?"

"Tell them the truth."

"What, that Davy Crockett served his ninety days in the ranks doing absolutely nothing more praiseworthy than the next man? That I went and sat out most of the next year? Or—wait, I know what I can tell them. I can tell them how this one time I got so spooked I saw savages behind every tree. Aye, and 'twas all I could do to keep from sticking my head between my legs to kiss my arse goodbye."

"Show me a man born of a woman who would have felt otherwise."

"We ain't talking about no such man. We're a-talking about the Great Bear Hunter. What in God's Kingdom is the Bear

Hunter supposed to be doing home with his wife and young 'uns when his comrades are getting shot at?"

"You went back, didn't you?" Chilton said. "Back to those comrades."

Crockett nodded. "'Twas nothing but more of the same, though."

"Well, then shall I fashion you into the second coming of General 'Swamp Fox' Marion. Would that suit you better?"

"That ain't what I'm a-saying. I just want folks to know I was out there doing my part. What they make of me is their own business."

"Then tell them what you did."

"I just told *you* what I did—and it wasn't much."

"Then tell them what you saw. Surely you at least *saw* something."

Crockett lowered his head a little, then looked up sheepishly as if he were just caught red-handed at something.

"Oh, I saw plenty," he finally said. "Too much, really. Fact is, twenty years have done come and gone and such things still disturb my sleep at night." He rubbed his eyes. "Once I saw a Creek squaw draw a bow with her feet and kill a man, the first man I ever saw killed with a bow and arrow—and by a woman, yet. She was setting in the door of a house that forty or fifty warriors had run into, and when we was finished with her, she had at least twenty balls blowed through her. Twenty balls, Chilton, and one of them mine, I reckon."

He cocked his head and snapped his fingers twice. Chilton, in response, poured them both a small portion of brandy.

"Then we shot them like dogs," Crockett went on. "And then we set the house on fire with all the warriors in it. And there was other women there too that was killed. And children too, Chilton, Some no older than yours."

He downed his drink and raised his empty glass for more. "There was this young boy I recollect that was shot down near the house. His arm and thigh was broke and he was so near to the burning house that the grease was stewing out of him. He was still trying to crawl along, but not a murmur escaped him, though he was only about twelve-year-old. An Indian would sooner die than make a noise or ask for quarter."

"You don't expect me to put any of that down, do you?" Chilton said as he poured his friend more brandy. "People are going to get the wrong impression of you. I mean, participating in a massacre, for heaven's sake."

"It was no massacre, damnit. A true battle is what it was—and we was all under orders. Now, I ain't proud of it, but such things do happen in war, and folks need to know I wasn't making stuff up for my own glory."

He started to take another sip but stopped himself. "And you can put this down, too," he went on. "When we come back there the next day, many of the carcasses of the Indians was still there and they was a terrible sight to behold all burnt up like they was. Then we found a cellar under the house filled with potatoes, and by God if hunger didn't compel us to eat them, though I had a little rather not if I could have helped it because the oil of the Indians we had burnt up had run down on them, and they looked like they had been stewed with fat meat."

"My God," said Chilton. "Who could blame you for having second thoughts about soldiering."

"Not a man who's ever seen what I done seen. Still, I wish I hadn't sat out so much of the next year. I reckon we'll have to fill it in somehow, though."

"That's your department, my friend."

Crockett shook his head. "You're the word-stringer."

"David, my words won't ring true. I mean, I have never fired a weapon at anything I wasn't prepared to eat."

"So talk to someone else who has. Go talk to Cave Johnson's friend over there at the Lottery Office. He was with Jackson at Horseshoe Bend. He was—"

There was a knock at the door. In walked their landlady with a covered bowl. "Ox-tail soup left over from supper," she said to

Crockett. "I know you favor it, so when I saw you come in late, I saved you some. When you weren't in your room, I tracked you here to Mr. Chilton's room like one of your bears."

"Thank you, ma'am," Crockett said handing Chilton his glass. He then propped himself up on his elbows and allowed her to place the tray and bowl on his lap. After she was gone, however, he had Chilton take it away.

"It's done slipped her mind," he said as he got up to put on his boots, "but once I got sick on a bowl of this very same soup. Still, I'll have to say this about Mother Ball's cooking: it tastes just as good coming up as it does going down."

Chapter Eight

Thomas Chilton picked up a flat jagged stone about the size of a biscuit from the towpath. *Kaintuck*, he dubbed it and pitched it into the canal. It skipped three times, then sunk in the murky water.

Three's a-plenty, he muttered. *Three's enough for any fool in this man's House.*

He pitched another stone. This one only skipped twice.

Maybe so, he responded taking it as a sign he should consider resigning at the end of this congressional session and deny himself a full third term. Aye, but then he would have to quit drinking for good again sooner than he had planned. Either that or figure out how to hide it from his family back home in Kentucky for longer than the summer-fall recess.

Chilton reached into the pistol pocket of his overcoat for the green bottle from the apothecary that had once held a foul-tasting tincture of something to aid his digestion. He didn't notice that his fingers were trembling until they went to unscrew the cap. Then he took a more generous sip of brandy than he had intended—his first of the morning—and walked a few steps closer to the canal. Garbage from Center Market was floating in the stagnant water: bits of newspaper and some kind of orange skimmy-scum.

"Vichyssoise," he said loudly enough to warrant looking around to see if anyone had heard him.

While the canal may have been an open sewer, Chilton still found it a fine place to walk along and ponder, particularly in the chillier months when it stunk a little less. In the warmer months the stench was nearly unbearable—even in his own bed chamber, for his rooms were but a stone's throw away. So he'd rise early, saddle-up and follow the Potomac up-stream past Georgetown until he reached some appreciable rapids. Once, he was tempted to wade-in at the ferry landing just below the Great Falls but then thought better of it as he'd been warned that the apparently still waters belied a deep undertow.

So he hiked farther upstream to just above the falls where the river was ten times wider—too wide for George Washington to have hurled a rock over (no, it wasn't a silver dollar; who'd be such a fool?)—and perched himself on the rocks high above the falls. Then, in an instant, all was right with the world; because such a spectacular view somehow could slow his racing mind to a decipherable speed and wash away the intrusive distracting ruminations with its current.

Funny though, he thought now as he continued to gaze into the canal, but communing with even a pathetically meager suggestion of a river sometimes *also* could clear his head.

Shame it's so filthy unclear, he thought.

The water, too, he added and chuckled at his accidental joke.

Chilton took another sip from his medicine bottle and then screwed the cap on tight, tight enough to keep him out of it the rest of the morning, he hoped. 'Twas true, he had far too much oratory to put to paper to allow himself to get pickled, even on a Friday when Congress was quiet. It was to be a follow-up of the most important speech of his political career. Who could say, it might even supersede it. He was scheduled to deliver it next Tuesday or Wednesday, but he had barely begun to compose it.

No doubt about it, if he had a lick of sense he'd be back at his writing table this very minute. But he was set to break bread with a delegation of Chickasaw Indians in but an hour's time. Then he had to tutor his landlady's grandson in Latin. Aye, and sooner or later after that—no doubt sooner—Crockett would grab him by the ear again. And he likely wouldn't turn him loose until they were knee-deep into the night.

Chilton took his first few sluggish steps back toward the marketplace five blocks distant. He shook his head and bared his front teeth—his *mad rabbit* face, as his wife called it. Ever since Senator Clay tapped him for the speeches—this one and the first one he delivered last month—the days sure seemed to be getting shorter and shorter, the hour hand speeding around his watch like a Kentucky racehorse. That was ten days before Christmas at the senator's home, and it had been a daunting experience.

When Chilton stepped into Mr. Clay's parlor, he found himself in the company of some of the most pivotal members of the Whig coalition including Senator Poindexter of the States Rights Party and Horace Binney, the U.S. Bank's spokesman in the House. Although this was Chilton's third term in Congress, it was the first time he had been included in a grand strategy session.

When Mr. Clay finished his first glass of bourbon, he set it down on the card table next to his silver snuff box and got down to business.

"It's up to you gentlemen," he said to his lieutenants from the lower house, his icy blue eyes fixed on Chilton. "The Senate shall take care of itself."

And the Senate probably would, Chilton thought, for there Mr. Clay and the now firmly united opposition held a decided majority. Was it large enough to override President Jackson's inevitable veto should Mr. Webster and his friends attempt to push through a re-charter bill for the Bank? No, but it was large enough to keep the question of America's first duly elected monarch's executive usurpation on the floor for the entire session if necessary.

The House would be another story. There the party lines were of roughly equal strength, the Jacksonian Democrats showing a slight advantage. The Whigs' chore was to reduce and possibly eliminate that advantage by creating a measure of doubt in the minds of the more conservative of King Andrew's minions of their chieftain's scruples, enough to free them of his spell.

"And this young man shall fire the opening salvo, won't you son?" Mr. Clay said, striking a pose, his left hand over his heart and his right hand on Chilton's shoulder. Chilton hadn't felt such a strong sense of foreboding since the day his preacher father called his twelve-year-old son to the pulpit to deliver his first sermon.

"You cocked and ready?" his father had whispered in his ear.

"I reckon, Pa—kinda sort of," the trembling boy had whispered back.

But the trembling man—deep inside, that is—of four weeks ago knew better.

"Yes sir," he replied to Senator Clay loudly enough for all present to hear. Then:

"*Hellfire* yes!"

And why had Mr Clay chosen him of all people? There were far more eloquent Whig orators in the lower house than he— Mr. Everett in particular. But Mr. Everett was from Massachusetts and drafting an Easterner to be the champion of the United States Bank, Mr. Clay said, his snuff box in one hand and the fingers of his other hand slowly flexing as if they were claws, would be like *"drafting a panther to expound on the gentleness of the feline species."*

No, it had to be someone like Chilton. Briar-picking Tom with his honest Western twang.

A brisk wind picked up from two or three different directions, or so it seemed. Chilton closed his overcoat and secured it with a single button. When he got to the bridge at Center Market, he paused to look down from it at some boatmen unloading their cargo. Their vessel was a canal barge of considerable size, the kind you were more likely to find plying much larger waterways. Six years ago, when Chilton first arrived in Washington, the only boats capable of floating this far into the city were crude flat-bottom rafts, the kind you broke up for firewood after you sold or bartered away the produce you carried off from the West. Six years ago, the water here at Seventh Street was at times no more than a few inches deep. Once, Chilton actually *walked* across the canal in pursuit of his new silk hat, which a northerly breeze had taken a fancy for.

Chilton leaned against the splintering handrail and waved a greeting to one of the boatmen. He felt sorry for them; they were so far away from their homes. And yet not a one of them could possibly be more homesick than he himself. Whatever had possessed him to come back to Babylon, back to worshiping at the altar of Mammon? That's what the Jackson press was calling the Bank of the U.S. these days, *Mammon*. And to give the Devil his due, they weren't so very far off the mark.

And yet it was something he thought he should do, defend the "hydra headed monster." Imperfect as it was, the B.U.S. was a far safer bet than were the wildcat state banks down whose drains the Jackson administration was pouring substantial amounts of federal funds. Chilton could tell you a thing or two about those banks. He had been a twenty-year-old law student when the bottom dropped out of the money market in Kentucky. Scores of those rag shops had flooded the state with their worthless paper that summer creating so much debt and devaluing the state currency to such an extent that within two years' time, all but a few of them had closed their doors. His father lost all he had when one of them failed, and Chilton was not about to sit idly by and watch the same thing happen again.

Aye, but with God's help perhaps it won't, Chilton now thought.

Indeed, things were looking rather propitious at the moment. So far, the president was getting most of the blame for the financial panic, this for withdrawing significant numbers of federal deposits from the National Bank and dumping them into the un-secured vaults of his pet state banks. And if things went as planned, public pressure on Congress would soon vote the B.U.S a new charter, and those funds would go back to where they belonged.

But if things did *not* go as planned? Well, then Chilton just might be shooting his congressional career in the foot.

As might a far better marksman than me, he thought and squeezed the air with his trigger finger.

Chilton of course meant his friend Crockett. Come summer of next year, should Jackson triumph, the two of them would limp home together never to return. Chilton was certain of this. He could feel it in his bones.

It seemed like they did everything together like clockwork, he and David. They had arrived here within a month or two of each other; they served two terms together as nominal Jacksonians; they both publicly repudiated the old man in 1830; they both lost their seats in '31; and they both won them back in '33. As for what the elections of 1835 had in store for them (should they make another go for it—an unlikely event, at least for Chilton), it was a year-and-a-half too soon to tell. And it depended upon who would get saddled with the blame for the burgeoning financial panic, Jackson or Mr. Biddle's Bank.

One of the boatmen caught Chilton's eye. He upended a jug of something, then faked a stagger—which confirmed it was spirits, not water. Up on the bridge Chilton waved his approval. The boatman waved back an invitation to come down and join him for a taste. Chilton shook his hand no, then held up a forefinger and reached into his pocket for the medicine bottle with his other hand. He unscrewed the cap, which wasn't nearly as tight as he had thought, upended it and returned the fake stagger. Upon examination, he found that he had swallowed close to half its contents.

So be it, Chilton thought as he started across the rest of the bridge.

"The prudent man looketh well to his going," he recited aloud as he stepped onto the usually muddy, but now cold solid ground. He sat down on a bench right there in the heart of the market grounds. A vendor was frying up some pork parts—everything but the squeal, as Chilton's father used to say. It smelled mighty good. It smelled like home.

'Twas but two months since Chilton kissed Franny and the children goodbye, but it seemed like a year already. He had grown accustomed to family life the year round since his defeat in '31. Moreover, the longer he stayed away from politics, the less need he felt to doctor his melancholy with spirits. If only Senator Clay hadn't flattered him into standing for office again, he'd have no need whatsoever to carry a medicine bottle around with him.

"Then carry you a flask," said his friend Crockett in mock-Scottish tones the other day when the subject of Chilton's future came up.

"My ears tell me that *your* future should be in the theater," replied Chilton.

Crockett shook his head. "Ain't right for two of me to take to the stage. That would only serve to confound the people."

"Two of you?"

"Me and that Wildfire creature whats-his-name. No, my future is right here just like yours is, where we can stand watch on the old man and the rest of the monarchists that aim to destroy our Republic."

"A noble endeavor that I am proud to play a part in," Chilton said, "but once we get the upper hand on him, I'm through."

"Speak for yourself."

"I just did. *Per ego sum.*"

"Well, I'm not finished. Not by a long shot"

"That's because you enjoy it. I don't."

"What's not to enjoy? Winning the hearts of those that

believes in you and living up to it by acting right. I've grown mighty fond of such things"

"If you want to know the truth ... "Chilton began slowly, "I've been thinking more about winning souls lately. Might even dust off my Bible and brush up on my parables."

"Well, then you go home and preach the Bible, Saint Thomas. Me, I still aim to preach the truth about Old Hickory-face to the Yankee folks up north—that is if you and me ever do finish my life's history. And as for my future, you keep your eyes peeled down Pennsylvania Avenue for my star. By the Eternal if it won't soon be a-hovering over the White House."

You'll be lucky if it hovers much longer over the House of Representatives, Chilton thought.

Not that he chose to repeat that aloud. Nay, he and his Western Whig colleagues had already poked enough fun at his friend's ambitions behind his back lately; far be it for him to attempt to burst his bubble any time soon.

But it wasn't the jokes that were going to bring down Crockett's star, neither David's own—most of which were charming—nor the cruel ones he imagined his enemies were telling on him. No, 'twould be the "serious talk" he was so dead set to inflict upon his growing public. Now that he had the whole country by the ear, he figured he could say whatever he pleased about anything from Andrew Jackson to the Bank of the U.S. without fear of retribution by his constituents at the ballot box. The only thing that mattered was that he sounded like he knew what he was talking about.

Chilton, of course, knew otherwise. He knew that as soon as his friend set out on his tour, as soon as the newspaper writers reported the homage he was heaping on the Bank and the derision he was heaping on the president (who, much more so than Crockett, was ever-yet his constituents' favorite son) his political career would be on the line. And teetering toward the abyss.

A tangle-haired stray dog took a few cautious steps toward

Chilton's bench, then thought better of it and headed toward the roasting pork.

Davy, Davy, Davy, Chilton said to himself. *Davy Crocko'shit.*

And that he *truly was* these days. Aye, the poor fellow really and truly imagined he was on the road to some sort of secular sainthood. And Chilton, in his fever-paced chronicling and his complaisant counseling, was daily affirming this for him. More likely, though, his friend was going to end up flat on his face.

And you don't have to be a calloused Easterner to share the blame for that.

Chilton reached down and picked up a few pebbles that were lying close to his feet. He removed his left boot and inserted—at the heel—a sharp-edged stone the size of an almond. Then he pulled the boot back on, rose and walked slowly and deliberately up the avenue to his lodgings.

Chapter Nine
BALTIMORE, APRIL 1834

R.C. Crabtree

The news is out, so I reckon you know by now that my friend U.S. Congressman David Crockett has commenced his tour of the Eastern states. He in fact should be in the city of New-York by now. I do hope that he's in a better humor than he was when I last saw him. When I saw Crockett last, which was here in Baltimore but a few nights ago, he committed himself to spending the night with my sister Sarah and me, only he never did. Instead, he stomped off down the road all by himself back to his hotel room without so much as a farewell to Sarah, who had gone to the trouble of baking him a frosted cake. And all because I expressed my concern that the rich Northern sharpers might be taking advantage of him.

Do you know what I believe? I'm beginning to think that if Crockett and me hadn't known each other so long. he would have broke a few of my bones instead of just hurt my feelings a little. I pity the poor Yankee stranger that says the wrong thing to him or even so much as looks at him the wrong way.

The hotel that Crockett stomped off to is called Barnum's,

and it was there that I first greeted him several hours previous. This was shortly after the dinner they had given him had broke up. He had finagled me an invitation, but I chose not to go, for all the guests were of the wrong political persuasion. By this I mean they are members of the Bank Party, the very party that gave us the hard times that we are all still suffering through. Hezakiah Niles of the *Weekly Register* was there and so was Mayor Small. I saw George Brown the banker come out the door just as I was fixing to enter and had to turn my head because if his eyes had met mine, I might have spit at them. Understand, I will say such a thing about few people in this world, but he is one of them, for he is the man who turned me down for a loan three months ago.

I must tell you how out of place I felt walking into that building. Barnum's is the most head to foot high-wrought hostelry south of Boston and New-York. It is seven stories high with great stone columns and two matched staircases leading up to a portico, and on the inside there is red velvet everywhere. By the time I stepped into the Long Room, most of the guests were gone. Those few that remained were off by themselves in the far corner. I took a look at myself in an eight-foot-tall gilt-framed mirror and felt like a field hand that had snuck into the Big House. Crockett appeared to be comfortable enough, though, all togged out in his finery. He was sitting by himself at the head table signing a copy of his book for a father and his small son. Six or seven others stood behind them awaiting their turns. I took my place in the rear of the line.

"*I leave this rule for others when I am dead*," Crockett recited, referring to his motto which is printed just beneath the title, "*be always sure you are right, then go ahead.*"

The boy looked up in wonderment at this hero he had heard so much about and asked him where his rifle was. Crockett told him he left it back home in Tennessee along with his ring-tail coon hat. Then he winked at the father and took his money.

"I'll take two," said I when I got to the head of the line. "One for me and one for my sister."

"Tree!" Crockett exclaimed at me. "I had plum give up on you. I had them set you a plate at the head table, but you never showed up."

"We had company over," I lied, "and we couldn't rid ourselves of them."

He reached under the table and brought up two copies of his book, the history of his life that he had wrote. He had to ask me what my sister's name was, which surprised me because even though he had never before met her, her name had come up in discourse more than once. He sat there for a moment or two trying to think of what to inscribe and finally come up with a line from that play he claims to hate so much.

"*To Sarah, the fairest flower in the forest*," he read aloud after he finished inscribing it. "Now, ain't that a dandy-line, Tree?"

For me he wrote another line from that same play:

To my old friend Crabtree. Stand up to the lick log, fodder or no fodder.

"I'm afraid there ain't been much fodder lately," said I. I then tried to give him two silver dollars. He refused them, but allowed I might could take him across the hall if I so wished and buy him a drink.

I told him I had a better idea. "I know this is going to sound mighty queer coming from an old pour-out man like me," said I, "but why don't you come back to the house with me for some coffee and a piece of frosted cake. My sister baked it up special for you. She's dying to meet you. Fact is, she'll kill me if I show up by myself."

If Crockett thought that was a good idea, I surely couldn't tell from studying his face—well, not till after I told him I had three jugs of homemade apple pie for afterwards, which I must tell you is not pie at all but sugared-up firewater. So we hopped into my one-horse shay and headed on home, which is two miles out Jones' Falls. Sarah and myself operates a cotton mill there and the house is located straight across a narrow lane from it. Quick as we got there, Crockett presented her with his book, and she brought it out back with her when she stuck the cake in the warming closet. But first she offered to put him up for the night.

"Unless you would rather stay at the big hotel. I suppose you have already paid for your room."

"No, ma'am, they give it to me. But this here is a whole lot more like home. Still, I really do hate to put you out."

"You won't be putting me out at all. My brother here will sleep on the floor, won't you, RC?"

"You took the very words out of my mouth," says I, although in truth they had been quite a considerable distance from it.

"No need for that, Tree," says Crockett. "I can tolerate a bedfellow if you can. As you may recall, I was raised with five brothers, so it wasn't till I got married that I ever got to sleep by myself."

We repaired to the parlor after that and had our coffee and cake, which was as good a one as she ever baked up. I'll tell you what, when I go back to Memphis this summer, I intend to carry her along with me and put her to work in the kitchen.

"So tell me, David," says she, "what do you think of our fair city?"

"It'll do, I reckon."

She assured him he would be a mite more enthusiastic if he had seen more of it.

"I'm sure I would, ma'am. It's just I ain't too partial to any big cities. And I *have* seen it already—four times, ma'am. Matter of fact, my mother was born but a little ways down the road from here, just across the state line from York."

"I doubt she would know this city today," Sarah said.

"First time I laid eyes on Baltimore you weren't even born," Crockett told her. "I'll lay you weren't neither, Tree."

I told him I probably wasn't, not unless it was more than a few months into this century.

"Might could have been," says he, "but I believe it was more like back in '99. Anyways, I was about thirteen or fourteen at the time."

"You came with your folks?" Sarah asked him. "To visit your mother's people?"

"Hell no, ma'am—pardon me, ma'am—I was a-running away from them. My pa, he was about to give me the thrashing of my young life, and I wasn't about to participate in any part of such business—least-ways not on the receiving end."

Sarah looked him straight in the eye like she was maybe his mother or his wife and told him he likely deserved it.

"I reckon I did," says he. "What I done, I was a-laying out in the woods when I was supposed to be in school. 'Twas on account of a fight I got myself into. Four days I did this. I knew the master would tan my hide once he got a-hold of me—and so would Father if he ever come to find out."

"Which I take it he did."

"Aye, and the first I saw of him after that he had him a two-year old hickory in his hand and was tearing after me like the devil. He would have caught me, too, if his game leg hadn't a-give out like it done and compelled him to head on home. He thought I would do so myself once I got hungry enough. I didn't, though. I made up my mind to cut out of there by guess or by God is what I done. So I spent the night at a friend's house, and then the next day we hired ourselves out for a cattle drove, me and my brother Billy did."

To make a long story short, Crockett and them set out with a drove of cattle down into Virginia. Somewhere along the way he had a falling out with the drover and I think maybe his own brother, too. Anyway, when the man left him, he was upwards of four hundred miles from home with only four dollars to bear his expenses. He never made it home, though. Not then, he didn't. He fell in with a wagoner that ended up carrying him in the opposite direction clear to Alexandria, Virginia, right there across the Potomac River from where Washington City now stands, and the following spring he took him with him on one of his short hauls, which is how he ended up here in Baltimore.

"I had never before been to such a place in my entire life-time," Crockett said, "so I said to myself: *'let's have us a look-see,'* and next day went down to the wharf to see the big ships with their sails all a-flying on account of such things I never before believed truly existed in nature. Well, before I knew it, I found myself on board one of those ships eyeball to eyeball with the captain, and what does he do, he straight out asks me if perhaps I might consider taking a voyage with him to London.

"'Hellfire yes, Captain sir,' says I, for I know'd not a better place I wished to go."

"Weren't you in the least bit apprehensive?" Sarah asked him.

"I was skittery as a long-tailed cat in a room full of rocking chairs, ma'am, but at the same time I was pretty much weaned from home. So after that, I went back to the wagoner for my money and the rest of my clothing such as it was, but he rued back and refused to let me have neither. `You are bound to me for the duration, son,' says he, and then he swears he must confine me and take me back to Tennessee with him. It took me several days to escape from him after that, but by then the ship had already done sailed."

Sarah asked him how he thought he might have taken to the seafaring life.

"Believe me, I've studied on that from time to time, ma'am, but I still can't truthfully say. One thing I surely do know, I would never have a seat in the Congress. And I misdoubt there'd be books written about me neither, on account of I never could have hunted up enough bear out there on the ocean to build me much of a reputation."

"You might have built your reputation at the expense of the whale," Sarah said holding up an oil lamp.

"You know, I never thought of that," Crockett answered her,

"but you're right. I might could've been swept into office as the man that lit up the entire country with his harpoon. Aye, a celebrated much-talked-about harpoon called 'Old Betsy'"

Right about then I tried to excuse ourselves so we could sneak across the lane and have us a taste of that apple pie, but Sarah wasn't about to let old Crockett get away from her that quick.

"I want to thank you for the book again, David," said she. "I've leafed through it a little already out back in the kitchen. I really do admire what you had to say about the Indians."

"You always read a book from back to front?"

"I like to find out what happened."

Crockett laughed. "Me too," said he. "One minute folks is talking about sticking me in a menagerie and the next minute they're a-talking about running me for president, so I'm just as ponderous as you are."

"You're clear enough about the Indians," Sarah said. "I'm sure you are aware that my brother and I once lived a-way down in Ducktown, so I know of which I speak."

"Cherokee country," said Crockett .

Sarah nodded. "Our daddy even married one after our mama passed. Most of them are fine decent people."

"Especially Johnny Stark," says I. "Daddy should've let you take up with him. Then you'd never a-been stuck with Elisha, God rest his crooked soul."

Sarah blushed red as the velvet curtains at Barnum's Hotel. "We were never more than close friends," said she, "but I near-about have a fit whenever I think of what they done to him and the rest of his people."

She was speaking about President Jackson's Indian Removal Bill, the law-bill that removed them to the far side of the Mississippi River. I have a mixture of feelings about that measure, but Crockett opposed it lock, stock, and barrel. Which never made much sense to me seeing as one set of his grandparents was massacred by a band of them.

"Makes me mad as hell, too, ma'am," says he. "You know, when it comes down to it, there ain't a ha'penny's worth of difference between them and us other'n the color of their skin. And I can show you dozens upon dozens of old farm boys that turn every inch as dark come summer."

Then he whispered to me that the best we could do for them was to get a-hold of their squaws and fuck their entire race white. Sarah inquired as to what he had said but he knew better than to tell her.

"Well, I believe it's time for me to show old Crockett around the mill," said I, for that is where I keep my apple pie firewater hid.

"And don't you change your mind about spending the night, David," Sarah said to him. "It's no trouble whatsoever. And I shall rouse you in the morning so you won't miss your stage."

"Steamboat, ma'am. Then it's the railroad up to Delaware City. I ain't never rode one of them before and I sure am a-looking forward to it."

"Then I shall rouse you so you will miss neither your steamboat nor your train of railroad coaches."

"If you're up with the chickens you might could."

"I am up before the chickens, sir."

Crockett considered this for a moment and then told her she had herself a bargain.

"Now *that's* a relief," Sarah said. "I don't admire my brother to go riding around at night when he's been a-drinking."

I made like I never heard her speak that.

"You looked like you just stepped on a snake," Crockett said to me after we walked out the door. And I probably did, for I had no idea that she knew I'd taken to communing with the spirits again. I had quit outright for several months last year, but like I told Crockett I found I missed it too much.

"I don't blame you," says he. "It's hard to get yourself up in the morning when you know that's as good as you're ever going to feel all day."

I agreed.

"I quit drinking once myself," he continued on out of the corner of his mouth like he wished to keep it a secret, "but not for long, on account of I never could figure out a better way to get it down."

So we walked across the lane to the mill, which I shall now describe in brief for you. It is a framed structure three stories high and a hundred foot long with a stair tower and a belfry over the top of it. My office is on the first floor. It's walled off from the rest of the room so I can open the window without having to worry about the wind blowing cotton fibers all over the place. Over the coat rack is a small likeness of Sarah's father-in-law who founded the business, and next to that is a locked cabinet with nothing more valuable to pilfer from it than three jugs of home-made apple pie.

"What was that figment you were dispensing to her about your great love for the red man?" I asked Crockett as I poured him a glass.

"It's the truth," he answered me, "every word."

"I never before heard you put it that way to the voters."

He looked at me like he thought I wasn't right in the head. "A public servant's first duty is to get himself re-elected—you know that," said he. "How ever else is he supposed to do any good for his neighbors red or white?"

I shrugged and poured myself a glass.

"Now, if I was a chowder-head Yankee, it would have been a far sight easier, but answer me this, Tree. If Everett and them lived out where we do, don't you reckon they'd be a-whistling a different tune?"

I had to agree. Believe me, it is far easier to stick your neck out for the Indians if you live a comfortable distance away from them. Fact is, I wondered how Crockett ever brought himself to take such a position that might jeopardize his career when the only folks it would help couldn't even vote for him.

"Because I wanted the world to see what a cruel un-human

bugbear that white-haired old man that calls himself The Government is," said he. "And I wanted my constituents to know that once King Andrew finished legislating the red men out of their land, they was next. I figured it was well worth the risk. You call that being bought over?"

Here he was referring to the Bank Party, which had led the opposition to the Indian Removal Bill.

"Not at all," said I, but really and truly I wasn't so sure. This is because when I was in Washington City four months ago, I come to find out that he received an interest-free loan from the Bank of the United States that he ended up never having to pay back. And as I'd made up my mind to confront him about it the very next time I saw him, I reckon you'd have to say it was time for me to either put up or shut up.

So there we were, Crockett and myself, warming up a couple of chairs in my office at the mill, and me trying to find the courage to confront him about the loan. I knew I had better pick and choose my words with careful deliberation on account of him having such a quick temper, so I started talking about my own troubles instead of his.

I began with my inventory and what a devilish time I was having trying to sell it off. Might as well try and peddle the entire mill itself flat-outright, I finally concluded. Well, easier said than done, I soon come to find out. Two years ago, the city went down on its knees before Sarah a-begging her to sell them her property for the right of way for their water supply, but she refused and now they won't so much as discuss the matter anymore. Then I spoke to the Abbots about them buying up our looms, but they didn't offer me a shadow of a shade. Between you and me, like as not I'll settle for that same shadow less twenty per cent, is what I told Crockett, but out of principle I was not about to jump at such an offer.

Then I told Crockett how I almost stepped into Mr. Brown of Alex Brown and Company at the hotel, the banker I could not get a loan out of.

"Maybe I should've had *you* speak to him," said I. "You don't seem to have much trouble with such things."

He asked me what I meant by that.

"The loan the U.S. Bank gave you," I answered. "Dickinson tells me you weren't even required to put up collateral for it."

"I put up my good name," says he. "Don't that stand for anything?"

"It must," says I. "I heard they forgave you every penny."

"That they did," says he, "but so what. They done it with others, so they might as well do it with me, too. You saying I'm bought over?"

I looked at Crockett, and he looked back at me like I was some sort of bug he was fixing to squash with his boot heel.

"Of course not," says I, "but it just may look like that to the voters."

Crockett stood up and folded his arms. "Let me tell you something, Tree," says he. "They's a heap of difference between accepting someone's heart-felt gratitude and being bought over."

"It's a mighty fine line," I replied.

"You don't understand," replied he to me. "They forgave me the loan only after I done some good for them, not before. And I'll have you know, anything I done was for no one else but my constituents. If it profited the Bank, too, so be it, I can't help it."

I told him I didn't think his rich Eastern friends had his best interests at heart.

He cocked his head down like he was listening to something coming up from the floor.

Then said he:

"What, you reckon every poor man is a saint and every wealthy one is a devil?"

"Ain't you worried about what your constituents may think?" I asked him. "You've always called yourself the 'Poor Man's Friend.' I sure hope they still believe that. "

"My constituents have been knowing me long enough to comprehend my true motives."

That was what I was afraid of—although I hope to God I'm wrong about those motives.

"So you think the Bank Party's done got me in their hip pocket, do you?" says he. Even in the candlelight I could see that his face was now a deep shade of red.

"No, of course not," says I, for I had lost all stomach to continue challenging him.

"I reckon you think I'm a supple and likely fellow to do their bidding," says he, "but let me tell you something, Tree. They may not know it just yet but they're a-doing *my* bidding. Drop in on me in '36, son, and eyewitness it for yourself."

Then he explained his party's strategy for the next presidential election two years hence. He had it all figured out. They would field a host of regional candidates—"favorite sons" he called them—to whip Van Buren piecemeal and toss the election into the U.S. House of Representatives. Then they would broker one of their own into the White House.

"Of course that ain't the way they put it to me," Crockett said—thank God he seemed to be calming down some. "They told me I'd have as good a chance as any of them to come out on top. And I like to believed it at first. Well, maybe for about a half-day I did—but I don't no more. One thing I still *do* believe is I can walk away from that canvass with a right considerable sack of votes. So I asked myself what that particular sack might acquire for me if it won't make me president. And what do you think I come up with, Tree?"

"The *vice*-presidency?" I asked, trying to lighten things up with sort of a mock un-tactful hamhandy-ness.

He looked at me like I was that bug again.

"Well, least-ways you didn't say they would give me another interest-free loan," he finally answered me and sort of laughed—which to me came as a great relief.

"I'm sorry I brought that up," I replied. And truly I was, for I had no intention of throwing our friendship out the window whatever he had done, nor did I relish the thought of him knocking my block off.

"You want to know what that sack of votes is going to fetch for me?" he continued on. "I'll *tell* you what. It's going to fetch me my land bill. Why ever else do you think I consented to go on this consarned book tour right slap in the middle of the session? The way I studied it, such a thing might could make me a larger man than I already am, which is more or less how come I wrote my book in the first place. And the larger I get, the more they'll be a-needing me rather than contrariwise. Mark you my words, Tree, it won't be long till every dirt-poor settler in my district owns their own piece of land free and clear."

"I'm happy for them," said I, although I wasn't so hopeful as he was.

He put his arm around me and apologized for losing his temper. I told him I had deserved it for bringing up subjects I had no business wading into and made him sit back down.

"We was speaking of loans," said he after he'd been sitting quiet for quite a few minutes.

Oh no, thought I.

My alarm must have showed loud and clear in my face, for he straight-off then said:

"Ease up, Tree. There ain't no need to re-hash what we already done put to bed. It just reminded me of a story, that's all. You ready for it?"

"Ready as I shall ever be," I replied.

"Now, it was round about electioneering time," Crockett began, "when some fellow down home asked me if I had any regrets about being so famous. 'Not many,' I answered, 'excepting in-laws and other kinfolk I never heard of are forever coming out of the woodwork so that they might gang around their famous connection.'

"Here I must tell you, Tree, that I was being completely truthful. And the more I thought about it, the more it begun to eat away at me. Well, like they say, 'necessity is the mother of invention,' so I come up with a method to make certain I would see very little more of them. Do you want to know what I done —I'll *tell* you what I done:

"I borrowed money from the rich ones and lent it to the poor ones."

We had us a good laugh and then I poured us some more apple pie. When we had drunk our glasses bone-dry, I took him up to the belfry to show him what a slap-up view of the city we have. It was almost full-dark, but you could still make out the taller buildings set off against the night sky such as Barnum's Hotel, Washington's Monument, and the shot towers. Now, the shot towers I knew old Crockett would find interesting. Like I told him, a friend of mine once took me up to the top of one of them—the highest building in these United States, he said—and showed me how they make the shot. What they do, they pour their molten lead from the top of the towers down into a pool of water at the bottom where it cools it off into ammunition.

Crockett asked me if I might could get them to make him up a special batch with some salt mixed in with it.

"I don't see why not," said I, "but why for the salt?"

"I always mix salt in with my lead," says he, "on account of Old Betsy's got such a range that when it's nice and clear outside and I can see as far as she can deliver, it takes me days to reach my kill. So I've got to make sure it remains preserved till I get there."

We both had us a good laugh, and I soon found myself more comfortable with him again. Then we reminisced about the old days back in Murfreesboro, Tennessee where I first met him. He was in the legislature back then, and I was keeping bar at the Sign of the Elk's Horn. I will spare you these stories all but one, the one about Judge Mitchell. Now, Judge Mitchell was a leader of the party that represented the great landowners and other such money men. This was ten-twelve years ago at the beginning of Crockett's first term in the legislature, so nobody was much familiar with my old friend yet. All they knew was that he was poor folks, this from the simple fashion that he dressed himself in.

Anyways, what happened was, he had just finished his first speech there in the General Assembly when Judge Mitchell rises up to answer him, and when he does, he refers to Crockett as the "Gentleman from the Cane." This fetches some considerable laughter, for you must understand that it was like calling someone here in Baltimore the "Gentleman from the *Slum*," which means the filthiest low-down part of the city. So Crockett takes Judge Mitchell outside and threatens to thrash him, but as the judge sees that it won't be much of a match-up, he gets down on his marrow-bones and begs Crockett's pardon. Now, this all was done in private, and the way Crockett saw it, he hadn't received full satisfaction. So he was bound and determined to get it some other way.

The way he did this was some several days later he happened upon a fine cambric ruffle blowing around in the street and noticed it was the same exact pattern that Judge Mitchell wore. So what does he do, he pins it to his own coarse cotton shirt, and the next time the Judge rises to deliver a speech, old Crockett rises to answer him. Or so it seems. Really and truly, though, he just stands there so the whole House can see how comical he looks in that ruffle of his. Well, pretty soon there was so much general laughter that Judge Mitchell couldn't suffer his own presence there any longer and had to walk out of the chamber.

"I sure come a long way since then," says Crockett to me.

"You surely have," says I.

It might have been the way I said this—either that or he was reading my mind—for right about then he got plum-awful quiet. What I was thinking was:

I hope you are still on the right path, for you are dressed today much like Judge Mitchell was back then—and not just the ruffle.

After that, I looked away from him for a mere moment and when I looked back, his face was all puckered-up into an expression of plu-perfect hate.

"Don't you ever misdoubt my character again," said he in a sorry viscous tone of voice. "By the Eternal if I'm changed. I'm still common as coon shit in a barley patch—and don't you dare forget that."

Then he walked out the door and stomped off to his hotel two miles distant—on foot and in the pitch dark he did this. He forgot his silk hat, though. Perhaps I shall return it to him some day and see if it still fits his head.

Chapter Ten

Private remarks to Edward Windust at the bar-parlor of his downtown New-York eating house: the Windust Tavern, late Wednesday afternoon, April 30, 1834

Dr. William A. Caruthers

Thank you, Ned. And it is my pleasure as well, sir, to have you keep company with me, busy as you customarily are. My expectation, however, is that business will resume its usual briskness before you get too comfortable sitting here.

My novel? No, it is not yet back from the binders, sir, but Mr. Inman at *Harpers* has assured me that he has every expectation that it will be on the shelves by June. I must confess I still have to pinch myself, for until six short weeks ago I yet had ever-diminishing expectations that I might someday be fortunate enough to migrate to the ranks of your *published* clientele from those of your eternal hopefuls.

Thank you again, Ned; your faith in me has always been greater than my faith in myself!

Oh, and I nearly forgot to mention my most recent spate of good news, this I suppose out of fear of being thought boastful. Just last week the Harpers agreed to publish my *second* novel, which is but half finished.

No sir, the *Cavaliers of Virginia* is what they intend to call it. And for good reason. What key word do you think would be more likely to help it fly off booksellers' shelves, *Recluse* or *Cavalier?*

Agreed, I never heard of a flying recluse, but I understand that most balloonists fancy themselves cavaliers.

Yes, the first one has been re-titled as well—by *my* insistence this time. It is now once again the *Kentuckian in New-York,* which truly does roll off the tongue more readily than does the *Three Southern Sojourners.* That, and it sounds suspiciously like what they now call the *Lion of the West,* to wit: *the Kentuckian or a Trip to New-York*. Perhaps some of Kirke Paulding's admirers will pick up a copy solely on his account!

Actually, these papers here are from neither. They are notes I took from Colonel Crockett's speech at the Exchange earlier today.

With all due respect, sir, I'd rather you did not. Besides, I hazard you wouldn't be able to decipher my hand. That, and I wish not to spoil it for you at the hotel tonight, as his speech there will be nearly identical.

No, they are not for the newspapers. The colonel's associates have hired me out to produce a journal of his tour, and that's what these are for. I shall with great pleasure provide you with a copy when it comes out, and of course the novels, too.

I do hope you can make it to the public dinner tonight, Ned. Colonel Crockett is quite the entertainer, and I predict you will enjoy yourself immensely. As for the bill of fare, well it's touted as bear steak, but I think it's actually some rough cut of beef. Regardless, it certainly won't compare to your wife's cooking, so you might want to have a bite here before you leave!

You know, 'tis amusing to me that just as my *Kentuckian in New-York* is on the verge of publication I find myself a chaperon of sorts for the "Tennessean in New-York."

No, I did not accompany him on the journey up, but he has provided me with an account of it for the journal, most of it no more than what you might expect from a curiosity-filled stranger in a strange land.

In Philadelphia, when he wasn't being wined—or, rather, *whiskeyed*—and dined, Colonel Crockett was shown the city-sights at which he marveled more like a small child than a member of Congress.

"You should have seen the waterworks, leech," said he—that's what he calls physicians like me: leech. *"A few wheels can toss up more in an hour than my whole district could use in a month. And such a scrubbing of steps—even the pavement under your feet! I'll tell you what. The housemaids in that town take to water such that I was compelled to look close to see if they had webbed feet."*

But most of all he marveled at the railroad, which he rode from the Chesapeake to Delaware City on his way to Philadelphia and then from the Delaware River to Amboy on his way here.

"It was a dozen big stagecoaches hung on to one machine," he told me as if I had never before seen a train of railroad cars. *"They said we run twenty-five mile to the hour. I could only judge the speed by putting my head out the side to spit. I did this and overtook it so quick that it hit me smack in the face."*

I tried to persuade him to synopsize for me the speeches he had given at his public dinners. He chose instead to synopsize the menus and the wine lists and to boast about the fancy new percussion cap rifle that was going to be made to his specifications and presented to him on the Fourth of July.

When he arrived here in New-York yesterday, I was down at the wharf to meet him. I looked around and found myself immersed in a crowd of thirty or forty merchants, bankers and other broadcloth gentlemen as well as a few dozen professional politicians disguised as common citizens, some of whom I recognized. The Young Whigs had recruited them. They tossed their hats and gave the colonel three cheers, and from the look on his face, I am quite certain that he mistook their well-orchestrated demonstration as a spontaneous burst of affection.

A third term congressman, thought I, and still a babe in the woods. Or, rather, a babe fresh *out* of the woods, for the first words I heard him speak were:

"Ain't never seen so many sailing ships in one place before. Beats me to all hollow. With the sails down such as they are, looks to me like a big clearing in the west with the dead trees left standing."

I didn't approach him until much later: in the evening after he and Mr. Verplanck returned from the theater. I met him at the bar parlour of the American Hotel. The Young Whigs have provided them with a suite upstairs, he and Judge Clayton.

Well ... and for me too—at least for last night. I must admit the couch there is ten times more comfortable than Charlie's.

Charlie Hoffman. That's where I am still camping out these days, sir.

Anyway, before I could finish my last glass of whiskey punch, there came from the street a cry of:

"Fire, fire!"

The colonel jumped from his chair and ran for his hat. One of the Young Whigs at our table told him to sit down, for the fire did not appear to be near us.

"Well, ain't you going to go help put it out?" the colonel asked him.

"No need to," he replied. "We have fire companies here, and we leave it to them."

The colonel walked to the window, shaded his eyes with both hands and peered out. "Back home I would've jumped on the first horse at hand," said he, "and rode full flight bare backed to help put a neighbor's fire out."

The Whig politician laughed. "I rather doubt you would here, sir. You can live a dozen years or more in this city and never make the acquaintance of your next-door neighbor."

After considering this for a moment, the colonel got his hat and headed for the door. He apologized on his way out for his rampant curiosity. The Young Whig party man and I decided it was best not to let him wander off alone, so we followed him into the street. When we got to the site of the conflagration the engines were still assembling, one of them huge and being dragged by twenty-five or thirty men.

The colonel? Oh, yes, he certainly did. The whole thing. And he watched it in *astoundment*; they put out a four-story blaze in less time than it took us to walk there. While the firemen were still at their tasks, he crossed the street to get a closer look, but as soon as he got there, they made him cross back. He must have told them who he was, though, for shortly after they extinguished the fire, he was shaking their hands and promising them copies of his book. The last I saw of him—until he finally wandered up to his rooms—he was walking down Broadway alongside one of the engines, a black leather fireman's helmet on his head, an axe in one hand and a speaking-trumpet in the other. The germ of a story for my chronicle? Not unless he rushed into a burning building and came out with some distraught mother's child.

Well, maybe he did. Who's to say he didn't?

Anyway, that was last night. It was 'round about noon today when he spoke from the steps of the Exchange. 'Twas, as I have said: the same speech you shall hear tonight. Unlike at the wharf, though, he drew a crowd of genuine curiosity-seekers who were truly captivated by him. I however did see a number of Young Whigs there whom I remembered from the wharf, and they made me feel sorry for the foolish trust he has placed in these people who profess to be his friends. I overheard two of them mimicking his Western patois—they broke up each time he mispronounced a word. I spoke with a third: an attorney and passing acquaintance from the Literary and Philosophical Society. He was convinced that it had been poor strategy on the part of the Whigs to have recruited Colonel Crockett to proselytize the Northern workmen.

"Even the wildest-eyed Irishman looks down upon the *trans montagne*," said he. "A half-eagle, Caruthers. A half-eagle says we'll throw him back in the stream by summer."

No sir, we did not shake on it. That would have been a poor bet indeed, Ned.

So after he was finished signing copies of his book, Colonel Crockett and I, along with Judge Clayton, took a coach back to the hotel, a dozen party men trailing behind us. The colonel said he wished they would go away. We both agreed, however, that wishing was not about to accomplish anything, so when we reached the hotel, we walked in the front door and out the rear. I suggested a stroll through City Hall Park and a cocktail right here at your fine establishment, sir, for we were not expected at the mayor's office for another hour.

"No need to waste our money in a tavern," Judge Clayton said —sorry Ned—and drew a flask from his coat pocket. He suggested Peale's Museum instead, and so there we sauntered.

"Well, Judge," the colonel said when we stopped at a large glass display case filled with a variety of insect specimens. "I just can't understand the curiousness folks take in sticking up whole rows of little bugs and such-like varmints."

"Most likely it's the same curiosity they have in seeing you," Judge Clayton said.

The colonel laughed. "I suppose you're right. Seems only fitting they should make a display out of me here, too. What you think folks might pay to see the *Wild Man from the Far West?*"

Not that anyone would have mistaken him for a wild man yesterday. In his sober black frock coat and high-crowned beaver hat, he could have passed for a banker or a prosperous merchant (if there are any left in this city) or even for the presidential candidate he claims to be. Mayor Lee certainly didn't patronize him when we visited him at City Hall a short time later. He, in fact, treated him with all the deference he might have accorded a Webster or a Clay.

Yes sir, even when the conversation turned to national and municipal affairs. I kept expecting him to make a tomfool of himself—but he didn't. On the contrary, he surprised me not only with his common-sense opinions on the state of the Union, but also with his familiarity with the intricacies of this city's politics. I suppose that comes from being so close to Mr. Verplanck when they served in Congress together.

Yes sir, I know he does. I have seen him here often. And I agree with you, Ned: Mr. Verplanck would have made an outstanding mayor.

Anyway, after we left City Hall, we walked over to one of the politician's abodes for some cold turkey and gingerbread with his neighbor Seba Smith, whom I might add, Colonel Crockett insisted on calling "Major Downing."

Yes, sir, the whole time he called him that. As if he existed anywhere other than in Mr. Smith's satires. Which gave me an idea for my own satirical piece. More about that later after I have finished it.

Well, by the time we left we were stuffed thoroughly to the gills. I suggested walking back to the hotel for a nap. Colonel Crockett wholeheartedly agreed.

"Napping comes easy to me any time of day," he said. "So easy I can even do it with my eyes closed."

I must tell you that as we walked down Broadway, the colonel wondered aloud if New-Yorkers had as many boxes and bags inside their houses as they did outside. I explained that tomorrow, being the first of May, was moving day and that the inevitable yearly rent increases forced families to move more often than they wished.

"Poor devils," said he. "I'll tell you what, leech. It'll take a ton of lead and a barrel of powder to move me out of *my* log house on any day of the year."

Seeing those boxes yesterday had their effect on me, too, Ned. Aye, they made me melancholy about my family. I couldn't help but think about the day that I packed my own traveling bags and toted them to Charlie's. I had thought it would be only for a few days, but that was the thirtieth of March and here it is nearly May Day.

Yes sir, I suppose you could say it concerned our friend Miss Green of the Park Theater Company. Yes, I know you are fond of her. I, of course am too. Far too much for my own good.

My tale of woe? No, I don't mind, but I shall be brief.

On the penultimate day of March, an agreeable but somewhat meretricious young lady about Ivy's age in a gaudily embroidered silk cape stopped by my desk at Uncle Rice's apothecary with a letter from her friend in England. And who should that friend turn out to be but the one woman on this planet I had hoped to never hear from again.

Correct again, sir. And the letter? Upon my word, it rendered me even more thankful for the three thousand miles of ocean that separate us. Because this is what our Miss Ivy Green had to say to me in that letter:

She said she was with child—and that *I* was as likely to be the father as any!

As *any?* thought I. Well, what about the rake you ran off with? I refer here to one James Strange French, or *Strange Jamey* French as some of us refer to him. You remember him. He was the big clumsy fellow who broke your punch bowl a couple of years ago. You may recall he elaborated about his efforts suppressing the Southampton slave insurrection in Virginia and how he subsequently defended a number of the accused in court. He, in fact, claimed to have headed the defense.

I don't know, sir, Jamey talks a lot. He had only just then finished reading the law. But then again, he has stage experience and is probably quite impressive before a jury.

No, that was his father who owned the theater.

In any event, Jamey is without a doubt the father of Ivy's child. Indeed, the day after my first, last and only night with Ivy in nearly a year, he whisked her off to London— where I hardly think they planned to live as brother and sister! In fact, he boasted that they were to be married there.

Well, he apparently chooses not to boast about his imminent fatherhood, though. Aye, because less than a week after Ivy informed him of it, he vanished. Ivy, in her letter, asked me if I knew his whereabouts—I didn't—and if I did, would I please be so kind as to inform her friend, the young lady from the Bowery Theater Company, who would bear me the letter.

Yes sir, the letter which I was just then reading.

Anyway, she went on to request that I warn Jamey—if I should actually see him—that if she didn't hear from him in two months' time, she would inform his parents of the situation. Aye, Ned, she did know where to reach *them*. She had been presented to them a few days before she and their irresponsible son departed the country. And then:

It is my hope that I shall not have to resort to such tactics with you, William.

No, she never got the opportunity. Because on Monday the 31st of March—the day I first read those words—my wife's friend Clara Weber at half-past noon spied Ivy's salacious-looking girlfriend and myself walking out of the apothecary together.

No, I don't expect you would know the girl, sir. She is very young, an understudy at best—possibly something much worse.

In any event, she followed us down Canal Street toward the Bowery, Clara Weber did. Understand, 'twas only because I declined to permit this young girl to walk back un-escorted that I was there for her to see. Clara, however, apparently did not trail us all the way down the Bowery to the theater, though. Because if she had, she would have observed us politely bidding each other adieu. Rather, she in her imagination pictured us on our merry way to a house of assignation in the Five Points for a daytime tryst.

Yes, a coincidence, Ned. But 'twas not as you say an incredible one, Clara happening on us like that. Because her husband's office is on Church Street just around the corner from mine, and it is her custom to carry his dinner to him every day at half-past noon. What I did not know, however, was that 'twas also her custom to spy on me at my wife's behest, which she apparently did on and off for the better part of two years.

No, she never saw me with Ivy—of this I am quite certain. Understand, I never permitted Ivy to meet me at the apothecary. But wouldn't you know that this this actress friend of hers upon whom I had never before laid eyes or any other part of my anatomy would choose precisely half-past noon to rendezvous with me there!

Yes, Clara did indeed tell my wife. And when Louisa confronted me about this day-working strumpet whom Clara had caught me with—I couldn't convince her she was one of my patients—I at length broke down and told her about my connection with Ivy. Thought I, she will find out anyway, and 'twould be best if she heard it directly from me first.

Aye, Ned. To put it another way: a dead-in-the water connection would be far less disturbing to her than an imagined on-going one—in this case financially less threatening, too. Because my truth-telling has effectively crippled Ivy's blackmail capabilities—except with Jamey, of course—and with Jamey, that really isn't blackmail at all. "Tis a righteous demand for the exercise of his parental responsibility, for God's sake!

Anyway, that was thirty evenings ago. I haven't had an undisturbed night's sleep since. But enough of that. This too shall pass.

Yes, sir. At least I hope so. Who knows, perhaps Louisa will whistle a different tune once I have established myself as a published writer. Anyway, I do truly hope and pray that she will. And if she does so for such reason, I have you, sir, to thank as much as anyone, for thanks to you, I have here made the acquaintances of all the literary lights of this great city as well as those editors and publishers that help keep those lights burning.

No, those two don't look like literary lights to me either, Ned. However, I do agree with you so do please go seat them! Thank you again my good friend, and I shall see you later this evening at the Crockett affair.

Chapter Eleven

REMARKS OF HON. DAVID CROCKETT OF TENNESSEE

On the Occasion of a Public Dinner Held in his Honor at the American Hotel in New York City On Wednesday Night, April 30, 1834

Judge Clayton, Mr. Verplanck, fellow Young Whigs—that is, if you'll permit a man two years shy of the half-century mark to call himself such.

Gentlemen, I find myself at a loss for words that might suitably express my thanks for the sentiments you just drunk to me. And now you've called on me for a speech. As a matter of fact, Colonel Webb here just told me he'd sooner hear me speak than eat—he's already had his fill of hearing me eat—so I reckon there's no getting out of it. Still, I have no doubt that I will owe you an apology before I'm done for this attempt, so don't say I didn't forewarn you. I only had but six months of schooling in all my life and I consider myself but a blockhead to be here addressing the most intelligent people in the world. Now, don't get all in a pucker, for I shall accommodate you a very short time, though I haven't the least idea that I can add anything to what has been so ably said by those that's already spoke.

First off, I'd like to tell you how much I've been enjoying myself here in the great city of New-York. I must admit it come as quite a surprise after what I've been told by some of my colleagues in the Congress. They said folks up here ain't friendly. They said they won't so much as give a stranger the time of day.

I'll tell you what I say now, sirs. I say:

"Not so, by God!"

Not that I didn't have my doubts at first like when folks down at the wharf started calling me "Goat-head." It soon come to me, however, that they was really shouting out my motto *"go ahead!"* But what really changed my mind about New-Yorkers happened yesterday the very first time I stepped out of this hotel. I hadn't took but a step or two when this old boy looks me straight in the eye and says, `*Evening, son,*' and right then and there I knew I been told wrong about you good people up here being stand-offish.

Well ... in all honesty I later did come to find out what he said was the name of the newspaper he was a-hawking, but that don't take away from the right friendly manner he put it to me, does it?

I suppose some of you gentlemen is wondering what on earth Old Davy's up to here among you good people. Really and truly, I come up north for my health. Fact is, if I know'd I was expected to haul off and deliver speeches, I like as not would have remained home in the woods where I'd be a sight less likely to embarrass myself with my ignorance. Seeing as I'm here, though, I believe I had better get on with it and commence my lie-tales for you about the Wild Man you done heard so much about. But don't for one minute expect the whole hog out of me. No sirs, because then you won't need to acquire a copy of my book. Not that I need the money. I don't, but the folks I owe sure enough does.

First off, I wish to clear the air about some unfounded rumors that are hovering over the country like a flock of buzzards. Whatever you may have heard to the contrary, I can assure you with God as my witness that both my parents is full-blooded human beings. The Jackson press notwithstanding, I know of no other species in my family tree. Aye, and to address the most specific allegations, no blood kin of mine to my knowledge has ever taken pleasurement in swinging from the branches of that or any other kind of tree by their tails.

I do have an uncle, though, that some folks say has a little potlicker hound in him. Now, I'll grant you that others much smarter than me and them all put together say that such a thing is not humanly possible, but they never met the man personally. Deaf and Dumb Jimmy Crockett is his name, and I'll tell you what: he could cold trail a coon better than any dog I ever owned. I didn't believe it myself till the day my father took me and Uncle Jimmy out a-hunting with him. I was only about ten-year-old at the time, but I recollect that day as clear as if it was yesterday.

We was down in a part of Sevier County where none of us had ever been before including Uncle Jimmy. After a while we come to a clearing in the woods, and he puts his nose to the ground, walks around in circles awhile, then takes off across the field in a considerable burnt hurry. When he gets to the middle of the field, he does something mighty peculiar. He stops dead in his tracks, then leaps two or three feet into the air, maybe higher.

After that, he took off towards the woods again. When we caught up with him, he was pointing at an old 'simmon tree and sure enough there was a coon there in a hollow spot where three limbs branched out. It wasn't much use to us, though, on account of nothing was left but bones—now that's what I call cold trailing, sirs!

And if that wasn't enough proof of what Uncle Jimmy's nose could do, we later come to find out that the reason he done leaped so high in the middle of the field was on account of there once used to be a fence there.

All seriousness aside, it was Old Tiger that done all that. Old

Tiger, now he's my number one beatenest bear dog of all time. All I have to do is carry my rifle-gun on my right shoulder and he knows that bear's indeed what we're a-hunting. Put it on my left shoulder and he'll go after coon. One time he observed my youngest son getting out his fishing pole and he set-in to digging worms, I swear he did.

Here I must apologize for my bragging, but when it comes to my dogs there's no stop in me. Fact is, I got to bragging so much on Old Tiger when I first arrived in Washington City that my messmates thought I was a bald-faced liar. Now, I know'd that was no way to commence my congressional career, so I decided I had better bring my big yeller friend back with me the next session, which I subsequently done. Well, one Sunday I thought I'd take some of the fellows into that patch of woods out back behind the Capitol to show them what Old Tiger could do, but before we got more than a block or two from my lodgings, that fool dog of mine runs around the corner and commences to bark at a hitching post. Now gentlemen, you can well appreciate how shame-faced this made me feel, for we all knew there weren't no game to go stalking after in the middle of the city. But when we got up to him, we saw it wasn't the hitching post he was a-barking at. It was the sign over the door to the house that said:

A. Coon, Attorney at Law.

From that day on I never misdoubted that animal's intelligence again. Not for one minute, especially when I take him out bear hunting. Now, whenever I'm a-hunting bear there's two things I always take along with me. Like I say, one's Old Tiger. The other is Old Betsy, my bear rifle. You better believe my messmates took in an earful about Old Betsy, too, that first session, and they all wanted to try her out—but I wouldn't permit it.

You want to know why—I'll *tell* you why. 'Twas on account of Old Betsy requires a certain knack that don't come easy to a man straight off. Not even to an experienced rifleman such as myself. She packs a mean wallop. Fact is, whenever I shoot me a bear I have to run for cover, because the ball I fire spins the critter around so fast that when it goes out the back of him, like as not it heads straight towards me. I mean, like it has eyes.

Gentlemen, I have a confession to make. This past fall I gave up bear hunting for good, like my wife's been a-trying to get me to do for ten year. Now don't get me wrong, it wasn't any of her doing. What happened was this big old he-bear broke into my cabin and got into a jug of molasses and spilt it all over the floor. When he was finished, he went down to the creek to wash his paws. At least that's what I thought his reasoning was at the time.

Well, I soon come to find out I was mistaken. He went to the creek to go fishing is what he done. He went into the water and held up his right paw and sure enough the molasses that still covered it attracted flies. Pretty soon some trout jumped up to get the flies and quick as they did, the bear knocked them out with his other paw and threw them up on the bank. If he didn't, I wish I may be shot. Then he looked at me and sort of nodded and went off into the woods where he come from. I figured he wanted to pay me back for the molasses. Now I ask you, sirs: how can a man live with himself with the violent death of a fair-minded critter like that on his conscience?

I told you that to tell you this:

Once, I thought that fine folks such as yourselves was my natural prey and my predators, too, and that the Jackson Party was my friends. But after a while I come to find out I was dead wrong. Some folks say I've changed, but I haven't. I still believe in doing what's right for the betterment of my constituents and other such poor folks in this great nation of ours. It's Jackson that's changed. He's fallen under the spell of the Magician. That little red-headed Judas from Kinderhook. The thing he calls his vice-president.

This reminds me of a story my brother James once told me about an old man in the barrens of Illinois. Now this old man, he took his young grandson out to plow, but there was no trees in those barrens to have him take aim at. So he says to the boy, he says:

Do you see that there red heifer down yonder, boy?

And the boy says, *Yes, sir, I surely do.*

Well then, says the old man, *you plow straight towards her, hear?*

So the old man left the boy all day and come back in the evening to see how he done. He was astonished, for the rows his boy had plowed was all crooked. Says he:

What kind of plowing is this you have done?

Why, says the boy, *you told me to plow to the red heifer and I been a-plowing after her all day ever which way she went.*

Gentlemen, I was one of the first men that crossed the Tennessee River with General Jackson to fight the battles of our country. I helped to give him all his glory. When he was at the Battle of Tallahatchee, I was there. When he was at Talladago, I was there. When he was behind the cotton bales at New Orleans, I was starving in Florida. But when he begun to plow after the red heifer of Kinderhook that was grazing in every direction, I quit him on account of his crooked rows, for I was learned to plow by an old Quaker whose directions was to plow straight rows and go ahead.

Sirs, when I first come into Congress in 1827, I was as honest a friend of Andrew Jackson as any man in the world, but when I come to find out his whole object was to serve party and reek his vengeance upon them that voted against him my bristles begun to get up. When I saw honorable Members of Congress creeping around the House with papers to recommend some man to office overlooking his qualifications but writing his Jacksonism in capitals, and when I saw them like jackals in the night a-prowling after those poor fellows in office that dared to think we was wrong and they was right but other than that done their duty to their country faithfully, I said to myself:

"God never made man upright to do so. I can't go it. There's no principle to the thing."

What I done was find out that I'd got off the path I set out on. And I had the good sense not to waste time debating the question with myself, so I straight-a-way turned myself around, went home, and took a fresh trail.

I had to pay for all this dearly, gentlemen. Every press denounced me as bought over. No matter. My bear-hunting knees was too stiff to bend to power. They hit me uncommon hard at home, but I bore it and fought shy till I got them out of wind and then brought them to a parley.

You all know they turned me out of the last Congress, and after that when I was in the woods, I'd lay down my gun, call in the pups and think over everything. One evening late while I was a-setting so, Old Tiger put his paw on my knee and seemed whining for me to go.

"*Well,*" said I to him, "*Honest Old Tiger, you never cried on a false trail and neither will your master. You always hold like death. When you take, you grip and so will I. You never forsaked your master, though I've used you hard sometimes, so by the help of God I'll not forsake my old constituents. And if I can only succeed in making them know one-half of what I've seen of men and things at Washington, why, they'll go about right.*"

I sprung to my feet, begun a new campaign and I stood up to the rack, fodder or no fodder. And so here I am again, friends. I've been whipped and cleared and restored to my station once more. And you can rest assured I'd sooner be sent packing again than be a coon dog yelping along after a party, right or wrong.

Like I said before, I was reluctant to speak to you learned gentlemen about the great issues of the day, for I am from the far West and have made but little pretensions of understanding the wheels of government. But the government these days, as you all know, is but one man alone—at least that's what Old Hickory-face has taken to call himself lately, "*The Government*"— and I've had an opportunity to study him up close for years, so maybe I really do know a little something about those wheels after all.

Gentlemen, I consider we are returning to the old days of

King George III as fast as possible, to the time when our fathers took up the sword and pledged their lives and their sacred honor that they might be rid of a government of one man. They laid their petitions before the king. They humbled themselves at the foot of the throne and what respect did they get?

None. So they declared war. They swore they would be free, and by the Eternal they were free. Aye, they and their children have been free now for fifty-eight years.

But in 1834 what do we see? We see one man holding the sword in one hand and the purse in the other and bidding defiance to Congress and the nation. That man is Andrew Jackson, the first king of this country. Now, a king we wouldn't think so bad of far across the wide Atlantic, would we, sirs? But to have one in our own country is a horse of another color. And I don't know what else you could properly call a man who has declared that unless two-thirds of Congress will vote for a measure—which, of course, is nigh near impossible these days—he will veto it.

Consider that, sirs—and consider it powerful hard. In my opinion, it's far worse a thing than George III or any other king of England would dare to do. My friends, over there it would cost him not only his cap, but his head along with it. Things have got so bad here I'm afraid we have but little need of the Congress at all. We may as well save the people's money and dismiss ourselves and go home.

Look back only a few months, friends, when you saw this country the picture of good times and blessed with the best currency in the whole world. And now? The currency is destroyed and along with it most of our commerce, and they can no more mend it than a small boy can repair his father's watch. I am no prophet, but it don't take a prophet to see that we'll soon have to give boot to our money when we travel from one state to another, each scrap of paper worth less than the next, and all because of the thing that calls itself president and his hundred little fly-blown rag shops. And what is all this for? It's for no other purpose than to gratify the ambitions of one man so he might reek his vengeance upon the United States Bank, because it refused to give him a leg-up and uphold his corrupt party.

Gentlemen, my colleagues and myself have seen petitions signed by hundreds of thousands laid before the Congress praying for relief and the restoration of the people's deposits to the people's bank. And what has become of those petitions? I'll tell you what, for I was there, and I know. They've been sent to a packed committee made up by a party speaker with his pay in his pocket. You are never to hear from those petitions again, sirs, and still this is what they call the days of democracy.

Well, I say *not so!* I say that Andrew Jackson has done worse than even King George did, for he's gone so far as to close the door of the palace against the bearers of those petitions. That's right, he has refused them entrance into his majesty's presence.

And what do the people think of all this? If you go into the country like I done and tell them what I just been a-telling you, and back-staff every word:

"Oh," they say, *"Jackson has been in office a long time, he must be doing what's right."*

Truth is, they reckon that no man was ever competent to administer the government but him. Never mind that we have had presidents before Andrew Jackson, some the selfsame men that once framed the very Constitution of our country. Strange to tell, the people have come to the conclusion that nary a one of those presidents comprehended its meaning. But when Andrew Jackson come in, why, they figured he was just the man to construe it like he so wished, to mould it and fashion it, to make a corn dodger or a johnny-cake out of it and bake one side or both and the people still cries:

"Amen, it is right. Jackson says so."

And now King Andrew's a-fixing to smuggle in the red fox as his successor. Aye, Martin Van Buren the Little Magician, a man whose political creed is no more moment to him than his liking light bread better than biscuit. He aims to do this in the same fashion that he smuggled him into the vice-presidency: in the seat of his britches. The little Judas expects to be wafted into office and get the crown on his bald plate.

Well, sirs, I aim to do something about that, though I don't know exactly what as of yet. I reckon most of you have heard by now that they's folks down south a-begging me to run for the presidency myself in '36. I told them they was more partial to me than I was to myself—and I still believe that, but who knows, maybe they know something I don't. I expect there is likely something in me I have never yet found out. Now if any of you Young Whigs find it, I say:

Go ahead and run me. If elected, I shall seize the old monster which they have attempted to fool the people by calling it the Democrat Party—aye, I shall seize it by the horns and sling it right slap into the Atlantic Sea.

Other than that, I'm afraid I can't give you any more notions that I might be expected to have about the great bulk of government matters seeing as the "Government" hardly stands in one place long enough to form any opinion of him—kind of like that red cow I done told you about.

Anyways, opinions ain't the things they's cracked up to be at all. They can get mightily in a man's way. Folks may take great pride in having them, but most ain't a-willing to put the hard work into thinking them through. So what do they do, they appropriate somebody *else's* opinions and act them out like they was their own. Which is like trying to live another man's dream instead of your own. And that, by the Eternal, is no life at all.

As for me, gentlemen, I choose to live my own life thoroughly and honestly. You all know my motto is: *be sure you're right, then go ahead*. Well, I choose to put the hardest work into the first part, so the second part comes easier.

As for the next presidential election, I have not yet come upon the *"go ahead"* moment. Therefore, I believe I shall go for non-committal just a bit longer and let you Young Whigs work it more to your own notions than my own. Understand, nobody can misconstrue my opinions when I won't express any!

All seriousness aside, I'm not so sure I deserve the attention and good will you fine people have been heaping on me here. But if it spins me around and hits you back full force like a piece of lead from Old Betsy, I'll feel like I done accomplished something worthwhile.

Gentlemen, I have already spoke more than I intended, and I thank you for tolerating my plain unvarnished manner of addressing you. And now, before I sit down, if you'll permit me three toasts:

Our liberties. May they be restored along with the deposits.

Martin Van Buren. A political Judas, may he sink to the level of his merits.

Andrew Jackson. May his soul be rocked in the bosom of Lucifer before he commits yet another act of high treason.

Chapter Twelve

The following morning, May 1, 1834

"Mr. Paulding is indeed here, sir," said the clerk in the anteroom. "Who may I say wishes to see him?"

"Dr. Caruthers" said Will. "And a friend."

"What, you don't reckon he'll see us if he knows one of us is me?" said Colonel Crockett as the clerk disappeared into James Kirke Paulding's office down the hallway. Kirke Paulding was the U.S. naval agent of New-York City.

"I guarantee he'll be pleased to see you, Colonel," said Will. "I have never known him to allow politics to get in the way of friendship. I am no more a Democrat than you are, sir, but he certainly seems fond enough of me."

"And I'll lay he is," replied the colonel, "but me he only knows from the newspapers. And the ones he reads up here don't much admire me."

"But *he* admires you. Maybe not for your politics, sir, but most definitely for your humor."

"You reckon so, leech? Well then you think maybe he'll consent to join us over yonder for my speech? I mean, it's just spitting distance from here, ain't it?

The colonel was referring to the Battery, where in a little more than an hour there was to be a May Day flag raising ceremony. Mayor Lee was expected to attend along with a host of other Whig politicians. Jacksonian Democrats, however, were expected to snub the affair. Therefore, Will was reluctant to encourage the colonel to invite Kirke to listen to him speak.

"I'll even work in a few Wildfire-style jokes just for him," Crockett went on.

"I don't know, sir."

"What, you don't reckon he'll be up for a joke-joust?"

"With all due respect, Colonel, jokes have nothing to do with it. It's just ... I mean: what, sir, if the shoe were on the other foot? Would you expect yourself to warm to the notion of attending a Van Buren assemblage?

"That depends how badly I was itching for a fight," replied the colonel.

The clerk returned and told them that Mr. Paulding would see them in no more than ten or fifteen minutes.

"But please do have a seat and make yourselves comfortable."

Will and Colonel Crockett sat down on some well-worn but indeed comfortable enough upholstered chairs, the colonel throwing one of his booted feet over his other knee and shutting his eyes. Will looked at him and chuckled to himself. This was the least likely place he ever expected to find himself sitting next to the bear slayer.

Well, until last night it was. Last night, just after Crockett came up from his post-speech holding forth at the Windust Tavern, he announced his intention to *track down Paulding* in the morning

"Really, sir?" replied a dumbstruck Will.

"Why shouldn't I. He don't bite, do he?"

"I thought you were angry with him for caricaturing you in his play."

"For what?"

"For ridiculing you, sir"

The colonel laughed. "No, I got over that a long time ago. I stood up in front of all them folks in Washington and took a bow to Jim Hackett up there on the stage a-making fun of me, didn't I?"

"I know you did, sir. I was there."

"Anyways, your Mr. Paulding done disclaimed in the newspapers that his concocted Wildfire fellow had anything to do with me at all. It ain't *his* fault if the public still makes the connection. I'll tell you what, though. I do believe I'd get a kick out of meeting that unwitting concocter of that connection face to face —I mean, wouldn't you, leech?"

Will nodded. However, he in fact was not so comfortable at all to visit with Kirke Paulding just now—that is, in Colonel Crockett's presence. And it was his own fault. Because when Will informed Kirke a few weeks ago about the flattering account of Crockett's tour he was writing for Matthew Clarke and the Whigs, Kirke responded with a counteroffer: to write a satirical broadside about Crockett for the Democrats. And Will didn't turn him down on the spot as he knew he should have.

"But don't you think that might be just a tad two-faced for me?" was as close as he had come. They were at Kirke's home just down the street, in his private office. Kirke did all of his literary work—and as much of his government work as he could get away with—there in his red velvet dressing gown.

"Rubbish!" said Kirke. "And I can assure you that nothing viscous is called for here. Trust me, it will be all in fun. And may I remind you that you yourself recently told me that 'twas your great fear that this journal you are compiling for him might help make him president. Well, here is your opportunity to reduce that risk!"

Short as ever of ready cash, Will un-enthusiastically consented. Nevertheless, he soon *enthusiastically* went to work on it—and on his competing client's time!

It didn't take him long to sketch the thing out. He got the idea at the luncheon yesterday. Right after the trip to City Hall.

It came to him while he was enjoying the table banter between Colonel Crockett and Seba Smith, the creator of the fictional character Major Jack Downing. They got on well, Smith and Crockett did. Both spouted-off in character throughout the meal as if they were upon the stage, Crockett in an exaggerated (even for *him*) English-mangling Western twang and Smith in an equally exaggerated down-east Maine dialect.

Smith's ever charming humor never failed to impress Will, particularly how he equipped the irrepressible major with it as a tool to attack and irritate President Jackson. He did this by presenting the major not as a critic, but as a *friend* of Old Hickory. Aye,'twas his hilariously inept *defense* of Jackson that singed the president!

And so Will decided to turn the major loose in an inept defense of Colonel Crockett. He thought it up all afternoon and started committing it to paper at the public dinner last night, conjecturing that if the colonel noticed him at all scribbling away at a distant table, he would assume Will was taking notes from the speechmakers. Then came some revisions, these while Colonel Crockett was safely away working up an inebriation at Ned Windust's. And later yet, Will re-read it on the sly for continuity, this when the colonel was dangerously closer and sleeping that inebriation off.

"Mr. Paulding will see you now," said the clerk in the naval agent's office. He then led Will and the colonel down the hallway to Kirke's private chamber.

"So good to see you, William," Kirke said standing up behind his desk and reaching for Will's hand. Then to Crockett:

"And you, sir, are you who I think you are?"

"I am indeed, sir," said Colonel Crockett. "And if I ain't, I wish I may be shot."

"Seems to me I have heard that line before," Kirk replied scratching his head. He stepped around his desk to shake the colonel's hand.

"So at last we meet," the colonel said grasping Kirke's

extended hand and throwing his other arm around Kirke's shoulder. "I already done shook hands with Wildfire. I figured it was high time I squeezed yours, too, sir."

He turned Kirke loose, then folded his arms and looked around the room approvingly. "My, what a quality place you have got yourself here, Mr. Paulding," he said. "I wish I had me an office. All they provides us with in the Congress is a paltry little writing table and some quills, but I reckon you already know that, sir."

They sat down, Kirke back behind his large mahogany desk and his guests facing him from the other side. Kirk then rang for his subordinate and had him bring a pitcher of iced water.

"You mention Wildfire," Kirke said while he shuffled through some documents. "That must have been 'round about Yuletide at the Washington Theater. I understand you caused quite a stir there."

"Me? No, it was the spectators doing, not mine. They give it to me when I walked into the building, and they give it to me again when we made our bows, Jim Hackett and myself. Twice we done that—at the start of the play and the finish—and for a while there I feared the rafters would give out."

Kirke sighed and looked up at the ceiling. "I'm afraid the play is doing more for you these days than it ever did for me. I defy you to find my name on a playbill."

Inexcusably true, thought Will. The original manuscript had been revised by others several times already. Even the title had been changed.

"In any event, you deserve all the accolades you've received, Colonel. I have always considered you to be a fine specimen of the American mountebank."

Will winced—inwardly, he hoped.

"Much obliged, sir," said the colonel, "I, uh ... reckon."

Kirke smiled. "The word means 'noble yeoman' sir. Whoever coined it must have been thinking of you."

The colonel crossed his legs and started nervously jiggling his foot and clearing his throat.

"Well now," he finally said, "I ain't so good at this, but before the doctor and myself heads on out of here I must first express my ... my heartfelt sense of ...

"Confound it, I had it all rehearsed. I reckon I'd better put it in plain unvarnished English seeing as that's all I can speak. What I'm a-trying to spit out is that I am truly in your debt, sir, for all that you done for me. My whole life I wished to be the man I find myself today, and it never would have happened if you hadn't wrote such a wonderful play like you done. Never in a hundred years. I'm tickled to death I finally got to see it with my own two eyes. And I must tell you, sir, it sent chills up and down my spine."

"That was probably your ague," said Kirke.

The colonel looked Will in the eye. "Talking about me behind my back, are you leech? Doctors ain't supposed to do such things no more than lawyers are, old hook.

"But like I was saying," he went on to Kirke, "folks never knew me from Adam till you wrote that thing—and don't you for one moment speculate that I don't appreciate what you done for me. I ask you, sir, how many back-country old boys such as myself wouldn't give their right arm to be where I am today?"

"Sir, you flatter me more than I deserve," said Kirke.

"I don't flatter you enough. The way I figure, people likes to laugh—you follow me so far, sir?"

"Like one of your hunting dogs, Colonel."

"Which one?"

"Sir?"

"Tiger? Old Rattler?"

The colonel held up his hand. "No, that was a joke," he said interrupting himself. "My apologies, sir, but when it comes to dogs and jokes there's no stop in me. But like I done said, folks really do likes to laugh. So what they need is somebody to laugh at—ain't that right, sir?"

"From time immemorial."

"And that particular somebody might just as well be myself."

"You do seem to enjoy that sort of thing."

"I do, and you knew it—God bless you, sir."

The colonel uncrossed his legs and leaned forward in his chair. "Do you mind if I tell you a funny little story about myself?"

"By all means please do, Colonel. I have always found your stories to be most entertaining."

"All right, then I shall go ahead full steam. Now, this is between you and me and the leech over here, so it don't leave this here room. Agreed?"

Kirke nodded, then stole a quick glance at Will.

"Good, then I shall take you at your word as a gentleman, sir. Now, when I first come to Washington, my dream by no means was to become president like folks is saying these days. No, sir—listen careful, sir:

"My dream, sir—and this is the first time I have ever told a soul—was to become the laughingstock of the entire country."

The colonel held up his hand again.

"Now wait, let me ask you the question I know you was fixing to ask me first," he went on. "Why on earth would I wish to become such a thing?

"I'll *tell* you why," he answered himself. "Because that way I might could make the voters so ashamed of me that they'd throw my sorry red-faced arse out of office. But try as I might, I could never fully succeed in this. I come close a few times, but it took your play—which I must say is the greatest comedy ever wrote since *Hamlet*—to make a perfect enough fool out of me to do the trick."

Will hadn't been prepared for such an ironic turn, and from the look on his face Kirke obviously hadn't been either; Kirke, who then reiterated to the colonel that he had never intended to model Nimrod Wildfire after him.

"I thought we settled that in the newspapers years ago," he said. "And need I remind you, sir, that you took me at my word."

"I had to," the colonel said. "I hadn't yet seen the confounded thing—and neither had no one else." His face was noticeably redder now, and he was opening and closing his right hand into a fist as if he were tossing a coin in the air and catching it.

"It was the truth," Kirke said.

"What was?"

"My dear sir, I had never even *heard* of you."

"The newspaper scribblers sure enough did. I suppose the next thing you're a-fixing to tell me is you don't read the newspapers Well then where the devil did you come up with `*I wish I may be shot?*'"

Kirke rubbed one of his frail wrists with the bony fingers of his other hand. "It's a common expression," he said.

"Common to *me*, sir—and you knew it."

"Upon my word, sir, the language came from sources other than yourself."

"Like my sworn enemies in the Congress, I'll lay."

Kirke shook his head. "Most of it came from a particular friend of mine. You know, the *half-horse, half-alligator* brag and such. The man's an itinerant portrait painter who has traveled extensively throughout the South and West. His name is John Wesley Jarvis. As I have said, I had never heard of you. But it is possible that he had."

"John Wesley," said Crockett. "Now that's my eldest son's name. And my father's name, too. But where else do I know that name?"

Will wondered what that had to do with anything, and why it shut the colonel up for a few moments. As for Kirke Paulding, Will knew he was lying through his teeth about having never so much as heard of Crockett when he wrote the *Lion of the West*. One morning four years ago, Kirke confided to Will over coffee about his latest literary endeavor: a farce about a colorful congressman from the wilds of the West.

"And might that congressman be one David Crockett of Tennessee?" Will had asked him then.

"The same," replied Kirke. *"Only I believe they call him 'Davy.' You don't happen to know him, do you, William?"*

"No sir, but I did meet him once. In Staunton, Virginia at the home of my uncle McClung. I've no interesting stories, though. Sorry, sir."

"No matter," said Kirke. *"I shall invent some."*

"And that there was when?" Colonel Crockett now said. Will thought he sounded like some half-educated backwoods lawyer.

Kirke closed his eyes. "What was when?"

"When you collected this here language."

Kirke replied that he'd been interested in language all his life. "I am a writer, sir," he said. "It's my stock and trade."

"I mean you a-squeezing this John Wesley for words and such like you figure we use out west, this according to you before you ever seen my name in print."

"The summer of 1830."

"The summer of 1830," the colonel repeated sarcastically.

Then he stood up and pulled a rumpled piece of yellowed newsprint from the inside pocket of his frock coat.

"Gentlemen," he said, "what I hold in this hand is a story clipped from the *Nashville Whig* in 1828 wrote by none other than you, Mr. James Kirke Paulding, two years before a time you said you still hadn't heard of me yet. Shame on you, sir! Here, leech: take you a look at this sorry piece of privy-work."

Will looked it over. The story mentioned Crockett by name, and if you believed the writer, he made a boor of himself at President Adams' dinner table shortly after arriving in Washington to begin his first term in Congress. The colonel is the supposed narrator of the anecdote, and practically every other line is *"I wish I may be shot."* He complains to the waiter about his having stolen the colonel's plateful of roast goose.

"Now read the last part of it out loud, about me eating soap from a finger bowl," Crockett said. "No, better yet give it here and I'll recite it, because it's me that's supposed to be narrating this blasted thing—ain't that right Mr. Paulding? Now you can hear exactly what I'd a-sounded like if I actually had uttered such a figment."

Still standing, but now about half-way closer to where Kirke sat, the colonel squinted at the paper, holding it at different distances, finally settling on a full arm's length. "Now keep in mind," he began, "I'm a-setting there at table with the president of the United States and several honored others. So what do I do? Well, according to Mr. Paulding here, and I quote:

"I filled my plate with bacon and greens—the waiter had just stole my goose—and whenever I looked up and down the table I held on to my plate with my left hand. When we were all done eating they cleared everything off the table and took away the tablecloth. And what do you think? There was another cloth under it. If there wasn't, I wish I may be shot.

"Then I saw a man coming along carrying a great glass thing with a glass handle below, something like a candlestick. It was stuck full of little glass cups with something in them that looked good to eat. Thinks I, let's taste them first. They were mighty sweet and good, so I took six of 'em. If I didn't, I wish I may be shot."

The colonel put the paper down on Kirke's desk and took yet another sweeping step toward him placing his hands on the back of Kirke's armchair. Then he leaned forward and stuck his face so close to Kirke's that Will thought he was poised to bite off his nose.

"Answer me something, sir," he said softly and evenly. "Do

you wish to defend yourself on the field of honor or (his face reddened as his voice rose) shall I thrash you here and get it over and done with?"

Will looked around for help should he need it, but Kirke's subordinate was gone, and the building seemed deserted.

Kirke tried to smile. "There is nothing to thrash me for," he said. "I never wrote that piece."

"Saint Clarke says you did."

"Saint Clarke?"

"Matthew Saint Claire Clarke, the Clerk of the U.S. House of Representatives. He just so happens to be a friend of mine."

"I don't care, sir, if he is your twin brother," said Kirke. "I have never heard of him. You say I wrote that folderol for the newspapers. What kind of sense, sir, does that make? Why would I have wanted to ridicule you in the Adams Party press? I am a Democrat, just as you were at the time. Why would I wish to ridicule a fellow Jacksonian?"

The colonel looked away for a moment, then grabbed Kirke by his shirt, just below the collar. "So you never so much as heard of me back then," he said. "Then how the devil did you know I was a Jackson man? How the—"

"Somebody ... must have ... told me at the time, I'm sure." Kirke gasped. "I mean, when I read the article. Yes, I remember it now. 'Twas then that I learned you were one of us. And you can rest assured that I condemned the anonymous wag who wrote it."

"Well, don't that make me feel good," said the colonel, who then loosened his grip a little. "But wait. If you knew me then, you knew me when you wrote that damn play two-three year later. Lies, lies and more lies."

The colonel's hands moved from Kirke's collar to his throat. Kirke's face was now red as a beet; Will thought he might have an apoplectic fit.

"All right," Kirke finally said, his hands on Crockett's wrists trying to loosen his grip. "All right, I admit it. I ... will you please, sir?"

The colonel let go, then wiped his hands on his trousers as if he had been handling a greasy hunk of meat.

"Yes, I had heard of you by the time I wrote the play," Kirke said, still gasping for air. "But I never meant to ridicule you. Upon my word I didn't. Do you know Dick Wilde?"

"Wilde of Georgia?"

Kirke nodded.

"I served with him in the House," Crockett said nodding back.

"A friend of his told me about you. I wish he'd had the decency to affix his name to the letter he wrote. If he had, then perhaps you would consider thrashing him instead of me."

The colonel smirked, then looked at Will so viciously that for a moment Will thought he was going to accuse *him* of writing the newspaper piece.

"You, sir," Crockett said turning back to Kirke, "are a monumental liar, a puppy and a poltroon. You wrote that sorry thing for the Adams papers despite anything contrariwise that you're a-saying now. It come out the first year of my first term, and nobody yet knew aught about me except for the folks back home. By God if that wasn't the first look the rest of the country got of me. I'll tell you what, I was never so shame-faced in my life. And then when folks was just about forgetting it, you had to go write that damn fool play of yours."

"That 'damn fool play' made you what you are today," Kirke said.

"What, a damn fool?"

"I didn't say that, sir. I merely—"

"It cost me the election that year, is what it done. And I've a mind it's going to cost you within an inch of your life, sir."

Will tried to calm Crockett down, but the colonel brushed him aside.

"I'm afraid I am going to have to ask you to leave, sir, "said Kirke.

"Stand up and face me like a man," said the colonel.

When Kirke demurred, the colonel lifted him out of his seat and set him down on the floor so hard that Kirke lost his balance. He lay there for a moment, stunned, then motioned to Will to fetch his walking cane.

The colonel stood over him with the strangest look on his face. Will couldn't read it, but he saw in it not a trace of contrition. Then Crockett crumpled up the newspaper story and tossed it at Kirke's feet.

"By the Eternal if I shouldn't make you eat it," he said and went for his hat.

"Oh, and one other thing," he said from the hallway. "Mountebank don't mean 'noble yeoman.' It means a vigorous, boastful scoundrel, you sorry little piece of shit."

Fom Kirke's office Will and Colonel Crockett walked across Whitehall Street toward the Battery for the flag ceremony and the speeches.

"Thank God you didn't him hurt badly," said Will.

"If I had wished to hurt him, I'd a-hurt him," replied the colonel. Then he accused Will of misleading him by not informing him of Kirke's frail constitution. But mostly Crockett was silent, with that same strange look in his eyes. It reminded Will of something, but he couldn't put his finger on it.

But then about an hour later, when some Whig politician was droning on to those assembled about something patriotic, Will noticed a scrawny gray cat making its way through the crowd, rubbing itself against a thicket of trousered legs and mewing. It reminded Will of one of his own cats from back home in Lexington—Tom Gray he used to call it because it was a gray tom.

One night, soon after Louisa had gone up to bed, Will heard a scratching sound at his front door. He opened the door, and in pranced Tom Gray with a field mouse in his mouth. He dropped the mouse at Will's feet, crippled but still alive, and began to play with it, preferring slow torture to a quick *coup de grace*. Unable to bear the sight of this disturbing but, alas, predictable feline behavior, Will distracted his cruel little friend with a bowl of milk in the serving kitchen, tossed the mouse outside and put it out of its misery with a pocketknife.

As soon as Tom Gray finished his milk, he ran back to the hallway in search of his prey. The look on his face when he found the mouse gone was that of a bully stopped in his tracks. That was precisely how the great Davy Crockett looked to Will hovering over poor Kirke Paulding.

Said Will to himself:

This is the man I am so concerned about maligning?

He looked across the park at this stalker of wild beasts and cripples and thought:

This man is fair game.

Chapter Thirteen

HOW I SAVED PRESIDENT CROCKETT'S REPUTATION—TWICE!

MAJOR ZACK UPPITY OF UPPITYVILLE

For JKP,

> *Please excuse the plagiarism. Somehow, I don't think "Major Down-ing" will mind.*

—WAC.

I've been a-hanging my hat here at the White House ever since last summer when I come down to Washington to stand guard while President Crockett was on his annual tour away up north and down east. When he came back in the fall, I told him I wished to remain at my post a while longer. Of course he could hardly refuse me. He figured he owed me a lot more than that seeing as I was the one that saved his reputation at the second Battle of New Orleans back in '36.

Who'd ever a-thought them bloody red Britishers would've cared to tangle with us'ns once again on the selfsame soil where we whupped them all to shreds nearabout thirty years ago? Fortunately President Crockett—"Colonel" Crockett, really, for he weren't the president yet—got wind of the scheme, so he and me was able to raise enough regiments and brigades and such to drive them back into the Gulf of Mexico.

Might could be that it wouldn't have turned out that way. Truth is, if it wasn't for me, we might all be British subjects once and forever again. Don't believe me? Well then you just listen. This here is the little-known history of what really happened right there at the beginning and the end of the War of 1836. I was there, so you can rest assured that this is the true and complete truth as I saw it— and experienced it.

Anyway, there we indeed was: way down south just outside of New Orleans and within plain sight of the whites of the enemies' eyes. The only problem was that the boys soon turned their eyes in the opposite direction and started falling back like scared jackrabbits. I looked around for Old Davy so's I could get him to rally the troops back to where they was supposed to be, but he was nowhere to be found. So I commenced to track him down. And find him I soon did. He was as far back in the rear as you could go and still be within clear earshot of the musketry. Fact is, he was back in his tent.

Now you may not believe any of this, but it is the gospel truth: when I found him, old Davy was a-trembling like a shaker man at a church meeting. So I takes him by both of his shoulders and shakes him back the other way, but all this does is make him tremble more. Thinks I:

Thank God no one has seen you like this, Davy. Aye, but once someone does and the word gets out, we are all doomed. How in tarnation can I get you out of this here tent so you can haul off and save the day?

Then like a bolt of lightning it come to me that he needn't have to do no such thing at all. No sir, for I would do the thing myself.

So what did I do? I thanked him kindly to give me his buckskin hunting duds that he was a-sporting and that famous coonskin hat of his. What he give me first, though, was that menacing look of his. Then he grumbled something and straightaway complied with my wishes. Anyway, when I left him standing there in the tent, he was naked as the day he was born'd. He didn't even have the common sense to put on the duds I left behind for him to wear.

So there I was, a half-hour later up front with the troops all decked out in Davy's duds. And just like I done planned, them troops all mistook me for him. Then, with the help of God and a dram of limber-leg applejack, I was able to turn the rout into a rally. I done this first by reminding the boys how brave they truly was and then by threatening to shoot their yeller-belly arses myself with Old Betsy if they didn't turn around and face the enemy again.

Anyway, by nightfall the day was finally ours. Before I knew it, there was huzzas for Crockett up and down our lines. I was about to shuck my disguise and claim the credit for myself like I deserved when the troops started huzza-ing him for president. Well, I know'd I didn't want no part of any president business, so I got out of my bear hunter disguise quick as I could and high-tailed in my long-handles to the rear to give Davy his duds back.

That was when I informed him that he was, like as not, going to be elected to the White House as the next president of these here United States come November.

"I figured as much," says Davy. "Andy Jackson don't have nothing on me no more."

Then he thanked me for what I done and asked me what I would like in return. I told him I didn't rightly know yet, but he would be the first to hear of it. One thing I did do, though, was I made him promise to let me lodge with him at the president's house as long as I pleased so long as it was understood that that alone didn't cancel out the debt.

And so I moved into the White House the summer after the election and stayed on. Now don't think for a moment that I ain't been earning my keep here at the mansion. Truth is, I been a great help to President Crockett all day long—and yet some. I get up at first light all primed to go, but half the time he is already moving about. The bark of his rifle is what usually rouses me. I'll tell you what, pretty soon there won't be ary a squirrel left alive on the White House grounds.

After breakfast, our workday commences. Davy fires up his corn-cob pipe and begins to think pretty hard, and I open up his letters. We sort them out like sardines in a packing yard, one pile marked *'red,'* another pile marked *'not red and worth nothing'* and a third marked *'red and to be answered.'* Then I commence to read them out loud with him looking over my shoulder sometimes and saying:

"Major, I reckon we best say so and so to that."

And me saying:

"Just so," or *not* as the notion strikes me, all the while not letting on that I know he can't read a lick of English or any other language.

Then come the cabinet meetings where them Secretaries of This-and-That pretty much handle him the same way I do excepting they ain't looking out for his best interests like I am. The only interest they's a-looking out for is their own—and Nicholas Biddle's, too, of course, who is president of the Devil's own Bank of the United States.

Here I must tell you how much I despised the way that the Bank people was using Davy for their own devilish purposes. Aye, and how much I wished to put an end to such mischief as soon as I could. The only problem was that I didn't have me a plan yet. And I probably still wouldn't if Old Davy hadn't gone and broke his specs.

It was close to sundown one evening when President Crockett called me into his office here at the White House and said I must help him find his best gold-rimmed spectacles. He had looked high and low for them and thought two pair of eyes would be better than one for such task. But that proved not to be the case.

He finally did find them when he undressed for bed a few hours later. They had fallen through a hole in one of his pantaloon pockets and was all stomped to bits in his boot. I told him I would go down the avenue and get them fixed, but he grabbed my arm and ordered me not to.

"These here was given to me for Christmas by Mr. Biddle of the Bank," said he, "and he told me never to let no one fix them but himself."

So he had me send them to Philadelphia, and all the while they was gone, he couldn't do nothing with business. He was as bad off as an owl in sunshine.

Well, a few weeks later them gold specs came back by express from Mr. Biddle. Davy tore into the package and put them on.

"Aha," says he. "These specs is good as new again! I can't see a thing with Vice-President Chilton's specs or nobody else's as good as I can see with these here."

Then he made me read the letter that came back with them. It said not to touch the screws. Now, them spectacles of his have a dozen such things—and half again as many springs, too.

I asked him if I could try them on. Said I, "I promise not to touch the screws."

Old Davy shook his head. "Mr. Biddle made me swear an oath never to let nobody else examine into them," said he. "Especially you, Major."

"Me?" said I. "Whyfore me in particular?"

"He didn't say," replied Davy, "but I reckon he has some good reason. But look here: even if he don't, I done took that oath and must abide by it."

Well, from that day on I couldn't eat nor sleep until I got a-hold of them there specs. It was the day the Congress sent the new Bank charter up to the president for him to sign that I got my nerve up. Davy was setting there at his desk a-studying that Satanic document. He had a broad grin all over his face as he made like he was a-studying it top to bottom. Like I said, he can't read a word to save his life.

Anyway, after a while he goes to bed and pretty soon, he commences to snoring like a nor'easter. So into his office I steal myself, and right there are them gold-rimmed specs still a-setting on his desk next to that re-charter bill, which I could see he hadn't put his mark to yet. So I clap them on and commence to look through them at the document. At first the letters and figures was blurry like the morning after a hard night of drinking. Then they begun to swirl around. Said I to myself:

"If old Davy can make out so much as a single letter through these specs, it's more than I can—and I done completed the third grade."

Well, the next thing I know, them letters and figures have turned themselves into a crowd of folks throwing up hats. And cashiers from the U.S. Bank are running around holding up banners and signs with *Glory* printed on them and *Huzza for President Crockett*. And there surrounded by the crowd is President Crockett himself with a Roman bedsheet wrapped all around him and rockets exploding over his head. I said to myself right then:

"If things look so to Davy like they do to me through these specs, I don't wonder no more why it is that he don't always see things like other folks does."

It was then that it come to me. I turned them screws every which way till I didn't see nothing through them specs but the words and figures like they was rightfully wrote. Then I took them off and put them back on the table where he left them and went back to bed.

Well, the next morning when old Davy put them back on again to have another look at the Bank charter, said he:

"There must be something wrong with these specs. Only last night this paper made perfect sense, but now I can't make heads or tails of it."

Said I to myself:

Of course it don't make sense to you, Davy. All you can read is pictures.

"These here specs must be sent back to Mr. Biddle for adjustment," said he.

I told him I would take care of that right away, but meanwhile he better not leave that Bank charter of his lying around like that.

"You had better put it in your pocket for safe keeping," said I.

"Major, that is an excellent idea," replied he. Then he folded it up and stuffed it into his coat pocket.

And that's where that bank charter remained for two months while I made like I was seeing to getting his specs fixed. Well, by the time we wrote the third letter to Biddle complaining that we still hadn't received the specs (I never sent them nor did I post any of the letters), Congress adjourned, for that was the short session right before the congressional elections. And that year the people finally threw the Bank Party out and elected a Democratic Congress again.

So that's how I tricked old Davy into pocket-vetoing the Bank re-charter bill and putting Nick Biddle out of a job. And that's how Davy squared things with me despite himself for saving his reputation as a fighting man. And that's how he got his reputation back as a man of the people even though he ain't been one for years.

Chapter Fourteen

Later that same day, May 1, 1834

"I say gangway, you snail!"

Dr. William A. Caruthers hung on to the side strap of his borrowed carriage for dear life as if he indeed were tethering himself to his gastropod shell. Will's driver maneuvered them away from the roaring teamster and his wagonload of furniture. When the teamster passed them, he turned his face toward them, his thumb at his hawk nose and his fingers wagging in their direction.

"Now, there's a bran-fire new one for me," said Colonel Crockett who was sitting across from Will in the carriage. He put his own thumb to his own hawk nose and shook his fingers at Will.

"You are fortunate, sir, that I find myself unarmed today," Will said with a dead-set straight face.

The colonel laughed. "I reckon so. All seriousness aside, though, but this here is a world of difference from May Day back home. You may not believe this, leech, but where I come from, all the little children goes out into the woods and gathers flowers. This is no more like May Day in Tennessee than a fly in a mess of grits is like a man on a steamboat."

Will nodded, sticking out his lower lip for emphasis, for his own May Days in Virginia had been much the same as the colonel's. And some of the little flower children had been close kin. Today in New-York, however, the streets were filled with empty carts and loaded carts rattling down the stone pavements and backing up to doors out of which strangers of all ages and sizes were lugging the totality of their earthly belongings stuffed as they were into boxes, barrels, chests and even wash tubs, pots, and kettles.

Will and Colonel Crockett were in the midst of all this now, inching along the Bowery in the emerald-green lacquered barouche that one of the party men had lent them along with his diminutive white-haired Irish coachman. Three blocks back they weren't even inching. At Spring Street a fully loaded dray had been smashed into firewood by an omnibus. It took twenty minutes to clear the street and allow traffic to start moving again.

Of all days to go sight-seeing! thought Will. And it was astonishing that the day wasn't even half through yet. Will had begun it at first light in Colonel Crockett's hotel room; the colonel and Judge Clayton had not yet returned from their night of carousing. Will took advantage of this by finishing up the dirty little piece of libel that Kirke Paulding had commissioned him to write about Crockett. He penned it in the colonel's bed with the aid of the Judge's writing box, blowing the ink dry and hiding it under the bed each time he heard footsteps in the hallway lest the colonel catch him in the act and do unto him as he had done unto Kirke.

After the colonel returned to his room (at nearly eight a.m.); and after he took possession of his own bed (from Will) to catch a few hours of much needed sleep; and after he delivered Kirke Paulding his dressing-down (to the floor); and then after he re-delivered his Young Whig speech (not long ago) to a considerable noon-hour gathering at the Battery he, Will and Judge Clayton took a foot-tour of the neighborhood with old General Morton, a relic of the Revolution. They walked down the flagstone sidewalks of Battery Place, then up State Street, stopping to admire the grandiose three-story row houses across from Bowling Green.

The colonel noted that the elegant black wrought-iron fencing, which matched the one that encircled the park, left no doubt to passers-by whose private preserve the owners of those houses thought it to be.

"But I say huzza for them," he went on. "And what a likely place to raise a family. Well, if you got you enough bullion stashed under your floorboards."

"There are not too many better families left around here," said General Morton. "These are mostly boarding houses now."

"Right fancy boarding houses, sir."

"That they are, Colonel, but they are much too close to the bustle of commerce for a family man. The people of consequence have moved up the country, some as far north as Greenwich."

The colonel stroked a side whisker. "So it's the rich that moves and the poor that stays."

"So it seems."

"Funny, ain't it sir?"

"Funny, Colonel?"

"Aye sir, because where I come from it's the other way around. It's the rich man that stays put and the poor man that leaves. Me, I ain't never been worth more than what I could stash into one pocket. I was born in East Tennessee on the banks of the Nolichucky River and now I'm nigh up to the Mississippi, which is as far West as you can go and still be in the state. Another ten year and who knows, I might be nigh up to the Pacific Sea, you can't ever tell."

Will smiled to himself; Crockett never missed an opportunity to identify himself with the downtrodden—particularly when he was out courting the wealthy.

The colonel took leave of General Morton. Then one of the Whig politicians in his party (who favored the actor Edwin Forrest so much that Will nearly addressed him as such) offered to drive him around the city in his private coach.

"So long as I can take my interpret-*tater* with me," the colonel said, gently elbowing Will.

They drove up Broadway to the hotel, where Judge Clayton took leave of them. Before he did, however, Will placed in his hands a package containing his notes for Colonel Crockett's journal. The judge was to assume Will's chronicling duties for the northernmost leg of the tour, which was to begin bright and early tomorrow morning.

"If you have an opportunity, sir, to look them over this evening," Will said, "I would welcome an honest critique"

"A critique, I regret to say, will have to wait until we return from Boston," the judge replied. "I won't have time to peruse them until we are shipboard. I do, however, intend to give them a thorough going-over."

From the hotel they drove to Hudson Street and St. Johns Park to take in more fancy wrought-iron work. The colonel stuck his head out the carriage window.

"Cottonwoods," he said pointing to a copse of young trees in the fenced-in park. "They'd like to make me feel at home if it wasn't for such clumping-up of them big houses all together. It's like they's in a warehouse awaiting to be hauled off somewheres one at a time."

Next stop was Washington Square and more clumped-up houses, these ones with Doric columns and white marble porches. Then, east on Fourth Street to Lafayette Place and the two-story colonnade that ran the full length of a long row of even more expensive structures, one of which, according to Edwin Forrest, Washington Irving had once called home. It had cost upwards of twenty-five thousand dollars, he said. They all did. He gave a detailed account of the financing of their construction. When the financier turned out to be a close friend, Will grew suspicious.

The sales-pitch came at Tomkins Square, a ten-acre park about a half-mile distant that afforded a clear view of the East River shimmering in the bright sunlight. Edwin Forrest offered to build Colonel Crockett a house there free of charge that he could occupy whenever he was in the city.

"While I must admit that I've always wished to see the great corporation of New-York," replied the colonel, "why ever would I wish to return now that my curiosity's done been satisfied?"

"To see your public, sir. And for your public to see *you*"

"To see me?" The colonel hawked and spat out the side of the open-air carriage. "After all they've read about me, I do believe they're in for a big let-down."

He didn't show any interest until Edwin Forrest suggested a statue of him in the middle of the square.

"In your frontier garb. With one of your hunting dogs, perhaps. And perhaps there will be a small menagerie. The park will celebrate the wilderness, sir, and everything else you stand for."

The colonel scoffed at this, but his countenance betrayed him; he was clearly enjoying the flattery. When he learned that he could rent the house out all year long and pocket the proceeds, his eyes brightened even more.

But only briefly.

"What's the set-off?" he said. "I'm supposed to go from door to door soliciting rich folks to buy lots on the square so they might could live next door to the Wild Man?"

Edwin Forrest shook his head. "The word will get out that you are building here."

"And you'll be the one a-getting it out."

"Words, sir, are my livelihood."

The colonel laughed. "I reckon they're mine, too, come to think of it."

He cleared his throat.

"Well, sir," he went on, "this is indeed an interesting proposition. My business manager here and I shall give it some serious thought."

He turned around to face Will, winked and then rolled his eyes; and in those simple gestures Will thought he detected in Colonel Crockett at least a glimmer of integrity.

"I am quite certain you will, Colonel. You seem to be a man who divines an opportunity when he sees one."

"I'm a creature of the woods, sir," the colonel said. "I know such things when I smell them."

That was four hours ago. Edwin Forrest, home now in his snug little mansion, nevertheless had been hopeful enough about Crockett coming to terms with him that he offered to lend him his coach and coachman to continue his excursion about the city. The colonel accepted; and now here they were, Will and he, stuck in traffic on the Bowery. They were on their way to the Five Points, the filthiest neighborhood in New-York.

"I wish to see where the *real* folks live," the colonel had explained to the skeptical Irish driver who, if he didn't currently live in Five Points, in all likelihood once did. "Folks like you and me who live by the sweat of their brow."

As they were but a few blocks from their destination now, Will suggested they get out and walk. So the colonel and he stepped into the street, and as they did, a shop clerk approached them. Will waved him away. He turned one of his coat pockets inside-out to show the man how broke he was, then laughed at how disingenuous that must have looked considering he had just alighted from a three-hundred-dollar barouche!

The colonel stepped up to the sidewalk and surveyed the piles of merchandise in front of the crowded shops: the cheap cowhide boots and heavy hobnailed work shoes, the ladies' caps and bonnets, the bolts of patterned fabric in colors more garish than any lady but a "Bowery Girl" would dare to wear.

"So this is where rich folks too idlesome to haul away their old chattels on Moving Day comes to stock up," he said.

"Not likely," replied Will. "Most of them wouldn't be caught dead shopping on the Bowery."

"You reckon? Looks mighty rich to me here, leech. Rich as three foot up a bull's arse"

The colonel removed his hat and wiped his forehead with a silk handkerchief. "I believe we had better move along before I spend all my drinking money," he said. "You think a man can find himself a drink of something stronger than cider where we're a-going?"

"With his eyes closed."

"Well then right face, forward march! Lead on, old hook."

They followed Bayard Street, then turned down Orange toward the Five Points. The rickety old frame houses that lined both sides of Orange Street, their once-white but now sooty-gray paint blistered and peeling, reminded the colonel of an old country village gone to seed. Will nodded, though he had never before seen such a village in any of his travels. Certainly not one where half the cellars on the block were thrown open and packed with the dregs of what seemed like every nation on earth stomping to the cacophony of untrained fiddlers and drinking themselves blind on whatever kill-devil the proprietors were vending without a license.

Half-way down the block, Will and the colonel had to step into the street to avoid a group of dangerous looking young plug-uglies just past school age passing a jug around. They were lounging in the middle of the sidewalk on several planks of rotten porch-wood. They were playing some kind of game with a barlow knife.

"I believe I'd sooner risk myself in an Indian fight than venture among these creatures after night," the colonel said. "In my country, when you meet an Irishman you find a first-rate gentleman, but these here are too mean to swab hell's kitchen. Come to think of it, it *smells* like hell's kitchen, don't it?"

Will looked up at the cloud of gray smoke that was wafting toward them. It was coming from a large bonfire in the middle of the intersection of Orange, Cross and Anthony streets: the heart of Five Points. On the Anthony side, two gray-haired women of indeterminate age in coarse rumpled dresses were tossing last year's straw from their old mattresses into it, and on the Cross side, a crowd of several dozen boys from under ten to barely under twenty were roasting potatoes on sticks. Across the street from them, on the sidewalk in front of a ramshackle grocery, sat a disheveled young couple on a torn mattress. They were guarding their possessions, most likely all they had in the world: two large, padlocked chests, a table and three unmatched chairs. The man held a sign that read:

The Lord Will Provide.

"Poor devils," said the colonel. "If they'd ask me, by God, I'd tell them what to do. I'd have them move to a bran-fire new country where every skin hangs by its own tail."

"I wouldn't waste my breath," said Will. "They're not going anywhere."

The colonel stooped and picked something up; it turned out to be a tiny pink wooden arm about six inches long from a child's plaything. He frowned and slung it over the crowd and into the fire.

"I reckon I forgot," he said. "Poor folks around here stay put."

"The poor Irish do," Will said.

Even when it's killing them, he thought. Two years ago, during the cholera summer, when nearly everyone—and not just the wealthy—deserted the city, it was only the destitute Irish of the Five Points who remained. One work-day noon in August, Will looked down Broadway and saw not one soul from Canal Street all the way to Fulton, but here at Five Points you would still see clusters of wretched humanity milling around in the filthy streets. And Will administered to as many patients here that summer as he did at New-York Hospital, many of them small children and their streetwalking mothers.

"Right there," Will said. "It was right there by the side of that little park. Three corporation wagons were lined up in a row there with their end-gates down. And the workmen were stacking white pine coffins as high as the lid would permit—sometimes two or three from the same house. Funny, but I was ten times more struck by those stacked coffins than I was by a whole hospital of patients. I don't know how I managed to hold up."

"But you done stood up to the lick-log, fodder or no fodder, didn't you?"

Will shrugged. "I *had* to—somebody did." He looked down at the sidewalk. He felt uncomfortably self-righteous. "Well, I suppose it was more like I already had suffered through too many moving days by then to pick up and leave."

"I reckon it was more than that."

"I don't know, sir. And I really did have my rent to pay."

The colonel pointed to the poor couple on the mattress. "You didn't get aught from the likes of them."

"I wasn't thinking about my rent then."

"You just said you was."

"Not while I was caring for my patients I wasn't. No more than a soldier will think of his pay while he is defending his country."

The colonel chuckled. "You ain't never been to war, leech, have you?"

Will shook his head.

"I didn't think so, but I'll tell you one thing I know about you now that I didn't five minutes ago. You got you a heart hid there under your shirt after all. And here I've been a-thinking all along you was just another blue-blood physicker with nothing but your bank account in your sights."

"My blood hasn't been blue for years." Will said. He knew his face was as red as a fireman's shirt, though.

"I was referring to your patients' blood, son."

"It's not so blue either. Not enough of it anyway to put me on the road to solvency."

"Aye, if there really and truly is such a thing," the colonel said with a trace of a smile. "As for me, by God if I ever in all my life done tread upon one. Tell me something, leech. What you reckon if that blaze there took off and burned down the whole plague-gone neighborhood?"

"Sir?"

"I mean, you reckon these folks here would be better-off or worse-off?"

"A leaky roof is better than no roof at all."

The colonel tugged at the lapels of his frock coat. "Maybe for you it is," he said. "As for me, I'd live in a damn tree in the middle of the deep woods before I would crowd myself up into one of these here, what you call them?"

"Tenements."

"Aye, tenements." The colonel stepped into the street and took about a dozen steps toward the bonfire. Then he stopped and turned around. "One thing I will say," he shouted back to Will. "If all this really did burn down, think how many barbecued bed bugs and fleas would go straight up to bug heaven in smoke."

Will sat down on a dirty old, discarded locker box, the word *Grandpater* scrawled on the lid. As for Colonel Crockett, he was soon with the children, working them as if they were bona fide voters who might help elect him president. He produced a penny from a half-naked little boy's ear, held it in his hand and made a fist around it. Then he passed his other hand over it, and it was gone, only to reappear a moment later in his mouth. He wiped it with his handkerchief and gave it the boy.

"I think we had better high tail on out of here before I spend what little I have on these tatterdemalions," he said after he had given away a dozen more.

"You won't need much. The place I have in mind will sell you a gallon of whiskey for twenty-five cents."

"I wasn't thinking so much about the whiskey. I was thinking more about hunting up some female company of the opposite gender. Lessen you know a better remedy for the horn colic, Doctor."

"Sometimes the old remedies work best," replied Will. "And you can rest assured that they, too, are priced to fit your pocketbook."

The colonel cut off the tip of a short crooked segar with a penknife and lit what was left with a lucifer. "I'll tell you what," he said. "My pocketbook ain't never accommodated more needful than'll feed a company of bed bugs for a week—and you can bank on that."

IT WAS THREE STORIES HIGH AND PITCHED A LITTLE SIDEWAYS. It was called the *Finish*, although no sign bearing that or any other name hung over its door. It looked less like a place of business than somebody's decrepit old home place, somebody who had long since lost the wherewithal to keep it up.

Or, rather, the *inclination* to keep it up, thought Will, now upstairs in the parlor. Aye, for on a good evening more money changed hands here than Will brought home all week. The upstairs parlor was large and drafty and was partitioned off from the rest of the second-floor space by coarse jute curtains. The half-dozen young women stationed there like so many nurses made it feel like an outlandish hospital ward. Queer, Will thought, but they looked more like patients in their flimsy white chemises. Two of them, both blonde, one with hair so thin you could see a red blemish on her scalp the size of a silver dollar, were conversing with a fidgety young fellow in his late teens.

But that little redhead, Will thought. The one in the corner by the samovar. She had an air of refinement to her; and despite the likelihood that it was just the book she was reading, it touched him. She was the only girl in street clothes. She wore a stylish carriage dress with huge leg-of-mutton sleeves, and when she crossed her legs you could see a calf-full of purple and yellow striped stocking. She turned out to be the niece of the proprietress—and not on the menu.

Colonel Crockett ended up with the proprietress herself, plump and closer to fifty than to forty. She confided to him that she had a weakness for public figures, many of whom she professed to be well acquainted with.

"If I were unscrupulous enough to mention their names," she said, "'twould not be the first you have heard them."

She took the colonel to her private chamber on the third floor. That was over an hour ago. Since then, Will had sipped more wine—astonishingly an 1825 Marcobrunner—than he had intended to as he stole glances at the red-headed niece. It struck him that a fully clothed female form should attract him more than a half-naked one.

Too many cadavers in medical school, he thought.

And then:

Well, she does look a little like Ivy.

Not that he actually missed Ivy. Good heavens, anything but! 'Twas in fact less than a week after she ran off to London with Jamey French that he apprehended how fortunate he was to be rid of her. And his uneasy stomach knew it before that, for he was able to eat three platefuls of stewed oysters at the Indian Queen Hotel the morning after he had discovered she was gone.

The proprietor's niece closed her book and straightened a striped stocking. Will closed his eyes and tried to think of something else.

Or, rather, *somebody* else, his wife being a far more socially acceptable subject for his daydreams. But all he could think about was how stupid he had been to confess to her about his entanglements with Ivy. After all, it wasn't Ivy whom Clara Weber had seen him with on the Bowery. Besides, Louisa well-knew that her husband, in his capacity as a physician, sometimes treated prostitutes who walked that same Bowery and lived right here at Five Points. What proof did she have that the young tart whom Clara had spied with him was anything more than one of Will's indigent patients who, perhaps, was just then leading her doctor to her bedridden parent or child?

"I think you *wished* to be caught," Charlie Hoffman told Will on their first night as housemates.

"That, in all due respect my good friend, is preposterous!" Will replied.

"Then you may have been of two minds about this without even apprehending it. To wit: how many times have you complained to me about your wife's belittling of your literary endeavors? Then, in the same breath, you would gush about how refreshing it was to have found someone who looked up to those endeavors—and the rest of you along with them."

"Perhaps, but that certain-someone now looks up higher to Jamey French—all six-foot two-inches of him. Why would I desire someone like Ivy Green who will always have an eye cocked for someone richer and better spoken of than I?"

"You don't. You want someone more like your wife, but who will worship you. And allowing Louisa to cast you away frees you from the pain of having to be deceptive and duplicitous with her as you continue your search for a more suitable replacement."

"My search for *what*?" cried Will. "There is no such search! My sole task is to somehow make Louisa see something better in me and fall in love with me all over again. If such thing is indeed possible."

Charlie thought about that for a moment and then offered another theory:

"Perhaps," he said, "your animal magnetism compelled you to confess for an entirely different reason. Perhaps you secretly wished that your confession might illuminate for her the fact that she had been blinded to aspects of you that were clearly evident to other women. Then she might come to her senses about what a treasure she had in you."

Will scoffed at such mesmer-ish babble. No, he didn't secretly-from-himself wish *anything* in his sleep. Fully awake, however, he clearly apprehended the task that lay before him. This is what he knew:

If his stature had any chance whatsoever of rising in his wife's eyes, 'twould first be necessary for Louisa to observe such rise not through her *own* eyes, but through the eyes of those she respected and admired who would one day soon read his published work, some of whom just happened to be among the brightest literary lights of—

"Can't take your eyes off her, can you?" The colonel pulled a chair up to the table and sat down next to Will. The proprietress breezed past them leaving behind a trail of rose oil. She wore a scarlet shawl that came down to her ankles. She turned once to smile broadly (she was missing an upper tooth not quite out of sight), waved her velvet-clad fingers at them and then took her niece by the arm and headed for the stairs.

"Right handsome woman, ain't she?" the colonel said.

"I hope she showed you a good time."

"She showed me some things I ain't even heard of before. You ever heard of 'brushing with Miriam,' leech?"

Will shook his head.

"I'll tell you what. If you ever wish to get a laugh out of her, just ask her if she would use a feather on you. Then when she says yes she would, ask her how much more it would cost if she uses the whole chicken."

"That's ... very funny, sir."

"But that ain't the one I meant. I was speaking of the young 'un with the stripe-ed legs. What ever would you give for a taste of that, old hook?"

"I'm afraid my taste buds aren't functioning properly today," Will said.

"What is it, she ain't pretty enough for you?"

Will smiled faintly and cast his eyes to the floor.

"By God if I wouldn't eat the corn out of her shit," the colonel went on. "You sure you don't need specs?"

"I can spot a pretty girl from as far off as you can, sir, without them," Will replied. "But I've other things on my mind at the moment. And from what I have already confided to you, I expect you know what they are."

The colonel squinted and raised an eyebrow. "Aye I reckon I do, but I'll tell you what. One thing I'll never comprehend is how come you never put up a fight. If it was me that got throw'd out of my own house, why I'd pick myself up and stomp right back in there and show her who she's a-cutting and shuffling with."

"I'm afraid that's not my manner, sir."

"Then get you another lady friend to occupy your time. That way you won't have the time to go beg at your own front door."

"I already tried that."

"Then try harder."

"I did. I tried *too* hard."

The colonel rubbed his chin. "Well, I reckon such a thing is possible," he said. "One thing I do know, love is like a fart. If you have to force it, shit is what it truly is. But I ain't a-talking about love. I'm a-talking about the likes of what goes on in this fine establishment."

"I can't do that to Louisa anymore," Will said scrunching up his nose in disgust.

"The hell you can't, leech. By God, this is the eighteen thirties! A man's wife expects that sort of thing nowadays after the bloom has done come off the roses. My wife, she don't like to fuck so I always went elsewhere for that. I will say this, though. I never did bring it home and rub her nose in it."

The colonel reached across the table for an empty glass and filled it with the dregs of Will's bottle of wine.

"Now my first wife," he said, "I never ventured no place else but her side of the bed. That was on account of I married her out of pure affection. And things remained that way even after we started having babies."

He took a slow thoughtful sip from his glass. "Tell me something, leech," he then said. "Your first wife, where'd you first meet up with her?"

"I met my first—and so far, *only*—wife in Philadelphia, sir," Will replied. "I was attending medical school, and she was attending the ladies academy there."

"So you went up north and got you a Yankee gal. Nothing wrong with that, son."

"No sir, a Southern belle is what I landed despite the geographic improbability. Louisa grew up on a plantation in the Georgia sea islands."

"Too rich for my blood," the colonel said.

Will chuckled. "For mine, too," he said. "Only, I didn't know that at the time. My father was the richest man in the county, so I never worried about my finances back then."

"You better believe I wouldn't neither."

"So I started throwing money at her—as if she needed it! 'Twas, I suppose, because I wanted her to accept me as her social equal. Even after the wedding I kept spending it recklessly. More so, really. On lavish parties and four-month sojourns throughout the South until it was all gone."

"Seems like the most rich pays the least mind to their bank accounts."

"That was true enough for us, sir. When my father died, he left his fortune to eight heirs; and believe me, none of us ever paid the scantest attention to how the others were spending their shares. I know I didn't."

The colonel folded his arms and cocked his head part-way down to his right shoulder. "I never had that problem," he said. "And Polly, she never did neither. Polly, now she was my first wife, the one I already done mentioned."

He leaned his head back, still cocked to the right. "I wish you could've seen her, leech," he went on wistfully. "Dark brown hair all done up in ringlets, and rosy red cheeks like mine, only they looked like they was round little apples in them." He puffed his out and pushed up on them with his fingertips.

"You want to know how I first met her?" he went on. "They was having this great reaping and flax pulling not far from my father's house, I'd say fifteen odd miles distant. I was nineteen-year-old at the time and sore as a beat-up old chanticleer fighting cock over this sorry little wench that done showed me the gate."

"Your former love interest?"

"Aye, and though I never did know it at the time, that was the very best thing she ever could've done for me, chucking me off like that. By the Eternal if it wasn't."

There was a knock on the half-opened second-floor door; in stepped a red shirted 'Bowery b'hoy,' his trousers stuffed in his boots. He waved at one of the girls who then trotted over to him in her bare feet, took him by the arm and led him to one of the improvised bed chambers on the other side of the curtains.

"It was her mama that introduced us, Polly and myself," the colonel went on again. "She walked right up to me and said, 'Lad, I have a real sweetheart for you.' Pretty soon she was calling me her son-in-law—I mean, on that very same night she was calling me that!

"Anyways, we got married in August of the following year, eighteen aught-six, Polly and me did, three days short of my twentieth birthday. It near didn't happen, though. Her mama done got dead set against me on account of she had found her another suitor a far sight further from the poorhouse than I was at the time. But you reckon that put a stop to old Davy?

"Hellfire no!" the colonel answered himself. "So I hunted me up a justice of the peace and come by the house with an extra horse for my little girl, her mama be damned."

He smiled and rubbed his mouth with the back of his hand. "You should have seen the look on that mean old woman's face when I come by to get her daughter. She looked at me savage as a meat axe. But by God if her husband didn't bridle her tongue right then and there and smooth things over for me. And we got married in that very house on that self-same day."

Will thought of his own early tangles with his in-laws. "It was the opposite with me," he said. "Louisa's mother was all for it, but her uncle—"

"I'll tell you what," the colonel cut back in, refusing to abandon the love of his life for a look at Will's. "She was a true beauty and I done my beatenest by her—Lord knows I tried to —but my beatenest wasn't much at all in them days. She give me two sons and a daughter, but me, I never did give her nothing but a heap of foolish talk and an early grave. She wasn't but twenty-seven the day she died, leech. Twenty-seven-year-old— the same age our boy Johnny is this very year."

He gulped the rest of his wine and wiped his mouth on his sleeve. "It was two years after I left the army that the fever done took her. There was nothing no doctor could do to save her. She just lay there all in a sweat a-looking up at me like she wished I might shoot her with my rifle-gun."

He slumped a little in his chair and fingered the blood-stone fob dangling from his watch chain. "I couldn't even afford a proper tombstone. Sometimes I wonder if her grave's still got a marker. I'll tell you what, though. I could find my way there on a moonless night blindfolded. Only, I've never been able to bring myself to visit it. Not ary a-once."

"She's in your heart, sir, not in the ground."

"I'd like to think she's in a far better place than my heart," the colonel said looking down at his feet. "Now don't get me wrong, son. I ain't much of a church goer, so I'll have to say that such things is above my knowledge. I can only hope and pray."

"What man on this earth can do more?"

Crockett shifted a few degrees more in his chair. "You know it's the children that makes things different," he finally said, his eyes still on the floor.

"You see what I'm a-saying?" he said an instant later, his eyes suddenly peering straight into Will's. "She done left me with the children she done brought into this world."

Will tried to think of something appropriate to say, something fittingly uplifting. "Maybe it's that your wife ... it's that Polly never really left you," he finally said. "She lives on in your children."

The colonel folded his arms and frowned. "That's not what I meant at all, son," he said. "No, she done left me, all right. Left me high and dry with my hands full, what with those three small children of ours—and one of them, mind you, was still a mere infant. So I made up my mind right then and there that I had better go out and find me another wife. And I didn't give a hoot in hell if old cupid didn't shoot me up with a quiver-full of his arrows this time. Or how pretty she was. I'll tell you what, old Betsy was never much to look at—even then she was big enough to eat hay—but like I said, love was not my prime objective."

"It wasn't, sir?" said Will. "Sounds like it was to me."

"My children needed a mother was all it was."

"Your children needed love, sir. A mother's love."

The colonel smiled and softly said:

"You ain't as dumb as you let on to be."

A servant came by and filled the colonel's glass with some kind of spirits. Will put his hand over his half-filled glass and declined more wine.

"She was a widow-woman a few years younger than me," Crockett began after recovering from too generous an initial gulp. "Her husband was a friend of a friend, and he was killed in the Creek War. He left her with two small children—one boy and one girl—about the same age as John and Billy, so really and truly we was in the same boat. We done the ceremony right there in her own home and—I must tell you this, leech:

"There we all was, a-setting there waiting for the bride to enter, and what do we hear but this grunting sound a-coming from the wide-open door. And who should march in but a big old sow. I won't tell you what I thought at the time, but all I could think of saying was—and this was straight to the hog:

"'Old hook, from now on *I'll* do the grunting around here.'"

He drew two crooked segars from his coat pocket and lit them both with a candle.

"I made myself a vow that night," he said handing one of the segars to Will. "I swore I would do better by my new wife than I ever done by my first. And I believe I done just that, after a fashion. Only, the way things turned out, she done me even better. Understand, I would never be the man I am today if it wasn't for her—and that's the gospel truth. And I could name you a dozen others that can say the same identical thing about their own wives, some of them larger men than I'll ever be in my lifetime."

A dozen and one, Will thought, for he would be in the poorhouse by now if it hadn't been for Louisa and her generous brother. And his children would be begging on the street.

"They're made of stronger stuff than we, the ladies are," he replied to the colonel.

"Aye, they are—and if you don't believe it, consider what it must be like to shit a watermelon." Crockett drew thoughtfully on his segar. "And talk about patience, I don't know how she ever put up with me and my thick skull. I mean when Betsy and I first met, I could barely write my own name. And yet one short year later I was made a legal magistrate."

"You must have been a quick study." Will said putting out his own smelly segar; he rarely smoked anything but an occasional pipe-full of black Cavendish.

"I was a slow study. It took me longer to read through but a handful of depositions that first year than it would take to plow a forty-acre field full of roots and rocks—and I had to get my constable to issue my warrants. But old Betsy, she stayed up nights reciting to me these verses she done composed in her head—she can barely write herself—and making me copy them down till they got to where they didn't look so much like our little son scrawled them. But more than that, she put ambition into my blood, said I could do whatever I set out to do. Well, she was sure enough right about that. It wasn't long before I was writing those warrants with my own hand. You want a roll?"

"Sir?"

"A roll. It's like a biscuit, only it's got sugar all over it. The lady give me three of them. I got them right here in my pocket. Go ahead, have one."

Will said he wasn't hungry, then changed his mind and took one. "Maybe it will soak up the wine," he said. "It's gone straight to my head."

"Mine, too—I mean this here has," Crockett added, holding up his glass of mystery spirits. "And I had me a few horns of something even stronger upstairs. What was we speaking about?"

"Your warrants, sir. The ones you wrote with your own hand."

"Aye, the warrants. That was about the time I begun to take my rise. I got myself elected colonel of the militia and town commissioner, too, but you reckon that was enough for old Elizabeth Patton Crockett? One cold winter's morning she wakes up with a notion that I should canvass for the legislature and rub shoulders with the governor. Well, you can imagine my uneasiness at such a prospect, leech. I had packed my belongings and moved numerous times since I reached my majority, but each hollow I done crept out of so far, it was just to creep into some other'n. She said I had the grit to do it, though. *'You sure you're right?'* I asked her. *'I know I am,'* she done answered me. *'So you just go on ahead.'* So that's what I done. And right there is where my motto first come from."

The colonel took a sip of his spirits, a more measured one this time. "So I set out electioneering," he went on, "and by God if I didn't win. That was August of 1821. I turned thirty-five-year-old that very month."

"Quite a remarkable gift for the occasion," Will said.

"Aye, leech—and a curious one, too. Up until then, I had attributed my rise to my wife's educating me, but from that canvass forward I come to suspect that 'twas more to do with me displaying my ignorance."

"Your *ignorance*, sir?

"My making a spectacle of it. By playing the agreeable jackass. I've said it before, and I'll say it again: the people likes to be entertained."

"The people knows ... the people *know* you are not ignorant, Colonel. Those who voted for you know that."

The colonel twisted a loose thread from his waistcoat around his forefinger.

"Some of them knows I'm not—I'll grant you that," he said at length. "And maybe I really do sell myself too short. But I ain't about to take credit for what I never could've done on my own. I'll tell you what, if I can make myself understood to an educated man like yourself without my mouth feeling like it's chock full of dry mush, it's all my wife's doing, not my own.

"And I'll tell you another thing, old hook: my children owes her the selfsame thing. Johnny, now he's my eldest and if he had to rely on his old father raising him alone, why he'd like as not be nothing more today than a poor dirt farmer. Now, don't get me wrong. I don't have a thing against such folks—hell, I ain't much more than a dirt farmer myself. But I'll have you know my boy John is Clerk of the Circuit Court today and teaching school at the academy, and that wouldn't have happened in a hundred years if he didn't have a step-mama with a head on her shoulders and a heart as big as the state of Tennessee."

"And if he didn't have a father in the United States Congress, sir, to admire and model himself after."

The colonel dismissed that with a broad sweep of his right arm that just missed Will's wine glass.

"You don't think you had anything to do with it?" Will asked him and moved the glass out of range.

"Not enough to make a differ, son—lessen you're a-talking about what we call 'horse sense' down home."

"It's a consideration," Will said. "And it's a gift that I'm afraid is beyond my power to pass on to my own children. Ask my wife. She'll tell you. And I must admit that she's right. I wish I had half the common sense that she has."

The colonel squinted and drew on his segar. "Then crawl on back to her," he said. "Who knows, maybe a lick of that horse sense will rub off on you."

Will laughed. "Getting myself to crawl back is not the problem. The problem, sir, is getting her to invite me back in."

"I know that only too well," the colonel replied as he balanced his segar on the edge of the table. Then he downed the contents of his glass in two or three gulps.

"Listen here," he finally said after recovering from the hundred proof kick. "My mind is to tell you something I ain't never told a soul other than my best of friends. If it wasn't for this here (he brandished his now-empty glass) you would never be a-hearing this neither."

"You don't have to tell me anything that you would rather leave unsaid."

The colonel smiled a little. "Much obliged for enlightening me on that particular rule," he said. "But do you know what I've been informing folks these past several years about Betsy and myself? I've been a-telling them it was *me* that cut out on *her* on account of she got so large that our bedstead could no longer accommodate the both of us, and that it would snow in August before I'd go ahead and sleep on the floor.

"But that ain't true, son. You may not believe this, but it was the other way around "*She* throw'd *me* out is what done happened." The colonel raised his right hand. "God as my witness, she did."

Will did not find that difficult to believe at all.

Crockett lowered his voice. "Now, exactly what come between us is nobody's business but mine and hers, but I will say it's a far sight worse than what's come between you and your'n. I mean, it's nothing to do with what I might've done with some other woman. It's more to do with what I done with, God help me ... with *critters*.".

Will found himself speechless.

The colonel laughed and slapped Will on the back. "No, I'm just a-fooling with you," he said, "and you should see the look on your face! It ain't true, though. I never committed an unnatural act with no critter in my life excepting maybe one time when I was a small child. But critters did figure into why my wife left me. Not like I made you think, though. She done got jealous on account of all the time I was spending with my dogs is what she done. I mean, in the deep woods a-hunting after bear and she left behind to take care of the children and the farm and all—and this after I spent so much time away from her in Washington taking care of the people's business. And speaking of Washington, she suspected I had spent more time there lifting a glass and tossing the dice than doing what I was being paid for—but she was wrong.

"Well ... not entirely," the colonel added sheepishly. "I must admit that once I had to borrow money from a friend to pay for my journey back to Tennessee after I lost most of my congressional pay at the faro tables. Anyways, that was when we broke up housekeeping. It's been, I'd say, three year since then. I sold all my property right about then to attempt to get myself out of debt—you know, from that election I lost time before last. I had to live somewheres though, so I leased a patch of woods, built me a cabin there along with a barn and a smokehouse, and cleared off some fields for crops as my part of the bargain.

"As for Old Betsy, she took our little girls and moved about forty mile south and settled in with some kin she's got down there. And then she made her old daddy from Carolina come join them—which was smart, on account of he was still a wealthy man. So he come up and bought him some more land down there in Gibson County—and just in the nick of time because he died about a year later."

"What about your children?" Will asked. "Do you get to see much of them?"

"Not at all when I'm in the Congress—you know that."

"Yes of course I do, sir. I meant—"

"You meant during the recess. I know you did—just fooling with you again, son. But the children, no I don't see them anywheres near as often as I should like to. That's all I hate about our coming apart, Betsy and myself. I mean, me not being able to live under the same roof as our three little girls. I'll tell you what, it really tortures me inside and out. But then you're getting a taste of that sort of thing yourself now, too, I reckon."

"Indeed I am, sir," Will replied.

"And if the likes of that don't aggravate your soul, nothing will. How long's it been—what, about a month?"

"About—but it seems more like a year."

The colonel placed his hands on his hips and puffed out his chest. "Well, what do you aim to do about it?" he asked menacingly.

Will shrugged. "If this had happened to one of my characters —you know in my writings— I'm sure I would come up with something. But it's not so easy in real life."

"Then make like you really are one of your made-up charac-ters. Or somebody else's like that sorry friend of yours, Paulding. Then draw you up a battle plan."

Will laughed. "Maybe I should take some laudanum and dream up a war council. I wonder what pearls of wisdom Colonel Nimrod Wildfire might offer me."

"Go west, I reckon."

"Seriously though, I have reason to believe that my own char-acters may at length make a difference in this, as you say '*battle*'. The better they do, perhaps the better I will do."

"So you aim to write you some happy endings?"

"They're already happy enough," Will replied, "but that's not what I'm talking about. What I mean is that the better my writ-ings are received by those whose opinions are well-respected in the literary world, the better I shall be respected by the general reading public."

"I thought it was your wife we was talking about."

"My wife is as well-read as any woman in this—well, perhaps not so much in New-York City—but certainly in any city south of here. And she values the opinions of those whom she reads in well-respected journals."

"What, like your sorry friend Paulding?"

Will opened his mouth, but nothing came out.

"In all due respect," he finally said, "I do wish you would get over that, sir. Kirke meant no harm. Upon my word he didn't."

"Who says I ain't over it?" the colonel replied. "I can get over things just like the next man can. And I didn't mean him no harm. Something about him just didn't set right with me and I let my demons get the best of me, that's all. But you was saying what about your wife?"

"I was saying that the higher my reputation rises in the literary world, the greater the possibility that Louisa will begin to look at me through different eyes. The eyes, that is, of people whom she respects."

"So she might come to respect you more so than you figure she does now."

"Something like that."

The colonel closed his eyes in thought. Or in inebriation— probably the latter, Will surmised.

"So it's a mite more than your prowling around that's got her back up," Crockett finally said.

"No sir, that was precisely it."

"Sounds more like the last straw to me."

"The last straw?"

"Aye, but it seems like 'twas more all the other straws that's like to break the back of that wife of yours. And the longer you wander around in the deep woods, the sooner that's a-gonna happen."

"Sir?"

"I mean you expecting to scribble your way to fame and fortune—that's *your* deep woods, leech. And it's a-doing you no more good than bear hunting is for me lately. Mark you my words: it's a-gonna tear up your family just like it's done mine."

"Not necessarily, sir," said Will. "My reputation, once established, should be expected to—"

"Your reputation? How many meals do you expect such a thing to provide your family with? And don't you forget that I done wrote a book, too—and I already *have* the reputation, but I'd be a fool to risk all I hold dear on more such endeavors."

Agreed, thought Will.

"You're a much smarter man than I am," Crockett went on, "so you know as much as I do that it's selling books, not writing them, that provides you with the money. And you can no more expect to make your fortune doing that than I can at the faro table.

"I'll tell you what: puffing yourself up like a woodcock on the prowl for a hen ain't all it's cracked up to be. I ain't saying it won't help you float your way up to some special heaven for famous folks when your time comes, but it sure-enough won't win you back your wife on this earth. Not in a coon's age. You want to know why it won't—I'll tell you why not. Because women don't care about being Mrs. *Big High and Mighty Know it all Done it all*. Least-ways not after they start having babies. You think my wife fashioned me into the man I am today for her sake? I mean, so she might be *Mrs. Congressman Crockett the Rich Man's Security and the Poor Man's Friend* and render everyone she meets awestruck in her presence?

"Not hardly, leech. She done it because she figured the higher I might take my rise, the better a life her children might have as a direct consequence. But let me tell something else: None of that counts for nothing once she believes you ain't personally looking out for those young-uns half as hard as *she* is. No sir, behavior like that will turn her against you quicker and nastier than I ever turned on Andy Jackson.

"I already done told you," the colonel went on, "that the only reason I agreed to permit those Young Whigs to throw my hat into the ring for the presidency is so I might obtain more power to keep my poor constituents from losing their homes. I'm a-talking about those selfsame homes where they are raising their children just like I done my best to raise mine. But like I said, my wife don't think that's what I'm a-doing for *her* children these days. And it don't matter how many hundreds or thousands of families I may help rise from poverty. No sir, not if she thinks I ain't so much as lifted a finger for my own flesh and blood.

"Anyways, I told you that to tell you this. You want to keep writing books? Fine, but you ought to be able to build up your doctoring practice in greener pastures than this sorry part of town. I mean, so when you do show up at your wife's door you wont have to come empty handed. But above all—and I'll say this ten more times if I have to—you must first show her how much you care about your children."

"She knows how important they are to me."

"That ain't near enough—not by a long shot."

Will thought about that for a moment. "What, sufficient words but insufficient deeds on my part—is that what you are suggesting, sir?"

The colonel held up his right hand. "No, that's not what I'm saying at all. Far be it for the likes of me to judge another man that's in the same sorry mess as myself."

He stood up and placed his left hand on Will's shoulder. "Here's what I *am* a-saying, son" he went on emphasizing each word with his right forefinger. "And I want you pay close attention. What I'm saying is that if you wish for your wife to truly want to take you back—and I mean with all of her heart—you must first convince her not so much how important your children are to *you*—for God's sake she already knows that—and besides, what does she care about your feelings at this moment? No, you must convince her how important *you* are to *them*. I mean, how their lives shall be improved one hundred-fold with you around."

The colonel placed his right hand on Will's other shoulder

"And since you already done brought up the subject of words and deeds," he went on, "I suggest you use both. Words is seldom enough. Me, I've been a-spewing out perhaps more than my fair share lately. Some of these days, though, folks will sure-enough come to expect a considerable portion of something else out of me."

WHEN COLONEL CROCKETT AND WILL RETURNED TO THE hotel later that afternoon, they were both ready to, as the colonel put it, *'hit the hay'* until suppertime. They hadn't so much as taken off their hats, though, when the agitated hotel manager accosted them and informed the colonel that he was scheduled to speak at the Bowery Theater in less than two hours.

"You must have the wrong Crockett," said the colonel.

"I think not," the hotel manager said and presented him with a handbill that advertised the event.

"I never consented to such a thing," the colonel said and tore it up. "Now if you gentlemen will excuse me, I'm retiring to my bedchamber."

The hotel manager, too timid to try to stop him, went next door to Mayor Hone's house for help. The former first-citizen of the city apparently had better things to do, but he sent two of his clerks. Whom the colonel grabbed by their coat collars and shoved out of his room. It took Mr. Hone himself to convince him to change his mind about delivering the speech, and it took him over a half-hour.

Better if he had been less persuasive, thought Will now. He was backstage at the Bowery Theater watching Colonel Crockett stagger toward the podium. The colonel chose not to stand behind it, though. Rather, he stood off to one side of it, his left elbow leaning against it, his right hand on his hip and his right elbow thrust out like a chicken wing.

"*My name is David Crockett,*" he began in a smug, slurry tone of voice, "*and I'm here to tell you folks a thing or two for your own good—that is, if you care to sit and listen to a rustic like me make like he knows what he's a-talking about.*"

He went on to dispense his medicine—and without the aid of his usual palliatives: the backwoods jokes and Western anecdotes for which he is so famous. He mentioned neither bear nor dog nor coon. However, he lambasted Jackson and Van Buren so viciously that Will would hardly have been stunned by the sight of foam oozing out of the corner of his mouth—as if he had just emerged rabid from his own kennel!

The audience for the most part listened in a whispering, mumbling but otherwise near-silence; clearly, they had come to be entertained, not preached to. He even drew some jeers from the galleries when he lit into Van Buren, for despite the fact that the Young Whigs had done a credible job of turning out the party faithful, there had been plenty of seats left for curious Democrats to fill. And the Tammany henchmen had no compunction about filling them with spirited Irish street fighters to remind the colonel at the top of their lungs that he was treading on the vice-president's home turf.

After the first few jeers, the colonel retreated to behind the podium and turned some of his invective toward himself.

"*I'd sooner be called a card-cheat than a politician—Whig OR Democrat,*" he cried out in his Western twang. "*But by God I reckon that's what I am, a vote-starved ballot-eater with a hand full of gimme and a mouth full of much obliged—and don't think I don't lose sleep over that.*

"*But with all due respect to you OK fellows up there a-snarling at me, you've got me dead wrong. Truth is, I care about your plight a far sight more than the man you done sworn allegiance to does, not to mention that thing which yet resides in the White House who has hand-picked him to be his successor.*

"And it's a sorry viscous lie, gentleman, that my legs is spread from the Hudson River to the Potomac. Because if they was, not only would my jokes all be gospel truth—which is impossible because everyone knows that joking means making stuff up—but my heart-felt sentiments about the hard-working farmers and mechanics of this great nation of ours would all be lie-tales.

"Which of course they are not.

"But if such a thing was possible, and they truly WAS made-up for my own selfish reasons, why then I wish I may be shot. And any man that suggests such a thing to my face will wish he may be shot too—and mighty quick—after I get through administering the truth into him. Because even though folks that knows me will tell you I ain't the arse-hole you apprehend me to be, when pushed I can be the brown around it."

There were few interruptions from the galleries after that, only that same uncomfortable near silence that one would hardly expect from a Crockett audience. His speech lasted no more than perhaps ten minutes, after which he and Will took a hackney coach back to the hotel. The colonel was determined to get to bed early, for he was expected to be in Jersey City for a shooting match sometime before noon the next day. Then it was on to Boston via steamboat.

Will accompanied the colonel upstairs to his room to retrieve his traveling bag. As he latched it, he thanked Crockett for providing him with an up-front view of current American political affairs.

"One additional favor, please," he continued after the colonel released him from his bear hug. "Would you be kind enough, sir, to remind Judge Clayton to return my sketches in care of the hotel manager when you return from Boston?"

"Your sketches?"

"My notes for your journal of the tour. And I do hope you have the opportunity to read them yourself. I shudder at the thought of you putting your name to something I have written sight-unseen!"

"I trust you, leech. As much as if you was close kin I do. And I still wish you'd reconsider and tag along with us."

"I wish I could," Will said, "but I am expected at the hospital tomorrow morning. They are considerably short-handed these days."

"*Se la vie*," said the colonel.

"*Bon voyage,*" Will replied in kind.

Then, as he turned to walk out the door, he smiled to himself at the far-Western pronunciation of a phrase he hardly expected to be part of the colonel's vocabulary.

"Now don't you forget those things I done told you," Crockett shouted after him.

THAT WAS TWELVE HOURS AGO. ACCORDING TO WILL'S WATCH it was nearly 8:00 a.m., which meant that Colonel Crockett was, in all likelihood, well on his way to Jersey City by now. As for Will, he was back at his temporary lodgings on Charlie Hoffman's couch. He got up, went to the kitchen and poured some still-warm water from the fireplace kettle into a basin that Charlie had provided for him there and cleaned up.

"I won't forget a word," he said aloud—a belated response to Crockett's parting entreaty of last night. That entreaty, Will was certain, referred to the marital advice the colonel had imparted to him yesterday at the whorehouse. And it was sound advice, if not entirely unfamiliar. Indeed, much of it had occurred independently to Will during long sleepless nights in this very abode.

No matter.

Aye, for even if you pride yourself in the power of your own independent reasoning, 'tis reassuring to hear corroborating sentiments from someone you respect.

Someone I respect? *Davy Crockett?*

As much as that thought startled him, Will had to admit he was changing his tune about the Bear Hunter now that he had seen a glimmer of the soul behind the comical—and sometimes crude and ornery—mask. Never before would he have credited Crockett with the possession of such an insightful mind. Not before he spent so much time with him these last few days.

Will unlatched his traveling bag and placed its contents on the couch. All, that is, except what was hidden beneath the false bottom.

Which he then unsnapped. Then he removed from underneath it the folder that held the satirical Crockett piece he had written for Kirke Paulding.

"Thirty pieces of silver," he said to himself. *"I shall not go through with this."*

And it didn't matter that Crockett was perhaps the least Christ-like person he knew. No, that wasn't going to make Will feel any less like Judas. Not if he didn't make immediate amends. Which meant that right now he was going to have to place those papers where they belonged:

In Charlie Hoffman's fireplace.

Will sat back down on the old familiar couch. He opened the folder for one last look at his diabolical handiwork before reducing it to ashes. But what he now held in his hands turned out *not* to be the satirical piece he had intended to burn. Rather, it was several pages of notes he had made about Colonel Crockett's tour. Notes that he thought he had given to Judge Clayton yesterday afternoon.

"Oh my God," he said aloud. *"Oh my dear, dear God."*

1835

Chapter Fifteen

WASHINGTON CITY

"Listen to this, gentlemen," said "Black Tom" Corwin to his friends and fellow members of Congress: "Long Tom" Chilton and "Blustering Ben" Hardin. He was sitting across the breakfast table from them at Brown's Indian Queen Hotel.

"I rested my rifle on my wife's back and fired at one of the panthers. It jumped up ten feet and fell down dead."

They all turned to the fourth congressman—"Colonel Davy" himself—who was sitting next to Corwin. He responded to them with a wide closed-lip mock smile.

"Wait, there's more," Corwin said adjusting the little booklet he held in both hands into better focus:

"My wife then gave the other panther a cut over the back with her axe, which broke his backbone and disabled him, so we made out to dispatch him. The third panther my wife then shot in the trap which he had got clamped in. We drug them home one at a time and skinned them. The largest weighed over four hundred pounds."

"Your wife did all that," Ben Hardin asked Crockett.

Crockett smiled, a genuine one this time. "My current wife I always thought might could do so if she took a notion to. But that's my first one they's a-talking about, and she wouldn't harm a fly."

Hardin opened his mouth in mock astonishment. "You mean you ... you actually *made all this up?*"

"Somebody sure enough did," Crockett said, "but it sure beats me who. Am I right or what, Chilton?"

"Oh, he's right alright," Chilton said with a yawn. "When we stepped into Mr. Thompson's bookstore to see how his *Memoirs* were selling, no one was more surprised than David here to find a foot-high stack of these *Davy Crockett Almanacs,* a dandified gentleman of color in a top hat on the cover with a fish hooked on one of his fingers!"

"I'll bet it struck you that folks might suppose that was you," Corwin said to Crockett.

"It did," Crockett replied, "but then I figured it would like as not make them even more curious about me and wish to see me in person. Then after they done heard me speechify, not only would their curiosity be satisfied, but at the same time they would walk away a far sight better informed about the evils of Jacksonism."

"And the virtues of making you president," said Hardin.

"You know I done put down that horse."

Thank God for small favors, Chilton thought, his sleepy head propped up in his cupped hands.

And thank God for Hugh Lawson White. With a well-respected United States Senator in the saddle, thought he, the Whigs now had a viable compromise candidate from the West should next year's presidential election be thrown into the House.

Aye, instead of an un-predictable, un-reliable and un-restrainable teller of tall tales.

Not that anyone with an ounce of sense had forecast a President Crockett in the near or even near-distant future. No one except David, whom Chilton thought only sometimes made it into that category. And David, oddly, didn't seem to mind being dropped by the wayside.

"More men, women and children knows my name than they do any other member of Congress," David had said as he and Chilton walked here from their boarding house—or rather, from Crockett's old boarding house—across the avenue for breakfast this morning. "I figure that's satisfying enough for a fellow with but six months of schooling, don't you think?"

"I wouldn't know," Chilton had replied, "seeing as I have never experienced such renown. But I *have* been wondering lately how one adjusts to being the most famous man in town."

"You'll have to ask *him*," Crockett said pointing up to the sign over the hotel's door which in foot-high letters read: JESSE BROWN. "Now *thar's* the best-known name in town. And the most generous—leastways when it comes to me. Folks here pays three times Mother Ball's rate, but I don't pay a penny more. Reckon he sees me as a first-rate pull for travellers looking to see a two-legged *bar*."

Chilton, his sleepy head still in his hands, his elbows akimbo on Jesse Brown's long table, regarded his friends and fellow congressmen, who were now discussing presidential politics. You'd never take them for the thoughtful public servants they truly were if you saw them later in the evening at the faro parlors down the avenue, some of which were embarrassing close to the Executive Mansion. Not that Chilton ever accompanied them there. While he may have backslid a little in the temperance department and had occasionally allowed Crockett to drag him to the theater, gambling was strictly out of the question for an ordained Baptist minister, even an inactive one such as he.

Inactive? thought Chilton.

Well ... perhaps not for much longer.

If the truth be known, Chilton, had indeed been thinking of taking up the cloth again for some time already. Ever since the last election, in fact, which was a year and a half ago. This is what sealed it:

On the evening of his first day home in Elizabethtown this

past summer, his seven-year-old son George Willie declared to him:

"I wish to preach the Gospel right soon, Pa. Just like you and Grandpop."

"Why ever should the people make *me* president," Crockett loudly intoned, beckoning Chilton back to the here and now, "when they can have Van Buren for not a penny more?" He bit into a biscuit and nodded repeatedly as he chewed.

Chilton looked up again, this time straightening himself up in his seat while Ben Hardin and Tom Corwin looked at each other and chuckled.

"Ain't no laughing matter," Crockett said, his mouth full of biscuit. "I now believe the Magician to be the next fitting man to General Jackson for the presidency, I swear I do. Judge White *pales* in comparison—no joke intended."

"Hell and thunder!" Corwin said. He raised his empty water glass. Jesse Brown, who was hovering close by, filled it about a third of the way up with Kentucky bourbon, then did the same for Crockett—Chilton, too, after he hastily downed the rest of his water. Hardin alone abstained.

"Although few refuse a julep with breakfast where I come from," said he, "I shall make this one exception. I have a few remarks to make this afternoon which unfortunately demand a clear head."

Corwin stood and re-raised his glass. "Gentlemen," he said. "To the Caesar of the East and the Caesar of the West: we who are about to lose our seats salute you!"

"Speak for yourself, you old black Tomcat," Crockett said. "I aim to keep mine and then barter it off for a larger one—and if I don't, I wish I may be shot."

"I wouldn't tempt the fates," Ben Hardin said.

Crockett reached across the white-clothed table for a candle, then lit a segar with it. "The next president, gentlemen, shall come from the Northeast," he intoned, "Kinderhook to be more particular—aye, the little Van himself—and I shall support him. Then I go with all my heart for a Southwest president. And that president, sirs, shall be myself."

Corwin kicked Chilton in the heel. "Intriguing," he said to Crockett. "Only, I wouldn't allow it to leave this room if I were you, sir."

"I don't intend to, sir. I aim to keep the people's eyes and ears shut and contrive them to think I'm a-barking up a different tree. I must make sure they don't forget me for five more year, that's all, and then it's biscuits and gravy for old Davy."

Ben Hardin made a motion with his fork; David glanced over his shoulder and there stood Judge Poindexter, President Pro Tempore of the United States Senate, looking as if he had just smelled something peculiar. Chilton had heard that Vice-President Van Buren was packing a pistol these days while presiding over that body because of threats to his own personal body from none other than Senator Poindexter himself. And now Crockett was endorsing the senator's mortal enemy?

Crockett turned around, half rose, and shook Poindexter's hand. "You fellows have got to quit hanging on my every word like they's the gospel truth," he said to his chums and sat back down. "All seriousness aside, Senator, that was just a burlesque I was inflicting upon these gentlemen here. It reared its ugly head in the *Intellegencer* last month I believe. I reckon you missed it, sir."

"I've always considered you to be a man of ... many talents," Senator Poindexter said. He gave Crockett an abbreviated bow and went back to his table.

"You boys hear that?" Crockett said a little above a whisper when the senator seemed to be out of earshot. "A man of *many talents.*"

Chilton gently shook his finger at him.

"All right," Crockett admitted, "Saint Clarke done wrote that one—but I come up with at least half of the other'ns. And they's all a-going into the Tour book, which we're dispatching to Philadelphia just as soon as all the t's is dotted, and the i's is all crossed."

Ben Hardin looked up. "The Tour book," he said. "Another gem from St. Claire Clarke, or so I have been told."

"Well, you been told wrong. Saint Clarke merely composed the newspaper letters, is all. Fish-lips done wrote the book."

"Fish-lips" was Representative William Clark. He was from Pennsylvania like the more erudite Clarke with the silent *e*. Chilton had known for months that he had been commissioned to chronicle Crockett's tour of the Eastern states, this after Matthew Clarke's man bungled the job. Chilton also knew that this other Clark had about as much of a sense of humor as a mackerel.

"It could have been worse," he said. "Better dull than scathing."

"You got that one right," said Crockett. "I assume you're referring to that pap-sucking leech and two-faced ink-spiller Caruthers and what he tried to fob off on the nation concerning me. Mark you my words: if that sorry piece of privy-work ever sees the light of day, by God if I won't be the laughingstock of the country. You saw it, Chilton. Now, ain't I right or what?"

Chilton raised his bushy eyebrows and shrugged. Dr. Caruther's satirical piece about a future President Crockett and how he won his laurels at the Second Battle of New Orleans, this despite his having comported himself there less than gallantly, was embarrassing enough, he thought, but no more so than any of a dozen others that had been circulated about his friend over the past seven years.

"I thought that sort of thing doesn't grate you so much anymore," he said. "What was that you said, you'd rather be the funniest man in the country than a great military chieftain like Jackson at New Orleans because ..."

"*Because the joke is mightier than the rifle-gun,*" Crockett said.

"And it is. Mark you my words: some of these days my humor is going to win me greater renown than ever did New Orleans for Old Hickory-face. Who knows, it might could even make me president—not next year, of course but maybe 1840. One thing I *do* know, though, is that what the leech Caruthers come up with about me and that fake second New Orleans ain't laughable at all. Pure poison is what it is. And that's on account of he contrived me to look like a coward quailing in the face of the enemy. If that ever got into print, Chilton, I'm afraid I'd have to beg a good friend like you to save me from myself. I mean, to keep me from hauling off and doing something reckless and foolish just to prove to the people that I've got me some hair on my chest. Which is why I done called him out."

"You challenged him to a duel? said Ben Hardin. "My good sir, that in itself sounds reckless and foolish enough to require intervention —at least to my ears it does. Chilton, you heard the man. Save him from himself!"

"Not so quick on the jawbone," Crockett said. "I gave the leech an escape clause. All he needs to do is write me a public apology."

"A what?" said Corwin. "The piece hasn't even been published yet. Didn't you tell me you've the only existing copy in your possession? So why whet the public's appetite for something they don't even *suspect* yet?"

"Because if it ever *does* find its way into print, I'll already have a sample of the man's disavowal to show my constituents. That way I won't have to waste my time a-tracking him down again."

Chilton shook his head as imperceptibly as he could. He wondered why his friend hadn't burned the offensive satirical piece yet. Perhaps he secretly appreciated the humor. Perhaps he was considering turning it around and using it on somebody else.

"But what if he picks up your gauntlet," Ben Hardin asked, "and accepts your challenge?"

"He won't pick up shit," Crockett replied. "I ain't heard

aught from him and I don't expect I ever shall. Truth of the matter, sir, I ain't so sure I even wish to. The way I figure, I already done took a year or two off the leech's life."

"Negligible harm," Chilton commented. "Doctors on the whole seem to live to a ripe old age."

"Aye, by not taking their own remedies," said Crockett. He polished off his whiskey in one prodigious swallow, some of it going down the wrong pipe.

"I'll tell you what," he choked out in a coughing fit. "When it comes down to it, he really ain't such a bad sort, that leech Caruthers. I'm a-willing to live and let live, I reckon. I done a thing or two myself to make a dime that I just as soon had a little rather not have."

Aye in spades, Chilton thought.

Then he stood up and tipped the hat he wasn't wearing. "I'll see you gentlemen later," he said. "I believe I'm going to give myself a head start on doing the people's business today."

> And it came to pass, that, as Jesus sat at meat in
> his house, many publicans and sinners sat also
> together with Jesus and his disciples; for there
> were many, and they followed him. And when
> the scribes and Pharisees saw him eat with
> publicans and sinners, they said unto his disci-
> ples, How is it that he eateth and drinketh
> with publicans and sinners?
> When Jesus heard it, he saith unto them, They
> that are whole have no need of the physician,
> but they that are sick: I came not to call the
> righteous, but sinners to repentance.

BY THE TIME THOMAS CHILTON REACHED HIS TWENTY-FIRST birthday, he was already considered a talented orator both in the courthouse of Bath County and in the Kentucky statehouse to which he had been newly elected. But by a year later he had had his fill of both places.

"You must change your attitude about the law," his mentor and sometimes courthouse opponent Benjamin Hardin—that same Ben Hardin with whom he had just had breakfast and who was now probably about five minutes behind him on their amble up Pennsylvania Avenue to the Capitol—had told him fifteen years ago. "Stop beating yourself up for hand-picking your evidence. Considering the case from all sides is the judge's task, not yours. You know that. Be proud of what you do, because you do it admirably for a man of your age. Hell, for a man of any age."

Chilton chose not to change his attitude; rather, he changed professions. He tried teaching for a while. At length, however, he settled upon preaching, initially in his father's church. It did not take him long to find his voice. He would begin his sermons in a calm friendly fashion to put his parishioners at ease. Then the lawyer in him would take over and make his point rationally, logically and convincingly, but still calmly.

Straight from the head, Chilton said out loud as he walked along the avenue.

But then, as if moved by the Holy Ghost—or by the power of his own arguments and the obvious (to him) emotional ramifications of them—he would work himself up into a frenzy transforming his oratory into the familiar Kentucky Baptist cadences. Not the flat emotionless singsong that you hear so often these days, though, but choruses filled with spirited eruptions of visionary prose punctuated by unexpected hacks and prolonged halts. Then it was back to the calm oratory of the head for perhaps a minute or two until the heart took over again.

One day, several of the elders from the Newcastle Baptist Church heard him there at his father's church, a Seperate Baptist church they usually shunned. They asked him wherever he learned to sermonize like that.

"From my father," Chilton replied.

The church elders looked at each other, then back at young Tom in disbelief because Thomas John Chilton the Elder rarely put such thunder into his own singsong evangelizing. What Chilton the Younger chose not to tell them was that he picked up the dramatic touch from watching his father entertain the Reverend Mr. Bailey's red-boned hound.

"You must try to be a good boy," his father would whisper into the dog's ear. "Because if you are *not* a good boy ... *HAH!*"

The startled dog would then take off on a tear around the house only to return to beg for another startle.

And so after but a single listen to Chilton the Younger at the pulpit, those elders hired him as their pastor. It didn't matter that he belonged to a wing of the Kentucky Baptist church that stood in opposition to some of their most basic core beliefs. It didn't matter because young Tom was so good at what he did.

"*I wonder if I still have it in me*," Chilton said to himself as he picked up his pace down the avenue, determined to be at his desk when the Speaker gaveled the House to order. "*Reckon there's only one way to find out.*"

For three years young Tom Chilton ministered to the brethren at the Newcastle Church. When he left, however, it was not of his own volition. The problem was he had felt strongly about giving them what they needed rather than what they thought they wanted. They were old-fashioned Calvinists who had been taught all their lives to shun sinners and to congregate solely with fellow righteous souls in order to keep their church pure and chaste. The Reverend Mr. Chilton, however, was intent upon converting the unsaved. And he was intent upon convincing those who already were rock-solid certain of their own salvation that it was their mission, too, to welcome struggling penitents into their fold. In this he was successful, for in his three years at Newcastle, the young preacher managed to convince over half the congregation to adopt his more inclusive point of view.

The best thing I ever did in life, Chilton said to himself as he looked up at the Capitol in the near distance. *Up to and including right now.*

The church elders obviously disagreed. Steadfast in their conservative beliefs, they grew increasingly apprehensive about a possible split in their church; therefore, they at length replaced him with a pastor more of the hard-shell variety who closely shared their views about this world and the next.

Frustrated, Chilton went back to practicing law, and then the following year to politics. This time, however, he ran as a Jackson man for a seat in the US. House of Representatives and narrowly won it in a second round of balloting after a contested election. During the electioneering, he accused Old Hickory's opponent President John Quincy Adams of being a spendthrift with federal funds. And he continued accusing him long after Adams packed his bags and departed the White House. But the main reason Chilton supported Jackson—the same reason that most western Kentuckians did—was because the Easterner Adams had favored his own sectional interests at the expense of the West, and the Old Hero could be depended upon to restore a fair balance.

Lord, was I ever beguiled! thought Chilton.

Indeed, President Jackson soon proved to be just as big a spendthrift as was his predecessor. Moreover, thought Chilton, he could no longer be counted on to defend the welfare of the West. This became crystal clear to him by the spring of 1830, midway through Chilton's second term, when Jackson killed the Maysville Road Bill for purely political reasons.

Aye, for reasons easily traced to a cynical magician from Kinderhook: the next president of the United States, God prove me wrong.

'Twas true: Martin Van Buren, soon to be vice-president, had convinced Jackson to veto that bill, a bill which undeniably would have greatly improved commercial transportation in Kentucky by providing strong competition to the Erie Canal in Van Buren's home state of New-York. And why should a Westerner like Jackson veto a bill so favorable to the West? Simple: because he owed a big one to the Magician. Because it was none other than Martin Van Buren who had orchestrated Jackson's triumphant presidential campaign two years previous.

So when Chilton canvassed for re-election again the following year, it was not only his congressional opponent that he ran against; it was President Andrew Jackson as well. Unfortunately for Chilton, the Old Roman was still mistakenly thought of by most Western Kentuckians—particularly the newly enfranchised frontiersmen and tradesmen—as God's gift to the West. Which meant Chilton got trounced.

Two years later, however, Chilton ran again and won. He won because by then the Jackson Party had been saddled with the blame for the burgeoning financial panic brought on by the president's attempt to kill the Bank of the United States, this by choking off its flow of funds and spending down what was left. This was why Chilton, soon after he arrived in Washington City in December of 1833, agreed to play a prominent role in the defense of the Bank.

'Twas my moral duty, thought he as he stepped even more deliberately and quickened his pace toward Capitol Hill.

Defending the Bank, however, was a toss of the dice for a man who had forsworn gambling. The odds were moving in his direction, though, for the newly united opposition—the Whigs in all but name yet—were growing stronger day by day: indeed, soon a Senate bill of theirs censuring the president would carry!

As for Chilton's risks at home, it mattered little to him that those who thought him flat-wrong on the Bank question now nearly equaled those who gave him at least the benefit of the doubt. He would minister to his constituents just as he had ministered to his congregants. Aye, he would do for them what he knew they needed, not what they thought they wanted. And he would *go ahead* because, as his friend and fellow Jackson foe from Tennessee would say, he was *sure he was right*.

That was a little over a year ago.

"Tis night and day since then," Chilton whispered to himself after tipping his hat to a clergyman whom he had momentarily regarded with envy.

Since then, Old Hickory and his henchmen had convinced the public that it was Mr. Biddle's Bank, not he, that had crippled the economy, this by contracting the money supply and shutting down the doors of commerce.

"Why do you come to me?" the president would say to insolvent White House visitors. "Go to Nicholas Biddle. He has the money. He has millions of specie in his vaults lying idle."

Upon his arrival in Washington this past December to begin the second session, Chilton received a letter from a Whig friend in New-York advising him to drop the Bank like a hot potato.

.Any candidate connected with the Bank is committing death, wrote he to Chilton. *Particularly a Westerner such as you.*

Although he agreed with his New-York friend, Chilton knew it was already too late for he himself to take any corrective measures. Indeed, he had as much of a chance for re-election this coming August as would a six-foot four Kentucky snowman for surviving the summer heat!

No matter, Chilton thought now as he crossed Fourth Street in front of a halted four-horse carriage. Indeed, he had had his belly full.

Well, in all honesty it had been the other way around: his constituents had had a belly full of *him*. This past summer, at a public barbecue for him not far from his Hardin, Kentucky home, no more than a dozen constituents (other than his family and close personal friends, who outnumbered them) showed up. And it was too fair a day to blame the poor turnout on the weather. His neighbor Beech Wirt provided a chilling explanation. Said he:

"You rued back your trust with the people."

"My trust?" said Chilton. "Upon my word I would never do such a thing. What in God's name do you mean by that?"

"The Bank," Beech Wirt replied. "You chose the Bank over

us. You chose the Eastern money men over honest everyday stand-up folks like us that you swore to look after."

Chilton attempted to explain himself but 'twas of no use. Said he, if he had turned a deaf ear to the East, sure as death he would have let down the West. And then under his breath: if his constituents were too hard-headed to understand that, he couldn't help it.

Well, perhaps I should have marched to my heartbeat instead of to the throbbing of my head, he thought. He stopped walking, loosened his overcoat and reached into his tailcoat pocket for his watch.

I should have declared all banks to be corrupt instead of defending the lessor of the evils.

He looked at his watch; it was fifteen minutes till high-noon and the calling of the House to order.

I should have known better. Backing Henry Clay (our favorite son, for God's sake!) over Andrew Jackson was one thing, but defending the Bank of the United States was unforgivable.

He continued to stand there staring vacuously at his watch.

It wasn't as if Chilton couldn't see the handwriting on the wall. Six months before he received that cautionary letter from New-York he was already suspecting that—

"I once had me a timepiece like that. My grandfather sold it to me on his deathbed."

"You like to scared the britches off me sneaking up on me like that," Chilton said to his friend Crockett.

"It comes from plenty of practice," David said proudly. "It don't always work, though, on account of as quiet as I might be in my moccasin feet, those bears and other critters like as not smell me a-coming. You would've too, Chilton, if I had waited but one more *leetle* month to scrub myself pretty."

"Oh, but I *did* smell you coming," Chilton replied. "From fifteen or twenty paces back. What did you do, splash on a full bottle of lavender water this morning?"

"Well ... I reckon that's as good a way as any to announce

that yes, I *indeed am* a civilized gentleman without having to open up my big mouth and boast about it."

Chilton shook his head and smiled a little. "Anyway, I'm glad to see you really did catch up with me as promised. After all, it's not *my* bill that's (God-willing) coming up today."

"It'll take more than God's will to get that piece of paper taken up and passed," David replied, the over-rusticated accent now vanished, as he and Chilton started walking up the avenue again toward the Capitol. "It'll take a pack of them stiff-necked Yankees living up to their word."

"What, their word of seven years ago?"

"Time don't make a difference. Their word is their word."

"Time makes all the difference."

"I stood up for them—and by the Eternal I still do. So why can't they stand up for me when I need them the most?"

Chilton thought about that for a moment, then chose one of his favorite sidesteps to such questions. Said he:

"There are as many reasons as there are members."

And then:

"Well, why do *you* think they won't stand up for you, David?".

"Ain't no good reason" David replied. "There's a wicked one, though. It's on account of they got Judge White now. I done all the sowing, but he gets to do the reaping. And now they've got no further use for me."

"I thought you supported Judge White."

"I do, but replacing me with him is no valid reason for them heap-biggity Whigs to shit-bucket my land bill. It's not like I done stopped getting my hands dirty going after Jackson and Van Buren. It's not like I've stopped caring about what's best for this country just because I won't be made president. And as I hardly must needs to tell you, Chilton, caring for my country today means—by the process of elimination it does—boosting their party as well, something that don't come natural to a stand-alone fellow like me What kind of fashion is that to treat one of their party's most dedicated foot-soldiers?"

"I agree," Chilton said looking David sympathetically in the eye as they walked, "but chew on this for a moment, my friend:

"You know as well as I do what our Eastern colleagues fear the most: that voting too much with us Westerners will jeopardize their chances at the ballot box. Aye, just as we too would be at risk if we voted too much with them. But here's the rub: it appears that when it comes to you specifically, David, they don't have to risk those chances at all. They observe how driven you are by such an overwhelming hatred of Jackson, and they consequently find it completely unnecessary to offer you *anything* to continue your predictable behavior."

"They can all go to hell."

"That is quite a sweeping sentiment."

"Aye, you got that one right."

"And maybe some of them *shall* go to hell someday—but you had better hope they stay around a little longer. Because right now you need them. Because without their good will, David, it shall soon be time for you to bid farewell to this city forever."

David's eyes were still locked with Chilton's. One of them, however, was squinting a little now as he replied:

"You saying I can't win again without my land bill carrying?"

And then with a semblance of a smile:

"What, my charm and good looks ain't enough?"

Chilton smiled back—but at his own traipsing feet now, not his friend's face. "I can't address your physical attributes," he said, "but I haven't seen much of your charm lately. Not on the floor of the House, anyway. I dare say even some of your chums are getting tired of your outbursts."

"I suppose that goes for you too, old hook."

Chilton directed his countenance back to his friend. "You know me better than that," he said. "I'm with you till the end. Of course the end for me is just two weeks away. Might be the case with you, too, my comrade-in-arms."

"Not if my land bill carries," David said. "I shall be a congressman for life. Might even be a senator if Judge White is made president. And think of all the newborn babes that'll be named after me: Crockett Jones, Crockett Smith, Crockett MacGillicuddy, Crockett Poffinberger. ..."

"That's precisely it. That is why it's so critical that—"

"What, I'm finished without it?"

Chilton placed a hand on David's shoulder; they were nearly at the foot of Capitol Hill. He motioned with his other arm to join him under a nearby poplar tree.

"Understand, my congressional career is over because I defended the Bank," Chilton said, one hand on the tree trunk now, the other gesticulating. "There you have it, pure and simple. You, however defended said Bank ten times more vociferously and publicly than ever did I. I ask you then: why on earth should you expect a rosier outcome?"

"They's other considerations," David replied, his arms folded in front of him.

"Aye, there always are. And granted, if that had been your only perceived transgression in your public's eye, perhaps your ... *charm and good looks* might indeed have saved you."

"I don't mean to be boastful," David began. "but folks back home seem mighty proud to know such a celebrated fellow as myself even though it's unclear to some of them—myself included—why and how I got that way."

"But that doesn't mean they will necessarily cast their votes for you again this time. And I am not solely referring to the Bank business. I'm referring to the book tour as well."

"It wasn't just a book tour."

"Well, whatever you choose to call it, you told me yourself that your opponent has already lambasted you throughout your district about all those roll calls you missed. I told you to put it off until the end of the session but no, you had to go listen to party operators who claimed they cared more about you than did your best friend. And that's what I am, or at least what I have always tried to be."

"And that you most assuredly indeed are," David said. "Aye,

you're my best friend, Tom Chitlins—there I done said it. But look here: you've been a-knowing me long enough to understand that just because you speak the truth to me don't necessarily mean that I'll pay my full mind to it. You know as well as I do how partial I am to running my life with an iron head."

Chilton smiled. "I know you are—but in this world of political give and take, you're going to have to start giving a trifle more and taking a trifle less—and the sooner the better. And while you are at it, I suggest you strike the word 'trifle.'"

"By God, I'm through with giving."

"I know you are, but do understand that if you cannot get that bill of yours passed—"

"My constituents know I'm a-working like a horse for them."

"Perhaps, but look at it this way: your constituents sent you to the halls of that edifice (Chilton pointed to the Capitol building looming large in front of them) to give them clear title to the land they 'improved by the sweat of their brow' I believe was how we put it."

"Aye, and that was one of the best speeches you ever wrote for me."

"But that was, what, seven years ago? *Seven years!* Which in your constituents' eyes means you have failed them. They may not say that to your face, but I'll tell you what they are thinking. They're thinking: perhaps it is time for someone else to try."

David rubbed one of his long side-whiskers. "So, you too have given up on me. *Et tu*, Thomas: my best friend in the whole world."

"I have done no such thing," Chilton said. "I'm just conjecturing what a considerable portion of your voting public might at this very moment be thinking. And you know what you have to do to improve their sentiments, don't you."

"Charge up that hill," David answered without hesitation. "and change a few minds about my *self-serving* piece of legislation,"

"Aye, and what innate tool of yours can you ill-afford to do that with?"

"I know you ain't referring to Old Betsy."

"Thank God I am not!"

David thought about that for a moment.

"My iron head," he finally replied. "And the steam-powered mouth attached to it."

~

"Point of order, sir,"

Several groans reverberated through the House chamber.

"The Chair recognizes the gentleman from Tennessee."

"Well ... this in truth is more properly a point of criticism," said Representative Crockett, who was standing ramrod straight with both hands on his desk, knuckles down. "Mr. Speaker, we are now within two weeks of adjournment and what have we done? Nothing. Last session, seven months were spent in talking —and two months more this session. I therefore am come to the conclusion that this a better place to manufacture orators than to dispatch business."

"That is not a point of order. The gentleman—"

"A great number of bills have been made special orders— among them one of great interest to my constituents—but on account of the long speeches they could not—"

"The gentleman is out of order."

"I hardly reckon," Crockett replied lapsing into his frontier voice. "Mr. Speaker, it ain't so much me that's out of order, it's the whole plague-gone *House* that's out of order. Throw in a few loose women and you have the biggest *disorderly house of ill repute* in this entire city."

He sat back down as, repeatedly, the Speaker pounded his gavel.

Chilton shook his head not only at Crockett's outburst, but also at the frustration that caused it. The Tennessee Land Bill was indeed one of those special orders to which David had referred. It was, in fact, next up for consideration. But "next up" could mean next week—if that—and the session was almost over. David was right; these prospective Acts of Congress had been talked to death. Not one vote on these questions would be changed if they were debated right up until the last day of the session.

As for David's bill, even if somehow it was voted off the table and called up for consideration before adjournment, it was fore-doomed. First of all, the president of the United States had made it a party mission to defeat the measure and rid the Tennessee delegation of the perpetual thorn in his side for good. Secondly, the Eastern Whigs, who were always embarrassed to have to break bread with their backwoods ally, but who nevertheless often had stood with him, now had no further use for him. And finally, he was now starting to annoy even some of his closest Western friends.

The Navy Pay Bill now came up for the third reading and consideration for its final passage. Crockett and a number of other members including his drinking and gambling chum Ben Hardin arose at once.

"The Chair skeptically recognizes the gentleman from Tennessee again," said the Speaker.

Referring to the Navy Bill, Crockett said:

"Mr. Speaker, this legislation has already consumed no less than three weeks in discussion. Now, as many of you gentlemen are already aware (I have been anything but close-mouthed about this) I have a bill made the order of the day following this bill. So it should not come as a surprise to any of you that, since speaking has become so fashionable here, I have discovered in myself a disposition to speak more on the subject so dear to the hearts of my constituents. I therefore move the previous question to do exactly that."

"Will the gentleman yield?" said Ben Hardin.

"The Chair recognizes the gentleman from Kentucky."

"I hope my friend from Tennessee will withdraw the motion." Hardin continued.

"I cannot do it, sir," Crockett replied. "I cannot in good conscience abandon my people like that."

"Nor can I abandon the good people of the West," said Hardin, "which the last time I consulted my map included your people as well—aye, sir, the good people of West Tennessee whose interests will be harmed if this bill is passed. I shudder at the thought of such funds that will be siphoned from the West to the East as a direct consequence of this half-baked measure."

Chilton had to agree with old Blustering Ben, for there was no Navy in Kentucky to fund; therefore he voted along with Hardin against Crockett's motion to cut off debate on the Navy Bill and open his own bill for consideration. However, he hoped debate would be short and Crockett's bill would soon get an airing. Indeed, Chilton had every reason to believe that would be the case. After all, Hardin himself had told him so.

Crockett's motion predictably failed—and fortunately for Chilton not by just one vote! Unfortunately, however, Ben Hardin went on to speak for upwards of an hour followed by more debate on the question and then several other questions none of which was the Tennessee Land Bill.

If it does not come up today, thought Chilton, *it will not come up tomorrow--or any other day this session. The votes against it have been cast in iron. And in iron has thus been cast the die that shall provide the deathblow to David Crockett's congressional career.*

"So you voted your conscience I suppose you're going to say."

"I always vote my conscience," Chilton said to a red-faced Crockett just after the closing thump of the gavel.

"All I know is you voted against me just when I needed you the most."

"I didn't vote against you. I voted for Hardin. And both he and I expected to be voting for you momentarily thereafter."

"He tied up business with his chin music so long that such vote was fore-ordained not to be."

"He swore to me that he wouldn't speak anywhere *near* that long, David. Otherwise I would have voted with you to muzzle him."

"The hell you say."

"Upon my word I would have."

Crockett thought about that for a good ten or fifteen seconds.

"In a pig's eye," he at length said and stormed out of the chamber.

But the Honorable Mr. Chilton of Kentucky remained there at his desk on the floor of the United States House of Representatives. Indeed, it looked as if he would be the last member to depart the chamber. All he could think about was his dear friend from Tennessee. Not about the parting insult—good heavens, no. That would be forgotten by both in but a day or two. This is what he was thinking:

I, Thomas Chilton, will be content to remove myself entirely from the national stage and to devote the rest of my life to my family, my community and, God willing, to my parishioners.

Amen.

Aye but will you, David Crockett, be content to live a similar life? Will you be content to live out the rest of your years in the deep woods you so love?

Quis potest dicere—who can say?

There was a time when David most certainly would have. Those woods, Chilton thought, had been what he was all about. But now that he was "*Colonel Davy of the Almanac and the Lion of the West,*" the living symbol of that untamed frontier, he seemed to be more about something else. He seemed to be happier in his newfound role of ambassador from that frontier to the rest of the nation, particularly to those more polished—if not wiser—folks who held the reins of power here in Washington City. And he no doubt secretly (and occasionally not-so secretly) wished that some of what *they* were all about might rub off on him.

As for Chilton himself, as much as he looked forward to leaving Washington behind him forever, the thought of such thing hardly cheered him. He, in fact, was daily growing more and more melancholy, this as adjournment was quickly drawing nigh. A part of him dreaded going home to Elizabethtown. If he had put his congressional career to an end voluntarily, that would be one thing. But going home an outcast was, as his frontier friend would say, was "a monstrously different creature." Aye, and the words of his neighbor Beech Wirt from last summer were ringing in his ears louder and louder these days:

"You have rued back on a trust, Thomas."

Chilton pressed his palms together.

"*Oh Lord,*" he whispered. "*My soul is full of troubles and my life draweth nigh unto the grave. Thy wrath lieth hard upon me. Thou hast put away mine acquaintance far from me; thou hast made me an abomination unto them. Lord, why castest thou off my soul? Why hidest thou my face from thee? As the deer panteth after the water brooks, so panteth my soul after thee, O God. My heart is smitten and withered like grass so that I forget to eat my bread. But I have eaten ashes like bread and mingled my drink with weeping. And those tears have been my meat day and night while they continually say unto me:*

"*Where is thy God?*

"*Mine enemies reproach me all the day. They are mad against me; they are sworn against me. But the Bible says, Blessed are they which are persecuted for righteousness' sake: for theirs is the kingdom of heaven. Blessed are ye when men shall revile you and persecute you and shall say all manner of evil against you falsely for my sake. Rejoice and be exceedingly glad: for great is your reward in heaven: for so persecuted, too, were the prophets.*"

Chilton rose from his desk and walked toward the cloakroom to retrieve his overcoat.

"*No thing by necessity ends as it seems,*" he said aloud in his full voice, for no one was left to hear him. And then once more in a whisper:

"*The stone which the builders refused now has become the corner-stone. May that be our fate, yours and mine, friend Crockett . . . Amen.*"

Chapter Sixteen

LEXINGTON, VIRGINIA, MAY 1835

She is blue-eyed, fair-haired and fair-complected, and there was once a time when you would have considered her petite rather than simply short and (her words)"a trifle squat." She parts her hair over her forehead in the Grecian manner these days to please her husband, for that was how she wore it in the days of their courtship.

Louisa Gibson Caruthers

This past Tuesday morning I received word that I had saved my husband's life. You can well imagine the unalloyed exuberance this gave me, but it also gave me pause for thought:

Would I have done such a thing a year ago, I asked myself, or would I have allowed him to fend for himself? I choose to think that I would have let bygones be bygones. Who knows, perhaps I am not as selfish and vindictive a person as I have long imagined.

What came between William and me was what all too frequently comes between a husband and wife these days: an unscrupulous unchaste woman. William has admitted that for the better part of a year, he carried on a connection with a young actress from the Park Theater Company. While I did not learn about this until several months after she had left him, I nevertheless had long suspected it, for his medical practice, meager as it was, still should have provided us with more of an income than it did.

But wherever did those eagles fly? Somewhere, I surmised, in the vicinity of the Park Theater, and you can well imagine how that made me feel. And yet when he sat down next to me on the divan to admit his inconstancy and to beg my forgiveness, my dwindling inheritance was as far from my mind as this Miss Green now is from my husband's body. (She is in London at present.) All I could think of was my crippled old mother.

I shall attempt an explanation:

When I was a little girl, I lived in a big house on Whitemarsh Island. Whitemarsh, which is situated off the coast of Georgia near Savannah, seemed to me a world unto itself, its reigning monarch being none other than my father. (Which, of course, made me a princess!) This is why I grew up expecting so much from life. And why I have been so sorely disappointed.

When I was eleven years old, I spied my father in the arms of one of our young servants, a girl not so many years older than I. I happened upon them in the chamber maid's room. I had stolen there to ask our dear old Nedda to tell me a bedtime story as she frequently did, but alas Nedda was not there. The room was dark, and I could barely make the two of them out, my father and this girl from the quarters, but even with my eyes shut I would have apprehended his presence from the fragrance of balsam in the air. At first, I surmised that he was examining the girl for ticks, something I had once observed an overseer do; however, it was soon quite obvious that he was doing nothing of the sort.

It took me several days to gather up the courage to confide in Dolly (my cousin Gibson's wife) I was so abashed. I asked her if I should speak to my mother about it.

"Pray don't, my dear," she said. "It is not the sort of thing one speaks about. And besides, your mother already knows."

Then Dolly continued about her business as if I had merely asked her the time of day. But later on that evening, to my horror Gibson questioned me about what I had seen. I knew not the appropriate low language to curse Dolly awake later that night—but I wished I did. Understand, to hear such things from a man—*any* man—cut me to the quick.

"Louisa," Gibson said. "What you saw is more akin to going to the necessary than it is to a display of affection. A man must do what a man must do. Surely you cannot envisage him with your mother in such fashion these days, can you?"

Verily I could not (even if Mother had been healthy I—like most daughters—still could not envisage such thing) for my mother, crippled with rheumatism, could by that time barely walk, and the last thing in the world she needed was to have a two hundred fifty-pound man crush her to death looking for ticks. When Father passed the following year, she no longer could walk at all, and somehow, I had it in my mind that his coactive manly behavior had brought about not only his death but her affliction as well.

As I have stated, this is what filled my mind when my husband begged my forgiveness for his infidelity: my insatiable father and my poor crippled mother. And I swear that, for a moment at least, I entirely lost the use of my limbs.

I can assure you, however, that I was soon up and on my feet; and that I remained upon them long enough to assist William with his packing and to escort him out of the house. That was the thirtieth of March 1834, fourteen months ago this very day. I took him back this past Christmas, for the children's sake. He came to visit them on Christmas Eve, and I permitted him to spend the night on the divan. He didn't return to his lodgings until two days hence, and that was merely to retrieve his belongings.

So is it forgive and forget? I dare say I shall have to forget first—and I have been blessed with a long memory. But if five years in New-York have taught me anything, it is that one needn't be a "Southern" to exhibit a predilection for self-solicitude. This, and my dearest lady friends have advised me that I likely would not do any better with another man; and that if William is truly penitent (which I believe he is), and if I have confidence that it won't happen again (I do), then I might as well bind up the wounds of my marriage and hope for the best.

Which brings me to this past Tuesday morning. As I have said, 'twas but four days ago that I learned I had saved William's life. Colonel Crockett apprised me of this in a letter which I received under cover of Mr. Gulian C. Verplanck. By way of an explanation, about this time last year, when the colonel was in New-York, my husband wrote an unflattering anecdote about him which William's employer intended to have published anonymously. Unfortunately, the piece was inadvertently placed in the colonel's hands; it offended him to such an extent that by the time he got back to Washington City he apparently had already resolved to challenge William to a duel.

William chose to ignore the colonel's demands (he received the colonel's first letter just after the New Year, although it was dated September 3rd) and to hope that they might go away like swallows flying south for the winter. I assure you that my husband is by no means a coward, but neither is he a marksman or any manner of grappler. And furthermore, he has his professional reputation to consider; to acquiesce to the colonel's demand that he apologize in public would be the death knell of his medical practice.

Therefore, unbeknownst to William, I wrote Colonel Crockett a letter, importuning him to spare his life. I informed him of Will's change of heart and that he had planned, on the very day that he inadvertently handed him the story, to burn it. I personally delivered my letter to Mr. Verplanck, who is both the colonel's friend and the uncle of one of my husband's closest chums Charles Fenno Hoffman, and this most erudite and clever gentleman swore that the letter would be our little secret. That was in late February of this present year, a few months before we removed to Lexington, Virginia, and as the congressional session was drawing to a close, Mr. Verplanck had thought it best to dispatch it to Colonel Crockett's residence in Tennessee. He had also thought it best to permit the colonel to believe that William and I still resided in New-York. As for the colonel's reply (in care of Mr. Verplanck), it was brief enough and to the point, so rather than paraphrase it I have chosen to include it here in its entirety:

Weakly County, Tennessee, 27th March 1835
    Mrs Wm Caruthers
    New-York City
    My dear Mrs Caruthers,
    I have just yesterday received your letter and have stayed up all night studying on it. Up until this time it was my Solemn wish to demand Satisfaction from your Husband upon the field of Honor. Indeed I have so repeated this to my trustful associates in the Congress and they have all concurred with me about this difficult and ominous decision. But I must tell you Mrs Caruthers that your letter has touched my Heart and powerfully convinced me to withdraw my Demands. So do not be uneasy about this matter. I can only hope that in the future your Husband will heed the words of my Motto and be sure he is always Right before he goes ahead. And a true Wife such as yourself should keep him on the right trace.
    I am your obedient servant,
    David Crockett

Well, now that I have saved my William's life, I feel it is my responsibility to ensure that he does something worthwhile with it. Regarding his literary career, however, I have little expectation that he will put an end to it in the near future. Thank goodness the public is not aware of his name (his novels are published anonymously) or rather of *our* name, for I would surely die of humiliation if his authorship ever became generally known. Understand, as far as I am concerned, novel writing is only a rung or two above play acting. William, of course, hardly shares my viewpoint, but he does affect to tolerate the anonymity.

"At least Mr. Irving knows who the 'Virginian' is," he said at Christmas dinner last, bursting with as much pride as the rest of us were bursting with our goose.

What *I* say is that at least the "Virginian's" first novel has yielded to us a return, albeit nothing much to speak of. William, however, insists that his second (*The Cavaliers*) shall restore his solvency—and who knows, perhaps it *shall*, for the first edition has already been exhausted. What's more, it has been widely and favorably reviewed in the newspapers and magazines including the *Knickerbocker* and, of course, the *American Monthly*, Charlie Hoffman's publication. William has copies of them all, and never have I seen him gloat so much as when he showed them to his friend James French (who has yet to finish his *first* novel) when he called upon us here in Lexington last month.

"Did you see the look on Jamey's face, Lou?" my husband said to me just after our house guest rode off. "He looked like he swallowed a live frog whole!"

I laughed and nodded my head in agreement, because if there is any man on the face of the earth who can stand to have his pride put in his pocket, that man is James Strange French. Never in my life have I met a more inveterate and transparent prevaricator. He even went so far as to claim he had been a pallbearer at General Lafayette's funeral. And that the Comtesse de Lasteyrie had fainted in his arms at the grave site!

One other thing we have from Jamey French (although in this I can hardly take him at his word, either) is that after having deserted the actress Miss Green, who at the time was with child, his conscience compelled him to return. He professes to have provided her with a good deal of money and would have remained by her side if another suitor had not emerged—some middling thespian from the Covent Garden theatrical company, says he—to woo her away from him. But in truth, surmises my husband, he was more relieved than upset about the emergence of a rival. Confided Will to me:

"He could have danced a hornpipe on his rooftop. And the child? Says Jamey, and I quote: *How can I miss something I have never beheld? Besides, where is the proof it's even mine?* I suppose we shall have to wait until he or she reaches the six-foot two-inch mark before we call his bluff."

As for Miss Green herself, oddly enough I now find myself feeling sorry for her. She is, after all, another victim of Southern self-solicitude.

There I go again. Condemning my heritage because of a handful of solitary experiences. Upon my word, there is much to say in favor of the South when it comes to charity and compassion. I dare say that if my family and I were to find ourselves destitute in Savannah—or, shall we say, in Atlanta where I have no connections whatsoever—we would be taken in far sooner than ever we would in New-York where greater numbers would seem to statistically favor us. Now, when I say "greater numbers" I mean that in New-York more people pass you by on the sidewalk in a day than ever would in a year anywhere in Georgia. As a rule, however, few so much as acknowledge your presence with a touch of their hat brims. There are plenty of exceptions to that rule, of course, all of whom I already dearly miss, but I will say this *without* exception:

I shall hardly miss those frigid New-York winters!

With that sentiment in mind, I undertook a fresh project with the new year. I resolved to convince William to carry us back home (*my* home in Georgia, of course!) before we had to face another wicked snow-blizzard in New-York. I even went so far as to threaten him with Charlie Hoffman's sofa. While I cannot imagine that he took my caveat truly seriously, we nevertheless found ourselves within six weeks' time as far south as his old hometown Lexington, Virginia. When I asked him the other night if he truly had no regrets about leaving New-York he replied:

"None whatsoever. I have made my mark with the Knicker-bockers and am now perfectly content to leave them to their own devices."

"Do you really mean that?" I queried him. "Or are you merely humoring me?"

"Of course I mean it," he insisted. "Who in his right mind wishes to remain a *picayune fish* in a huge icy pond?"

"The water is yet warmer a-way down yonder," I told him, alluding of course to Savannah, for I was—and still am—deter-mined to see my old home again as soon as 'tis conveniently possible.

"We shall pack up and go wherever you wish just as soon as I finish up," he promised. William here was referring to his third novel, which he calls *The Knights of the Golden Horse-Shoe*. If it is a pecuniary success, he will continue to write; if not, he promises to put down his pen forever.

"And how far along are you?" I asked him. Honestly, I had no idea. I leave him alone with his writing and he is circumspect about discussing it with me.

"Not far," he replied. "Seventy-five pages or thereabout. I can't seem to find the time."

"Why don't you ..."

I had to stop myself. And I had to turn my head from him to hide my involuntary smile. Consider this, if you would: there I was, about to suggest that he take some time off his medical practice to finish his novel!

Isn't that queer? thought I. *What a lady won't do to reclaim her lost heritage!*

Chapter Seventeen

DAVID CROCKETT

He has been home for nearly a month already. During the first several weeks he drank a good deal more than usual as he roamed the woods with his dogs feeling sorry for himself and trying to shed the ten or fifteen pounds he put on in Washington. And trying to sort things out in his mind, some of which he put down on paper in a letter to R. C. Crabtree.

Weakly County, Tennessee 20th April 1835

My Dear Crabtree,

This is the first I have had an opportunity to write you with convenience. I am glad to hear you are blessed with good health and settled once again in your own little Tennessee home. It is a great personal Pleasure to once again have you in my District though for how long that District will be mine, I cannot rightly say.

You say in your letter that you made your journey west in the month of November last which can only mean we surely must have passed each other along the road. I am mighty sorry we did not get to meet up at some Tavern along the way to have us a horn or two and then brush aside the old differences. When I received your letter of February 2, I meant to write you without delay but as I spent the last weeks of the Session trying to get the plague-gone House to take up my Land Bill I had precious little time for nothing else. So I decided to wait until I arrived at Home which I am ashamed to say was over three weeks ago.

I cannot begin to tell you how joyful I am Tree that you are a large enough Man to have forgave my uncalled-for behavior the last time that we met and give our old Friendship a fresh start. I had no right to trifle with my old Friend like I done for questioning my Integrity and also my love for my Constituents that I can assure you has never left me.

Well Tree, I suppose you have heard that the great travesty of our Republican Institution of free elections now has took place. It is a pity you were not still there in the city of Baltimore so as you could see first-hand that what I have been telling you for Years is come true that Jackson has chose to ignore the wishes of the People and chose instead to call together this sorry Caucus to impose his wishes upon the Electorate and nominate the little Van. This is why I support Judge White. Here I must tell you how much it does gratify me to hear that you do as well despite your fashion of turning a blind eye to the great evils of Jacksonism.

One thing I do know that you may not be aware of Tree is that Old Hickory-face is trying to put the entire blame of the White candidacy upon none other than my shoulders. He must truly believe that his Collar boys in the Congress would never have deserted him on that Question or any other if it was not for Old Davy's persuading them. Apparently, he is more aware of my Abilities than I myself am! And he seems to have forgot that up until the Judge agreed to enter the race, I was a presidential candidate myself. Why would I instigate a movement to defeat myself? It goes against all laws of Nature!

All I can say now is 'So much for the Presidency' for I expect in all probability to have my hands full just trying to keep my Seat in the Congress. Now if all I had to contend with was Peg Leg Adam Huntsman I would not be so uneasy. He is a right clever fellow but no kin to Solomon and he does not make much of an Opponent by himself. But I must tell you Tree that I am not just running against Old Timbertoe this summer. I am also running against the full force of the president of the United States and all the powers of the Throne. It was just yesterday that I come to find out he has franked the entire *Globe* with a prospectus in it to every Post office in my District with a record of my absences from roll calls in the Congress. I knew it was a mistake to commence that Tour before the end of the Session like I done. I suppose that is what great ambition for higher office will do to a man. Right now I will settle for another term in Congress, and it is my fond wish that I can once again rely upon your services in helping me to accomplish this.

I plan on making a two-weeks Canvass in mid-June and as usual find myself short of funds. Still I do have a great hope that I may yet come up with them. If I do, I shall once again require your services to dispense of them. Do you remember the time you got old Fitz so drunk he could not find his mouth without a leading string, and he was an hour late for his own speech? I do believe I shall require more such tactics this time out. I have told those who have inquired as to my prospects that I have a considerable chance of gaining an easy reelection, but you are my friend, Tree, and I must tell you the Truth. The truth is that I am not so sure I can triumph over the grand rascalry of my Opponent this time. My son John has been in every County but one, and, after I have drug it out of him, I come to learn that I am everywhere losing ground. I dare say that all Hearts has turned to gizzards for too many of the People believes the Lies which they have been hearing from the Enemy camp: that I have been bought over by the United States Bank.

Now believe me Tree I am well aware that putting a chokehold on all such folks that has swallowed this lie-tale will not likely gain me their votes, so I had better try my hand at convincing them that the Facts remain otherwise. It is certain I will have but a small trace of Voice left by the end of my Canvass for I intend to go the whole hog with it these next three months.

If only the Congress enacted my Land Bill this year, I would not be in such a devil of a hobble. At the beginning of the past Session I had the greatest hope that it would. I seemed to have patched up my differences with my Delegation thanks to Judge White's candidacy and if King Andrew could not collar them on that question I didn't expect he could collar them one and all against my Land Bill neither.

But what do you think the Tennesse Delegation done—the ones that once agreed to the compromise language of my measure? All but two voted with their arses and refused to be counted either way. As for my so-called Whig friends they left me out on the limb too—the selfsame one they had once talked me into venturing out upon. And after all I done for them. I had voted for their pet measures even though my Constituents might have a little rather I did not. I went on the Boston Tour and put doubts in the minds of friends of Jackson and his little Magician. I cooperated in the publication of a book about that Tour and also did lend my name to a scurrilous biography of the little Van that will be coming out this summer.

Understand, Tree I have done all this at the great risk to my Career. Aye but what thanks did I get from my so-called Whig friends? They would not accommodate me so much as to vote to consider my Land Bill—and them knowing all along that, like as not, it might be the only thing that could save me at the ballot box this summer. I reckon those Blackguards figured they had no further use for me now that they have mustered in Judge White. They have concluded I am a Pigeon no longer worth the plucking and would now willingly send me to Hell to pump thunder at three cents a clap.

So much for spilt milk. I am more concerned about the welfare of this Country. Let us hope and pray the People unites behind Judge White for I do not think there is a single Man that can defeat Van other than him.

What I shall now tell you Tree I have said more than once in the course of this past Session and to a good number of people. If the little red fox is elevated to the Presidency next year, I will leave the United States for I never will live under his Kingdom. Before I submit to his Government I will go to the wilds of Texas. I will consider that Spanyard Government a Paradise to what this will be.

But I have not given up Hope yet Tree. And if the little Van is stopped in his tracks by Judge White, I may instead remove to Alabama with my friend Chilton. You may remember him from your visit to Washington. He is a tall fellow and also my mess mate of so many years. This whole last Session and after he has been drinking to a great excess and acting most strange. He has turned entirely to the Bible—which in and of itself come as no great surprise to me for he was once a Baptist Preacher. But this last Session he was much given to parables that even our Lord Jesus Christ would not understand. And when I would ask him what he meant by such things as a two-headed billy goat at Heaven's gate he would just stare at me like I was even more doltish than I truly am and then laugh like the Devil and pour himself another glass of Rum.

Therefore while it may have struck me all of a heap, I nevertheless was not so bewildered as you might allow when I come to find out that he made up his mind to take his own life. This was within a few days of his arrival home in Kentucky, and it was his brother William that wrote me concerning this. I already had known that Chilton was bad plagued by his Constituents giving up on him as their Representative in the Congress. But while this may have been enough to drive him deep into the bottle, I knew it surely was not enough to drive him into the grave. It took the Church to do that—the same

Church that he did love so well and wished to serve as Minister of the Gospel.

As I have said when Chilton returned home, he could not keep a handle on his drinking and most embarrassed himself and his family in public on several occasions which I shall not inconvenience you with. You can imagine how that set among the Church Elders. It was not long before Chilton was banished from the very Pulpit he did covet so well and was denied all Fellowship of the Church. If it was not for his Brother who was visiting him at the time and some good Friends as well I do verily believe that he would indeed have thrown himself into the Ohio River as he so threatened. I can only pray that they have truly convinced him of the errors of his ways for it is my fond Hope to see him again in this World.

Chilton's brother has since asked him to join him in Alabama so that he might be of help in his Law office there in Talledego while he calculates what to do with the rest of his life. Perhaps I shall join them down there too some of these days. The way I figure Chilton has done me a world of good over the Years and I now owe him whatever I can do for him. Besides which that is a mighty pretty Country down that way. As you may recall I was there with the Army some twenty years ago and I remember it well.

So if I am indeed defeated by Peg Leg I say: so be it, for I am sick to death of politics. If I never again set foot in Washington I will miss it not for one moment. I expect you will find this hard to believe coming from the same Man that boasted he was going to be the next president one short Year ago, but it is the Gospel truth. I find myself a Changed man.

Now don't for one minute think I am not going to fight my Opponent with my gloves off this Time as always. I aim to gain my Seat back if at all possible if only to again try and get my Land Bill passed so that it may bless many a Poor man with a Home.

Now I must close in haste for it is late and I must get a good night's rest as I have some serious plowing to do in the morning. I hope to see you in June if not sooner. I eagerly await your reply.

Your friend and Obedient servant,
David Crockett

1856

Chapter Eighteen

He turned fifty-six this year along with the century. His face is lined, and his head is as bald as the upside end of a broom, but there's not a fleck of gray in his dragoon mustache. If you should ask him if he feels as old as he looks, he will straight-face tell you to ask MRS. Crabtree.

R.C. Crabtree

Back in Murfreesboro, Tennessee where I spent the earliest years of my majority we had a saying:

"*Scratch a Tennessean and you will find a North Carolinian.*"

I'll bet it's been thirty years since I heard that old saw, but I'll tell you a fresh one I heard but yesterday:

"*Scratch a Texian and you will find a Tennessean*" is what the people here in Fannin County, Texas now say. And it's true, for I am by no means the only such creature young or old that ever lost his heart to the Red River country. I once swore that I would never again leave the banks of the Mississippi, but that was two decades ago.

It wasn't my idea to pick up and leave for good. That distinction goes to Clayton, my sister Sarah's husband. The two of them migrated three years before I did. By this I mean the fall of 1836, shortly after the revolution. I hardly reckon I'd have made the move myself if it had not been for a four-foot eight-inch senorita half my age by the name of Magdalena Cabrera Paz. I met her in '38 when I came down to visit Sarah, and the next year I found myself being two things I had never previously been: a Texian and a husband.

I should tell you that I'd already been down here once before with my friend Crockett among others, and it was only after hearing my report that Clayton and Sarah decided to make the journey themselves. Before I go on, I must first inform you that I feel a little peculiar mentioning Crockett's name and mine in the same breath. This is on account of the heroic stature he has grown into since his death, which has numerous times caused folks to consider me a braggart for claiming we were friends as I do. I'll tell you what, may God strike me dead if we weren't.

One other thing about Crockett I must tell you. He may have died as brave as any man that ever walked this earth, but if you are like most folks and think the reason he went to Texas was to fight Mexicans and die for freedom, then you are dead wrong. I am telling you this first-hand, for when me and him pulled out of Memphis we had no idea that hostilities had already commenced. If we had, we most likely would have turned around and headed home. Least-ways I know I would have.

If you're wondering what exactly *was* on Crockett's mind, I'll tell you that, too. It was to explore the country and pick out a piece of land to settle upon once Texas won her independence. And if you believed what you read in the newspapers, it looked like independence and annexation was both just around the corner. This was a constant topic of conversation in my tavern in those days. It was a common belief that if you migrated to Texas, you would become richer than John Jacob Astor—and in half the time—once the Mexican overlords were booted out. Crockett thought so. As God is my witness, when it came to indepen- dence he was ten times more intent upon reaping it than cultivating it. I know this is contrary to what you may have read in his so-called Texas diary, but that piece of work is nothing but pure figment. Crockett's brave death speaks entirely for itself and will never need the help of a hackneyed scribbler in a money-man's employ.

Funny how things work out, one thing leading to the next. What I'm thinking about is him losing his seat in the Congress like he done the summer before he got himself killed. If he had won, he most likely would still be alive today and trying my patience all over again with one of his get-rich-in-a-hurry schemes. If I could go back in time and change things, I might would wish for that, but like as not I would then still be a stern old bachelor emptying slop-buckets at my tavern in Memphis.

Well, it wasn't my fault that he lost. I gave away as many jugfuls of whiskey in two weeks' time following him around from one stump speech to the next as I normally sold in two *years* at the Sign of the Crabtree. It was his mad-dog hatred of Andrew Jackson that done him in. He blamed him for everything that was wrong in the world—I'd hardly be shocked to learn that he even blamed the weather on him. And there was just so much mean spirited talk that the president was willing to put up with, so he electioneered as hard against Crockett as he did against Henry Clay in the previous presidential contest. I don't mean to say he actually went out and delivered speeches. What he done was use his friends in the newspaper business to do his bidding.

What kind of Representative of the People takes a three-week pleasure trip through New England during the middle of the Session? one newspaper story I still recall went. *One who is more concerned about his silk-stockinged Yankee cohorts than he is about his own constituents.*

Do not mistake me. That kind of writing soon had its effect, for the people were getting sick and tired of the company Crockett was keeping. Nobody out west had any great love for the U.S. Bank except some of the most flat-out moneyed men, and it was beyond the poor folks' understanding how he expected Biddle's Monster to secure for them clear title to their land. I know it was beyond mine.

All throughout the two weeks canvass that I accompanied him on he made like he still had a chance, but I believe he knew it was a lost cause. You could see it in his face. He rarely cracked a smile anymore—and when he did, it looked like it was forced open by a horse bit. When he told a laughable story, it sounded more like preaching at a funeral. This he must have apprehended, for after a while he stopped telling them. He would just rant and rave and vent his spleen all over Andrew Jackson. And that was about the most foolish thing he could have done, because trying to turn a Western farmer against Old Hickory was like trying to turn a drowning animal against Noah.

So it was a mighty sad two weeks' time for me. The only amusing thing that I can recall about it was a prank he played on his opponent Peg-Leg Adam Huntsman. I know some of you won't believe this, but it is the gospel truth. We were over in Hardeman County. Crockett and Huntsman had delivered their speeches from the same platform that day and were now lodging in the same room of the same house. I was outside asleep in my whiskey wagon when Crockett in his bare feet and a nightshirt roused me and asked me to come witness some devilment he had in mind. I protested, but it was to no avail. So before I knew it, I found myself following him back to the house. I hid in the bushes by the veranda to witness whatever it was he had in mind.

Now, the owner of that house happened to have an unmarried daughter whose room was at the other end of the veranda from where Crockett and Peg Leg was put up. So what does Crockett do, he carries a straight-back chair to her door and makes a considerable amount of commotion like he's trying to force his way in. Then he places one foot on the rungs of the chair and hobbles across the porch to his room and I make a beeline for my wagon. Needless to say, the girl thought it was Huntsman and his wooden leg—and so did her father, who threatened him with a sawed-off rifle gun.

Crockett later told me he apologized to his host for his opponent's scaley behavior and made himself security for him until morning. I reckon that was at least one vote he lined up on that canvass of ours. He claimed he got upwards of a dozen more from the man's kin. Maybe so, but even if he did, they weren't enough to win him his seat back, so it was goodbye forever to the great state of Tennessee that he had always claimed to love so well. And goodbye forever to me, too.

Or so I thought, for it was but a few several months before I learned how determined he was to take me along with him. This was in Memphis during the first week of November 1835. I was thirty-five years old along with the century. Crockett was fifty or thereabouts at the time and was starting to look it. He had developed that soft, swag-bellied, idlesome middle-aged lawyer look. *"Reckon I'm a-getting ready to sprout crops,"* he would say while drumming at his gut. To tell you the truth, he looked like he needed to sleep for a solid month what with those bags under his eyes he now had. He wasn't about to do such a thing, though, for he was on his way to Texas, to see the country that he had heard so much about. As for me, I was doing everything in my power to resist being talked into accompanying him. He had already invited me in a letter, but I hadn't given him my answer yet.

Here I feel I must clear the air about something. I am referring to an ugly story that I've heard too many times over the years. There are those that say Crockett left his home without so much as saying goodbye to his family. This is entirely untrue. As a matter of fact, two of his traveling companions happened to be kinfolk. One was his brother-in-law Abner Bergin, and the other was a Patton—his wife's nephew, I believe. The third member of his party was his neighbor Lindsey K. Tinkle, who Crockett liked to call 'Twinkle-Star.' Aye, and who later became a close friend of mine and a Texian as well.

I shall never forget the day I saw them come riding into town. I was over at McCool's Grocery when this young boy that used to lend me a hand at the tavern runs up to me and cries:

"He's a-coming up Front Street this very minute. Davy Crockett himself, I swear."

I followed him out the door and sure enough there they were, hitching their horses in front of the Union Hotel. Crockett was dressed head-to-toe in deer leather. Well, not so much his head, for sitting on top of that was something I had never once seen him wear in the fifteen years I had known him: a raccoon hat with both the head and tail still attached. I suppose he intended for the Texians to know him at first sight from pictures in the almanacs or from folks who had seen the famous play about him.

That night we all had supper at the Union Hotel. There was upwards of two dozen of us including my friend Major Marcus B. Winchester, who had helped foot the bill for Crockett's political campaigns. After supper, they all asked Crockett to give them a speech. He obliged them, though I hardly reckon it was what they expected. I was there, and I do believe it was the ugliest ill-humored grumble I ever heard out of him. He accused the president of being a feeble-minded old tool of the Kitchen Cabinet that had run Peg Leg Huntsman's campaign direct from the White House. And he claimed that the Union Bank in Nashville had rascaled him out of the election by paying citizens twenty-five dollars apiece to vote against him. But most of all, he lit into the plain honest folks that voted him out of office, the folks he had betrayed without knowing it by choosing the wrong friends in Washington. I can still see him sitting there—not standing, mind you, like nearly all public figures do when delivering a speech—at the head of the dining room table as he gave us these closing remarks:

"And to my former friends and constituents I say this: Since you have chose to elect a man with a timber toe to succeed me, you may all go to hell and I will go to Texas."

That was about seven or eight o'clock. By midnight we had

dropped in on every taproom in Memphis, and with the exception of mine he gave a shortened version of the go-to-hell speech at each one. The reason he didn't deliver it again in *my* taproom was that by the time we got there, it was just me and him. That was when he set his sights on convincing me to tag-after him to Texas. I put up a fight, but after my fifth or sixth horn of corn I finally consented. I had already known I would, deep down inside. I was barely eking out a living in those days what with the larger establishments crowding me out of the hostelry trade, and I knew I needed a change. I just wanted to make certain we wouldn't get mixed up in the revolution that was brewing down there.

"My word as a gentleman," says he. "We'll take us a look, then turn around and come back, simple as that. Come independence, we'll carry everyone we know down there and start up a settlement. I'll tell you what let's do. We'll name the town after you, Tree. Crabtree Texas. How's that suit you?"

"Suits me fine," says I, "but I reckon they'd sooner name it after you."

"Me?" says Crockett. "Hell, they're going to name the *county* after me."

So it was off to Texas—and me along with him. The first leg of the trip was by steamboat, and I'll have to admit that I looked forward to the folks up and down the river taking notice of him as much as Crockett did—and them taking notice of me too, right there alongside of him. Which they did all up and down the river before we even got to Texas. At Little Rock, Arkansas there must have been two hundred folks come by to hear him perform the go-to-hell speech. A dozen or so had copies of his book for him to sign, and one small child had a Davy Crockett Almanac. He played up to them and acted out the rustic character they all thought him to be, claiming he knew nothing about anything.

"If you don't believe me, just ask me," he would tell them and then commence to reel off one of his laughable tall tales. The way I see it, he finally came around to the conclusion that if the people liked him better as the half-horse, half-alligator that could wring the tail off a comet rather than as the bitter, beat-up politician that he truly was, then maybe he would like himself better as such, too.

At Little Rock we heard the news that hostilities had broke out in Texas. A newspaper writer asked Crockett if he planned on volunteering.

"If they're a-needing me, who am I to refuse?" Crockett said off-handedly as he picked at his fingernails with a jackknife. "I reckon they's worse things to die for."

Die for? I thought my heart was going to fly out of my mouth and sail clear across the taproom we were sitting in. I tried to get Crockett to explain himself, but he wouldn't utter so much as a single word on the subject until we went up to bed—and then he tried to make light of it.

"Ain't no part of nothing," said he. "I just told them what they wanted to hear."

"Like you're telling me what *I* wish to hear."

"What I'm telling you, Tree, is the truth. Like I always done. Anyways, you read that thing same as I did, so just hush up and go to sleep."

What he was talking about was a newspaper story that one of the townspeople showed us earlier in the day at this shooting match that they had arranged for us. It said that the Texians under General Austin had whipped a portion of the Mexican Army at Gonzales, which is in the southern part of the state— killed forty of them without losing a man—and they were now marching on San Antonio to take on Santa Anna's brother-in-law and the more considerable portion of that army.

"So the war might be over and won by the time we get to it," Crockett said. "And even if it's not, we won't be anywhere near it."

True, thought I—but only if we stuck to our plans. Crockett had laid it all out. We were going to explore the Red River Valley, which is in the northeast portion of the state, because that was the country we had heard so many wonderful things about.

"Ain't no need to proceed farther once we done found the Garden of Eden," he said now.

"You sure that's all we're doing, exploring the country?" I asked him.

He raised his right hand like he was taking a solemn oath.

"And then we're heading straight home?"

"Before the bears wake up," said he. "But I'll tell you what I'm fixing to do right now." He blew out our candle. "I'm going to have myself a look at the inside of my eyelids. We have a heap of traveling to do tomorrow and the sun ain't a-waiting for us."

Then I did something I should have known better than to do. I took him at his word and agreed to continue along with him.

We started out early the next morning. We were a party of seven or eight by then, for when there is a famous man out-and-about, you can rest assured there will also be tag-afters. It was all horseback from then on. A few others and myself purchased our mounts in Little Rock, strays mostly, that cost us no more than thirty-five dollars apiece. Mine pulled up lame no more than a dozen miles into our journey, so I had to purchase another—which only goes to show you get what you pay for.

We first struck the Red River at Fulton, Arkansas and lodged at a place between there and the Texas border called Lost Prairie. The fellow who's house we lodged at carried us to his neighbor's *ranchero* the next day for a chicken dinner, and it was there that I had my first taste of tequila, which is a Mexican sort of spirits and mighty potent. It was at this man's house that Crockett swapped the fancy gold watch that the Whig Party gave him in Philadelphia for an inferior one plus twenty or thirty dollars, for he was by this time short of funds. I asked him what his Whig friends would think of what he had done if they ever found out.

"They can all go to hell, too," said he.

So be it, thought I. I cannot begin to tell you how good it made me feel to hear him voice such a sentiment, to direct his ill feelings towards the very blackguards that had caused him to lose his seat in the Congress by making him stick up for the U.S. Bank. It must have made him feel good, too, for this was a time I remember thinking how much younger he was starting to look than a few short weeks before. He was smiling a whole lot more. He had finally got politics out of his blood and looked so much the better for it. Said I to myself:

Here is a man who has been in the wrong occupation all his life—or at least as long as I have known him—for he has not the cunning and treacherous nature that such an occupation requires. I am not saying that he couldn't be deceitful at times. For instance, he was hardly one hundred per cent truthful with me back in Little Rock when he claimed he had no idea of joining up with the American volunteers, as I was soon to find out. Still I never knew him to inflict misfortune upon another man, whether he deserved it or not.

From Lost Prairie it was but a morning's ride to the Texas border. From then on, we followed the Red River to the north and west and had us a close look at the countryside. And what a beautiful country it was. Flowers of all variety were in full bloom, and so were the peach trees. It seemed more like mid-summer than mid-winter. I was expecting all of Texas to be nothing but dry desert but how mistaken I was. We found clear water every-where—the best springs and wild mill streams—and plenty of timber. Later we came upon the place where I eventually settled and where I still call home today. We were on a hunting trip— Crockett was determined to get him a buffalo—but it was at this place that we decided to turn back, for we come to find out that the Comanches were close at hand and on the warpath. I should tell you we named the place Honey Grove on account of there were bee hives on nearly every tree. And so it is still called today.

After escaping that country with our scalps still in place we proceeded due south to Nacogdoches, which was the seat of one of the departments of Texas and the nearest one we could get to for the purpose of laying claim to some land. We got there shortly after the first of the year, 1836. Nacogdoches is a dirty little drinking, gambling and trading town that goes way back to the old Spanish times. Twenty years ago it had less than five hundred souls, I'd say, unless you count the Indians that drifted in and out to trade their blue-jerk deer meat for whiskey. We were greeted by Judge Hotchkiss and Colonel Forbes who gave Crockett a salute with the town's cannon.

We hadn't been there for more than three quarters of an hour when Judge Hotchkiss put his arm around Crockett and took him into the Old Stone Fort (which is really not a fort at all but merely a large house where they held court at the time) for a discussion of some sort. When they came back out, Crockett was all lit up like a young boy of today that's just been promised a visit to the county fair.

"I have a great hope of finally making my fortune," he reported to me after the judge went back inside. "You've been a-knowing me a considerable time, Tree. You know full well that when it rains my dishes is forever bottom upwards. But not this time, old hook. They're wanting to give me forty-four thousand acres—that's over fifteen thousand dollars—and all I have to do is be their land agent."

After that, I breathed a whole lot easier—if only for a short while—for no one was happier than me to learn that he was more intent on hawking real estate than collecting Mexican scalps.

That night they gave him a public dinner at one of the taverns, a shabby little Mexican mud hut. The room had no windows and was long and narrow like a coffin for the whole lot of us, and it smelled of the earth. Crockett gave them the go-to-hell speech—which I had pretty much memorized myself by then without wholly intending to—only this time he didn't get so worked up over it. I reckon he was too filled with hope and good will to harbor any more hard feelings.

After Crockett had finished speaking, and before he had a chance to sit down, Colonel Forbes rose to his feet and shook his hand. "I have an announcement to make," he said. "Colonel Crockett has just informed me that he intends to take the Oath of Allegiance and will be joining our volunteers in a few days. This is splendid news indeed and it calls for a toast."

He raised his glass.

"Colonel Crockett," he said. *"May he `go ahead,' for we are sure he is right."*

I couldn't believe my ears. This was Little Rock all over again. Until that very moment, he hadn't expressed the slightest interest in the revolution other than what fruits it might bring him, and now he was going to be riding plumb-square into the middle of it.

"By the Eternal if I am," he whispered to me a few minutes later and looked around to make sure no one was listening. "The way I figure, it's all over and done with."

He told me that Colonel Forbes had just spoke with some returning volunteers who claimed that they had whipped the Mexican army not only at Gonzales, but also at San Antonio and sent them packing just like we had heard it rumored on our way up. Then they were congratulated by the government, dismissed and sent home.

But there were other rumors flying about, I reminded him. We had also heard that a powerful effort was being made in Mexico to raise another army to re-invade Texas and that their supreme leader Santa Anna was going to lead this one himself.

"By God if the first one of them Spanyards shows his ugly face in Texas before spring," says Crockett. "Might not even be till summer—and we'll be back home by then."

"I'll be back home long before then," said I. "And if you had any sense at all, so would you."

Then I asked him why he was in such a hurry to join the army if he had no intention to stick around and fight. He wouldn't answer me. He just sat there in silence like he done in

Little Rock sipping his whiskey and listening to the sorry excuse for music they had provided us with: two out-of-tune violins and a triangle. Then he made Judge Hotchkiss take us over to the Mexican quarter on the other side of town where they were having a fandango, which is sort of a Mexican ball. The music there was much livelier. And so too were the women, although I was too bashful to get to know any of them.

It wasn't until we got back to our lodgings that I had an opportunity to press Crockett about his joining up with the volunteers. It must have been three o'clock in the morning, and we were both drunker than two *picaros* on pay day. On the way over, we sung an entire verse of some love ballad that we forgot by breakfast in Spanish, a tongue which neither of us could understand. I'll tell you what, though. I sobered up mighty quick when I started thinking about him fixing to sign up with the army.

I asked him point-blank if he really meant to do such a thing. He said he did and then tried to arm-twist me into tagging after him. This time I stood up to him, for I apprehended that every foot southward he had taken me so far was one more foot closer to calamity. I told him that under no circumstance was I going to utter one word of that government oath, so help me God.

"And neither is Lindsey and Abner," I added lest he think me the possessor of the only faint heart in the lot.

"That ain't what they say."

"They told you what you wanted to hear," said I.

"You reckon?"

"I'd bet my best suit of clothes."

He folded his hands behind his back and looked down at the floor. "Well, I'm a-going anyway," said he at long length. "Even if it's by my own lonesome self."

"All right, then go," said I. "Go get your head blowed off. I'll get up a petition to make sure they name that county you done mentioned after you."

"I ain't going to get my head blowed off," says he. "I'm a-going to San Felipe, is all—and you could do a world of good for me there if only you'd come along."

San Felipe, thought I. "I thought you was going to join the army, not the government."

"I am," says he. "You've got to join one to join the other."

I should have known. San Felipe was the seat of the provisional government of Texas back then, and after all his talk about giving up politics for good, there he was: ready to plunge into the same old cesspool again. I reminded him that not six months previous I had sworn off any further electioneering on his behalf, and that he had made the same oath to himself the morning after he found out he had been booted out of Congress. I reminded him how fed up he'd said he was of having to enter into unholy alliances in order to contribute anything to the public good in politics.

"But things is different down here, Tree," said he. "We're all on the same side, so a man don't need to barter his vote for what's right."

Colonel Forbes had sketched it out for him. He told him that in order to earn the right to vote, not to mention the right to stand for office, he would first have to sign up with the volunteers. Not that he would actually have to fight. First off, there didn't seem to be any enemy around *to* fight; and second, the Constitutional Convention was scheduled for the first week of March, less than two months away.

"A man of your political talents shouldn't waste them too long in the military," Colonel Forbes had said.

"I have a great hope of getting elected as a member from this province," Crockett informed me. "Forbes and Hotchkiss both thinks I can't lose. Let me tell you something, Tree. I'd sooner be in this present situation than to win a seat in Congress for life, I swear I would."

I wished him the best of luck but informed him that I didn't have as much faith as he did that the Mexican Army would roll over and play dead while he carried on with his electioneering.

The next day was the last I ever saw of him. He and his nephew headed out for San Augustine to meet up with some other volunteers, and the following morning I cut out for home with Lindsey and Abner. You would think that I'd remember the last words we spoke, but like that Mexican love ballad that I sung and forgot, I can't for the life of me.

One thing I do recall most clearly about that day was him taking the oath shortly before he rode out. He did it in the Old Stone Fort. What struck me then as it still does now, but in another way, is how he refused to swear allegiance to the government unless it was truly republican in form. This he actually had inserted in the document before he put his name to it. I remember thinking that at last he had put both his feet on the side of the people. I had no idea that his mind was still working in the same old misguided way as always until some fifteen years later. This I came to find out when I was shown a letter of his, no doubt one of the last he ever wrote.

The man who showed that letter to me was the Reverend Thomas Chilton of Houston, Texas. After he did this, he told me a story that gave me what I believe is the true picture of my friend's last days on earth.

It was five years ago, Christmas Day, 1851 that I met up with the Reverend Mr. Chilton. I was visiting Clayton and Sarah (who had moved to the southern part of the state two years previous shortly after the end of the War with Mexico) and Reverend Chilton was their new preacher. I had accompanied them to church on Christmas Day, and as soon as I laid eyes on the Reverend, I knew I had seen him some place before—something about his thick eyebrows and the old-fashioned manner which he clubbed-up his hair and, of course, his great height. I couldn't place him until Clayton told me that he once had been a member of the U.S. Congress and had known my friend Crockett.

Then it came to me. Why, this was the same Thomas Chilton who had been Crockett's messmate in Washington City and who had helped him write his life's history. I had met him on a previous occasion, which was during my visit to Washington in the early thirties. I even heard him speak from the floor of the U.S. House of Representatives defending the Bank of the United States of all things. What a difference it was to hear him deliver his sermon, though. I could scarce believe this was the same person, although I now knew him most clearly. When I heard him twenty years previous, it struck me how slick-polished and cityfied he sounded; but upon listening to him in church, I now thought he sounded more like some twangy hard-shell Baptist brimstoner from way back in the hills.

When Clayton introduced us, Reverend Chilton knew me straight off, too--or at least he made like he did. After he finished shaking the folks' hands, he invited us to his abode. We had other plans for that day but took him up on his offer for the day after. When we got there, we had plenty to talk about, most of it concerning Crockett as you might have expected. I was hardly surprised to learn that folks treated him—Reverend Chilton that is—with the same wonderment that they did me when they found out he was once as close a friend as Crockett ever had in this world. And I have but little doubt that he obliged them, for he was blessed with a friendly nature and a ready sense of humor. By the end of our visit, I found I truly liked this man whatever his politics might once have been and looked forward to visiting with him again on our next journey to Houston.

Before I go on, I wish to first mention something about that subsequent Houston journey, the second one. It took place two years later and once again at Christmas time. When we got there, I come to find out that Reverend Chilton had been forced to resign from his ministry on account of the strict rules he tried to force down his congregants' throats against such things as drinking and dancing. It was rumored that he had removed to Montgomery, Alabama where he had previously lived, which was much too far away for us to go see him again.

But last year Sarah come to find out that it was Montgomery, *Texas* that he had gone to, a place no more than forty miles northwards of Houston and along our pathway home. But by then it was too late to ever see him again in this world, for he had passed on to a better one the year before.

But back to the day after Christmas, 1851. It was right after dinner that Reverend Chilton showed me that last letter which Crockett had sent him. It was wrote about two weeks after I last saw him in Nacogdoches. He composed it in Washington-on-the Brazos, which is upwards of one hundred and twenty miles to the southwest of where I left him. I made myself a duplicate, which I still have in my possession. I provide you here with a true copy of it:

January 23, 1836
    Washington, Texas

My Dear Chilton,

This is the first I have had an opportunity to write you with convenience. By now you have likely read in the papers that I have gone to Texas. I have indeed done that and am now blessed with excellent Health and am in high Spirits. I have got through safe and have been received by everyone with hearty welcome. The Red River country where I have been until this week is the Garden spot of the World. I do believe it is a Fortune to any man to come here and hope you will settle here too someday.

This little settlement of Washington on the Brazos I find it amusing to have such a name and am reminded of how the Yankees from such large cities as Boston and New-York looked upon Washington City when we were there. The Town is but one street in the middle of the woods with a dozen cabins including this tavern where I sit here writing which is now sleeping thirty men in but one room. I do believe that the only reason there is any interest to make this place the next Capital of Texas is its name.

Chilton, I must tell you I have taken the Oath of Government and have enrolled my name as a Volunteer. I had every intention of setting out to join the brave men that had rid the Country of the Mexican Army and are now set to bring the war across the Rio Grande to Matamoras in Old Mexico but I have since heard something about that Expedition that sticks in my craw.

Sam Houston, that pap sucking white-skinned Indian that refused to lend his helping hand to the fight at San Antonio did everything in his power to prevent the Matamoras expedition but now that there is every expectation of Success he has assembled his own private brigade in that same vicinity to reap that Success and claim all credit for it. I have also been told something that I suspected all along. Houston—this man who I once called my Friend—is Jackson's agent in this Country and doing all he can to block the efforts of the General Council of Texas. This is indeed distressful news and like as not will effect my plans for I have no intention to add to his Glory. I have therefore decided not to set out for the Rio Grande and instead I will see what service I may be to the Government—and it must be a Republican one for that is the only kind of Government I swore to uphold when I took the Oath. If Gen'l Houston ever <u>becomes</u> the Government as Andrew Jackson did before him I must then leave this Country too for I will not bend my knee to a tyrant King.

I must close now. Write to me in care of the General Council in San Felipe. And do consider Texas. The Government here could use a good man like you and I would very much like to see you again. Until then I remain your Friend and obedient servant.

David Crockett

WHEN I FINISHED READING THIS LETTER FOR THE FIRST TIME, I was struck by how much hate that Crockett was still filled with. Here is what was clear to me straight off:

Houston was a friend of Jackson, and any friend of Jackson was Crockett's enemy. Of course there is also the other side of the coin, which is that any enemy of Jackson was Crockett's friend. This is why he bed himself down with the General Council, for those rascals hated President Jackson as much as he did. They knew that both the president and General Houston wanted to annex Texas to the Union, and that was the last thing in the world they wished to happen on account of they were all rich landowners and had done fine up until recently as Mexican citizens. They merely wished for things to be like they was before Santa Anna trampled on the Constitution. Believe me, the worst possible thing for them short of a victory for Santa Anna would be a victory for Houston what with the Convention coming up so soon. The Houston forces would push through a Declaration of Independence, and then it would be only a matter of time until Texas joined the Union and their huge Mexican land grants might be called into question.

The reason why I've told you these things is because those rich landowners of the General Council were the selfsame men that sent my friend Crockett to his death. And you should also know that they were cut out of the same mould as the Eastern money men, by which I mean the Bank Party that had put him into such a state of mind that he had but no other choice than to martyr himself at the Alamo.

Just how this all came to occur I had no idea until that day I spoke with Reverend Chilton. I could not for the life of me figure out why Crockett would go risk his life in San Antonio when so few others were willing to risk theirs. He never saw himself as a military man, at least as long as I knew him he didn't. He wanted to get elected to the Constitutional Convention, not massacred. It didn't make a lick of sense.

"It didn't to me, either," said Reverend Chilton. "Not until a few years ago."

The Reverend then commenced to inform me that when he yet lived in Alabama, a parishioner of his told him that he had a brother who was lodging in the same tavern in San Felipe that Crockett put himself up in shortly before he set out for the Alamo. Now, it just so happened that this brother of his was a member of the General Council. He was also a friend of the lieutenant governor of Texas, who lodged there with him. The lieutenant governor's name was Robinson, and from all that I've heard, he was a true blackguard and in the pocket of the rich landowners. He was also the head of the General Council as well as being an enemy of General Houston and the old governor, who they had overthrown.

What transpired between Crockett and Robinson was later passed on from Robinson's friend who was there to his brother, then to Reverend Chilton and finally to me. It has been passed on by so many tongues that there is no way to say for sure exactly how accurate it is, but it has the ring of truth to it. And it does go a long way to explain what was running through my friend Crockett's hard head to lead him to go get himself killed like he done.

So there they were, Robinson and his friend on the Council holding forth in the public room of the tavern when in steps Crockett and his companions. They get to talking and Crockett repeats much of what he had to say in his letter of but a few days before about planning to march to the Rio Grande but changing his mind on account of Houston scheming to grab all the glory.

So Robinson says he fully understands Crockett's predicament, but that the Matamoras expedition is too important to call off just because that rascal Houston might make some political hay from it. This is when he advised Crockett to go to San Antonio. Said he:

"The volunteers there loath Houston just as much as you do."

"I heard they pulled out," says Crockett.

"Where on God's earth did you hear *that*?"

"Washington-on-the-Brazos. I heard they was a-heading east to join up with the rest of the army."

"Well, you heard wrong," says Robinson. "It's nothing but wishful thinking on Houston's part."

He then informed Crockett that General Houston had ordered San Antonio abandoned and the Alamo Mission blown up so as to prevent Santa Anna from fortifying it against the Texians. Not that Houston had any authority to do such thing, for the General Council had already stripped him of his command. He likely didn't know this yet, though.

"But the brave men of San Antonio do," Robinson continued on. "And they are not about to abandon their posts. The only man I'm worried about is Colonel Neil."

Here Robinson was speaking about the commander of the troops at the Alamo, which at that time numbered less than one hundred men. Colonel Neil was a Houston man and couldn't be trusted. The Council was planning on replacing him with one of the leaders of the Matamoras campaign once that was over with, but until then someone had better keep an eye on him.

"And the more I think about it," says Robinson to Crockett, "I believe that someone, sir, ought to be you."

Crockett protested. He said he had no intention of being anything but perhaps a high private of sorts. He said he didn't come this far to ride into a hornets' nest.

"Maybe that besotted old rascal Sam Houston is right," he continued on. "Maybe we ought to blow up the place and re-group somewheres else when our numbers is greater."

Robinson wouldn't hear any of that. He tried to convince Crockett that volunteers from all over Texas were at that very moment saddling up for San Antonio.

"In two weeks' time Santa Anna will find himself outnumbered two to one," said he.

He showed Crockett the message he had wrote himself and then had got printed up in the San Felipe newspaper. I have since seen a copy of it. It told that Santa Anna was some eighty miles from San Antonio and coming up quick, but if the true freedom-loving Texians would only rally to the standard of constitutional liberty and ride to the aid of the brave men of the Alamo, it would be a short but glorious campaign.

Victory awaits you, wrote Robinson.

"The regulars will be pouring in before you know it," he said to Crockett. In truth, however, he made no effort to round them up from the Matamoras campaign that he still had his heart set on.

"Maybe so," says Crockett, "but they ain't there yet."

"True, they are not—and I admit it's a gamble. But I believe it's one that is well worth the risk."

"Whose risk? *Yours,* sir?"

"This whole country's, sir. San Antonio can mean the difference between liberty and dictatorship."

"Now *that* makes a bundle of sense! What the devil difference does it make what day of the year and what spot on the map Santa Anna is knocked off his high horse? If you're asking me, I'd sooner postpone this initiative until we are better prepared."

"I am not talking about *that* dictatorship," says Robinson. "I'm talking about Houston."

"Houston? You already done told me you took away his army."

"On paper I did, but too many of his men are still loyal to him. The last thing we need is for him to win the war in the east when we can win it at San Antonio without him. And we *must* triumph before the Convention convenes lest he march into town at the head of his victorious private army and legalize his planned dictatorship."

Whether or not Robinson truly believed such a hateful lie-tale I have no way of knowing, but it must have had its effect on Crockett, for David was always saying that Andrew Jackson could never have got himself elected president if it hadn't been for his great military triumph at New Orleans. A heroic victory for Houston at Matamoras would be more than he could stomach.

"You hardly intended to come this far to live under the same yoke as you did under Jackson, did you?" says Robinson.

"No sir, I did not," says Crockett.

"Then you owe it to yourself to do everything in your power to prevent that from happening. For that, sir, is exactly what life will be like under *SAMUEL the FIRST: KING of TEXAS.*"

Then Robinson continued on, buttering Crockett up about the courageous stance he took against Jackson in the U.S. Congress. He insisted that the General Council could surely use somebody like him to stand up to the Houston men fodder or no fodder.

"I want you to ride herd on Colonel Neil," said he. "I want you to rally those men, Crockett—those brave men of San Antonio de Bexar. And once your work is finished, sir, all of Bexar shall send you to the Convention as their delegate. And all Texians shall be thankful that a *true republican* came to their aid in their hour of need."

At that point Crockett said he would sleep on it, but as far as Robinson's friend was concerned, he had already made up his mind. And I believe him, for I could have told, too, if I was there. Because if you dealt David a winning hand at a card-table, you could always tell instantly that's what you just done by what the corners of his mouth were doing.

"It's the same old story," Reverend Chilton said to me. "Once you have supped with kings, it's difficult to be a simple country man anymore. Do you know what his fondest wish was the day he set out for San Antonio? They say he wished to be appointed Minister to the United States while Jackson was still in office so he might compel the old man to sit down to dinner with him at the White House."

"I'm sure he had his sights set higher than just minister," said I, and the Reverend had to agree. Like the lieutenant governor had said, it was a gamble. Poor Crockett must have figured that what Jackson did at New Orleans, perhaps he himself could do at the Alamo: catapult himself to the presidency if not of the

United States, then at least of Texas. I can think of few other reasons for his disposition to accept such unlikely odds against the Mexican Army.

Now, before you rise up in protest to such an idea, consider the following:

My friend Crockett could have been every inch as patriotic somewhere else. The Alamo sure didn't corner the market on that precious commodity. Not by a long shot. He could have joined up with General Houston's men in the east and fought a more sensible war. Aye, but that would have been adding to another man's glory—the Devil's himself, as my friend was fast coming to believe.

Sometimes, though, I figure there was more to it than just that. Sometimes I feel it was more like him having to prove something to himself. This is because for his last five years on this earth he was such a larger-than-life personage in the minds of the people from all over the country without having done the first thing to deserve such celebrity. Well, if he was anything like me in that respect—and I do believe he was—he must have got sick and tired of seeing himself as an ass in a lion's skin. It was high time to show the people he could be just as brave in true life as he could in a book.

"It was my fault as much as any man's," Reverend Chilton confided to me. "James Robinson may have sent David to his death, but I helped whet his appetite for it."

"By the Eternal if you did," I replied and then apologized for my oath.

I then assured him that whatever was troubling his conscience had no business remaining there. I told him I could say this with considerable weight because I knew our friend even longer than he did, and that if there was ever a man in this world born to cook his own goose, that man was David Crockett. I said this not so much because I believed it—which I did—but because Reverend Chilton was the only Bank man I ever heard big enough to admit that he had contributed to Crockett's sad fate.

Now I will tell you what I truly believe:

It is my deepest conviction that there is a special place in hell for the men who chose for their own selfish reasons to make of my friend a public curiosity. I say this not just because they gave him something too big to have to live up to. I say this because when they made him several feet taller than he really was, they also mis-rendered him as several times more ignorant. Understand, this meant that he now had something to have to live *down*. And as if that wasn't enough, they had to go fill him up with enough hate to poison a whole pitful of copperhead snakes.

Here is another thing that I believe with all my heart: if those false friends of his hadn't poisoned him so much with their figments about Andrew Jackson, he might have found a way to patch up his differences with the president and get his land bill enacted instead of getting himself booted out of Congress and butchered to death. Here I must tell you that at least one of those devils that set my friend on the pathway to his doom met his comeuppance while still walking upon this earth. I have learned from Crockett's own son that Matthew St. Clair Clarke, the man that poisoned him the most, lost everything he owned in the Panic of '37. His chickens came home to roost, I reckon.

There is one other thing I have to say about that land bill of Crockett's—which was something that he lived for and in a way also died for:

He turned out to be worth more to his former constituents in Tennessee dead than alive.

This I shall now attempt to explain. All through his political career, he put the interests of those poor neighbors of his first and foremost above any others, but still he couldn't do a thing for them. This was because he did not have the temperament to be a successful politician. Understand, he took things too personal. He carried grudges too long and too far. Because of this, on the day he died his poor neighbors were no closer to owning the land they had settled on than they were the day they first elected him.

I'll tell you what finally got them their land. It was his heroic death and the great national mourning for him that done it. The first that these things done for them was to get his son John elected to his very seat in the Congress. That was just four years after he left it. The second thing was it allowed John to at long last get his father's land bill passed. If there is such a thing as purgatory like the papists say, I am sure this was enough to get David clear of that place and any other worse place as well.

I never truly knew John Wesley Crockett, but I made his acquaintance once in Memphis. This was the summer before we went down to Houston, Magdalena and me, and seven or eight years after John retired from the Congress. He was lodging at the Union Hotel and looking for some property to build him a house on. As for me, I had come up to visit some old friends and I was staying at that same hotel. It was in the dining room of that establishment that I met him.

When we got to talking, John Crockett and myself, we both agreed how mighty queer it was that we had never before met, seeing as I had known his father for so long. Then he reminded me that David never took his family to Murfreesboro back in the legislature days when I was around him the most often. After that, John had been a grown man and living under a separate roof in a different town. Another curious thing was that although I was only seven years older than him, I felt like I was more out of his father's time than his. I reckon you are only as young as who your chums are.

While I was sitting there across the table from old Crockett's son, I reminisced to him about the last time I sat with David in that very room. I told him about how hopeful he had been about the future, but I also told him about how I had to suffer through the go-to-hell speech. Then it struck me how things was mighty different in Tennessee now concerning his memory. I continued to think of such things long after John retired to his bed chamber.

Thought I:

Once, for every four or five people that loved the man dearly, there was four or five others that hated him. By this I mean folks that thought he had been bought over by the rich Easterners. Aye, folks that never forgave him for turning against Jackson. But now, not only was he just as famous as Jackson, he was by far more generally loved. In fact, so much so that I am surprised no one has started up a church in his name as of yet! That's what's a-coming next, I reckon.

Well, that's about all I have to say right now about my friend Crockett. I wish to close on a more uplifting note like preachers these days are so fond of doing. With this in mind, I don't believe I can beat the last words on the subject that John Wesley Crockett had to say to me that night at the Union Hotel. I leave you now with his very words as best as I can recall them:

In his death, like Samson he slew more of his enemies than in all his life, for even his most bitter foes have long since buried their hard feelings and joined us in our grief.

—finis --

Afterword

The author, in 1955, wearing a Crockett shirt

This is a work of fiction; nevertheless, my characters (with the exceptions of R.C. Crabtree and Ivy Green) have been drawn from real life. How they behave and interact with one another, however, are products of my imagination. Dr. William Caruthers, the author of the Crockett-inspired *The Kentuckian in New-York*, for instance may never have even met David. And although Caruther's biographer Curtis Caroll Davis suggests that he was a spendthrift who inadvertently deprived his high-born wife of her accustomed lifestyle, there is no mention of Will ever having been unfaithful to her.

As for Matthew St. Clair Clarke, I have followed the lead of Crockett's mid-20th century biographer James A. Shackford who credited Clarke as the anonymous author of the 1833 campaign biography *The Life and Adventures of Col. David Crockett of West Tennessee* (later retitled *Sketches and Eccentricities of Col. . . .*) even though it was registered for copyright by James Strange French. Shackford suggests that Clarke as a known Eastern Whig operative was loath to put his name on the Crockett book as that might have carelessly linked David to the Anti-Jackson party in Jackson's home state. Which of course is also why Clarke omitted any mention of the political pact he allegedly forged with his host when he visited David at his backwoods home in Tennessee; I filled that vacuum and wove my inventions into some of Clarke's descriptive passages about that visit.

I used that same approach of weaving and borrowing from David's autobiography: *A Narrative of the Life of David Crockett of Tennessee* (1834) ghostwritten by Thomas Chilton. As much of the *Narrative* was likely dictated to Chilton by his friend and congressional messmate, I seized the opportunity to use Crockett's own words where fitting, especially from his tall tales, his electioneering stories, and his recounting of the early days of his military and political careers. In a similar manner, I pieced together his 1834 American Hotel speech to the Young Whigs. His 1835 letter to the altogether fictional R.C. Crabtree, though, is as fully imagined as is its recipient; and so is his 1836 letter to the true-life Chilton.

I would be remiss if I did not credit James K. Paulding with the colorful on-stage lines of "Col. Wildfire" in Chapter One. I lifted them all from his *Lion of the West*.

Finally, I would like to thank the noted Western historian and Crockett authority Paul Andrew Hutton and the late Dee Brown, whose Crockett novel *Wave High the Banner* predated his immortal *Bury My Heart at Wounded Knee* by three decades, for reading and critiquing an early draft of my manuscript. As did my late mentor Robert Bausch and my fellow "lifers" in his Northern Virginia Community College creative writing workshops in the late '80s and early '90s. I must thank Bob in particular, as he once instructed me in front of the whole class: "If you ever get this published, you must say you owe it all to me!"

About the Author

David Barnett Goldman, born in Chicago and raised in Highland Park, IL, received a B.A. in American Studies from George Washington University in Washington, DC. in 1973. Two decades later, he studied Creative Writing with acclaimed novelist and short story writer Robert Bausch at Northern Virginia Community College. A retired custom framing shop owner, he lives in Rockville, MD with his wife Kathy and their two children/stepchildren.